FAIR GAME

FAIR GAME

R.D. NIXON

This edition produced in Great Britain in 2022

by Hobeck Books Limited, Unit 14, Sugnall Business Centre, Sugnall, Stafford, Staffordshire, ST21 6NF

www.hobeck.net

A CIP catalogue for this book is available from the British Library.

ISBN 978-1-913-793-60-9 (pbk)

ISBN 978-1-913-793-59-3 (ebook)

Cover design by Jayne Mapp Design

Printed and bound in Great Britain

 Created with Vellum

Are you a thriller seeker?

Hobeck Books is an independent publisher of crime, thrillers and suspense fiction and we have one aim – to bring you the books you want to read.

For more details about our books, our authors and our plans, plus the chance to download free novellas, sign up for our newsletter at **www.hobeck.net**.

You can also find us on Twitter **@hobeckbooks** or on Facebook **www.facebook.com/hobeckbooks10**.

To Tonya: rock-solid bestie, trusty road-trip companion; sharpener of pencils... my sister in all ways that matter. T – we will do that research tour one day soon!

The Macnab Principle

The Macnab Principle is a prequel to R.D. Nixon's Clifford-Mackenzie Crime Series.

This was originally published as a standalone novella.

Part I

10 December 1987

The flat, spitting sound of the gunshot was almost lost in the snap of Duncan Wallace's collar as the wind stepped up a level. But the faltering shape in the sky told him his aim had been true; the grouse tumbled, graceless, to the ground, to be triumphantly borne back in the laughing mouth of Duncan's Gordon setter.

'Good lad, Spark,' Duncan murmured, handing the bird to his underkeeper.

'Nice shot.' Alexander's voice lacked conviction as he lined up his own, but Duncan took the compliment; it *had* been a tough shot in this wind. He allowed himself a moment's satisfaction as he watched his underkeeper fasten the kill to his previous one.

A glance at his other three companions, ranged across the hillside, showed them eyeing their own totals with less satisfaction – particularly Will, standing at a conspicuous distance from the others. The five of them had been at the same school at roughly the same time; Rob and Duncan had always been close, as had Sandy and Mick, and the four of them had, from mildly rebellious boyhood, together enjoyed the freedoms that well-off family connections afforded.

Will Kilbride was a decent enough bloke too, but he was… superfluous, really. He'd started hanging around with them as they'd hit their teens, and had been tolerated well enough, but no-one noticed, or minded, if he wasn't there. Besides, he was new money, and it showed. For all that, Duncan quite liked him. He had a certain tenacity about the way he was determined to become part of this inner circle of Highlands royalty, and a bluntness of manner that appealed to Duncan's sense of devilry.

Anyway, today was the last day of the grouse season, and Duncan was feeling expansive. It was a time for goodwill, not elitism; for celebration, and perhaps a little well-earned gloating now, too, since the sun was dipping too low for the others to catch up.

He let Sandy take his shot, then broke his own gun for the last time. 'That's it, lads! Time to call it a day.'

'Are we stopping for a dram before we head back?' Rob asked. 'Bit of a wind-down?'

Duncan looked back along the path, to where the gillie's wooden hut nestled halfway down the hill by the fast-flowing river, overshadowed by trees so it was barely visible. There would be a paraffin lamp, camping chairs, and some half-assed attempt at whisky waiting in there. He pulled a face. 'Prefer a proper drink,' he said. 'What do you say, Mick, how's that home brew of yours? We're closer to yours here anywhere.'

His friend looked up at the lowering sky. 'Aye, okay,' he agreed. 'All back to mine, then.'

Duncan looked at Will, since none of the others did. 'Coming?'

Will shook his head, affecting a fairly convincing regretful look. 'I've got to pick up Donna from her granny's.'

Duncan and Rob exchanged knowing grins. Will had made no secret of the fact that, if he had to sit through Mick banging on about his family's prized gem collection once more, he'd nick them himself, and distribute them to all his most gauche aunts for Christmas. Little Donna Kilbride had probably just deprived her great aunts of some interesting gifts this year.

That thought led to Duncan's own daughter, and he scanned the hillside. 'Have you seen Sarah?' he asked Rob, who took his godfatherly duties seriously. 'I assume she's buggered off to that old cottage again.'

Rob nodded, swinging a brace of grouse over his shoulder. 'She sloped off at the start, as usual.'

'And she'll have spent the whole afternoon skulking in there, but will still take her beater's fee,' Duncan said, reluctantly impressed. Sarah was a one-off. Angry little miss sometimes, sweetest thing ever at others, but at all times she had her eye on any prize that offered itself. He could hardly reprimand her; she was just a chip off the old block after all. It was just that, at sixteen, it was becoming less 'cute' and more problematic.

Will set off back to Duncan's house to pick up his car. The four remaining friends put their guns and birds in the back of Mick's Land Rover, and Mick let down the tailgate so Spark could scramble in next to his own dogs. The walk took only around ten minutes from this end of Duncan's land to the neighbouring Drumnacoille, locally known as the Spence estate, and they were soon in Mick's porch, peeling off coats and easing off boots.

'Get that moonshine going, Mick,' Duncan urged, rubbing his hand in anticipation.

'You keep calling it that,' Rob warned him, 'and that's exactly what he'll give you one of these days.'

They settled into the two deep-seated sofas on either side of the fire, and for a while all was quiet contentment, but for the sounds of Mick's two kids charging around like bull elephants upstairs. Duncan heard them laughing, and wondered again if he and Mary had been wrong in deciding to stop at one; perhaps a sibling or two might have calmed Sarah a bit. Too late now though. He put it from his mind, accepting the tumbler of vintage Drumnacoille whisky from Mick's butler with a deep sigh of contentment.

'This is the stuff.'

Mick patted the table at his side. 'Good man, Rafe. Leave the bottle.'

'Here's to another good season,' Duncan said, raising his glass. The look that passed between the other three did not escape him, and he grinned. 'Some better than others, of course.'

'Here's to you, ya bastard!' Rob lifted his own glass, and Mick and Sandy followed suit just as a shout and a thump drifted down from the room above.

'Keep it down!' Mick bellowed at the ceiling, and shook his head at the others. 'Nearly the end of Christmas term,' he explained. 'They've got the bug.'

'Ah, leave them be,' Sandy said, with all the indulgence of the happily childless, 'it's nice to hear.'

Alright for him. Duncan's thoughts turned slightly sour; when Sandy went home tonight, to the grandest pile of them all, it'd be to blissful peace and quiet. Duncan was already on edge, thinking of Sarah demanding unearned money, and knowing he'd give it to her anyway. Sometimes he wondered why he was such a pushover.

'So, you're all free for Hogmanay then?' he asked, to deflect those unwelcome, morose thoughts. 'Only three weeks to go now, and Mary's wanting numbers.'

Rob and Sandy nodded, but Mick looked down at his glass. 'I can't, not this year.'

Duncan tightened up at once. 'What do you mean, you can't? You were all for it when I mentioned it before.'

Sandy looked equally disappointed. 'Bloody hell, Mick, I was counting on you to keep me out of the clutches of that nutty Martha what's-her-name.'

'Who?' Duncan asked, momentarily distracted by that surprising nugget. 'Not that it matters,' he added. 'If I don't know who it is, you probably don't need protecting from her at my party.'

'Oh, he does,' Rob said, laughing. 'She's that divorcée who's moved into the old malthouse on the far side of Abergarry. Set her sights on Sandy right away, so his mother says. Your Mary will have invited her, Dunc, they all three go to the same book club.'

Mick finished his drink and picked up the decanter. 'I don't know how you'd think I could help.'

'She knows you're a widower,' Sandy said, sitting forward earnestly, 'and it won't take more than an offer to show her the gems, to keep her glued to your side all night.'

Duncan and Rob exchanged another look, this time with rolled eyes, and Duncan looked pointedly at his watch. 'Twenty minutes from the moment we walk in, to the first mention of the Spence jewels. I didn't think it'd be you though, Sandy, you traitor.'

'Oh aye?' Mick gave them a mock scowl. 'What are you trying to say?'

'Good thing Will's not here,' Duncan pointed out. 'You know what he's like about your collection.'

'No worse than he is about his sodding phone,' Mick grumbled. 'Waving it under our noses every chance he gets.' He adopted an exaggeratedly high-pitched tone. '*Oh, look at my brand new Naawkia, it cost two grand, don't-you-know?* Tosser. Who wants to carry a brick like that around with them, anyway? And I'd rather not be reachable twenty-four hours a day, thanks.'

Duncan forced a short laugh. 'Forget him and his *Naawkia*. More to the point, why are you and your family snubbing the only Hogmanay knees-up worth attending?'

'Hardly snubbing!' Mick took a generous mouthful of his drink, and shook his head. 'It can't be helped though, sorry. We've been invited over to Inverness, to a family do.'

'And that's more important, is it?' Duncan kept his tone teasing, but he still felt the sting of rejection.

Mick shrugged. 'Sometimes family comes first, especially when it's the Spence side. After all I owe Claire's family a lot.'

'If you say so,' Duncan said, putting his glass down. 'I'm away to shake the snake.' He didn't want Mick to see he was genuinely annoyed, but it rankled that the man was still a slave to his deceased wife's family, no matter what he'd been bequeathed in her will. Besides that, Mick was an influential bloke as well as a friend, and there were always plenty of opportunities to be had while whisky and good cheer were flowing; Duncan had already told several of his well-connected guests that they'd meet Mick at

New Year, but he'd be lucky to see any commissions sealed only by a handshake, and a promise that would soon be broken. The bloody man would cost him in the hundreds of thousands, just because he felt he ought to snivel to his in-laws.

He wandered down the familiar passageway to the ground floor bathroom, listening to his friends' voices as they began wrangling over who'd shot the most since August the twelfth – besides him, of course. The air was see-your-own-breath chilly down here, since tightwad Mick had a thing about turning on the radiators. In a month or so, once winter really hit, the thin yellow curtains would be stuck to the inside of the single-glazed window for the duration. Duncan shivered as he closed the door, shutting out the sounds of chatter that drifted down from the sitting room; he'd have used one of the upstairs bathrooms instead, if it hadn't meant listening to those boys raising the roof up there.

On the back of the low-level cistern, there was the usual dog-eared copy of Buchan's *John Macnab*, its curling pages and almost white spine a testament to the hours Mick must have spent in here avoiding family life. Most of the pages had been marked at some point, with the corner folded down to indicate Mick's place, and it looked as if he was mid-way through it yet again.

Duncan's resentment faded a little as he picked the book up and flicked through it, smiling as he remembered the earnest boy Mick had always been, practically forcing them all to read it during the holidays. Even at that young age he must have known, deep down, that they'd one day become the same bored, wealthy landowners as the protagonists in this book. And yet he was shunning the party of the year? Couldn't be that bored then. Duncan tossed the book back onto the cistern with a sigh, and attended to matters before his frozen equipment snapped off in his hand.

Back in the sitting room, the others had been given a taste of the newly bottled Drumnacoille 25, and Mick had apparently called down for some dinner. Duncan lit a cigarette, accepted his own glass of the new single malt, and felt his annoyance further melting away in the relaxed atmosphere. There was every chance Mick's plans would change, anyway, and he'd come to the party after all, so it was pointless putting off those businessmen who'd accepted his invitation; the frustration would be ten times worse.

The remainder of the evening passed without further mention of either the Wallace Hogmanay party, or, thankfully, the Spence collection, and, by the time Rob and Sandy, who lived nearest to one another, were ready to leave, the four of them were at least three sheets to the wind. The stovies they'd enjoyed were sitting warm in their stomachs, having been slow cooking for most of the day, and they'd moved from whisky to red wine, and then on to brandy.

Duncan was feeling replete and mellow, and had made up his mind to tell Sarah she'd not earned her beater's fee, so wouldn't be getting it. Time the wee spitfire learned the value of money. He felt braced, but not entirely convinced he was ready, and didn't join the other two as they stubbed out cigarettes, ready for the off.

'Can we get a lift home, Mick?' Sandy asked. 'We're not fit to drive.'

'Or to walk back to Dunc's for our own cars, even if we felt like risking it,' Rob added, patting his pockets to check he had his keys, fags and lighter.

'You'll find Iain in the factor's office,' Mick said. 'He'll drop you home in the jeep.'

Duncan pointed to the clock. 'You might want to glance that way, before you go volunteering your staff without asking them. Again.'

Mick did so, and laughed. 'That late, eh? Well, never mind. He leaves the office key under the water trough, and you'll find his home number on the board. He'll come out to you, no problem.'

'I'm not ready to go yet,' Duncan told the other two, 'but I can walk back later, anyway. Your cars'll be fine overnight where you left them.'

'I don't remember if I locked mine,' Sandy said, levering himself, with evident reluctance, off the sofa.

'Bloody hell, you'd better stop off and do it then,' Duncan said drily. 'What with all the marauding car thieves prowling Glenlowrie, it being only a twenty-minute drive off the main road and all.'

'Sarky sod,' Sandy grinned good-naturedly. 'Fair enough, I'll leave it.'

He and Rob took their leave, and tramped away across the yard to the factor's office in search of their ride home, leaving Duncan and Mick to talk. As usual, their conversation centred on the relative difficulties involved in running a regular working estate like Glenlowrie, versus a tourist trap like Drumnacoille.

The distillery was the main draw here, but several of those executives Duncan wanted Mick to meet were interested in one of those newish kind of team-building events; shooting, fishing, and the like, living the life of the laird for a few days before they hustled off back to London, or Manchester, or wherever. They'd pay top whack for it, too, and Duncan felt it wouldn't take a lot of persuasion to convince Mick that's where the future lay. He brought the subject up, without telling Mick he'd already volunteered him, to gauge the response.

'Sounds bloody awful,' Mick opined, his eyes closed as he puffed contentedly at his cigar.

'But you can see the financial benefit.'

'Aye, I can see that.'

'I mean, with a whisky-tasting thrown in, it couldn't hurt the distillery side of the business either.'

'I said I can see it. Doesn't mean I'd want it for Drumnacoille.'

Duncan gave up. All he could hope for, assuming Mick didn't turn up at New Year after all, was that he'd be able to talk the execs into a meeting later in January, and use the intervening time to convince his friend he was sitting on a gold mine.

The evening crept on, and finally Duncan accepted the inevitable. Though, with luck and a following wind, Sarah would have gone out with her friends by now, and he could put off that particular confrontation until tomorrow.

'I'd better start back,' he said regretfully. 'I'd not meant to leave it this late, and Mary's not going to be happy.'

Mick eyed him for a moment, then seemed to make up his mind about something. 'Before you go, I've got something to show you.'

Duncan looked at him in sleepy surprise. 'Really? Why me and not the others?'

'Because you'll...' Mick broke off, frowning, then shrugged. 'I don't know. I just think you'll get it better than them. Even Sandy.'

Intrigued, Duncan followed in Mick's slightly weaving wake, to the little office off the library. When Mick crouched by the safe and started punching in his familiar combination code, Duncan groaned.

'Not those bloody Spence trinkets again!'

'Just wait a minute.'

Duncan leaned on the desk, trying to curb his impatience. The walk home might not take long, but now he was aware of the time he felt it slipping away at a tantrum-inducing rate. Mary knew how to make a life miserable when she wanted to.

Mick rose again, clutching something wrapped in black silk. He laid it on the desk, and carefully folded back the covering until he'd exposed what lay within. Then he wordlessly lifted his eyes to Duncan, who suppressed another impatient sigh, and shifted his attention to it.

'Holy shit,' he breathed, when his lips would move again. 'What is it?'

'An opal, from Lightning Ridge.'

'Where?'

'Australia. Stephen Spence, Claire's grandfather, brought it back with him.'

Duncan squatted beside the desk, so his eyes were on a level with the stone. It was big enough to fill the palm of his hand, though he daren't touch it. Its smooth surface had looked dull and opaque at first glance, but the second he'd moved, and the light hit it, its fierce beauty had him in its grip. He didn't know how long he remained in that squatting position, mesmerised, but when he was able to move again a spear of pain shot up his thigh and into his hip, and he was quite prepared to believe he'd been there long enough for his youthful thirties to have become arthritic eighties... Time, which had been slipping away so fast before, had meant nothing while he gazed into the heart of that stone.

'It's called the Fury.' Mick's voice seemed to come from another room. Inconsequential.

It didn't matter what the opal was called, but the more Duncan stared at it, the more the name made sense. It was a glorious riot of colour, captured inside a dull black stone from the other side of the world, but the warmth that flared, every time he moved his eyes a fraction, made him feel that the chaos could not only be controlled, but that the stone would reward him for it. He reached out a finger, only to find it brushing black silk as Mick folded the covering again.

'Let me,' he found himself whispering, and it sounded horribly like begging, even to his own ears. 'Just for a second?'

'No. You'll smudge it.' Mick picked up the opal and put it back into the safe. Now that he knew what that safe protected, Duncan wondered how he could be so stupid as to be still using his phone number as a combination.

'I wanted to show it to you,' Mick said, 'that's all. So you'd understand a little of why I'm still indebted to the Spence family.'

'It *is* yours though?' Duncan rose, feeling a new chill in his fingertips, so abruptly denied the warmth they had been offered.

'Not technically, no. Claire's grandmother gave it to Claire along with the collection, but this belongs solely to the boys. She doted on them.'

Duncan remembered the carefree yelling, and stampeding up and down the upstairs landing, and felt an unexpected, and disturbingly violent, surge of jealousy.

'She died then, did she?'

'Aye, a week ago. They're holding a special memorial for her, that's why I've had to change my Hogmanay plans.'

Duncan's irritation twitched again, remembering that. 'Do the boys know about this Fury?'

'The wee one used to spend a lot of time with Granny Spence in her room, doing puzzles, after his mother died. I assume she'd have shown it him then. When they're old enough, they'll be told it's theirs.'

'Well, they're good lads. They deserve it.' Duncan heard the words coming from his own lips, and wondered how he could lie so smoothly; those kids couldn't possibly appreciate the Fury the way he did. 'You're right though, I do get it.'

'I knew you would.' Mick smiled. 'You'll be away now, then?'

Duncan nodded. The last traces of pleasant, drink-induced wooziness had vanished now, and all he wanted to do was get out into the clear night air and feel the wind on his face. He needed to think.

Part II

New Year's Eve, 1987

The downstairs rooms had been opened up, and the hallway of Glenlowrie House transformed into as close to a ballroom as the Wallaces could make it. The wilting Christmas greenery had been thrown out and replaced with fresh, glossy holly, artificially studded with berries where it fell short of perfection. Two enormous Christmas trees, one at either end, twinkled with tiny white lights, and more lights were draped over the stags' heads that adorned the walls.

The Glenlowrie Hogmanay parties traditionally started in the late afternoon, and it was still early when Mary Wallace signalled for music, rearranged her red tartan sash, and swept everyone away from the dining table and into the makeshift ballroom.

Will Kilbride was around somewhere, but, contrary to his

usual attempts to include the relative outsider, Duncan drew only Rob and Sandy into his office and poured them drinks.

'To absent friends,' he said, raising his glass. 'To Mick.'

'Mick,' Rob and Sandy echoed.

'You've forgiven him, then?' Rob asked after he'd drunk.

'Nope, he's made me look a proper fool tonight.' Duncan shrugged and sighed. 'Aye, of course I've forgiven the annoying little gobshite. He's still our friend.'

'I saw him yesterday,' Sandy put in. 'Took the boys' presents over. You know he asked his family to buy him a mobile phone for Christmas? A Cityman 1320, exactly like Will's.'

'No!' Duncan couldn't help laughing. 'The only thing that does surprise me is that he didn't buy it himself.'

'Probably didn't want to admit he wanted one,' Rob said. 'This way he can deny everything.'

'Turns out Will was telling the truth about what it cost, too,' Sandy went on. He put his glass down to dig around in his wallet. 'He gave me his number, asked me to share it with you.'

'To do what? Call him and tell him he's missing the party of the century?' Duncan shook his head. 'Serves him right!'

'It's not his fault,' Sandy said, predictably loyal. 'He's never missed one before.'

'And he won't miss one again,' Duncan said, with deliberate emphasis.

Rob eyed him suspiciously. 'Meaning?'

Duncan re-filled his glass, and offered a top-up to the others. 'Meaning I think we need to teach him a friendly little lesson.'

Rob and Sandy looked at one another, then back at him. 'Go on,' Rob said, clearly interested, while Sandy just looked uncomfortable.

'Is he staying overnight at that shindig he's gone to?'

'No, he's got meetings first thing. He said he'll be heading back soon after midnight.'

Duncan put down his glass. 'Right, now don't go interrupting, just hear me out.'

'Sounds ominous,' Sandy murmured.

'Shut up!' Rob and Duncan said in unison, but both were smiling.

Sandy grinned and held up his hands. 'Fine! Stop beating around the bush and get on with it then!'

'Okay. We've all read *John Macnab*?'

'Aye,' Sandy said, but Rob pursed his lips.

'Remind me?'

'The John Buchan story Mick was obsessed with, about the rich Scotsmen who were all feeling in a bit of a slump. You know, successful, but missing excitement. Three of them used the one name, and the fourth set up the prank, whereby he'd warn his neighbours that "John Macnab" was going to poach something from their estate: salmon, stag, that sort of thing, and then return it, without the owners even knowing they'd taken it to begin with. Then the others set about it.'

'Ah yeah, I remember it now. There was a TV programme I think, a few years back.'

'Right. So my idea is that we break into Mick's place—'

'No way!' Sandy ignored Duncan's raised eyebrow. 'No breaking in,' he said firmly.

'Alright then, *gain entry*,' Duncan amended. 'The staff will all be off for Hogmanay. Thanks to Mick we know there's an office key we can get hold of easily enough, and there's sure to be spare house keys in there. So, we take it in turns to go in, and...just do something that'll piss him off.'

'Such as?'

'Ah, I don't know.' Duncan waved a vague hand. 'Maybe turn all his paintings upside-down, or strip the beds. Turn on all his TVs. Whatever you like.'

'So, just a prank,' Sandy pressed.

'Like I said, he's still a mate. Anyway, as soon as one gets back it's the next bloke's turn, and the last one to go leaves a note saying John Macnab did it, and lists what's been done. It's still Mick's favourite book, you've all seen in it in his bathroom. So he'll get the joke, and he'll know it was us.' He picked up his drink again. 'What do you say?'

Sandy frowned. 'If I remember the Macnab story correctly, there was *some* sportsmanship in it, since the landowners were told what would happen. They had a chance to stop him.'

'We're not stealing anything,' Duncan pointed out, 'just letting him know we're thinking of him, even though he can't be here.'

'Don't try to make it sound like we're doing him a favour!' Sandy protested, but Duncan could tell he was warming to the idea of the fun to be had.

'It'd keep you out of Martha what's-her-name's way,' Rob urged, nudging him. 'And if the first of us goes now we'd all be back well before midnight.'

Sandy looked from one to the other, then smiled. 'I like it,' he admitted.

'Good man!' Rob punched his shoulder. 'And it's a dry night too, so we won't get back here drenched, and have to answer a lot of awkward questions.'

'Who wants to go first?' Duncan asked.

Sandy still looked hesitant. 'Why can't we all go together?'

'Because the other two need to be able to cover. If we all vanish for more than a few minutes at a time it'll be harder to explain away.'

'True enough.' Sandy finished his own drink. 'Shall I fetch Will in?'

'No.' Duncan looked reflexively at the door, but it was still closed. 'Not this time. He won't get the joke, and he's greedy. God knows what he'd get up to in a place like Mick's.'

'Fair enough,' Rob said. 'Dunc, you go first, then you can't back out and drop us in it.'

'Oh, your lack of faith wounds me!' Duncan put down his empty glass and looked at his watch. 'Right, it's nearly seven. It'll take me a bit longer, since I'll have to get the key from the factor's office first, but I'll be no more than an hour and a half. That'll leave plenty of time for you two, at about an hour each.'

'What do we tell Mary if she asks where you are?'

Duncan shrugged, and plucked his woollen jacket from the back of his chair. 'You can tell her dinner has given me the runs.'

'Charming,' Rob grimaced. 'Go on then. I'll go next, just in case of delays. I'm first-foot this year, so I can't be late. Sandy can go last, and leave the note.'

Duncan took a slim torch from his desk drawer and slipped it into his pocket. 'Have fun, lads, but don't drink too much. No backing out allowed.'

It had been dry for a few days now, and the ground allowed plenty of shortcuts that weren't always usable. Duncan chanced a few, and found himself approaching the back of Mick's house relatively unmuddied, and before he'd even broken a sweat. It squatted in its huge grounds in total darkness; most of the staff were probably pissing it up in Abergarry or Fort William tonight. Duncan grinned as he thought about what they'd return to tomorrow, there was no way Mick would bother to put it all straight in the small hours when he got back.

What *would* they return to though? It was time to give that some thought, but, as he picked his way across the grass by torchlight, he instead found himself thinking again about that breath-taking opal that Mick kept, criminally, locked away in his safe. It shouldn't be in there in the dark; it should be out where it could be seen.

But even as he thought this, Duncan felt a pinched, secret corner of his mind whispering, *no!* For however long he'd been lost in the Fury's depths, all thoughts of conflict with his daughter, and with Mick, and Mary, had vanished, and he'd felt utterly at peace. If he'd only been permitted to touch it, he was strangely sure he'd never have had that knock-down-drag-out screaming match he'd had with Sarah when he'd got home. It was all Mick's fault, for showing him a glimpse of the possibilities, and then hiding it again – the frustration had been immense, and it was biting again now.

Duncan moved confidently around to the front of the house, and, groping around beneath the stone water trough with his gloved hand, he quickly found the key. The factor's office was tidier than Duncan's own estate office had ever been, but then this estate's reputation was more for house parties than shooting ones... Not that there had been many of those since Mick's wife had died, either; she'd been the one to draw the visitors in, while Mick was happy in the background. He would often slope across to Glenlowrie to shoot Duncan's game instead, which was good for them both, since he paid well for his kills.

Duncan's frustration grew, as he realised there was no convenient house key hanging on the rack alongside those for the bothy and the logging shed. Now what? The minutes were ticking away; he couldn't go back now and say it was all off. He left the office and crunched across the gravel path that led around the side of the house, to the passageway that housed that poky little, ice-cold bathroom. They'd be able to replace a small, single-glazed pane in half an hour, and it *would* be more of a shock for Mick, to think he'd been broken into, after all. More value for time spent, it was simple business economics. Mick would get that if anyone would.

'Sorry, Mick,' he whispered a few minutes later, as the tinkle of glass echoed through the hallway on the other side of the door. He stuck his arm through the broken pane, and twisted the lock, stumbling a little as the door opened under his leaning weight.

Once inside he listened carefully, but it was clear there was no-one home, and after he'd kicked the broken glass aside, he hesitated in the hallway, still not sure what he could do that would piss Mick off as much as Mick had pissed him off. The fact that they'd been in the house would probably be enough, but where was the fun in that? It had no *finesse*.

His first stop was the bathroom, but this time it was only to fold down the corners of several pages of *John Macnab*, and straighten the one that indicated where Mick had got to in his most recent re-read. Small stuff, but it was amusing to think of his friend's annoyance. It would most likely be the last thing he found, after everything else had been straightened, which made it funnier.

Satisfied, he made his way to the big front sitting room, with the vague idea of rearranging some furniture. He spotted the cut crystal decanter in its usual spot on the sideboard, and glanced at his watch; seven-forty-five. As long as he was back at Glenlowrie by eight-thirty, Rob would have plenty of time to come over and do his part, so that gave him almost half an hour before he had to leave. He poured a generous slug of Mick's prized new whisky, and drank it off in one gulp, grinning to himself as he pictured the look on Mick's face.

'This here's *sippin'* whisky, you lousy sonofabitch,' he told himself in the mirror, in an exaggerated drawl. He laughed at himself, then started to take knick-knacks off a small table in preparation for moving it, and noticed a framed photograph of Mick's dead wife. A flash of guilt nearly stopped him, but it was eclipsed by the brightness of a much better idea. By the time Mick got this far, he'd already be thinking he'd been broken into, so why not go the whole way? He could take the prized Spence collection back to Glenlowrie, returning it, in the true spirit of the John Macnab prank, before Mick even realised it had gone.

He abandoned the sitting room, in favour of Mick's office, and went straight to the safe, where he began to enter Mick's phone number. Nothing. Damn! He sat back on his heels, frowning. Why would the man have felt the need to change the combination now, after all this time? The frown cleared almost immediately the question crossed his mind, replaced by cold realisation and a wholly unexpected, and sobering, anger. Did Mick think Duncan would come after that opal? Did he *really* think that? After all the years they'd known one another? Well fuck him. Fuck him, *and* that precious black stone of his.

But the memory of it kindled that need once again, just to see it. To touch it. He'd never have thought about stealing it before, but the thought that Mick believed he might have, was enough to make him consider it now. Even if it were only for an hour. It would serve Mick right to think he'd lost everything, and he'd feel pretty shit when Duncan handed it back to him. He thought, too, of the look on Will's face when he later found out they'd done what he'd always joked about, but without him. Priceless.

So, this combination code. If not the phone number, then what? He tried to recall the date of Claire's birthday, but gave that up almost immediately; Mick wasn't the sentimental type, or he'd have used it before. He looked at his watch again; almost eight. He had to figure it out fast, or it'd be too late for Rob and Sandy...

Duncan straightened slightly. Sandy had Mick's new number, it had to be worth a try.

The irony came through loud and clear, as he found himself wishing there was a quicker way to get hold of Sandy than calling his own home and getting someone to find him. He was halfway to the phone on Mick's desk, when he realised he couldn't risk Mary picking up and realising he wasn't at home. Frustration quashed his elation at the brilliance of his plan. It would have been perfect; prankish, but with just enough edge that Mick would know for sure it was because he'd embarrassed Duncan tonight, and cost him money.

But it could still happen. Sandy would stuff it up royally, out of pure nerves, and he'd probably argue about it for so long the moment would have passed, so Rob would just have to do it. Mick would still know Duncan was behind it, and, more importantly, why.

Duncan returned to the sitting room and spent the next ten minutes dragging pieces of furniture a few feet out of their usual positions, and, for good measure, he replaced the Drumnacoille 25 in the decanter with cheapo blended stuff from the kitchen. Then, with fifteen minutes in hand, he left through the same side door, and made his way back to Glenlowrie.

Walking into his own home was like stepping into a furnace. The heating was on high, and the crush of bodies was almost overpowering after the freshness of the outside air, and he realised with a groan, as he pushed through it all, that he hadn't arranged to meet Rob anywhere specific on his return.

'Good bash,' a voice yelled in his ear, and he turned to see William Kilbride, his arm around someone who definitely wasn't his wife.

'Martha,' the woman supplied, clearly interpreting his blank look as belonging to someone who cared. Duncan remembered: Martha what's-her-name, the gay divorcee. Will was evidently making the most of being allowed out alone, which was good news for Sandy, if not for the Kilbride marriage.

'Seen Rob?' he asked Will, ignoring the woman's proffered hand.

Will jerked his head towards the back of the house. 'Conservatory, I think, with Sandy.'

'Thanks.' Duncan turned to go, but spotted the cloud crossing Will's face. He understood it, and while there was no time to worry about who was feeling left out of which gang now, he clasped Will's arm in a show of comradeship.

'I have a message for him. Don't go anywhere, I'll be five minutes.' He belatedly smiled at what's-her-name. 'Nice to meet you. Mary's talked about you.'

He left them slightly mollified, and found Rob and Sandy in the conservatory. He caught Rob's eye above the crowd, and as Rob made to break away and begin his mission, Duncan pointed at Sandy too, and then towards his office.

'What?' Rob asked impatiently, as they joined him. 'You're cutting into my time.'

'Sandy, give me Mick's phone number, quick.'

'He won't want you calling him,' Sandy said, fishing in his wallet again. 'The Spences eat late, they'll be in the middle—'

'I'm not going to call him.' Duncan took the piece of paper. 'Why would I want to do that? Rob, I'm pretty sure the last four digits are the new combination for Mick's safe. You need to grab the Spence collection, and—'

'You can't do that!' Sandy breathed. 'He'll go mad!'

'He won't even know we did it, until we give it back. The safe will still be locked. He'll think he's had a break-in. Well, he will have, I suppose—'

'You broke in?' Rob interrupted. 'You said we'd not be doing anything like that.'

'Aye, well needs must, there was no key in the factor's office. It was only the little window in—'

'Bloody hell, Dunc!' Sandy said. 'This wasn't what we agreed.'

'Can I get a word in?' Duncan rolled his eyes, and turned back to Rob. 'Get the collection, and bring it back here, we'll keep it safe until we hear from Mick.'

'Why do you want to do this?' Rob wanted to know. 'Just to teach him to shut up about it? I mean, he already knows it pisses us all off, so it's hardly necessary.'

'The point of the Macnab story is to prove that they *can* do it. Same for me.' Duncan grinned, and added, 'The chances are he'll blame Will, anyway, until we own up.'

'Bonus,' Rob agreed, relaxing into an answering smile. 'Okay, I'll do it.'

I don't like it,' Sandy said quietly. 'Not the Spence stuff, anyway.'

'How do you know? You've never seen it.' Duncan gave him an exaggerated smile, complete with jazz hands, but Sandy still looked miserably unsure.

'If my family get to hear *any* of this, my life won't be worth living.'

Duncan began to wish he'd left Sandy on the outside, with Will. The man spent his entire life trying to live up to his family's frankly frightening standards, it was the main reason he was still single; he appreciated spirited young women, but no-one with an ounce of gumption was prepared to surrender to the Broughtons' ideals.

'Your family won't find out,' Rob sighed. 'Stop fannying about, Dunc, and give me that phone number.' He glanced at it, and shoved it into his pocket. 'Right, which door do I use at Mick's?'

'The side door, by the back stairway. Pick up my canvas rucksack on your way out, it's on the hook behind the oilskin.' Duncan ruffled Sandy's hair and put on a soothing voice. 'Aw, don't fret, little one, Mick'll see the funny side once he gets the collection back.'

'Piss off.' Sandy punched him in the shoulder, but a reluctant grin was starting to surface. 'If Mick goes off the deep end I'm blaming you.'

Duncan turned back to Rob. 'When you get back, come straight in here, put the bag under the desk, and come and find me.' He pulled a face. 'I'll probably be schmoozing some disappointed executives, trying to recover a bit of dignity.'

Part III

'So, he's not coming at all then?'

'When *will* we be able to see him?'

'You're saying I've wasted a ten-hour journey, on New Year's Eve...'

The complaints were wearing, and Duncan was growing tired of repeating the same platitudes, but he kept his smile firmly in place and managed to sound equally regretful each time.

'I know, but there's nothing he could do. Family emergency. He sends his deepest apologies, and hopes to fix something up in the next few weeks, if you're still interested.'

He was speaking now to Andrew Silcott, the CEO of a sportswear company that was fast becoming one of the ones to watch. Silcott had travelled up from Kent on the understanding that he'd be introduced to Mick tonight, and Duncan assured him he'd be taken on a tour of Drumnacoille tomorrow, followed by an exclusive whisky tasting, including the new '25.

Of course, then he'd have had to stay the night, by the end of which they'd all have ended up winners.

'In the next few weeks, *if I'm interested?*' Silcott repeated slowly. 'Wallace, it's a day's travel either side. That's four days that a two-minute phone call could have saved me. I've left my own celebrations, and my family, and spent a *hell* of a lot of money getting here. Do you have any notion of the cost of hotels over Hogmanay?'

'I do understand,' Duncan said smoothly, making sure he sounded suitably sympathetic, but without the contrition that might indicate he was at fault. 'Believe me, I'm as disappointed as you are. Mick's a great friend, and I was looking forward to introducing you.'

'Ah, there you are, Dunc.' Will appeared at his elbow, minus Martha what's-her-name now, and held out his hand to Silcott. 'Pleased to meet you, Mr Silcott, I'm William Kilbride.'

They shook, and Silcott looked ready to resume his complaint when Will spoke up again. 'I gather you'd hoped to visit Drumnacoille while you were here?'

'I had, yes.'

'Rotten shame. I thought Duncan here would have called to let you know.'

Duncan tightened up, and tried to send a *shut-the-fuck-up* signal with his eyes, but he kept his tone even. 'It *was* a bit short notice, Will.'

'Three weeks?' Will shrugged. 'I wouldn't have said so, but you know best.'

'Three weeks?' Silcott repeated, his eyebrows lowering as he looked back at Duncan. 'You said it was sudden.'

'Oh!' Will said smoothly, 'yes, of course, I was mistaken.'

But Duncan saw the glint in his eyes and, for the first time ever, wanted to punch him. Hard. The bastard knew exactly what he was doing.

'Actually,' he said instead, with a kindly smile, 'though I don't expect him to have told *you*, Mr Kilbride, but he'd cancelled the plans you're talking about, in favour of this party. He fully intended to come, as he does every year, being such a close family friend.'

'I see.' Will turned back to Silcott. 'Anyway, since you're here now, I know an excellent estate a little farther down the glen. It's a bit smaller, but at least the laird's here tonight. In fact, why don't you come and have a chat? I'm sure he'd be happy to discuss your needs, to save you making the trip all over again. I know for a fact that he's open to the idea of executive...'

The friendly chatter faded into the music as Will led Silcott away, and Duncan watched thousands of pounds in commission vanish into the crowd. What the hell was that sod up to? They were supposed to be friends; Duncan was the best mate he had, for crying out loud!

He rubbed his forehead. People would be starting to say he was unreliable, couldn't deliver on a promise, and wasn't to be trusted in matters of business. He'd gone to all the trouble of contacting them, and stoking their interest in the Scottish estate team-building idea, only to have them drop like ripe apples into the waiting hands of William Kilbride.

He caught Sandy's arm as he passed on his way to the buffet table. 'What's up with Will, tonight? Why's he so intent on sabotaging my business?'

'Is he?' Sandy looked around. 'I don't know why he would.'

'Really?' Duncan frowned. 'You're looking a wee bit shifty, if I may say so.'

'Just looking for Rob, nervous to get going. Isn't he back yet?'

'He's barely been gone twenty minutes,' Duncan pointed out, with rising impatience. 'Look, I've still got one or two people to see, why don't you come over and back me up? Your family connections will make it harder for Will to put the boot in.'

'I wouldn't worry, he's still busy with Silcott.' Sandy side-stepped as Duncan's daughter and her friends cut through the crowd searching for some kind of diversion, probably in the shape of the sons of Duncan's acquaintances. Sarah was, like her friends, wearing too much make-up, and dressed like Madonna; what was her mother thinking, allowing that skimpy top that looked more like a corset? As he reprovingly followed her progress through the room, Duncan caught sight of one of the few CEOs he'd not yet had chance to speak to, and grabbed Sandy's sleeve.

'Come on.'

But word had clearly got around, with the cold efficiency so often reserved for character assassination. The thin, nervy-looking man, unlikely head of a chain of hiking shops throughout the lowlands, had evidently caught sight of Duncan coming towards him, and he visibly braced himself. Not a good sign, and Duncan uttered a curse that was thankfully swallowed up in the music as Sandy slipped away with a sympathetic shrug.

Enough. Duncan just couldn't be bothered anymore tonight, and, if he were honest, he supposed he couldn't even blame Will for cashing in on it; he'd have done exactly the same. It was Mick's fault, no-one else's, and Duncan wished he could re-live punching his elbow through that little window in the side door at Drumnacoille – he'd enjoy it a lot more this time.

Around half an hour later he was relieved to see Rob Doohan's dark head bobbing in the crowd, searching for him. He caught Rob's attention and indicated the office, then hurried there to meet him, Sandy at his side, and this time he locked the door. Just in case.

'Got them!' Rob put the canvas rucksack on the desk. He looked both elated and a bit worried, and Sandy, predictably enough, voiced his own concern as he put his hand over the buckle, preventing Rob from opening it.

'We took them out of the house,' he said. 'Isn't that still stealing, even though we're planning to give them back?'

Duncan waved a dismissive hand. 'It's only Mick. And he's still got those two Eric Clapton CDs he walked off with last year, if we're talking about borrowing things without asking.'

But with the reality sitting in front of him, and in the bright light of the undecorated office, the festive air was dissipating, and he too felt the first creeping tendrils of trepidation; could it really be classed as a prank, purely because they knew the victim? If Mick was angry enough to press charges, they were all in the soup. He gently pushed Sandy's hand away from the rucksack, then loosened the buckle and lifted the flap.

Inside was a jumble of velvet boxes and loose chains, many of them tangled in one another, where a panicky Rob had pulled them from their neat compartments in the safe, and thrust them all together in his haste to be away. It was a glorious mess. And somewhere in amongst it lay the Fury... The need to reach in and search for it almost burned, but Duncan couldn't let either of these two know about it; he felt absolutely certain that sharing knowledge of it would somehow diminish it, and too many people knew already. It stopped with him, it had to.

He flipped the top of the bag closed again, and chewed at the inside of his lip for a minute, battling with his conscience. When he looked up to gauge the mood of his friends, he was struck once again by Sandy's inability to look at him properly.

'What is it?' he asked, nerves making him snappish. 'Come on, Sandy, you've been looking like a rabbit in headlights for an hour now, and it's your turn to head over to Mick's. You don't exactly look equipped for this.'

'It's only... I was talking to Will for a bit, earlier.'

'And?'

'And...' Sandy flushed dully. 'I might have told him what we were doing tonight.'

Duncan stared. 'You *what?*'

'Not the jewels,' Sandy rushed on. 'We didn't know about them at that point, it was when you were over there. We were just chatting, and he asked where you were. So... I told him.'

'Jesus!' Rob's voice rose, and he shot an exasperated look at Duncan. 'What the hell did you do that for?'

'I just said we were playing a wee joke on Mick, moving stuff about to freak him out a bit.'

'I'm guessing he wasn't best pleased to have been left out,' Duncan said, remembering how the man's brittle good humour had given way to blatant client-poaching. 'No wonder he was so pissed off earlier. Seriously, Sandy, you really are a prize pillock.' He dragged a deep breath; at least that had taken the dilemma out of what to do next. 'Well then, we're just going to have to put these back,' he said, gesturing at the bag. 'We can't risk him telling Mick there was any malice involved. Which we all know he would, in his present mood.'

'Aye.' Rob nodded reluctantly. 'Right, Sandy, off you go.'

He pushed the backpack across the desk, but Duncan stayed Sandy's hand when he reached for it.

'Wait a sec. I'm not giving up that easily.' He moved around to the business side of his desk, and took out his Polaroid camera. 'We'll take a picture of it here, in the office, to prove what we did, and leave the photo in the safe.'

'Hah!' Rob smiled at last, and the tension eased. 'Brilliant!'

Sandy looked equally relieved. 'Perfect, Dunc.'

'And I'll go with Sandy to replace this lot,' Duncan added. He didn't need to explain his lack of faith in Sandy, but at the same time he didn't want to leave the poor bloke out; it wasn't his fault he was so paranoid.

'Are we going to be in the photo?' Rob asked. 'What about you?'

'You two can be in it, and he'll know this is my office. That puts all three of us in the frame. Literally.' He gestured to the other two to shuffle together. 'Put the bag there, next to the photo of me and Mary. Open it first, you numpty!'

The photo taken, Duncan put it on the desk to dry while he re-fastened the buckle on the rucksack. Once again, he felt the fading of that little burst of joy at the closeness of the Fury, but there was no help for it. And if he was especially nice to Mick from now on, he might persuade him to let him hold it next time.

He checked the time as he and Sandy slipped out through the back kitchen; they'd make it back in time for the count-down to midnight, but it might be tight if they wanted to be seen around before that. A snuffling at his side made him start, and look down.

'Spark, home!' He pointed, but the dog just looked up at him, no doubt awaiting the same kind of fun that usually occurred when his master left the house with a friend. Duncan sighed, and cupped his hands pretending to prepare to throw a ball, and Spark panted and dropped to his belly in anticipation. 'Fetch!'

Duncan let the imaginary ball fly, and while Spark tore off into the dark, the two men hurriedly continued on their way. Their torches played over the uneven, rock-strewn half-path created by years of visiting the next-door estate. The wind was getting up now, December-cold gusts, that buffeted them and made it hard to hear each other, heightening the sense that each was alone out here. When they reached the Spence estate, Duncan noticed Sandy hanging back a little, and gestured impatiently.

'Do you want to be part of this, or not?'

'Of course I do!'

'Well come on, then! Rob can only keep Mary at bay for so long, we need to get back.'

With Sandy trailing him, Duncan hurried around to the side door, and reached once more through the broken pane to release the catch. 'I'll put them back,' he said, as they moved quickly down the short hallway, 'you go and do whatever you were going to do.'

'I hadn't thought of anything,' Sandy confessed. 'What did you do?'

Duncan told him. 'Why don't you go upstairs and turn the telly on in Mick's room?' he suggested. 'He hates Channel 4, so put that on. In fact, put them all on Channel 4.' He stopped, one hand on the door to the main house. 'Can you hear something?'

'Like what?'

Duncan didn't reply. He pulled open the door and stepped into Mick's lobby, and his heart skipped sickeningly as he saw, through the fluted glass panelling either side of the front door, the sweep of headlights on the carriage turn. Sandy had followed him, and shunted into him so he almost dropped the rucksack that dangled from his suddenly numb fingers.

'Is it Mick?' Sandy asked, breathless and panicked sounding.

'How the hell should I know? It's just lights!' He gave the rucksack to Sandy. 'Here, hold this.' He clicked off his torch and shoved it into his jacket pocket, then loosened his scarf, which suddenly felt restrictive and tight around his neck.

'What do we do?' Sandy whispered, as if Duncan had all the answers, and Duncan bit back an irritable response; it wasn't as if he'd ever done this before either.

'It must be him,' he murmured instead. 'Get back in there.'

He pushed Sandy back, and they slipped into the passage seconds before they heard the front door open. He clapped his hand over Sandy's torch, which was sending violently trembling shadows dancing along the walls. 'Turn it off, you twat!'

They stood in the dark, both trying to breathe normally while Duncan strained to hear what was going on in the house. Mick was alone, that much was clear; there was no sound of his kids, or anyone else; he must have left them at the party and come back in a hurry. It crossed his mind that the game was up, and they should reveal themselves to Mick and admit what they'd done. It was still pretty funny, although it would have been better if Mick hadn't come home early and spoiled it.

He was about to say as much to Sandy, when Mick spoke. For a moment Duncan thought he was talking to himself, but soon realised he was on his new mobile phone.

'I'm in the house now. No, I probably shouldn't have, but the front door was still locked, and I can't see anyone...' A pause, then, 'Of course I called them! They'll be here any minute.'

Duncan almost swore aloud, as Sandy clutched at his arm and whispered harshly, 'Is he talking about the *police?*'

'Who else?' He felt his own insides churning, and could see why the characters in that Macnab book had gone to such lengths; this was the way to get the blood pumping, alright. But the police? That was another matter; if he'd worried about losing some lucrative commissions tonight, he could kiss goodbye to them forever once his name was blackened by an arrest. Even if it all came to nothing in the end. It was too risky.

He leaned close to Sandy's ear and spoke calmly. 'We'll be fine, we've just got to get back over the Glenlowrie boundary before they arrive. Leave the bag, just go.'

It was pitch dark in the passageway, and as they started to shuffle back down towards the door, feeling the wind reaching through the broken glass, Duncan heard Mick finish his phone call.

'Aye, cheers, Will. Appreciate this.'

Kilbride? 'Shit!' he whispered furiously to Sandy, who had reached the door now. 'He's only on the phone to Will!'

'What?'

Duncan sensed Sandy turning to him in his dismay, but there was no time to speak now. And the time for silent caution was long past too; he heard the door at the other end of the passage open, and then Sandy had yanked open the door at their end and they were spilling out into the night. Duncan heard a shout, thanked God for darkness, and then he and Sandy were away.

A tiny bobbing light from Sandy's torch showed them a few square inches in front of them, and at any moment Duncan expected to go sprawling on the stony ground, but he somehow kept his footing. More through luck than agility.

'Go left,' he gasped. Mick would still be able to see the faint torchlight, and Duncan didn't want him to see it heading in the direction of Glenlowrie; they could make a circuit and turn back onto that path when they were safely out of sight.

Through the rush of the wind in his ears he heard another car somewhere behind him, and the faint light from its headlights briefly illuminated the night as it climbed the hill to the house; he heard Mick's shout, but not the words. Presumably he was telling the police which direction the burglars had taken, but they were increasing the safety zone with every passing minute.

The police car's engine had died, and the muffled sound of slamming doors drove them both onward; ahead of him, Mick saw Sandy stumble, right himself, and keep going, and heard the sobbing of his friend's breath in counterpoint to his own. But, as he followed Sandy over the low part of the wall that separated the Wallace Estate from the Spence, he realised that they were away, free.

Once Mick found the bag in the passageway there wouldn't even be a real crime to answer, bar a broken window. They'd done it! Exhilaration took over, and he began to laugh, but switched to a string of curses as his foot caught in a tussock and he had to flail to keep his balance.

'Okay,' he gasped, holding his side as a stitch sank into him. 'Wait, wait...' He stopped, but gradually the discomfort began to ease, and he took longer, slower breaths.

The smile was still on his face though, as he straightened, and each panting breath carried a short laugh with it; what a night! What a cure for boredom, and a satisfying way to show Mick he was annoyed. No harm done, a replacement windowpane, and a story they'd all be sharing for the rest of their lives. He threw up his hands and let out a feeble, but heartfelt, cry of triumph.

'All hail, John Macnab!'

He'd found a new lease of life tonight, for sure, and all his annoyances with the various friends who'd pissed him off had blown away with the last blustery winds of 1987. Mick, Sandy, even Will, were all good blokes really; he was lucky to have them as friends.

Sandy came back towards him; Duncan could hear the scuffling footsteps in the grass, and saw the fading pinpoint of light from the dying torch. He patted his pockets until he found his own torch, and switched it on. Sandy flinched as the light swept upwards, and put one hand out to shield his eyes.

Duncan's smile froze as he looked at his friend's other hand. 'What the fuck, San?'

Sandy looked down, seeming surprised to see he still clutched the rucksack. 'I... I don't, I didn't—'

'I said *leave the bag!*'

'I didn't hear you!'

'Even if you didn't, surely you'd... Je*sus!*' Duncan struggled for the right words, but there were just too many of them. 'Christ on a bike!' he groaned at last. 'You do realise what you've done?' He looked around helplessly. 'We're going to have to get these back in the house now, without being seen.'

Sandy shuffled his feet and looked down. 'Do you think Mick's already checked?'

'It'll be the *first* thing he checked! And no note or photo, to say it was all a prank.' The photo was still sitting on his office desk, Duncan recalled, incriminating them all now, unless Rob had seen sense and moved it. He could only hope, but Rob had his brain switched on, at least, which was more than could be said for this other clothead.

'But Mick'll know, won't he?' Sandy sounded almost pleading. 'Since it was only us, I mean.'

'I shouldn't think for one minute Will would have told him who it was, that was in his house,' Duncan said, his voice grim. 'Not in his present mood. If he had, Mick would've brushed it all off as a joke right away, and not come rushing back.'

'But he'll drop the charges when he does find out, won't he?'

He might have, Duncan thought, *but I have a feeling taking the Fury was a step too far.* He kept that to himself, however. 'Maybe,' he allowed, 'but if he takes it seriously, he's got real grounds to turn nasty, now we've taken the collection off his land. Whatever our motives are, we're thieves now. We could *actually* go down for this, and Rob too, if they find the photograph. The very least we'll get is a criminal record.'

'God, my family...' Sandy clutched at Duncan's sleeve again. '*Shit,* Dunc! What are we going to do?'

Duncan gently disengaged the cold fingers. 'Don't panic! Just...give me a minute.' He shone the torch around them, satisfied they weren't being followed, and gauging their position. Away to their left he heard the waterfall that was the Linn of Glenlowrie, which meant directly ahead lay the river, and to their right, the road that snaked its way back down the mountain into Abergarry. He shone the torch at his watch: nearly eleven.

'Right,' he said at length. 'Let's not blow this out of proportion. We did something stupid, it went wrong. We've got to get these back into the house. Somewhere we can pretend they were, all along.'

'Right. Where, then?'

'One of the kids' rooms, maybe, he's not likely to have checked there.' Duncan nodded as he thought it through. 'Then we just need to show them to him, and convince him it was all just a bit of nonsense, Macnab-style. He'll be fine, I'm sure, once he's had a dram and time to cool down.'

'And how long will that take?'

'For Christ's sake, stop talking as if I know all the answers!' Duncan glared at him, though Sandy probably couldn't see. 'He's more likely to listen to you than to anyone. You go back the longest out of all of us.'

'That's true.' Sandy took a deep breath, and nodded. 'I could tell him Will's just been winding him up out of jealousy.'

'Which is true,' Duncan pointed out. 'But he won't listen to reason tonight.'

'Why not? It's only—'

'I just...don't think he will,' Duncan finished lamely. 'Look, he's had the police out, he's going to have to save face somehow, and he's not going to want to get a reputation for crying wolf, just in case. Go back to the house for now, and let Rob know what's happened. There might be questions from the police, and we need to have our story straight. The three of us have been playing poker in the office, okay?'

'Right. I'll make sure the photo's gone, too,' Sandy said, showing the first ounce of common sense Duncan had witnessed all evening.

'Good. And don't let anyone see you going in, whatever you do, or it's tatties o'er the side. I'll join you in a bit.'

'What are you going to do?'

'Give me that,' Duncan said, taking the bag. 'I'll stash it, and once midnight's done and out of the way we'll meet up and work out how to get these bloody things back into the house.' He looked around again. 'The gillie's hut. We'll make our separate ways there by twelve thirty. Don't let *anyone* see you, especially not Will. He might not have told Mick it was us, but he's still a risk; we'll have to handle him with kid gloves from now on.'

'I'm sorry about him,' Sandy muttered, shivering as a gust of wind whipped his coat collar up around his ears. 'I swear, I didn't think it'd be a problem.'

'It's not,' Duncan assured him, privately wondering if that was still true. He gripped the rucksack tightly as he watched Sandy pick his way carefully back towards the rough path, and remembered once again what lay inside, dark among the diamonds and emeralds. He itched to take it out right now, and shine his light onto it to release those shifting, fiery strands, but the possibility of dropping it somewhere in the dirt, and somehow losing it, filled him with a cold, sick feeling.

He wondered if it was worth hiking all the way up to the old crofter's cottage, where Sarah so often spent her days, but there was no time; that place was up near the top of the waterfall, and he had to get back in time to clean his shoes and be present for the midnight celebrations.

Instead he went to the gillie's hut, and hid the rucksack there, as best he could beneath the pile of canvases they usually used to form rough shelters on shoots.

He checked the lamp, and hissed in annoyance at the dry, dusty sound when he shook the paraffin can. It would be hard to find any to bring with him later, either, without making a costly detour via the old byre where the tools now lived. He shone the dying torchlight onto the shelf, but it was too high up to see, and he fumbled the length of the shelf with blind fingers, breathing a sigh of relief as he touched the waxy ends of a cluster of candles. Something scuttled away beneath his questing fingertips, and he gave an involuntary shudder and pulled back, then seized the candles and put them on the table, along with the box of matches from beside the redundant paraffin lamp.

To save time later, he lit one, and dribbled three maddeningly slow blobs of wax on the top of the tea chest, then stood each candle firmly in place before switching back to the torch. Its light was growing even feebler now, and as he left the hut, he cast a glance back, as if pulled by the wishes of a single black stone. He already knew there was no way those jewels were going back to Drumnacoille, it just remained to convince his partners in...yes, in crime.

The torch died just after he reached the path that would lead him back to his house. It flickered a few times, and he swore and smacked it into the palm of his hand, but it was no use. There were batteries in his desk drawer, he would have to remember to grab some before he made his way back, the others would just have to sort themselves out.

He pushed the torch into his pocket and peered through the darkness, trying to pinpoint the familiar shapes of the mountain range behind the estate, and after a minute he got his bearings. He felt ahead with one foot, to reassure himself he was on the path properly, and was about to set off again when behind him he heard someone clearing their throat, and a voice drifted out of the dark.

'What *have* you been doing, Mr Wallace?'

Part IV

'What did you get?' Will came closer. It would have to be him, of all people, but what the hell was he doing out here?

'Get? Nothing.' Duncan recovered from the shock, with an effort, 'it was just a joke. We rearranged some furniture, that's all. Sandy put all the TV sets on, and I swapped the '25 for some cooking whisky. That sort of thing.' He could only see a vague silhouette behind him, and felt another pang of guilt at leaving Will out of things, so he went on, sounding deliberately defensive. 'All a bit beneath you, really.'

'Beneath me?' The shadow came closer. 'What makes you say that?'

'Well, it's just schoolboy nonsense, isn't it? No gain, just harmless fun. We knew you wouldn't want to get involved. You haven't even read the Buchan novel, have you?'

'Oh, *that's* why.' But there was no belief in that voice.

Duncan didn't want to pursue it, he was starting to feel vulnerable and cold now, and there was something about Will tonight that sounded more dangerous than annoying. 'Have you got a torch?' he asked instead.

'No, I've been using the light from yours.' Will sounded faintly amused now. 'That's how I know you're lying about what you *didn't* get.'

Duncan had been prepared to move off, but now he stilled. 'How long have you been following?'

'Since you and Sandy left the party, of course. Couldn't hear much of what you were saying, thanks to the wind, but I'm not completely stupid either.'

'You were at Mick's? But he was talking to you on the—'

'He didn't know I was there, either. I called him, after Sandy told me what you were up to, and told him I saw a light on at his place. That's the beauty of the mobile telephone, my friend, you may mock them, but they have their uses. So, what's in that bag you left back at the hut?'

'Beats me why you didn't just break the door down after I left,' Duncan said, growing cross. 'That'd suit your sense of drama, wouldn't it?'

'It was more important to follow you.'

'Of course it was.' He'd intended for it to sound scathing, but it came out weak-sounding, and something strange was happening to his skin. It seemed to be shrinking on his bones, tightening, stopping the flow of blood to his brain. All he could think of was stopping Will Kilbride from seeing the Fury. From touching it. Maybe even taking it...

'Well I'm not telling you,' he said, calmly now, though it sounded as if someone else were speaking. 'If you want to know, you'll have to go and look.' It was a desperate bluff, and he could only hope Will wouldn't call it.

The shadow stopped moving from foot to foot, and shuffling around in the long grass. In the darkness the silence swelled, the wind hissed through the trees, and, somewhere in the distance, someone let off premature fireworks.

The sound seemed to galvanise Will, and Duncan watched the man's outline shrink abruptly as he turned and walked back the way they'd come. His feet seemed to find the path easily enough, and Duncan's own legs began working without conscious instruction, carrying him after the retreating shadow. His heart began to beat hard, as if he were running, but he was surprised to find he was only moving at a steady, brisk walking speed.

'You'll feel pretty stupid when you find a pair of my wellies and an old cagoule,' he called, but got no answer. He picked up his pace. 'Mick won't thank you for dragging him away from the Spences, for no reason!'

Now and again his feet knocked a tussock or slipped into a puddle, but he kept upright, and by the time he reached the place under the overhanging trees, where the gillie's hut stood, his entire body felt disconnected, alien to him. His eyes, slightly more accustomed to the dark now that he'd been without the torchlight for a while, were able to pick out Will's white hands reaching for the door of the hut.

He stepped forward and saw his own arm rise, his own hand outstretched, his own fingers close on Will's shoulder. Will spun around, throwing up his arm and knocking Duncan's hand away.

'Get off me!'

'You're not having it,' Duncan said, his voice still sounding faraway, but quite reasonable, he thought.

'It? What's *it*?'

'Come away, Will,' Duncan said, and now he was coming back into himself. The night came alive around him again, and he felt the chilly December wind lifting his hair and creeping beneath the cuffs of his coat. His skin expanded once more so it fit him properly, and he heard more fireworks exploding in the sky over Fort William. He turned instinctively to look, the boy in him unable to resist, and even as his eyes picked out the dying sparks drifting down over the town he heard the shed door rattle.

'I said come away!' He grabbed at Will, who turned, and pushed. Duncan stumbled backwards, his arms flailing for balance, and hadn't even realised he'd fallen until the impact knocked the breath from his body. His teeth clacked together, and his head bounced off the ground, sending more fireworks flying across his vision.

After a brief, stunned moment, he struggled onto his elbows and peered through the dark, in time to see Will prise open the shed door. He knew he should have said something then, should have been honest. He should have told Will about the Spence collection... He could have left out all mention of the Fury, and instead brought the man into the group, promising him whatever he planned to promise Sandy and Rob. But all he could do was utter a wordless, almost anguished cry, that made Will turn to him in astonishment.

It was that look, that sudden understanding on Will's face that there was something more going on than he'd thought, that propelled Duncan to his feet. He threw himself at his erstwhile friend, who, caught by surprise at the vehemence of the attack, stumbled against the side of the hut. Duncan seized him by the arm and the back of his coat, and spun him away from the shed, his own balance thrown off by the ease with which he was able to do it.

'Dunc! Come on, man, what's—'

'It's mine.' The two words, punctuated by a short, sharp

breath, sounded impossibly obsessive, even to Duncan, but it was too late now to try and lessen the impact of his reaction.

'You've nicked the collection, haven't you?' Will said in wondering tones. 'Fuck me, Dunc, you've actually *nicked* it!'

'It was a joke,' Duncan insisted, but Will laughed. Loudly, and with surprised admiration.

'Show me,' he said, losing all his former antagonism in the face of this revelation. 'Mate, this is epic! I wish I'd thought of it.'

He turned towards the door again, but Duncan found the torch in his pocket and dragged it out. Before he realised what he was going to do, he whipped it around in an arc, ending with a hollow smacking sound, and an agonising impact that ran up his arm into his shoulder, and made him cry out.

His fingers spasmed and flung wide, and the torch tumbled to the ground, while in front of him Will Kilbride's knees buckled, and he reached out to grasp the door jamb. 'What?' he muttered stupidly, his head drooping. Duncan knew there would be blood somewhere over his right ear, but he couldn't see it, and now everything became blazingly clear and real again.

Will's voice was thick and slurred. 'You bastard.'

Before Duncan could say anything in return, Will lurched towards him and Duncan felt hot pain as fingers hooked into his cheeks and mouth, pulling his lips wide as Will's thumbs slipped between them.

He stumbled back, carrying Will with him, and they fell together, the impact mercifully jerking Will's hands from Duncan's face. Duncan balled his fists and drove them repeatedly upwards, but the thickness of Will's clothing rendered the blows ineffective. Will rose up over him, preparing to roll away, but Duncan grabbed at his coat and pulled him back, unable to risk letting him get far enough away to begin kicking. He lashed out with his other fist, getting a lucky blow beneath Will's chin.

Will faltered, and Duncan could smell the blood strongly now, as it streamed from Will's head down his cheek, and warm splashes fell on Duncan's forehead. Revolted, he twisted away, and with a desperate cry, he clasped his fists and drove them up into Will's groin. Will froze for a second before falling, groaning, onto his side.

Duncan scrambled free, and stood up. He blinked, confused, and backed away, breathing hard and with an apology on his lips; this was a *friend!* Not the best, and certainly no Rob Doohan, but a friend, nevertheless. What had he been thinking? He'd been in thrall to some ridiculous lump of black stone... This wasn't him, not anything like.

'Will, I'm sorry,' he said, when he could speak. 'I didn't mean, I thought you... Look, come in on it with us. I'll show you what we've got.'

There was no answer, and Duncan moved closer. 'Come on, I'm sorry.'

Will lay motionless, and Duncan's blood chilled. He knelt beside the prone form, and bent his head close to Will's face. He felt the faint stirring of breath on his skin, and closed his eyes in relief. But the relief was short-lived; this close, he could see Will's face was slick with blood, and more was matted in his hair. He'd gone too far. This much blood must surely make it attempted murder, and even if Mick eventually saw the funny side of tonight's activities, there was no way Will would. If he even survived.

Duncan sat back on his heels, his head lowered. He didn't know how long he'd stayed there before he looked up again, but the fireworks were growing more frequent now, and on that

evidence alone he knew it must be getting close to midnight.
Will had not moved, and Duncan reluctantly accepted that he
wasn't just stunned by the pain of that final blow; the effect of
the head injury must have taken hold.

The night breathed. Beyond the wind, he heard the
rushing of the river that sped by past the hut, and a dim and
horrific thought began pushing insistently at the edges of his
clouded mind.

The thought became clearer, and he fought against it, but
with ever-weakening resolve. No solution he could think of was
enough to banish it entirely, and he finally stopped trying. He
rose to his feet again, but as he bent to take hold of Will's feet a
familiar snuffling, growling sound came from a few feet away,
and he looked up to see Spark, busily licking the blood from the
side of Will's head.

He tried to remonstrate with the dog, but instead a rush of
dizziness and revulsion made him turn away and retch helplessly; the rich Hogmanay dinner, mingled with Mick's
precious Drumnacoille 25, rushed up through him, stinging his
nose and burning his throat, before splashing onto the grass,
and his shoes. The smell rose, rank and sour, and he convulsed
again, adding to the hot pool on the ground.

At last he felt the trembling subside, and he knew he had to
do it now, before he let himself think about it any longer. If he
did that he might just crawl away into the trees, curl up, and
simply let everything go. He shooed Spark away, took a fresh
hold of Will's feet, and pulled.

His burden slid horribly easily over the grass, but with
every inch they covered, Duncan waited for Will to come to his
senses again. He half hoped for it, for anything that would stop
him from carrying this sickening deed through to its conclusion. But nothing did. Will remained unconscious and unmov-

ing. Spark hovered a few feet away, down on his belly, but his eyes following every move his master made, until Duncan stopped at the edge of the river, and, with his own eyes firmly shut, knelt down and rolled Will off the bank.

There wasn't even a significant splash to mark the moment; it was white water here, roaring over rocks and roots, on its way to the quieter spot below, where he and Will had often fished. Someone would find him there, see the head wound, assume he'd slipped and fallen in on his way home. There was no reason to suspect anything else.

Duncan remained on his knees for a while, thinking with renewed sorrow about little Donna, and the rest of Will's family, but when his knees started to ache with the coldness of the wet grass, he pushed himself to his feet and stood up. Just as he did so, fresh fireworks burst into the sky from the direction of the house. The real thing, this time, shooting upwards into the dense black, single silver threads that burst into riots of colour and sent sprays of stars across the vast empty canvas, welcoming a new year. One which Will Kilbride would never see.

God, what had he done? Fresh tears stung as another wave of disbelieving horror swept over him. The colours melted and swam in front of his blurred eyes, dying away only to be replaced by more, brighter, higher. He could hear the shrieks of his guests, followed by the laughter as they mocked one another for their excitement, quickly drowned out by more hissing, crackling, and ear-splitting booms.

He twisted to look back at the shed, his eyes dragged there by a force even more powerful than the plunging white river that had pulled Will out of this grey and thankless life. Inside that plain wooden hut, more colour and beauty were contained within a hand-sized black rock, than in the whole of the skies tonight. And it was all his.

His terrified tears dried on his cheeks, leaving his skin salty and stiff, and a smile even touched his lips as he turned his back on the river and its grim passenger. He began once more to walk back up to the house, Spark trotting contentedly at his side. A tune found its way out into the cold night air, and it wasn't until he'd hummed the first few lines that Duncan realised what he was singing, and began again, this time with conviction.

Should auld acquaintance be forgot, and never brought to mind...

Prologue

Three Sisters, Glen Coe, Scotland. Thursday 15th November 2018

HE STARED out into the darkness beyond his windscreen, icy hands jammed between his knees, but reluctant to leave the heating on in the car; if there was ever a time to risk flattening a tired battery, this wasn't it. The quarter-moon played fitfully with bulging clouds, occasionally outlining the menacing volcanic peaks that rose all around, and the time dragged on, but still there was nothing else out there except the rain.

For the millionth time since he'd arrived, his glance was pulled to the tyre lever nestled in the semi-darkness of the passenger seat footwell, inviting him to pick it up and admire its weight. For the millionth time he looked away again. No violence here, not tonight. He'd been a fool, that was the long and short of it, but there was a faint hope that he might at least buy himself some time, and, faint or not, he was going to grab it.

Popular in the daytime, even at this time of year, this beauty spot was always deserted once darkness fell, but the road that cut through the glen was still one of the main arteries from Glasgow, and several cars had passed by since he'd arrived. Another set of headlights lit up the rock face of the mountain, this time from the Fort William direction, and a car slowed. He sat up straighter, feeling sick, but the driver had only wanted to peer more closely at the famous Three Sisters mountain formation before carrying on up the winding road out towards Rannoch Moor.

The nausea remained, and he twisted the ignition key and buzzed his window down to let in some fresh air; rain blew in with it, and he welcomed the cool spray on his burning face as he thought over what he would say when Kilbride's man finally turned up. Kilbride wasn't an idiot, nor would he send one to collect his dues; he knew he'd get what he was owed, eventually, and that the interest alone would keep a roof over his head for months... Of course he'd wait. He had to.

The next car did not pass by. It slowed and turned in to the tourists' viewing point, and as the terrified man watched it creep slowly closer, his hand, acting independently from conscious thought, dipped down into the footwell after all and tested out that tyre lever's considerable weight. He slipped the lever inside his jacket, and yanked the zip back up just as the BMW Roadster drew up behind his own car.

The Roadster's window whined down, and the face that glared out belonged to Craig Lumsden, Kilbride's top enforcer, who bent and examined the back seat of the man's car through the rear window. He appeared satisfied no-one lurked there.

'All right, get out.'

The man did so, watching warily as the BMW circled away and returned to park more neatly next to him. He held the tyre lever tight against his side beneath his jacket, and hoped his movements didn't look too obviously stilted as a result. 'Where's Kilbride?'

'He's not likely to be coming out here himself, now, is he?' Lumsden got out of the BMW and studied him across the bonnet. A police issue nightstick was hooked into his belt, and sour bile crept once more into the back of the waiting man's throat. The solid presence of the tyre lever should have been a comfort, but he found himself wishing he'd left it where it was; before he could even draw it into the open, Lumsden would have that baton out and extended, it would be just the excuse he needed.

He lifted his chin. 'I need to talk to him.'

'He doesn't do talking,' Lumsden said. 'Not once the agreement's been signed.'

'Well if he wants his money he's going to have to.' He sounded stronger than he felt, even over the Beamer's running engine, and that in turn bolstered his confidence. He met Lumsden's eyes with something approaching calm.

Lumsden smiled, looking more shark-like than ever in the headlights as he passed in front of his car and came closer. 'Are you going to bring your account up to date, or am I going to have to remind you who's in charge here?'

'If I can't talk to him, maybe I can talk to you? Look, if you're prepared to wait, I could cut you in...give you extra, when I've got it, to keep for yourself.' He could feel the sweat, both on his palms and cooling on his temples as the wind blew into his face.

Lumsden studied him for a moment, then shook his head. 'William said you'd try that one.' He unclipped the nightstick in a disturbingly leisurely motion and flicked it to full length. 'Now—'

'Take my car!' He hated the harsh desperation in his voice, but couldn't hide it.

'*That* pile of shit?'

'You can tell Kilbride I never turned up, and then—'

'Shut up.'

'I'll not even report it stolen.'

'I said shut *up*!'

He did. He watched the debt collector, feeling all his muscles tense to the point of aching, and wondered where the first blow would land. He folded his arms tightly across his chest and felt the outline of the tyre lever under his right hand, but there was still no way he could draw it out before the stick put him out of action.

Kilbride's man was still watching him, his face all shadows in his car's headlights, rain falling on his lashes, but he didn't blink. He gave that smile again, the one that elongated his mouth but touched no other part of his face, then he stepped back and made his way around to the open door of his car.

'It's your lucky night,' he said, twirling the stick. 'I was just instructed to pass on a message, should you prove difficult.'

'Whatever he wants.' The man followed him, all caution fled in his relief. 'What is it? Tell him I'm getting the money together right—'

'You talk too much. And back off – you're crowding me.'

'Sorry.' He stopped a few feet away and quashed the urge to ask again what the price of his reprieve would be.

Lumsden seemed to be thinking hard about his next words. Trying to recall the exact message from Kilbride? Or maybe he just enjoyed screwing with people's heads. His phone beeped, he ignored it. Then he shrugged.

'Mr Kilbride says that if I go back empty-handed, he'll take something of yours to the value. Or possibly a teensy bit more.'

His smile was thin as he laid his hand on the door of his car, then he turned away. 'Isn't it traditionally accepted that the sons must pay for the sins of their fathers?'

The clang of the tyre lever hitting the ground, some unknowable time later, brought the man out of the howling tunnel into which Lumsden's words had driven him. He stared, numb, as the steel bar bounced twice on the gravelled ground and came up against the sprawled leg of Kilbride's debt collector, and then he dropped to his knees, vaguely aware of the sting of tiny stones through his jeans.

Hands clenched on his own thighs to keep from touching anything, he forced himself to look at Lumsden, slumped half in and half out of his car, and he wasn't sure whether he was hoping for a sign of life or not. But there was nothing. Lumsden's head lay twisted on the car seat, where he had been struck down even as he scrabbled for safety. Streams of blood pooled in the open eyes and ran in rivulets down over cheekbone and jaw; the rain diluted it and sent it moving faster, dripping into the open mouth and staining the teeth.

The killer — he was no more or less than that now — stood up and stumbled away from the two vehicles, until their light no longer illuminated the blood on his hands. How often had he hit Lumsden? Once? Twice? More? Christ, he couldn't even remember. And what now? What if someone had driven by, while he was lost in the throes of whatever it was that had consumed him, and seen what was happening? Taken his number plate? Taken photos, or even a video on their phone?

He tucked his hands under his armpits and sat on the grass at the edge of the viewing point, staring up at the lumpen masses above him as if they held all the answers. But even the skittish moon abandoned him as he watched, and the Sisters were absorbed into the black void above them. As another car passed by, he belatedly came to his senses; there was no chance he would have been Lumsden's only appointment tonight; no-one would come out here for one lousy collection. The next car might well be the next pickup.

He stood up again, on shaking legs, and gingerly picked up the tyre lever from the puddle of rain and blood in which it lay. He laid it quietly back in its footwell, and, leaving the BMW untouched and its engine still running, he drove home.

Chapter One

MADDY CLIFFORD GUIDED her scruffy little Corsa through the Friday afternoon traffic and out of Inverness. It was finally over, and her sentence was passed: a revoked firearms licence, a month of cleaning council toilets – or some such delight – for six hours a day, plus a year of keeping her nose clean, and that was it. Apart from the nightmares, of course.

She still had to keep telling herself that she hadn't killed Sarah Wallace on that horrific weekend back in August; shooting the woman through the window had saved young Jamie Thorne's life, and if it also gave Maddy recurring nightmares in which the bullet had missed Wallace and hit the child instead, well, they would fade in time. Someone else had fired the fatal shot, and they would never know which of the woman's supposed partners in crime it had been, but she herself had acted to save a life, not take one.

The community payback order reflected that, and was a small price to pay in the grand scheme of things. Having the interview today, directly after the trial, had eaten up the rest of her day off, but at least it meant her allocation could start straight away rather than waiting a week or so. Soonest begun, soonest done... She'd got off extremely lightly, all things considered.

By the time Maddy reached Abergarry she was calmer than she had been in a long time. The sight of the quiet streets, and the steadily falling drizzle, had its own soothing familiarity; tourists brought colour, life and much-needed income to her home town, but when they left, it felt as if she'd had a houseful of guests throughout summer and autumn, and now she was allowed to walk around in her pyjamas again.

She went up the narrow staircase to the office she shared with Paul Mackenzie, and automatically straightened the forever-crooked sign on the door: *Clifford-Mackenzie Investigations*. It never failed to make her proud to see it, but it likewise never failed to irritate her that she kept forgetting to fix it. Then again, today wasn't a day for irritations, and her smile widened as she pushed open the door and stepped into her familiar home-from-home. There would be no fanfare, but she was confident of a warm welcome here, at least.

Paul was frowning at his laptop as she came in. 'Seen this?' He pointed at the screen.

'It went very well – thanks for asking.'

He looked up, and his distracted look vanished. 'Shit! Sorry, I was... What did you get?'

She hung her raincoat on her chair. 'Two years, suspended for twelve months, and a hundred-and-twenty hours community payback for the council.'

He gave a low whistle. 'Cleaning? Your twelve-year-old self's bedroom would never believe it.'

'Says the man who needs a Sherpa to find a pen.' Maddy gestured at the mountain of paper on his desk.

He grinned. 'Good result though. Thank God it wasn't custodial. Remand was bad enough, from what you said.'

'Aye.' Maddy shut down the memory of those few horrendous weeks, before they could spoil the good feelings that had been sneaking back. 'What's happening here then?'

Paul spoke more gently. 'It's still your day off, Mads. Go home to Gavin and Tas.'

'I'm not quite ready for that yet,' she confessed. 'I'm too strung up. I'd only wind Tas up. D'you want a coffee?'

'Oh, yeah, that'll really help de-stress you.' He raised his eyes briefly to the ceiling. 'Go on then. I presume you've called Gavin?'

'Of course, as soon as it was over. He was...relieved.'

'He should have gone with you.' Paul scowled. 'I'd have had Tas here, if child-minding was the problem.'

'It wasn't.' Maddy switched the kettle on and spooned instant into two mugs. She didn't want to discuss her fiancé, who'd been touchy for days now; this morning he'd been talking to her as if he thought the next time he'd see her would be as a result of a visiting order. She could have done without that negativity and told him so, quite bluntly. Her father had been there for her, and that had been enough.

While she waited for the water to boil she cast a covert glance at her partner, assessing him, as she did every day, without comment. Since the bike accident that had shattered his collar bone he'd undergone complicated surgery to pin everything back into place, and he was moving a lot more easily now. More to the point he was allowing himself time, which was a relief. She watched from the corner of her eye as he rummaged in the pockets of the jacket that hung on the back of his chair, and while he favoured his left arm, there was a definite improvement in his range of motion.

That little firebrand, Charis Boulton, no doubt had a lot to do with it, Maddy acknowledged with a faintly grudging appreciation; she'd been relentless with the physio once she'd learned what to do. The fact that Paul not only put up with it, but defended her methods, told Maddy that the great lump had fallen hard for the woman since getting tangled up with her after Jamie had gone missing. Seeing him gradually allowing her into the space reserved for his late wife and son had actually been quite heart-warming, despite Maddy's initial reservations.

The fact that Charis had subsequently moved herself and her son into Abergarry, but not into Paul's home, was another good sign; any relationship born in a time of intense fear needed time to evolve more naturally, if it were to survive the humdrum of normal life. And life was certainly humdrum these days.

Maddy brought the drinks over to the desk, and Paul took the mug with *Everton FC* on it – a gift from the firebrand herself, knowing he was a committed Glasgow Warriors rugby fan.

'Have you seen or heard the news at all today?'

She shook her head. 'I didn't want to catch anything about you-know-what, on the local radio.'

'This has gone national,' he said. 'They found a body at Three Sisters this morning.'

'A *body*?' Maddy came around the desk and peered over Paul's shoulder. 'What the hell?'

'Craig Lumsden. Found with his head caved in. Halfway into his car, too; he must have been trying to get away from whoever did it.'

'God, that's brutal,' Maddy breathed, when she'd read the

brief report. 'Poor Donna.' She shut her mouth tight as soon as the words were out, but it was too late.

'You know his widow? She's William Kilbride's daughter, right? You never said you'd met her.' Disapproval was leaking through his mild words, and Maddy sighed inwardly. Kilbride was known to skate around the very edges of legality when it came to his business practices, and there was well-founded suspicion that his methods had crossed a line more than once. Paul would have nothing to do with him.

'We've met,' she admitted, 'but only once.' She started to move away, but Paul deftly plucked the coffee mug from her hand, and she stopped. 'Look,' she said, seeing by his expression that she wouldn't be able to brush this one under the carpet, 'I don't know the Lumsdens themselves. Not really. I just did a...a bit of work for Kilbride, back in August.'

'You *worked* for him?' He gave her back her coffee. 'That's even worse. How didn't I know about it?'

Maddy felt the heat as her cheeks coloured. 'I put it through the books under a different name.'

'What name?' Paul frowned and opened the Excel file on his laptop. There weren't that many jobs to scroll through, and he highlighted one of them. 'Is this it? John Macnab?'

'Kilbride suggested it,' Maddy said quietly. 'It's from the Buchan book and means something to him, apparently. I told him I didn't want his real name on our books, due to his...questionable tactics for recovering what he's owed.'

'Questionable?' Paul snorted. 'The man's a thug.'

'I know. And I'm sorry, but we needed the money then. It was before you got your inheritance back. And Gavin... Well, he wanted to keep Kilbride on side. He was doing some work for him too, at the time, and he recommended us. Or rather, me.'

'What did Kilbride want an investigation service for, anyway?'

Maddy looked sideways at him again, trying to gauge if his calm tone was really resignation, or whether he was about to blow a gasket. 'Evidently someone who worked for him owed him a lot of money and had given him a convincing sob story. He was totally sucked in, because he trusted the bloke, gave him an extension, and the bloke promptly vanished. Sort of.'

'And you helped Kilbride find him?'

'No, but I uncovered the alias the man had been using. And *that* bloke had no shortage of money to pay back what he owed. So no broken legs or missing ears required,' she added, knowing exactly what he'd been thinking. 'Kilbride was grateful for the info, so he paid up. I put it through our account, the electricity got paid on time and no-one got hurt.'

'Can't say the same for this one.' Paul closed Excel, and gestured to the news item now showing on his screen again. 'I wonder which debtor finally got fed up with being chased by Kilbride's bloodhound?'

'Maybe it started out as self-defence,' Maddy mused, 'and Lumsden had the tables turned on him.'

'Could be, I suppose.'

Paul shut the laptop and picked up his coffee. Maddy couldn't help noticing the little grin that lifted his expression as he caught a glimpse of the blue lettering on the mug, and wondered again at the way he and Charis seemed to fit so well together. She and Gavin were much more visually obvious, she supposed, Gavin being tall and slender, like her; they were both red-haired, to varying degrees, and possessed a certain elegance of manner.

Paul and Charis, though, were total opposites. Both were dark-haired, but that was it, similarity-wise; Paul was well over six feet and built like the rugby player his younger self had aspired to be, whereas Charis barely came up to the middle of his chest, and would blow away in a strong wind. Paul was quiet, most of the time, his humour well hidden from all except those who knew him best, and with a manner that often seemed morose to strangers; Charis was...well. Not like that.

'How's the mouth on a stick?' she asked, knowing it would get a rise out of him.

His dark eyebrows drew in, but there was an amused glint in the hazel eyes that regarded her over the steam coming off his coffee. 'She's fine. How's the yawn in a suit?'

She laughed just as her phone chirped, and she took it out of her pocket. 'This is him,' she said. '*Don't* do your usual.' She pressed to answer.

'Maddy?' Gavin's voice was tight. 'Have you seen what's happened to Kilbride's son-in-law?'

'Just now, aye. Are you all right? You sound...weird.' She could see Paul gearing up to shout something about a runaway leopard, or a spaceship that had just landed on the roof, and shook her head at him quickly. He seemed to sense this wasn't the time, and subsided.

'Well, it's just a bit of a shock, don't you think?' Gavin said, a little lamely.

'In his line of business, the shock's more that it hasn't happened sooner.'

There was a pause. 'That's true enough.' After another brief silence, Gavin got onto what had presumably been his real reason for calling. 'So... Are you on your way home yet?'

'Any minute.' She suppressed an irritated sigh. 'I'm just having a cuppa with Paul, before I pick up Tas from school.'

'Of course you are. How silly of me. What time will you be back?'

Her mouth tightened and she briefly closed her eyes. 'Around half an hour. I'll just finish my coffee.' She replaced the phone in her pocket and muttered, 'and burn the skin off the roof of my mouth while I'm at it.'

Paul raised an eyebrow. 'Everything all right?'

'He was just wondering if I'd seen the news about Lumsden.'

'I suppose it's a bit close to home, with Kilbride being a client of his,' Paul said reasonably.

'*Ex*-client,' Maddy pointed out quickly. 'As far as I know Kilbride hasn't retained Gav for any reason. So, this CPO,' she went on, keen to move away from the subject of her fiancé. 'They offered weekends instead, since I have a job, but I'm not giving up my time with Tas. Which means you'll probably have to draft someone in to help out while I'm wiping up puke and scrubbing down walls.'

Paul pulled a face. 'Good point. What is it, six hours a day?'

'Aye, for four weeks.'

'Crap. How far did you get with the background checks for Robinsons?'

'Almost all done. Just one candidate left, who says he went to Plymouth University, but he's lost his transcripts and certificate in a house move. He won't order more through their e-store, and Plymouth won't confirm his attendance until they've heard from him that it's okay to release the information, so I'm just waiting for that.' She had a sudden, awful thought. 'Don't for one minute think about employing Charis!'

Paul laughed. 'She'd run a mile, don't worry. Anyway she's still temping for maternity-leave cover at the council. Would Tony step in for a few hours now and again though, do you think? Just for office stuff and the odd bit of digging about?'

'Knowing Dad he'd jump at the chance.' Maddy threw the rest of her drink away and rinsed her mug under the tap. 'I'd better go, before Gav sends out a search party.'

'Don't be too hard on him,' Paul said, surprising her. 'He probably thought he was going to lose you. Spend some time together, aye?'

Maddy looked at him for a long moment, then bent down and slipped her arms around his neck. 'You're a rough gem, Mr Mackenzie.' She kissed his cheek, remembering a time not so long distant when such a gesture would have led to something warmer, more exciting. They'd been good together, and despite her faint regret that it had ended, it had left a residue of trust and closeness she valued above everything else in their relationship.

'I'll talk to Dad,' she said, crossing to the door. 'I'll call you later and let you know what he says.'

'Aye, great. Thanks.'

She looked back to see him opening the laptop again, the light from it spilling across his face, his expression showing he was already absorbed again in what he was reading. She smiled to herself and pulled the door closed behind her, straightened the sign again and started off home.

Chapter Two

IT WAS ALMOST nine on Friday evening by the time the detective sergeant gave Donna Lumsden one final look of sympathy, and then she and her colleague went home to their own families and their own comforts, and no doubt put the new widow, and her shell-shocked grief, out of their minds until tomorrow.

Donna heard the front door close, and her stepmother came back into the sitting room, her face still registering disbelief, especially now that the madness had died down. It was as if the closing of that door had been the switch that had shut off the TV programme and left them with only the truth: Craig was dead.

There was no mistake, and it had been no accident; someone had taken a blunt weapon to him, smashing his skull in from behind even as he'd tried desperately to claw his way into the safety of his car. Whoever it was hadn't stopped when they'd killed him, either; various reports throughout the day, filtered through the family liaison officer who'd just left, had confirmed what appeared to be a frenzied and unnecessary attack.

'What was he doing up at Three Sisters at that time of night?'

'Were you aware he wasn't at home?'

'Did he have plans to meet anyone there?'

'Would he have been alone?'

The questions had been endless, despite Sergeant Muir's half-hearted interventions on the family's behalf; when someone like Craig, the husband of a successful restaurateur, is murdered in cold blood in the middle of nowhere, answers can't simply wait until everyone's got over the shock. Even less so when he's the son-in-law of William Kilbride: Scotland's worst-kept secret. Donna had always known that someday someone was going to trip her father up, and his shadier dealings would be laid bare, but he'd been too clever to let that happen. Until now. It would be hard to keep it hidden once the investigation began in earnest.

Her father had come over immediately he'd heard, and surrendered willingly enough to the same barrage of questions, but Donna could see all he wanted to do was tell the DI in charge to fuck right off and leave them to process the news. Now they were alone again, he looked over at Donna and held out a hand.

She stood up and went to him, crouching beside his wheelchair and seeking comfort in his familiar embrace.

'Who was he meeting, Dad?'

'I'll have to check the book when I get home. But we don't know if it was a scheduled meet anyway; everyone who's dealt with him would know where to find him.'

'I don't get it, though,' she mumbled against his shoulder as he patted her back. 'Why was he on his own?'

'Martha,' Kilbride said over her head to his wife, 'leave us, would you?'

As always, Donna's stepmother melted away without argument, and Donna took her seat on the sofa again. 'Why wasn't there anyone with him?' A horrid thought struck her. 'Or was there? Was it *Ian* who did this? Or did he stand by and let it happen?'

Kilbride shook his head quickly. 'No, put that thought out of your head. Ian's not... He's left, that's all. I'm a man down, and Craig said he'd be fine to go alone.'

'Well he wasn't, was he?' Anger flashed through her again, fuelled by the horror of her imagination. 'You shouldn't have let him.'

'What was I supposed to do?' Kilbride slapped the arms of his wheelchair. 'I wasn't fit to step in! And there *was* no-one else. Craig knew the—'

'Don't you dare say he knew the risks!' Donna jumped up, a jangling bundle of nerves and raw grief. 'He was working for you! You owe him justice for this, Dad.'

'The police are on it. Let them do their job.'

'They'll play the self-defence card.' Donna stared out of the huge picture window at the darkness beyond. It suddenly seemed filled with moving shadows, and she shivered. 'You heard them; Craig had his baton on him, and it was found opened. Someone will pour out a sob story, point to a bruise, and they'll get off with a warning, or even a suspended sentence or some such crap. Dad, they don't *like* us.'

'So what are you suggesting?'

'I'm suggesting we prepare ourselves for that, and get ready to step in if needs be.'

Kilbride was silent for a moment, but in the reflection in the window Donna saw him give a brief nod.

'At least I was able to tell the truth when they asked me if I knew where he was last night,' she said.

'You genuinely didn't know he was out?'

'I was working,' Donna pointed out. 'Thistle Inverness had a golden wedding do last night, and it ran over. I didn't get home until almost four.'

And even then she had lain awake, scowling in annoyance that Craig hadn't responded to her text, and waiting for him to return with some half-baked excuse to cover another casino night. But of course, he hadn't. Instead there had been the clanging of the doorbell and the shattering of her world.

People thought she was cold, she knew that; even her children had been more likely to turn to their dad for anything important. And yes, maybe she *was* a bit detached, but Craig had been the one person who had seen far enough into her soul to touch it, and the pain of his loss, sweeping down in savage and unpredictable arcs, would have surprised everyone but Craig himself.

'I'm going to bed,' she said. 'Tell Martha goodnight, and thank her for me.'

'She'll be back in a minute,' Kilbride said. 'Stay down here and talk to us. You shouldn't be on your own.'

'But I am,' she said, her voice hollow. 'I need to get used to it.'

'What about Chelsea and Myles? You still have them, and they'll need you.'

'They'll need me to be a functioning person,' she said, 'which I won't be if I don't get some sleep.'

'Do you have anything to help you?'

Donna looked around at the drinks tray and picked up a bottle of Malbec. 'This'll do, until I get something from the GP.'

'Donna...' Kilbride looked at her helplessly, then rolled closer and gently took the bottle back. She didn't stop him, but it had only been a show of bravado anyway; she had no intention of allowing oblivion to steal her thoughts tonight, not when Craig deserved them. She bent to kiss her father goodnight and left him alone in the sitting room.

On her way up to bed she passed Martha, who squeezed her arm and gave her a troubled look, but didn't try to make things better; she clearly knew it would be pointless. Donna lay down, fully dressed, on the bed she'd shared with Craig, and turned onto her side, staring at his pillow and wishing for once that she'd bought cheaper ones that might still have carried the indentation of his head. She reached out and traced the shape of his face, as if she could see it, and could almost hear him telling her to stop being such a daft sod and let him sleep.

She smiled through the tears that blurred his outline, and laid her hand flat on the cool cotton. *Never.*

The following morning she watched her distraught children leave in the back of her mother's car.

Barbara Kilbride had turned up before breakfast, and immediately decided her grandchildren needed to be somewhere else, at least while the police were sniffing around the house and into their parents' lives. A quick telephone call to DS Muir had confirmed that it was allowed, provided they were reachable, and before Donna had really had time to think it through, Chelsea and Myles were on their way to the Trossachs. She already missed the noise, and even the stress, of having two kids around.

Another half an hour passed before Muir arrived, along

with DC Forbes and some more details that had come to light since last night's post-mortem.

'We believe the murder weapon to have been a chrome-plated steel bar of some kind, probably a tyre lever,' Forbes said, lifting the cover of his pocket notebook. 'We found flakes of the plating in the, in his...uh...' He broke off and cleared his throat. 'The only prints on the baton we found nearby were your husband's,' he went on. 'Where did he get it – do you know?'

'Ebay, I expect. He's carried one ever since some little scrote tried to mug Dad in the Rose Street multi-storey last year.'

'Mr Lumsden was your father's driver – is that correct? And presumably acted as a sort of bodyguard at the same time?'

'My father doesn't need a *bodyguard*,' Donna said, trying not to sound snappy. 'He's an accountant, for Christ's sake! But,' she conceded, after taking a breath, 'there are people who'll see someone in a wheelchair, who dresses nicely and wears a good watch, and take them for an easy target.'

'So Mr Lumsden fulfilled a sort of—'

'He's...*was*, Dad's personal assistant.' Donna swallowed another of the many tight lumps that had risen in her throat since yesterday morning. The sting of tears made her blink hurriedly; anything to avoid those looks of mingled pity and suspicion the two officers were so fond of giving her. 'I want to know exactly what happened to him,' she said. 'I'll hear about it at the inquest anyway, so you might as well tell me everything.'

'Okay.' Muir consulted her notes. 'We found bruising on the underneath of your husband's arms and wrists, which suggests he was first attacked from the front and raised his arms like this.' She demonstrated, crossing her own wrists above her forehead. 'His right wrist was broken, suggesting he was struck with some force.'

Donna flinched. 'And he didn't use the baton to protect himself?'

'From its positioning it seems likely he dropped it before he raised his arms.'

Donna nodded, part of her wishing she hadn't asked for details after all. 'Go on.'

'There was also some slight bruising to his forehead,' Muir said, 'which we believe was a result of his own knuckles coming back into his face when his wrists were struck, and it's possible he stunned himself by knocking his own head back against the door surround. There are traces of blood and hair there that we're having checked. That's probably when his attacker got through his defences and struck the blow to the top of his head.'

'And Craig tried to get away,' Donna managed, swallowing hard again, 'but the murderer came after him.'

'That certainly seems to be the way of it. So it's unlikely any claim of self-defence would stick.' Muir tucked her notebook away and touched Donna's arm. 'I'm so sorry, Mrs Lumsden. We're doing all we can to find out who did this to your husband. We're checking his laptop and phone, to try and find out what he was doing out at Glen Coe last night. Are you sure there's nothing else you can tell us about that?'

'Of course I'm sure!' Donna took a calming breath. 'I was working at the Inverness restaurant; we were late finishing because of an anniversary bash that went on longer than planned. I texted Craig around eleven or so, when I knew I'd be late, and when I got home and he wasn't here. I assumed he'd stayed at Dad's.' That last part was a lie, of course, but she saw no reason why she should mention Craig's habit of frequenting the casino. It was clearly irrelevant now.

'Did he stay with Mr Kilbride often?'

'Sometimes, if Dad had been out late and they'd had a chat and a drink after Craig had driven him home.'

'Do you mind me asking,' Muir said, opening her book again, 'what's the nature of your father's disability?'

'He's paraplegic. He spent a year in hospital a long time ago, after an accident where he fell into a fast-flowing river and broke his back.'

'When was this?'

'1987. Well, '88, technically, I suppose, since it was New Year's. He spent a bit over three months in a coma, and never walked again.'

Muir wrote quickly, though what relevance it had, Donna couldn't imagine. 'And how long had Mr Lumsden been working for him?'

'Since we got engaged, in '96.'

'A good while, then.'

'Aye.'

'Clearly he was trusted.'

'Clearly,' Donna said, her voice hardening again. 'Look, I don't mean to be rude, but I've got arrangements to make, and I don't see what my father's disability has to do with what happened to Craig.'

'Just rounding out the picture.' DS Muir pocketed her book. 'We'll get off now and leave you to it, but we'll be back as soon as we have any news. You must call if you need anything. Or remember anything,' she added pointedly.

Donna nodded. 'Of course. And thank you.'

She watched at the door until Muir and Forbes had vanished down the hill, and then went back inside, feeling emptier and more helpless than ever. With the children gone and her parents returned to their own home, the house felt even more enormous than usual. She tried to fool herself that she enjoyed the quiet, and that Craig would have pissed her off anyway by suggesting sex, when all she wanted to do was watch the telly, but it was no good. Even for the thirty seconds she believed it, she still felt cold and distanced from everything.

She went upstairs and curled into the pillow on Craig's side of the bed, hot-eyed and hollow. But the helpless feeling of loss gradually gave way to rising anger against whoever had taken him from her. If the police didn't find them, she would.

After a moment she rolled onto her back, frowning. Her father *had* to have known who Craig was meeting... She had no idea why he'd lied last night, but since he obviously had his reasons, it was pointless to hope he'd actually tell her. She swung her legs off the bed and sat still for a moment, thinking hard, then she reached for her phone, and tapped a name in her contacts.

'Martha, hi. Is Dad there? No, it's okay, it's you I wanted to talk to anyway; I'm feeling pretty low, and he'd only worry. Can I come over?'

Chapter Three

Maddy studied Gavin across the table. Saturday mornings had always been a time of calm for them, but today, when there should have been an air of celebration in the house, her fiancé looked distant and tight-jawed, and the eyes that met hers were the reddened eyes of the sleepless.

'You've been like this for days now,' Maddy said. 'I thought you'd be pleased it's all over.' She glanced through the open door to the sitting room, where five-year-old Tas sat with his Lego, and lowered her voice. 'I could have been in *prison* now, Gav!'

'I know that!' He snatched the toast off his plate and took a half-hearted nibble at the corner before dropping it back down. 'Obviously I'm glad you're not.'

'Then what's the matter? I understood it up until yesterday morning, but surely now there's no—'

'For God's sake, Maddy! Go in to work if you want to question things. I'm sure there's an insurance scam somewhere just begging for your brilliant investigative mind.'

Maddy stared, a hundred furious responses building

behind her tightly set lips, but she couldn't phrase a single one with enough cutting edge to satisfy her, so she sat silent.

Eventually Gavin sighed, and looked at her again. 'I'm sorry. That wasn't necessary.'

'No it wasn't.' Her phone rang, and she gave him another glare before she stood up and walked to the worktop. 'Sort yourself out, or you can bugger off to your office yourself. I'm not having you spoil today.' She picked up her phone and looked at the screen, then forced a smile into her voice. 'Nick! Hi.'

'Good news,' her brother said. 'I'm being seconded to CID for the Lumsden case.'

'Wow. That's great!' And just what he needed to persuade him to stay on in the service, too, she hoped. 'Might it become permanent?'

'Probably not. It's only because Alison Muir's been appointed family liaison, so the team's temporarily split. And Mulholland's still out, of course.'

Maddy winced at the name; the dead-eyed sergeant had been one of the darkest parts of what had happened in August, yet he had turned up for work the following week, shining and innocent, as if nothing had happened. Naturally he'd been immediately suspended, but there had been nothing to connect him to any of the violence, when it had all come down to it; he'd simply been assisting a superior officer to locate a missing child.

'Has anyone seen him since his suspension was lifted?' she asked.

'He's apparently put in for a transfer, but he's still on leave for now. DCI Kwambai asked for me specifically though,' Nick went on, 'which was pretty good.'

'Ah yeah, the new bloke. What's he like?'

'Dunno yet – seems okay though. And he clearly has good judgement when it comes to his team.'

Maddy laughed. 'Tas was asking if you were coming over later. I think he wants a bit of help with a list for Father Christmas.'

'That's about six weeks away!'

'Five. And believe me, you'll appreciate the extra time. So are you coming? Dad's talking to Paul this morning. He's stepping in at the agency for me, so maybe you could both come over together, when he's finished.'

'I'll give him a ring and come over after work,' Nick said. He was silent for a moment, and Maddy was about to begin the usual wind-up of the call when he spoke again, his voice hesitant. 'I meant to ask you yesterday, when you called after the sentencing, but it didn't feel like the right time. Is Gav okay? He's been weird lately.'

Maddy just stopped herself from looking over at her fiancé, who she knew would be watching her; he hated knowing he was being discussed. 'Fine, thanks,' she said. 'Just a bit tired.' Which could apply to herself as easily as to anyone else. 'Text me when you know what time you'll be here. I'll get the kettle on.'

She didn't return to the table; she'd had as much of Gavin's moroseness as she could stand, today of all days. Instead, she left him to clean up the breakfast things and went to play with Tas. Gavin joined them after a few minutes, and Maddy felt herself stiffen up as he sat down and ruffled Tas's hair.

'What are we building today?' he asked, in a too-jolly voice.

'Space station.' The little boy looked from one parent to the other, and Maddy could see he'd already picked up on the tension. 'See, that's where the spaceships go.' He pointed. 'I need a window,' he went on, 'so the captains can watch out for their spaceships when they're having dinner.'

'I'll find one for you,' Gavin offered, and Maddy turned a few bricks over, pretending to help but keeping a close eye on him. He too seemed to be only going through the motions; his expression was still distant, his mind clearly anywhere but on Tas's space station.

'Uncle Nick's coming over later,' she told Tas, to distract him. 'And Grandad too. They'll help you with your Santa list, I'm sure.' She knew she hadn't talked much about Christmas; she hadn't been able to bring herself to think about it, in case she ended up spending it in Cornton Vale; now she felt not only able to begin the traditional long build-up, but eager for it. Once more the enormity of her good fortune threatened to manifest itself in tears, but they would only have frightened the lad, so she blinked furiously and re-engaged herself in the search for a long window for the spaceship captains.

'Dad!' Tas said, exasperated, and Maddy looked up to see Gavin staring at the floor, one hand loosely covering a small pile of bricks but not moving.

'Why don't you make us another cup of tea, Gav?' Maddy suggested. 'I let my breakfast one go cold when Nick rang.'

He shot her a look that was part gratitude, part desperation, and it left her baffled. 'Keep looking,' she told Tas. 'I'll go and help your dad in the kitchen.'

She half-closed the door and waited for Gavin to speak. When he didn't, she took the kettle out of his hands and filled it at the tap. 'I swear to God, if you don't tell me what's wrong I'm going to blow a fucking fuse!'

'Keep your voice down!' He glanced at the door, then closed it fully. 'You and your friend might think it's edgy and cool to use that language, but I won't have it near my son.'

Once more Maddy was unable to fully express her anger, so she said nothing. She threw tea bags into two mugs and switched the kettle on, then gave Gavin a look he could hardly fail to interpret correctly and sat down at the table.

'I didn't mean to snap,' he said quietly. 'I'm sorry.'

'You keep saying what you *didn't* mean,' she pointed out. 'So are you going to talk to me, or are we going to have this day ruined?' Her eyes followed his as they went to the morning paper. 'Does this have anything to do with that murder out at Three Sisters? Don't tell me Kilbride needs a solicitor and wants you?'

'No! I'm not even a criminal lawyer; why on earth would he?'

'You tell me. You were the one working for him on some fraud thing in the summer. Is it connected with his son-in-law?'

Gavin shook his head. 'It's nothing like that. It's... Look, I know you're going to find out sooner or later, but it's best you hear it from me first.'

Maddy felt a chill crawling down her spine. 'Go on.'

He shot another look at the closed door, then sat down opposite her. 'The reason I was working for Kilbride last year was because I owed him.'

'Money, I take it, not favours? Is that why you encouraged me to take on that job for him?' He nodded, and she frowned. 'But he paid me for it, and pretty well, or I wouldn't have done it.'

'He just added the money onto what I already owed,' Gavin said in a low voice.

Maddy blinked. 'So...*we* paid me?'

'Never mind that now.' Gavin looked down at his fingers, knotting and twisting on the table in front of him, and separated them deliberately, laying them flat. 'The thing is, I went to meet Lumsden up at Three Sisters on Thursday night. Well, early Friday morning.'

Maddy snatched a painful breath. 'Jesus, Gav—'

'He was dead when I found him!' Gavin lowered his voice, and now his eyes burned into hers. 'You have to believe me, Mads. I went there, *with* the instalment I owed, and found his car with the lights on and the engine running. When I went around to talk to him I found him—' He broke off and closed his eyes. 'I found him lying with his head on the driving seat and his feet sprawled out behind him. It was...' He stopped again, and wiped the back of his hand across his mouth. 'It couldn't have happened too long before I got there,' he finished.

'Why the hell didn't you report it?' Maddy stared, disbelieving. 'Of all people, you should know how that looks.'

'I just—'

'If you're going to say you panicked, don't!'

'No, I thought about it,' he confessed. 'But if it got out that I'd been involved with Kilbride, which it would, that'd be it; if I didn't lose my licence, I'd lose all my clients. It just seemed... easier to drive away.'

'So you weren't out boozing with your team after all, then.'

'I was with them,' he insisted. 'I didn't lie about that. But I left them to it after the third pub. They knew your sentencing was happening on Friday morning, so they didn't question me leaving early.'

Maddy sat very still. Her instinct was to believe him; surely he wasn't capable of not only bludgeoning a man to death, but then lying so convincingly? Then her certainty wavered. He *was* a good liar, professionally. Top level. And if Kilbride had ordered him to carry out a hit on his son-in-law, for some reason known only to them, would he do it then? *Could* he, to pay off his debts and protect his future?

There was too much to take in. There she was, thinking he'd been behaving oddly because he thought she'd be going back inside, and all the time it was his own freedom he'd been frightened of losing. She didn't know how long it was before Tas came in looking for her, but the kettle had boiled and switched off, and Gavin was still sitting motionless opposite her.

'I'll be right there,' she told Tas cheerfully. 'Do you want some juice?'

'Aye!' Happy again, the boy went back into the sitting room, and Maddy made herself move, just to break the heavy spell of unreality that hung over her. She made the tea and poured Tas some juice, and all the time Gavin just sat there, looking as miserable and scared as she'd been herself ever since she'd pulled the trigger on Sarah Wallace. The resentment she felt at the way he was dragging them back down into that darkness was unfair – she knew that – but she couldn't help it. Just when things should have been getting back to normal.

When she'd taken Tas his juice and promised she'd be in again to play soon, she sat back down at the table and wrapped her hands around her teacup, for comfort rather than warmth.

'Did you touch anything?'

Gavin stared at her blankly. She repeated the question, more harshly, and he shook his head, but it was more of a wake-up than a negation. 'I...might have done. I don't know. I definitely didn't touch the murder weapon,' he added quickly, seeing her incredulous look.

'Which was what?'

'There was a night-stick. Like a police one. It was lying on the ground, and I nearly picked it up. But I didn't! That's how I know for sure I didn't touch it.'

'But you don't know about anything else?'

'Like what?' He shook his head helplessly again. 'It was such a shock. I might have... I don't know, I can't remember much else. There's no blood on my clothes or anything. I didn't touch Lumsden himself. I nearly threw up, though. Thank God I didn't.' His eyes widened, though only for a split second, and she frowned.

'What?'

'Nothing. Just thinking about what would have happened if I had.'

She nodded, suppressing a shudder. 'So how did you come to owe Kilbride in the first place?'

'It started when I won that hundred or so quid at the casino night last April, remember?'

She did – it had been one of their best nights out in ages. His firm had managed to poach a top barrister from Glasgow onto their team, and had taken them all out for a celebration, beginning with a posh meal at Thistle and ending with a night at the casino. Gavin had taken to it all like a kid to conkers, and had come out the only winner of the night. He'd been his old, carefree self that night, the way he'd been when they'd met, and she couldn't remember laughing so much. Whenever she'd wondered, since then, if she and Gavin had a future together after all, she only had to remember that night to feel reassured.

'I went back a week or so later,' he said now, 'with a couple of the others, and won again. Not much, but enough to pay for that city break in Rome.'

'You told me that was a bonus,' Maddy broke in. 'You said it was because you'd won the industrial sabotage case.'

'I'm sorry. I knew how you'd react.'

'Oh, so it was *my* fault you didn't have the balls to admit you were...' She held up a hand and took a calming breath.

'Let's not get into that. So, you decided you liked it, started losing, and went to Kilbride, of all people, for money?'

'He came to me, actually. It's how he does it. He's got eyes and ears all over the place, anywhere someone might find themselves struggling. His son-in-law spent a lot of time at the casino and must have reported back—'

'Presumably one of those nights you told me you were working through, or sleeping at the office.' It wasn't a question, and the dull flush that crept up his neck told her all she needed to know.

'Kilbride's daughter made an appointment with me through work,' he said quietly. 'She told me Kilbride could help, and that they'd make sure it was discreet. And so he did, and so it was. And I was *paying it off*, for Christ's sake! It wasn't as if I was struggling to make the payments.'

'Mum!' Tas's voice called through, and Maddy had to force herself not to snap back, but her blood chilled as he followed up with, 'There's a police car outside!'

She looked at Gavin, whose face had turned to putty. 'Could they have known you were going to meet Lumsden?'

'Unlikely they'd know for—'

'*Could* they?' she hissed, half her attention on the footsteps approaching the front door, and half on Gavin's grey face.

'Well I shouldn't have thought Kilbride diarises these bloody things!'

She ignored the sarcasm. 'Tell them everything. Tell them the truth, Gavin, okay? Promise me.'

The doorbell went, a harsh buzzing ring that cut through the silent house and made Maddy flinch. 'Coming!' she called, hoping she sounded more casual than she felt. She opened the front door and frowned in assumed surprise at the two officers who stood there. The woman was looking at Gavin's towering

Blue Arrow junipers by the door with open admiration, as if life hadn't suddenly turned to uncertain sludge beneath Maddy's feet; the calm, everyday attitude nearly sent Maddy through the roof, and it was an effort to keep her voice even.

'How can I help?'

'I'm DC McAndrew,' the woman said, 'and this is DC Byrne. We're here to speak to Mr Gavin Galbraith. Are you Mrs Galbraith?'

'Miss Clifford,' Maddy said. 'We're not married.' She stepped back and gestured to the kitchen. 'He's in there. Go through.' She suppressed the temptation to follow; she'd only be dismissed anyway, which, in her own house, would make her angry. Instead she went into the sitting room, where Tas still sat surrounded by his Lego, and tried to engage her mind in playing while she strained to hear anything at all from the kitchen.

After only a few minutes, however, Gavin appeared in the doorway. 'Mads, I'm just going to pop into the station, okay? It'll be easier to talk in there.'

She scrambled to her feet. 'They're taking you in?'

'No. My choice.' His smile was wide and completely false, and Maddy wished she'd listened at the door after all; at least she'd know if he'd told them the truth or not.

'See you later, Tas.' Gavin gave his son a cheery wave. 'Save me some sandwiches if I'm not back by tea time.'

'Oh, I'm sure you will be,' McAndrew said, but her smile didn't quite ring true either. 'Thank you, Miss Clifford. Mr Galbraith will show us out.' She turned back. 'Are you by any chance related to a DS Nick Clifford?'

'He's my brother.'

'I see the resemblance.' McAndrew gave her a bland smile, and then they were gone.

Maddy took out her phone and tapped her father's image on the home screen. He didn't answer, which meant he was probably driving over to the office, so she dialled the office phone. That rang out too, and in rising desperation she called Paul's landline, cursing the hopeless mobile signal up where he lived.

'They've taken Gav in for questioning,' she said, as soon as he answered.

'What?'

'I need to talk to you properly, but I've got no-one to look out for Tas. Can you come over?'

'Your dad's waiting for me at the office,' he pointed out. 'Look, why don't you meet us there? You can pick up your raincoat at the same time; it's making the place look untidy.'

She almost smiled at that, which was doubtless his intention. 'What about Tas?'

'I'll see if you can drop him with Charis.'

Maddy closed her eyes. *Charis? Really?* 'Would she mind?'

'He'll have a great time,' he said, nimbly sidestepping the question.

Maddy gave a resigned sigh. 'Okay. I'd bring him with me, but since this is about—'

'His dad. Aye, I know. She'll understand. Let me call her, and in the meantime you grab whatever Tas needs.'

A few minutes later he called back, but now he sounded distracted. 'Yeah, she says you can drop him round whenever you like. I'll get the kettle on for when you get here.'

Maddy was surprised at how easy it was to leave her son with the Boultons; Charis didn't seem to mind at all, and Maddy knew Tas liked her. Possibly because she was small and loud, and laughed a lot, but also, Maddy suspected, because Jamie's bedroom was an Aladdin's cave of comics, spy gadgets and goodness only knew what else. Jamie himself liked playing the 'big brother' too, which helped.

She handed Tas over in the doorway, promising to call as soon as she knew how long she'd be, and the boy barely looked back as he vanished inside. Normally Maddy would have felt a pang about that, but today she was grateful; her mind was back on Gavin, turning over everything she'd learned in the past hour.

At the office she found Paul true to his word. He'd seen her car park up on the street below and was already pouring the drinks; he never needed to ask what she wanted – it was always tea at home and coffee at work. Maddy gave her father a hug and took her mug to the back of the room, to the seating area they used for longer conversations with clients. After taking a moment to organise her thoughts, she told them everything Gavin had told her. She didn't want to look at either of them while she spoke, but felt immeasurably better for getting it all out.

'It was all pretty vague,' she finished. 'He just said he was going with them to answer a few questions. I mean, they didn't put his clothes in bags or anything, and they didn't arrest him.'

'Where did he say he was, on Thursday night?' Paul asked.

'His team was having a leaving do for one of the juniors. Pub crawl around Inverness.' Maddy rubbed her eyes. 'He wasn't drinking though, so it was no problem for him to have driven out to Three Sisters the same night. It's only a couple of hours, and the roads would be quiet this time of year. They're probably talking to loads of people.' She realised she was babbling, and stopped.

Her father nodded. 'Where've they taken him – do you know?'

'I didn't even think to ask.'

'They've likely set up the incident room in Glencoe nick,' Tony mused. 'They'd not let you see him anyway, so I don't think—'

'I don't want to go out there,' Maddy said. 'I just want to know what to *do*! He's got himself mixed up in some pretty nasty business.'

'But you're sure he's not responsible for what happened to Lumsden.'

'Of course he's not!' The reply came fast and heated, but she remembered the doubts she'd had, and Gavin's ability to lie so smoothly. 'He's not capable of that sort of violence,' she added, wondering if she was seeking to convince herself or her father.

'They'll see the coincidence though,' Paul said. 'You know that.'

Maddy nodded. 'They'll have a lot of questions for him, but he's fairly sure his name won't come up as a...a *client*, I suppose you'd say.'

'No,' Paul said, shooting her a dark glance. 'We know Kilbride likes a pseudonym, don't we?'

'What's this?' Tony looked from one to the other. 'Have you two dealt with him yourselves?'

'Only a background check on someone,' Maddy said quickly. 'It suited us both that we didn't use his real name when I put him through our books.'

'And did this have anything to do with Lumsden at all? Or Donna?'

'It was all Kilbride. Nothing to do with his daughter; she didn't even know I was working for him until I told her.'

'How do you know that?'

'I went there to ask her about Sarah Wallace, back in August. They were roughly the same age and went to the same school, and I wanted to find out if she knew who Sarah was having a fling with. She didn't know who I was, or what I was doing for her dad.'

'Well that's something.'

'So,' Maddy ventured, after a brief silence, 'do you think I ought to go to Kilbride?'

'No!' They both spoke together, and Paul went on, 'But if the police ask, you're going to have to tell them who *Macnab* really is.'

'Of course I will.'

'And you're sure that whatever information you supplied Kilbride with wouldn't have resulted in anything...dodgy?'

'I told you, it just meant that bloke couldn't keep pretending he'd no money to pay Kilbride back.' Maddy put down her drink and knitted her fingers. 'If he kept refusing after that I don't see how that's down to us.' She was aware she was sounding defensive, and that Paul was looking at her a little askance, but Gavin was the one in trouble now. She needed to think about him, not some joker who'd been stupid enough to think he could put one over on William Kilbride. 'I did nothing illegal, and I *helped* Kilbride. So it's all in Gavin's favour, when you think about it. Do you think I ought to go to the police and volunteer the information, or wait until they come to me?'

'Wait,' Paul said at once. 'The connection between Gavin and Kilbride is through him, not you. What you did was totally separate. And you can't afford to have something else come to light now, not with a suspended sentence hanging over you.'

'Oh God.' Maddy let her head fall forward into her hands.

'Why the hell did I get myself involved?'

'You didn't,' Paul reminded her. 'You didn't go looking for that job with Kilbride; Gavin passed *your* name to him.'

Tony nodded. 'And considering he hates the agency for taking up so much of your time, he was pretty quick to do that.'

'I'd have thought he'd be happier to see us go under,' Maddy agreed grimly. 'Then again, Kilbride did add our fee to his debts. Pretty galling to be paying myself to work.'

'At least he paid up first, before trying to claw it back off Gavin.' Paul cleared his throat. 'Look, Mads, I have to go out for a bit. Are you going to be okay?'

'Aye, I'm fine. All I can do is sit tight and wait until Gav gets home and tells me what's going on.' She looked up at him and noted that the distraction was back on his face. 'What's the rush though? Got something interesting on?'

'Possibly. He usually has.'

'Who?'

'My brother Ade. Apparently he's back in the country.'

'For good?'

'So Charis told me, when I called her to ask about Tas. He'd been to see Dad when he didn't find me at home, and Dad gave him Charis's address, assuming I'd be there.'

'So he's at Charis's now?'

'Has been for a while.'

'Ah,' Maddy said, suppressing a little smile. 'So *that's* why the look.'

'What look?'

'Like the kid with the sweets, who's just seen the school bully across the playground.'

'Paul gave her a wry, resigned look. 'No bullying needed; knowing Ade like I do, two minutes and the sweets would jump straight into his pocket.'

Chapter Four

WILLIAM KILBRIDE WATCHED the two family liaison officers carefully as they gave Donna the latest news about the investigation. DC Forbes checked his notebook.

'Do either of you know anything about a Gavin Galbraith?'

'He did a little advisory work for me, back in the summer,' Kilbride said. 'Why do you ask?'

'Advisory?'

'My accountancy firm,' Kilbride clarified smoothly. 'We'd had a little dispute with our usual legal team, and were a bit concerned about a possible fraud case. We thought we ought to be ready with a backup, just in case. I suppose you'd say more exploratory than advisory.'

'And what led you to choose Galbraith?' The officer was scribbling in his book, and Kilbride grew increasingly irritated by the scratching of his pen.

'We just got chatting one night, after he and some of his firm dined at my daughter's restaurant. It was a question of seizing the moment. Exchange of business cards. You know.'

'But the fraud case never arose, you say.'

'Happily, no.' Kilbride shifted in his wheelchair. 'You never answered my question, constable. Why are you asking about Mr Galbraith?'

DS Muir jumped in, addressing Donna. 'Was the fraud involving your chain of restaurants, Mrs Lumsden?'

Donna shook her head, a little scowl appearing on her brow. 'Of course not. And before you ask what it *was* to do with, I don't know anything about this Galbraith bloke. He and his mates just happened to be dining at Thistle that night.'

'Mr Kilbride?'

'That has no bearing on my son-in-law's murder,' Kilbride said, trying not to let his annoyance show. 'Just tell me why you're bothering about a solicitor we never even used.'

'His car was spotted near the scene on Thursday night,' Muir said. 'We're checking it now.'

'Spotted by whom?'

'A cyclist, taking part in a local challenge of some kind. She saw the report in the paper and remembered a particularly slow-moving vehicle in that area, because she was actually obliged to overtake it on her bike. She was able to give us a partial plate; the letters apparently had a personal significance, and stuck in her mind.

'And what's her name?' Donna wanted to know.

'It came via the form on our website. Anonymous.'

'Will you check her out?' Donna's tone was mild, but Kilbride knew every nuance of her voice and realised with a little chill where the tip-off had come from. But where the hell had she got Galbraith's name?

Muir stood up and gestured to Forbes to do the same. 'If the investigation isn't hampered by any false evidence, there'll be no need. Why do you ask?'

'I might owe this woman a great debt of gratitude,' Donna

said. 'Perhaps when it's all over she'll come forward and I can thank her then.'

When she returned from seeing them to the door, Kilbride folded his arms and spoke bluntly. 'How did you find out about Galbraith?'

'Find out what? You heard what Muir said; someone witnessed him at Three Sisters.' She shrugged. 'They'll check out his car, find the... I dunno, the right kind of gravel in his tyre treads, or whatever they look for, and he'll get what he deserves.'

'So you posed as a witness, *just* to make sure they checked out his car.'

Donna sighed. 'Congratulations.'

'You're sure it was him, then,' Kilbride persisted. 'Why?'

'Because I found his details in your little black book.' Donna sat down. 'Well, your little green book,' she amended.

'But there's nothing on that spreadsheet about him, or about anyone else involved in that side of the business.'

She gave him a thin smile. 'If you say so.'

'It's true. I'm not stupid enough to keep records of—'

'White text on a white background? Come on!'

Kilbride scowled. 'I suppose Craig let you in on that little secret then?'

'Oddly enough, Dad, it's not *that* brilliant a ruse. It would have been more fiddly if you'd hidden the text properly, but I could still have done it. In the end I just highlighted a few random columns and changed the text colour.'

'Okay,' he conceded, 'but you don't know Craig was going out to Glencoe to meet him. It definitely doesn't say anything in there about collection dates.'

'I'm not stupid either. I can work that much out for myself. Craig was out there on Thursday the fifteenth, and Galbraith's the only one with an original agreement made on the fifteenth of the month... It doesn't take a genius.'

'But how did you get into my office in the first place?'

'Don't blame Martha. I told her I was looking for a CD I'd lent you.'

Kilbride scowled. 'Sneaky.'

'I learned from the best.' Donna looked at him squarely. 'Why did you lie to me and say you'd no idea who it could have been?'

'Because... I was...' Kilbride shrugged. 'I thought you'd blame me, for misjudging what Galbraith was capable of. That you'd think I'd failed Craig by letting him go alone.'

'You did.'

Kilbride flinched at the harshness in her voice. 'I know,' he said softly. 'I really thought the man was just some weak, scared fool. I'd no idea. But I'll make it up to you somehow.'

'Then see that Galbraith gets what's coming to him,' Donna said coldly. 'You can do that, at least.'

'Only if he's charged.'

'Of course he will be. He did it! We both know it; we just needed to guide the police in his direction. So I did.'

'Is this likely to come back on you? The false evidence?'

'Like Muir said, only if it hampers the investigation. After all, who's going to say there was no such cyclist? And I filled in the online form at the library. They can't prove it was me.'

'I wouldn't bet on that.'

'Even if they could, it's hardly the crime of the century.' She paused. 'Dad, where did Ian George go?'

Kilbride blinked at the change of subject. 'You know where he went. He moved down to Stirling.'

'It was him that woman was investigating, wasn't it?'

'Why ask, if you already know?' Kilbride shrugged. 'Turns out Ian did the sensible thing.'

'Buggering off and leaving his own brother to be arrested?' Donna looked sceptical; she'd always been fairly pally with the George brothers, who were relatives on Martha's side somewhere down the line. 'That was the sensible thing, was it?'

'Aye,' Kilbride said. 'Whatever stunt the pair of them were pulling, I wasn't about to let them do it with my money. But to be fair I owed him the chance to get away, at least. After all the years he worked for me and kept quiet about it.'

He didn't say any more. The scenes that had followed Clifford-Mackenzie's investigation had been far from pretty, and Ian George's face even less so by the time Craig had finished with him. But the mention of his former employee focused his mind: there was no-one left now that he trusted. It was all very well being the name behind the unspoken threats, but Kilbride was well aware of his limitations when it came to carrying those threats out. He needed a driver, and he needed muscle. Fast.

In the meantime at least he had his adapted Qashqai to get about in, and that evening, as he left Martha at Donna's place and drove the familiar road home, his mind turned to those in his company who might be built from the right stuff. Ian had learned a harsh lesson about loyalty going both ways, and Craig had known which side his bread was buttered on; protecting his wife's father had come with the job, and he'd been good at it.

But Kilbride had never found it easy to make the kind of loyal connections he needed now. Even as a kid he'd never been a true part of the gang he hung about with, Duncan Wallace's lot, but still, he'd tried with them. And look how that had turned out... He flung an angry look at the disassembled wheelchair on the seat next to him. No. He'd never really belonged to that exclusive set, despite the weekend shoots, the fireside drinking sessions and the mutual commiserations over the various antics of teenaged daughters.

It had taken a good long time for him to remember why he was in hospital, when he'd finally struggled back from the thick darkness he'd been in, but it had come to him quite suddenly one quiet afternoon when his mind had been elsewhere: the fight by the river on New Year's Eve.

He'd heard about some kind of prank the others were playing on their friend Frank Mackenzie, a prank from which he'd naturally been excluded. So he'd followed Wallace and found him, around midnight, in the process of hiding something in the gillies' shed. It had turned out to be the Mackenzie family's famed gem collection, and Kilbride had actually been impressed by the way his then-friends had planned and carried out the joke raid. He'd also been interested in how they'd planned to replace it without being seen, in the spirit of the book by John Buchan, which had inspired the escapade. He remembered that Wallace had come up behind him as he'd attempted to look at the spoils, and that he'd half-turned in surprise at Wallace's anger.

There'd been nothing then, until Kilbride had woken in hospital to find it was spring, and that he'd spent three months being washed, shaved and changed by strangers. Evidently he'd been found by Wallace's underkeeper the next morning, sprawled on the shingle at the wide point of the river on the Glenlowrie Estate. Happy New Year, my friend...

Wallace visiting him in hospital had seemed like a step in the right direction, especially when he learned that poor old 'Mick' Mackenzie had suffered a stroke in the aftermath of everything; that Rob Doohan was serving five; and that Sandy

Broughton had committed suicide in prison. Perhaps Wallace had realised he'd lost three of his best friends and was clinging on to those who remained.

But no. He had sat amiably at Kilbride's bedside and announced that he now had a pet copper on side, a bloke by the name of Don Bradley. He'd pointed out that young Bradley was a dab hand at making accusations go away, so Kilbride might as well take a cash sum and say he'd slipped and fallen into the river on his way home. A confused, angry and pain-wracked Kilbride had been in no fit state to fight him; it had seemed easier just to put it all behind him. So he'd sold the family home and moved to the other side of Inverness, cutting every thread that had tied him to his younger life. Apart from Wallace's blood money, of course: the foundation for his own business as well as his daughter's.

Kilbride pulled up outside the home that business – and its darker sister company – had afforded him, and couldn't help giving a grimly satisfied smile. Here he was, living in secluded splendour in a place that put even Wallace's family pile to shame, and where was smiling, conniving, back-stabbing Wallace now? Nowhere. Same as his vile, spoiled brat of a daughter, who'd managed to cosy up with that so-called *loyal* pet copper, right under her father's nose. And while she'd been getting herself shot dead in the mountains, Donna was flourishing.

Or had been.

Kilbride pushed open his car door and began re-assembling his wheelchair, his mind turning towards how to make sure Galbraith knew he'd have to plead guilty. When the second wheel had clicked into place he swung himself out of the driver's seat and into the chair, but he paused before pushing the car door closed and twisted to look behind him. Something felt off.

He frowned and slipped his hand into the pocket on the inside of his chair, feeling the small but reassuring weight of the Glock 42 as his fingers closed around it. He looked slowly around the grassed area that spread away from the drive, following it down to its edge and then back up to the house itself; modern, glass-built and always, *always* lit.

He knew better than to telegraph the fact that his home was unoccupied at any time, and from here it was possible to see into most of the rooms at the front, which was how he liked it; since Hogmanay 1987 his tolerance for surprises had, naturally enough, faded to non-existent. But although the comforting light spilled out onto the smooth, tarmacked drive, the front door suddenly seemed too far away, and he felt an uneasy prickle at the back of his neck.

He carefully pushed the car door shut with his free hand, keeping the pistol gripped inside the wheelchair pocket with the other, and pressed the keyless lock button in the handle. Then, feeling a bit foolish, he nevertheless spun the chair around to face the way he had driven in.

Either side of the open gateway were groups of trees that fanned out along the perimeter of his property, giving it that secluded air that so impressed visitors and suited his lifestyle. But tonight, though the leaves had long since parted ways with the branches, the bare bones of those trees seemed to hide a hundred eyes. It was a long time since Kilbride had felt real, mortal fear, but he had made a lot of enemies over the years, and he felt the absence of his personal assistant more keenly tonight than ever. The branches creaked and swayed as a powerful gust of wind streaked across the moor, and Kilbride felt his palm sweating against the grip of the gun. His heart suddenly seemed too big for his chest, making it hard to breathe.

He peered into the trees, and then spared a quick glance at the warm safety of his home. The wind pulled at his hair, tugging it in several directions at once and making him shake his head irritably as his vision was marred by grey strands that flicked into his eyes. He swallowed, though his throat was dry and tight, and his mind began running through names of people who'd be only too glad to take advantage of a gap in Kilbride's protection. Pretty much his entire 'little green book', as Donna called it, particularly those in white text.

He glanced again at his porch; large, welcoming, tantalisingly close. He drew the Glock out of the pocket and held it on his lap while he pushed the lever on his wheelchair and turned, maddeningly slowly, towards the door. As he rolled up the gentle slope of the drive to the ramp that lay parallel with the front of the house, he kept turning to look back into the shadowy trees, convinced he could see movement that was caused neither by the wind nor by any of Martha's three cats. His heart was thudding uncomfortably hard and fast, and image after image passed through his mind of the things Craig had told him... No wonder late payments were rare. Sometimes he cursed his own vivid imagination.

Rolling into the brightly lit porch, he realised he'd been concentrating so hard on having the gun to hand that his keys were still deep in his coat pocket. He let out a muttered curse and rummaged past phone, tissue pack and chewing gum; as his fingertip hooked through the ring that held his keys, his breath stopped in his throat. A second later the gun was wrenched from his grasp and placed against the back of his neck

He moaned in terror and, oddly detached, felt a warmth

spreading across his thigh and matting his trousers to his skin. This was it; at the grand age of sixty-four he was going to die, just inches away from the safety and comfort of his own home, and having soiled himself. The gun pressed against his skin, and he closed his eyes, knowing there was absolutely nothing he could do about it. He had time for a flash of sympathy for Martha, arriving home to find him, and the brief regret that she would then discover why he had died and how many people would rejoice—

'I'll take that, pal. Now fuck off. And don't let him see your face, or you'll never recognise it again!'

It took a moment for Kilbride to realise that the barrel of his gun was no longer rammed against his neck; he could still feel the phantom pressure of it. But the appearance of the Glock at the corner of his eye, passed to him over his shoulder, woke him up. He grabbed at it, but the voice behind him spoke again, more gently now.

'Relax, Will. He's gone.'

'Ian?' Kilbride twisted and looked up at the man who'd saved his life. The last time he'd seen Ian George he'd been barely recognisable, but now he looked more or less the same as he had before his instructional encounter with Craig. Albeit with a new, livid scar running down the side of his face, from brow to chin and just skimming his left eye. All the bruises had gone, and the swelling had now disappeared, leaving only that hideous reminder of treachery, and its price.

Ian gave him a half-smile. 'Bad penny, eh?'

'Who was it?' Kilbride peered into the distance. 'Where did he go?'

Ian waved a hand. 'Doesn't matter. He won't be back. Well, not tonight, anyway.' He came around to the front of Kilbride's chair, and Kilbride frowned.

'Why did you step in? I'd have thought you'd have been happy to see my head blown off, after what happened.'

Ian shrugged and sat down on the edge of the porch. 'I might have wished that on you a few months ago,' he admitted, 'but I got what I deserved.' He touched the scar, and looked up at the house. 'Martha in?'

Kilbride tightened up again, but the gun was back in his hand, and it was Ian who'd put it there; he was pretty sure he had nothing to fear. 'She's staying at Donna's tonight.'

'Ah yeah. Poor Donna. Nasty business.'

Kilbride gave him a sharp look. 'Is that why you're back, then? Because Craig's gone?'

Ian met his gaze, and held it steadily for a moment. 'I think we probably need to go inside for this, don't we?'

In his own sitting room, and about to transfer himself from wheelchair to armchair, Kilbride became aware once more of the wet patch on his trousers. He felt the heat of shame creeping up his neck, but there was no reason Ian should have realised what he'd done. He excused himself and went to change, while Ian made himself comfortable at the generous drinks tray. When he returned to the sitting room, feeling in control of himself again, he settled into his chair and accepted the drink Ian passed him.

For a split second, as the tumbler reached his lips, he froze, suddenly certain Ian was out to get him after all, but with something more subtle than a noisy gunshot. He caught Ian looking at him, and saw the light of amusement around the younger man's eyes.

'I've not poisoned you,' Ian assured him, and took the glass away. He drained it himself and poured Kilbride another. 'Go on – it's safe.'

'So then.' Kilbride took a sip, blessing the warmth that trickled down his throat. 'Why are you here?'

'Lucky I was,' Ian pointed out. 'Or you'd have been—'

'Not the issue. But yeah, thank you.' He suppressed a shudder, but felt the ice-cold spot on the back of his neck again, and closed his eyes as he thought about how it could have turned out so differently... The comforting sense of being able to see right down the drive, and across the lawn, was abruptly replaced by a wish to shut out the night and the dangers that came with it. He picked up a remote on his side table and pressed it; the heavy velvet curtains swished slowly across the huge picture window and the sensors on the lights immediately dimmed as well, turning the room into something altogether cosier. Safer feeling.

'Right then.' He looked at Ian, who sat forward, rolling his glass between his palms.

'You were right. I came back when I heard what had happened to Craig. I didnae like the man – you know that, especially after what he did to me. But... Well. No-one deserves that.'

'And why did his death bring you back?' Kilbride was pretty sure he knew the answer, and how Ian would respond, but he was curious to see how the man would couch his proposal.

'Look. What Neil and I did was stupid. Risky, and disloyal. And you had every right to have me investigated. But you don't know the half of it.'

'Don't I?'

Ian looked uncertain for a moment, then shook his head. 'He'd not have told you,' he muttered, finishing his own drink.

Kilbride wondered if Ian had driven up from Stirling, and if so how he was going to get home if he carried on sinking the single malt like that.

'Told me what?' he prompted.

Ian stared into his empty glass for a moment. 'Craig was blackmailing me,' he said at last. 'He knew I was skimming and hiding the money under that other name.'

Kilbride didn't answer. He wasn't sure how to feel, or whether to believe what Ian was saying, but it made a grim sort of sense. 'Go on,' he said, after a long silence.

'I'm pretty sure Neil said something that made him suspicious. So he started watching me more carefully, and when he was sure he'd figured it all out he didn't come to you, he cornered Neil instead. Gave him a bit of a going over – put the fear of God into him. You know the score.'

Kilbride nodded. 'Go on.'

'Then he told me everything, and said he'd keep it to himself if I paid him. We had to stop taking our cut of your profits, so it became...difficult. Things were getting tight, and it meant I couldn't carry on paying the money back into *your* account either, so that was when I came to you for a loan.'

'Which I was happy to grant you,' Kilbride reminded him tightly. 'And at very generous interest rates I seem to recall, due to your previous good service.'

'Ironic, eh? You were paying yourself back.' Ian gave a short laugh, but Kilbride didn't see the humour in it and his glare made that clear to Ian, who subsided.

'Anyway, it got so I couldn't keep up Craig's blackmail payment, not even with the loan, and then I couldn't pay you back either. That was when you got that investigator in on it.'

'She found your other name, and the life that went with it,' Kilbride said. 'You were still maintaining that okay.'

'We weren't though. It just looked like it. Have you never done that whole "fake it 'til you make it" thing? I bet you have.'

Kilbride chose not to answer. 'So that was it? You're telling me that everything fell apart because your brother couldn't keep his mouth shut? That my son-in-law kept it to himself and lied to me, and to Donna?'

'That's about the size of it, aye.'

'Then I suppose it would surprise you to know that Craig's the one who told me what you were doing.'

'What?' Ian's composure slipped, and Kilbride offered him a faint smile.

'Left out the part about blackmail, of course. Why do you think I got the Clifford woman in?'

'The double-crossing bastard...' Ian's expression said, quite clearly, that if Craig wasn't already dead, he soon would have been.

'We fought about it,' Kilbride said. 'I didn't believe him. Didn't want to.'

'Just as you don't want to believe me about him now?' Ian rose and gestured to the cut-glass decanter. A wordless request.

Kilbride nodded. 'Get me a re-fill too. I think I need it.'

'You *do* believe me though?' Ian poured them both generous shots and returned to his seat. 'I mean, I've no axe to grind with the bloke, not now. But it's only right that you should know what he was really like.'

'Now he's not here to defend himself.'

'Or to confess. Look, Will – Donna has a right to know, doesn't she?'

'You leave Donna out of this,' Kilbride warned him. 'I need to think about what you've told me.'

'Aye, well. Do that. But if you're in the market for someone, particularly someone who owes you big time, to stay at your side and make sure things like that,' Ian pointed towards the window, and whatever lay beyond, 'don't happen again, you know how to get hold of me.' He pulled out his phone.

Kilbride frowned. 'Who are you calling?'

'Ghostbusters,' Ian said glibly. Then he sighed. 'A cab. Unless you're going to offer a bed for the night?'

'Call away. Get it to pick you up from the village in an hour.' Kilbride waited while Ian arranged for a taxi to Bught Park.

'You're staying at the caravan park?' he asked, when Ian ended the call.

'No, a B&B on Torvean Avenue.'

'I wonder if I know it. What's it called?'

Ian shrugged. 'Christ knows. Something bland. Park View, maybe? Look,' he went on, shifting uncomfortably in his seat. 'Craig was a shifty bastard, you know that, and he went behind your—'

'Hold on.' Kilbride pursed his lips. 'I'm not saying I believe Craig *was* using his position to score off you, but if he did, he took advantage of *you*, not me. Unlike you and your brother.'

Ian subsided. 'That's true enough. And he did what you asked of him.' He touched his scar again. 'Even if he did enjoy it a bit too much.'

'Don't push me.' Kilbride scowled. 'You want to come back to work for me then, is that it?'

'I never wanted to leave,' Ian pointed out. 'Even after what happened. You were a good boss, and I was the one at fault. I might not be Stephen Hawking, but I'm not thick. I know when I've done something stupid.'

'Like coming back here and risking ending up in the big house with your brother? You were safer down south.'

'Neil's the one they were after. I kept myself clean. They'll find it hard to make a charge stick; it'd be a waste of their resources. The Procurator Fiscal will never approve it.'

'You seem pretty sure of that.'

'I am.'

'They had to have a good reason to arrest Neil.'

'Aye, but that won't hold up in court with me, and they know it.'

Kilbride studied him in silence. He'd known the George kids since his second wedding, when Ian had had to be fished out of the ornamental fountain following a dare. They were enterprising lads, but not as clever as they thought they were; he'd known that even back then. It was one of the reasons he'd felt safe offering Ian a job when Martha had pleaded the lad's case years ago. Kilbride definitely had the upper hand, intellect-wise, and Ian's physical presence did the rest, even at just twenty years old. It had worked back then.

'How do I know I can trust you?' he said at last.

Ian gestured to the wheelchair, where the gun was once more tucked into the pocket. 'What better way? I saved your *life*, man!'

But Kilbride didn't follow the pointing finger. Now the shock had worn off, and the humiliation of sitting in urine-soaked trousers was fading, he was starting to wonder at the convenience of Ian's arrival in the nick of time. He allowed a little smile to lift one corner of his mouth, so Ian would see he hadn't fooled him after all, but didn't see the need to mention it.

'I can think of a way,' he said instead. 'Not yet, but maybe soon.' He glanced at his watch. 'You'd better get going. You've a good walk ahead of you to the village, and you don't want to keep that cab waiting.'

Ian stood up. 'How do things stand with us then?'

'I'll call you.'

A flicker of frustration passed across Ian's face, but was gone in an instant. 'Aye. Okay.' He put out a hand. 'I'll just sit tight then.'

'Do that. I'll be in touch. And don't forget, *you* can call *me*. You know,' he added cryptically, 'if you should suddenly need someone.'

'Thanks.' Ian gave him an odd look and went out to meet his taxi.

Around an hour later Kilbride reached for the phone. After a further moment weighing things up, he dialled the local police station.

'I had an intruder on my property this evening, and I believe it's someone you're looking for. No, he's gone now.' A little smile crossed his face. 'But I know who he is, and where he's staying.'

Chapter Five

MACKENZIE REPLACED the landline handset in its charger and
returned to the sofa. His brother lowered his mug of coffee and
gave him an enquiring look.

'All okay?'

'Aye. Gavin's back home, and Maddy can relax a bit now.'
He sank onto the sofa and rubbed his face. 'Where were we?'

'You were asking me where I was staying, and I was about
to say the pub at the bottom end of town by the library.'

'The Twisted Tree?'

Ade grinned. 'D'you remember us getting chucked out of
the pub garden for climbing that oh-so-sacred tree, when we
were kids?'

'I remember you and your mate lobbing acorns into some
big bloke's drink, and then pointing at me when he turned
around.' Mackenzie shook his head. 'You could be a proper
bastard at times.'

'It's what big brothers are for.'

Mackenzie laughed. 'Well you can always doss down here,
save a bit of cash, until you find a place.'

'Thanks. Thing is, I've got a place fixed up. Sort of.'

'Well that's good. Isn't it?' Mackenzie noted the hesitant look on his brother's face. 'I knew it; you and Charis are getting married, and you're moving in with her.'

Ade gave him a broad grin. 'She wishes!'

Mackenzie grinned back, but couldn't help reflecting on how well the two of them had been getting along when he'd gone to pick Ade up; people just took to him, always had. He himself might be a younger, slightly taller version of his brother, but it was hard to overlook Ade's brighter temperament, his readiness to laugh and his total confidence as he breezed through life.

'I don't know why you're not living with that girl yourself,' Ade said, taking a gulp of coffee. 'She's a wee cracker.'

'Early days,' Mackenzie said. 'It was a weird time to meet. We have to make sure there's something else there first.'

'She's the first one you've really let in since Maddy.'

'You knew about Maddy?'

Ade shrugged. 'I heard. I don't know that we ever met, though.'

'What do you mean, you don't *know*? Surely you'd remember?'

'Possibly, but the last time I was back here it was because of what happened to Kath and Josh.'

Ade had a wary look about him as he said the names, but Mackenzie shook his head; there was no longer that immediate flare of pain at the memories, just a familiar ache, and even a comforting kind of warmth.

'I know she was a nurse back then,' Ade went on, 'and you met while you were recovering in hospital, so... I might have seen her, I might not. And by the time you joined Tony Clifford's agency I'd already been back in New Zealand for months.'

'Mackenzie nodded. 'Yeah, well, it was short-lived with Mads. I wasn't ready.'

'But this Charis girl seems to have changed all that.'

'She does seem to.' Mackenzie allowed himself a little smile. 'But like I said, early days.'

'It's about bloody time.' Ade raised his coffee mug in salute. 'To Scouse dynamite.'

It was an apt description, and Mackenzie echoed the toast. 'So where are you moving, and why's it put that look on your face?'

'What look?'

'Like you're about to break the news that this house is actually yours, and you're throwing me out.'

Ade laughed, but it still sounded a little strained. 'Okay, you're going to have to give me your word you're not going to flip your lid when I tell you.' He sighed and put down his cup. 'This is to do with you, me and Dad.'

'Dad?' Mackenzie looked at him, startled.

'He said you visited every Friday, practically without fail. Said it made his week.'

'Did he?' Mackenzie was as surprised as he was touched; his father had never been demonstrably pleased to see him. He was glad now that he'd made the effort, since it had clearly had some impact after all. 'That's... Well, it's good to know.'

'Yeah.' Ade picked up his mug again, but it was clearly just for something to do. He peered into it, swirling the coffee until it slopped over his hand and brought him back. 'Okay, it's like this. Him getting the Spence collection back after all these years has—'

'Ah.' Mackenzie sat back, deflated.

'*Ah* what?'

'Ah, so that's why you came back.'

'Is it bollocks! I didn't have any idea about it until I saw Dad this morning. That's the truth; you can ask him.'

Mackenzie was inclined to believe it. He himself had never told Ade about the return of the family's valuables, and didn't imagine his father would have at that time, either. There was no-one else who could have. 'So why *are* you back?'

'I just thought it was time.'

'Weak.'

Ade shot him a rueful look. 'Okay. Jules and I got divorced. You know she has a huge family, and I'd been kind of absorbed into that. But it got me thinking about you, and Dad, and how the two of you are basically all I have left now.' He shrugged. 'There were decisions to make, about whether I want to stay out there or start a new life here.'

'And have you? Made a decision, I mean.'

'I hadn't,' Ade confessed. 'But then I spoke to Dad, and he told me about the money.'

Mackenzie tightened up again. 'That's his money,' he pointed out, 'not ours.'

'It's our inheritance though. And there's the opal.'

'You're not selling the Fury!'

'Everyone knows that's yours,' Ade said, raising a hand. 'No question. Even Dad knows it. Granny Spence had a soft spot for you, and you went through hell before you got that thing back.'

'I wasn't looking for it. I just—'

'No, that's what makes it all the more right that you should get to keep it, like Gran intended. Some weird kind of fate put it in your hands again, and we know you'd not sell it. We wouldn't want you to.' Ade sat forward in his chair. 'But since you *do* have it, Dad wants to put the rest of the collection to good use, rather than have it sitting in a vault.'

'By giving it to you?'

Ade was silent for a minute or two, and Mackenzie was about to prompt him when he spoke again. 'Do you remember much about that night? The night of the robbery?'

'Not really.' Mackenzie had only been ten at the time, while at five years his senior, Ade had naturally been more aware of everything. 'I remember staying over at Granny Spence's place,' he said, 'and that she'd died not long before. Then I remember being told we'd have to stay there a bit longer because Dad was ill.'

'He'd had the stroke,' Ade reminded him, and Mackenzie nodded.

'I didn't really know what that meant until a bit later.'

'But do you know it wasn't the robbery that brought it on? Not directly.'

'No, I didn't know that.' Mackenzie frowned. 'What was it then?'

'It was the accusation of fraud. That was what ruined us in the end. Dad's name was in the papers as being part of the robbery himself, for the insurance. The safe was still locked, see? The police questioned him, and word got out, and *that's* what did for him. For us all. Sandy Broughton tried to return the jewels, but it just made Dad look even guiltier, and then Sandy and Rob Doohan were arrested.'

'That was why Broughton killed himself in prison then,' Mackenzie murmured. 'Not just that his own family was disgraced, but that he'd ruined his best friend's as well.'

'Anyway, you know the rest,' Ade said. 'Dad was eventually exonerated, but by then it was too late. The working side of the estate fell into ruin, and you and I were packed off to the

Spences' place for good. Dad was taken to The Heathers, home sold. End of.'

'And now he has the jewels back, and he wants to sell them and give you the money?'

'Not quite. Rob Doohan had them valued for him, and yeah, they're going to be sold. He's no use for them now, after all. But he's not *giving* me the money, so much as investing it.'

'In what?' Mackenzie was starting to become irritated with the way Ade was dancing around the issue.

'Land I can build on. That way I'll have somewhere to live, and so will Dad. He can have a live-in nurse, and get out of that place on the hill for good.'

'How much do you think you're going to get?' Mackenzie couldn't help feeling a little amused. 'The collection's not worth *that* much!'

'Combined with my own savings and Dad's other, more bankable assets, it'll be enough.'

'Other assets?'

'Didn't he tell you?' Ade raised an eyebrow. 'You know the whisky that reached maturity just before it all happened, the *Drumnacoille 25*?'

Mackenzie had heard something of it, but not much. 'What of it?'

'There was enough of it left in storage to trickle into the market as a special reserve, and he's found a new distributor for that, and for a lesser vintage as soon as we have one ready. We're going to start up the distillery again.'

Mackenzie felt a little tug of regret that his father hadn't seen fit to tell him about this himself, but perhaps he'd thought his younger son wouldn't care. After all, Ade had been allowed to taste the stuff at least. 'What do you know about whisky distilling?' he asked, genuinely curious but aware it sounded a bit dismissive.

'Very little,' Ade admitted, freely enough, 'but I'll be learning from the best, won't I? You probably don't remember much about Dad's expertise there, but he's not forgotten a damned thing, let me tell you. Besides, that's only part of the plan. Anyway, what I wanted to know is if you're okay with it all?'

'What's it got to do with me? Like I said, it's Dad's money.'

'But like *I* said, it's our inheritance.'

Mackenzie waved a hand. 'You and Dad knock yourselves out. I don't want anything to do with that collection.' He saw the doubt on Ade's face and took a less defensive approach. 'Look, the opal's acting as collateral for the secured loan we needed to keep the business running while I was out of action, and Maddy was on remand, but once that's paid off it's all mine again. I don't feel for one minute as if I've been denied anything. I meant what I said: you and Dad do what you want to do.' He offered a small, faintly embarrassed smile. 'It'll actually be good to have you around again, believe it or not.'

'Good. And it's great to be home, *gille beag*.'

Mackenzie grinned. 'You can knock that on the head,' he said. 'I'm three inches taller than you.'

'You're still a little boy to me.'

Mackenzie pulled a face. 'Where's the land, anyway? Have you found somewhere yet?'

'I'm...looking into it.' Ade looked at his watch. 'I ought to go.' He stood up to take his mug to the kitchen, but Mackenzie leaned forward and blocked his path.

'Oh no you don't. You're hiding something. What is it?'

'I've been back in the country less than a day,' Ade protested. 'What could I possibly be hiding?'

'I don't know, but you are. Sit down.'

'The detective will see you now, eh?' Ade hesitated, then obeyed. 'Okay. I was checking out estate agents in town, online before I left NZ, and saw they were selling off a parcel at the bottom of Glenlowrie. The...the part that abuts onto the bottom half of Drumnacoille.'

The place where he'd almost died. Mackenzie replaced his mug on the table carefully, glad to note his hand wasn't shaking despite the way his gut twisted. 'Right. Okay.'

Ade reached out unexpectedly and laid a hand on his arm. 'How are things with you, Paul? Really?'

Mackenzie didn't answer for a moment; he just looked at his brother's hand on his wrist, and was dismayed to find himself struggling with a surge of emotion at the sight of it after all these years. 'It's fine,' he said at last. 'Really.'

'How can it be? Must have been fucking terrifying.'

Mackenzie gave a short laugh. 'I've stopped enjoying those "flying" dreams quite so much,' he confessed.

'Hardly surprising.' Ade sat back. 'And physically?'

'I'm getting there.'

'Good.' Ade fixed him with a direct look. 'Paul, this piece of land... It doesn't *have* to be that place. I'm sure I can find somewhere else.'

'No, it's perfect. And after all,' Mackenzie pointed out, a little wryly, 'I've travelled that road plenty of other times without flinging myself off the side.'

'Aye,' Ade said, 'in the back of Dad's car when you were a kid. Then the first time you're let loose on it under your own steam, look what happens.'

Mackenzie relaxed into a smile, grateful for Ade's dark humour. 'Can't be trusted, evidently.' He reflexively rolled his shoulder, feeling the familiar, dull ache across the top of his chest that he lived with daily now, and trying not to remember too vividly how it had felt, putting a hand up to his collar bone and feeling the shifting, grating mess that had lain beneath the skin. Surgery had more or less straightened him out, but the memory of that feeling still made him want to throw up, and the pain still caught him unawares sometimes when he tried to do something too quickly.

'So, you're buying Glenlowrie,' he said, to take his mind off it.

'The land agents have approached the owners of Drumnacoille on my behalf, too,' Ade went on, still hesitant. 'They never kept the estate up the way Dad did, and from what I saw when I went out there, that bottom end is an overgrown mess. Out of sight, out of mind, I suppose.'

'So if they agree to sell, you'd join the two estates together into one new one?'

'I want to create a thriving Highland Experience centre. The whole shebang, but very exclusive. Four rentable cabins, no more than that.' Ade started to sound more enthusiastic now he had got past the difficult part. 'The usual guided shooting and fishing, but with the whisky distillery at the heart of it, just like it used to be. What do you think?'

'Dad will love it. He's a lot more physically able than he makes out, by the way.'

'I know.' Ade gave him a brief grin. 'He started in with that line about not being able—'

'To brush his own teeth,' Mackenzie finished with him, and smiled. 'That's a familiar one.'

'And when I looked back through the window as I left, I saw him storming off towards the dining room like Mo Farah.' Ade's grin broadened. 'I'd love it if you came in with us, but I know you're happy doing what you're doing for now. Maybe in a few years though?'

Mackenzie studied him, and remembered that rush of fraternal feeling he'd felt a few minutes ago. He wasn't ready to give up Clifford-Mackenzie yet, but...

'Maybe,' he said at last. 'Keep a nice outdoorsy job open for me, just in case.'

Ade's grin softened into a real smile. 'Careful what you wish for,' he warned. 'Right, I really do need to get back if I want to catch last meal orders. Why don't you come down? They do a great steak and ale pud.'

Mackenzie shrugged. 'Why not?' He stood up to get his jacket. 'Where's this place you're moving into before the land sale goes through?'

Ade looked shifty again. 'Actually I wanted to talk to you about your bit of garden out the back. Does the kid play in it much?'

'The kid? You mean Jamie?' Mackenzie gave a short laugh. 'You really are out of touch. No, *the kid* does not play in my garden. He's eleven, Ade, not three. Why, have you got a tent you want to pitch?'

'Not quite.' Ade cleared his throat. 'I've not been idle since I left Dad earlier, and I've managed to get my hands on an old caravan. I'm picking it up on Wednesday. When I've sorted out the land business I'll move it there, of course, so I can supervise the site. But until then...' He raised a hopeful eyebrow.

'You want to pitch a caravan on my twenty-by-sixteen bit of garden?'

'Just for a few weeks. Would that be okay?'

Mackenzie regarded him for a moment, but they both knew the answer. 'Steak and ale, and most importantly, *ale*, is on you.'

'Of course.'

'Then lead on, prodigal brother. I'm starving.'

———

Maddy finished reading Tas his story and pulled the bedroom door halfway shut. She dreaded going back into the sitting room, but Gav was a wreck and he needed to talk, so on her way she took a bottle of Sauvignon Blanc from the fridge.

'I think this is in order after today, don't you?'

'No,' Gavin said. 'I'd better not. I need a clear head.'

His refusal meant Maddy felt guilty breaking the seal on the wine. She did it anyway, and sloshed out a generous amount, focusing on watching the glass form a satisfying layer of condensation.

'You'd better tell me everything,' she said. 'What did they want to know?'

'They've impounded my car,' he said in a tired voice, 'and they wanted me to tell them where I'd been on Thursday night.'

'And you told them?'

'Of course.'

'The truth, I mean, not just what you thought they needed to know.' He gave her a cool look, which she ignored. 'They know you saw the body, and left it?' she persisted, and the look became a scowl.

'Don't be—'

'Don't you *dare* tell me not to be stupid,' she warned, her voice low but hard, and Gavin looked away.

'I told him I was due to meet Lumsden, on business,' he said, 'but not that I found him. And I definitely didn't mention Kilbride. D'you think I have a death wish?'

'But everyone knows Lumsden was Kilbride's enforcer anyway.'

'They might know it, but no-one can prove it. And that's what matters. Look.' He stared earnestly at her. 'I know a bit about this stuff. They can't pinpoint time of death *that* accurately, especially when it happened outside. I told them the truth about what time I was there, but said I waited in the car for ten minutes and then buggered off when he didn't turn up. The window of time was probably miniscule anyway, if the bloke who was there before me did it. I must have missed him by, what? Twenty minutes at most.'

'Didn't they ask why you were conducting business in the middle of the night, and more to the point, the middle of nowhere?'

'Of course they did.' Gavin sent her an annoyed look. 'I just said it was convenient for us both, due to our individual scheduling, and the fact that I'd be on the road late anyway.'

Maddy closed her eyes; was he living in a dream world? 'What kind of legal business is ever conducted like that, Gav? The first thing they'll check your car for is drugs!'

The annoyance turned into a glare. 'Good. There won't be any. I don't know what you think I—'

'And how do the police know you were there at all, anyway?'

He shrugged. 'Presumably cameras along the road. I didn't ask, didn't want to sound defensive.'

'Those cameras don't record video, they overwrite the images every five minutes or so. I asked about it ages ago, when Paul and I were looking for—'

'Well *I* don't bloody know! There was no-one there to see me though, I'm certain of that. There's nothing at all to connect me to Kilbride, beyond the work I did for him in the summer.'

'Officially.'

Gavin snatched up his glass and the bottle, and poured himself a drink. 'They wanted to know whether I'd told you I was out there.'

Maddy took a quick breath. 'They'd better not think I knew anything, or I'll be back inside like that.' She snapped her fingers.

'I told them you didn't, but they'll probably still want to talk to you at some point.'

'I'm not lying to them.'

He stared. 'You'd drop me in it?'

'You want us *both* in jail?' she countered. 'At least, since you're innocent, you won't be there long. I'd have to do the full two years.' Maddy shook her head, horrified at the thought of leaving Tas for that long. 'So how was it left?' she asked, before he could respond. 'I mean, you were there nearly all day.'

'There was a lot of waiting around. The actual interview took about an hour, tops. They said they needed the car, and... Well, then they came back for the clothes I'd been wearing Thursday night.'

'What?'

'You were out, presumably still having your cosy little chat with Mackenzie.'

'I was talking to my dad about you,' she said icily. 'And yes, Paul too, but there's nothing cosy about explaining that your fiancé is up to his eyeballs in debt, and has been lying about it for months!'

'Well I'm sorry if I embarrassed you,' he snapped, and drained his glass at one gulp. 'I'm going to bed. It's been a long day.'

'Gav, wait.' Maddy reached out a conciliatory hand. 'I know it's been tough, but you have to let go of this dislike you have for my job, and especially my partner. We might even be able to help you.'

'Help me how?'

'By finding out who actually *did* kill Lumsden.'

Gavin gave a short laugh. 'Mads, you find missing puppies and mediate between squabbling neighbours. You don't find murderers!'

Maddy looked away, stung. 'We're investigators,' she reminded him, trying not to rise to the bait. 'You seem to have forgotten we managed quite a big case in the summer.'

'*You* managed it, did you? As I recall, your friend got run off the road by a disgruntled ex, and you ended up being charged with manslaughter. That loud-mouthed Scouse girl and her ten-year-old son *managed it*, love, not you two.'

Maddy slammed down her glass and stood up. 'Fine. You figure it out then.' She went into the hall and looked for her raincoat, hissing in frustration as she realised it was still in the office.

Gavin followed her. 'Where are you going?'

'Out.'

'To Mackenzie, I suppose?'

'To my brother, if you really must know.' She gave him a thin smile. 'He is on the investigation team, after all.'

'And that will achieve what, exactly?'

'A grown-up conversation, if nothing else. Don't wait up.'

Halfway to Nick's house, she slowed the car and started to look for a place to turn around. This was a stupid idea; Nick wouldn't tell her anything even if there was something to tell. He'd always played it by the book, just like their father, and he'd been beyond thrilled to be selected for his new boss's investigation team. He wouldn't risk that, and she couldn't ask him to.

The car once more on the short drive outside their house, Maddy sat for a while, trying to calm herself down before going back inside. The last thing they needed tonight was a row; her first day of real freedom had turned into a nightmare, and it would only bounce back onto Tas if she and Gavin couldn't square this together. She'd tried, but *Christ*, he was being unreasonable! She'd give it one more go, and that would leave her conscience in the clear, at least.

Even as the thought crossed her mind, the front door opened and Gavin stood there, outlined in the light from the hall. She could see, from the stoop of his shoulders, that he'd dropped that snippy attitude and was sorry. She got out of the car and went up to him.

'Can we talk properly now?'

He nodded. 'It's just... I don't know. Nerves. Delayed reaction. All of it.'

She leaned against him for a moment, until the wind caught the back of her short coat and lifted it, making her shiver. She was standing in the relative shelter of Gavin's prized junipers, but rain dripped off the winter skeleton of the Virginia creeper around the doorway and slid down the back of her neck. 'I'm not standing here all night,' she muttered, too weary to argue any further. 'Let's get inside.'

She woke with a start at a loud bang on the front door and looked reflexively at the clock. Six a.m. On a Sunday? The bang came again, and she realised whoever it was had ignored the knocker and was hammering on the panel between the glass panes. She shoved at Gavin to wake him, and grabbed her dressing gown, shivering as she hurried down to the front hallway. It must be serious, whatever it was.

Four police officers stood there, and one stepped forward. 'Mrs Galbraith?'

She blinked as a piece of paper appeared in front of her face. 'Clifford,' she began. 'What are you—'

'We have a warrant here to search your property.' The officer stepped back and waved two of the others forward; as they pushed past, he looked over Maddy's shoulder and called out, 'Mr Gavin Galbraith? We're here to arrest you for the murder of Mr Craig Lumsden.'

Maddy turned to follow his gaze. Gavin stood on the stairs, looking oddly young and helpless in his boxer shorts and T shirt, one arm halfway into the sleeve of his bathrobe. He looked from the officer to Maddy and back again, and she stood in numbed shock as he came down the rest of the stairs and swapped his robe for his coat.

'Will you cuff me?' he asked in a low voice, as if every neighbour they had was out there in the street, watching.

'Do we need to?'

He shook his head, and a look passed between the officers. They put the cuffs away, and instead guided him firmly out into the dark, windy dawn. 'Follow me when you can,' Gavin called back over his shoulder. 'I'll not be in long, and I'll need my own clothes for when you bring me home.' The smile he gave her looked as though it had been painted on by a child.

Maddy knew for certain then that everything had fallen apart, and she didn't have the faintest idea how to put it back together.

Chapter Six

JAMIE WISHED his mum wouldn't feel she needed to accompany him to the door; she could easily have just dropped him in the road and shoved off to Mackenzie's place. But no, here she was, practically holding his hand, as if he were five and going to a friend's birthday party.

He stifled a sigh; he couldn't really blame her. She didn't really know Ethan Cameron and hadn't met his mum properly yet, and after everything that had happened in the summer, her protective shield had gone right back to the way it had been when his dad had still been around.

Ethan's place, Wester Dean House, was about twenty minutes out of town and looked more like a small farm than a house. Big-ish and standing in its own grounds, it had a couple of different-sized yards at the front, a decent back garden, and even a paddock, with a path that led into woodland. His mum looked around with a sort of envious expression, but it was actually a bit like Mackenzie's place, though bigger, and she said she had no plan to move in there, so she couldn't really complain.

The door opened and Ethan's mum smiled at them both. She was one of those young, bouncy kinds of mums, dressed in jeans and trainers, and with her hair tied up in a high ponytail.

'Hi,' she said brightly, 'you must be Charis. I've seen you at the school. Hello, Jamie. Ethan's upstairs – you can go on up. It's the first door you come to on—'

'Jamie!' Ethan had appeared and waited halfway down the stairs, gesturing to him frantically as if worried the grown-ups would force them to stand and talk, or something equally awful.

'Hi, Mrs Cameron,' his mum said, holding out her hand. 'Thanks for having him over.'

'Justine,' the woman said, and as Jamie gave his mum a brief smile and followed Ethan upstairs, he heard the two of them making the arrangements for Mackenzie, who'd pick him up that evening.

Ethan Cameron was the first friend Jamie had made when he'd started school in Abergarry. Mum had managed to get him in not too long after the start of term, but he'd been annoyed to find out they went back about three weeks earlier up here than he would have done if he'd gone back to Liverpool. Worse still, as he'd yet to turn eleven at that point he was still going to be in primary school, instead of moving up to secondary. What kind of mad idea was that? He hardly dared think what his old class-mates would say if they found out... Thankfully they'd never know.

Jamie had soon found himself the centre of attention in the small school, as word got out that he'd been *that* kid; the one who'd been kidnapped from his hotel and held prisoner up at the old Glenlowrie Estate on the bank holiday weekend. Ethan, with whom it turned out he shared a fascination for detective, and spy stories, was one of the more popular kids at Abergarry Juniors, and he and Jamie had hit it off okay, so things had gone pretty smoothly after that.

This was his first invitation to Ethan's home though, and his mother had spent the whole drive instructing him in what to do and what not to. Did she think he was going to spray-paint the walls or something? He'd listened and nodded, and assured her for the thousandth time that he would say 'thank you' whenever he was offered anything, and not leave any veg on his dinner plate.

Ethan's bedroom door was standing halfway open, and Ethan himself had gone back to sorting through a stack of X-box games. He picked the top two off the piles.

'FIFA or Sonic Mania?'

'Sonic,' Jamie said at once. He looked around the room and was faintly disappointed to see it was pretty much a copy of his own, except he didn't have his own X-box in his room; he only had a PlayStation, and had to keep it downstairs, so his mum could keep tabs on what he was playing. His gaze landed on the only photo in a frame, which sat on Ethan's overcrowded desk.

'You never said you had a dog.' He picked up the photo, and was surprised to find it snatched from his hand and replaced. 'What kind is it?'

'We *did* have one,' Ethan said. 'A beagle. He died in the summer.'

'Oh.' Jamie frowned. 'Sorry. What was his name?'

'Pickles. Short for Tommy Pickles.' Ethan seemed to sense Jamie's puzzlement. 'Named after the kid in Rugrats,' he said with infinite patience, as if he'd had to explain it a hundred times that day already. 'He was my brother's dog really. Mum and Dad gave him to Kyle when I was born, and back then Kyle was only five, so it was either that or Pingu.'

'How'd he die?' Jamie accepted the controller Ethan handed him, and sat on the bed.

Ethan concentrated on setting the game up for a moment, then looked up. 'He was hit by a car.'

'Ah, that's nasty. Did you see it?'

'Me, Mum and Kyle were staying at our cousins' place, and Dad was here looking after him. But Kyle sneaked back on his moped, to get a game he'd left behind, and he found out what had happened. *On that actual day.*' Ethan shook his head at the unjustness of it all. 'He's been in a right state ever since. Dad's not been much better,' he added, and an ever-alert Jamie gave him a sharp look, but there didn't seem to be any fear there, just a sort of puzzled sadness.

'That's...horrible,' he said, a bit lamely. He cast another look at the picture, which showed a small-ish brown and white dog with a laughing face, and a younger version of the now sixteen-year-old Kyle. Jamie had only ever known Ethan's brother as a brooding, sulky presence by the school gate, when he'd met Ethan to take him home on the back of his moped, but in this picture he was clearly happy, his arms about his dog's neck, his eyes squinting against the sun as he grinned at the camera.

Ethan pressed to start the game and nudged Jamie. 'Come on. And after, I'll show you that spy kit Mum and Dad got me for my birthday.'

Jamie cheered up at the thought, and for a while he and Ethan happily lost themselves in their game, but his gaze kept stealing to the photo. Kyle looked like a whole different person when he was with his dog, and Jamie found himself wondering if he could fit a dog basket in the corner of his own bedroom...

'Boys!' Mrs Cameron's voice carried easily up the stairs a little later. Jamie and Ethan put down the miniature telescope and walkie-talkies they'd been experimenting with and went down to lunch. Jamie was relieved to see it wasn't a traditional Sunday roast, and tucked happily into fish fingers, peas and mash.

Midway through it, Ethan's dad came in. Jamie had met his mum before, at school drop-off, but his dad was never there, and it took him a moment to work out why he looked familiar. Then the man smiled, and he remembered.

'You run the shop at the bottom of town,' he said, as Mrs Cameron introduced him. 'You sold my mum a china kitten, and got paint in your hair!'

'So I did,' Mr Cameron said. 'I heard about what happened to you both,' he added, and the smile flickered a bit before it came back. 'Glad everything worked out okay.'

'Jamie saw the woman who was shot,' Ethan put in excitedly. 'It happened right in front—'

'Not at the table,' Ethan's mum said quickly. 'Finish up, lads. You don't want to waste what play time you've got left, eh?'

Jamie noticed a look pass between her and Ethan's dad, but he couldn't decipher it. It seemed neither of them was keen to talk about what had happened, but there was more to it than that. It wasn't until he and Ethan went back up to Ethan's room that he began to understand.

'I think my dad knew that woman a long time ago,' Ethan said, closing the door carefully. 'I heard him and mum arguing, after it happened. We weren't here, but Mum thinks Dad saw the woman just before she died.'

'Was that the same weekend your brother's dog was run over then?'

'No, that happened the weekend after. Dad had told us to stay at Sam's for another week. Kyle was proper crabbit about that too; it meant he missed the last week of the holidays, and his girlfriend got stinky about it and dumped him.'

Jamie had the feeling he was trying to change the subject. 'But your dad *knew* the woman who got me kidnapped?'

'A long time ago,' Ethan repeated. 'I mean, the rest of us had never met her, and she'd lived in America for years. They were kids together, I think.'

'Do you think he knew she was coming back, and that's why he sent you to stay with your cousins?'

'How should I know?' Ethan sounded bored now. 'Look, your mum's fella's picking you up in a couple of hours, so let's take this stuff out before we run out of time.'

He began packing the spy kit away into its smart carrying case, and Jamie helped, trying to remember what had been said in that cottage when it was all coming to an end. Then it hit him: just before he'd spoken up, saying he knew where to find that black opal they'd all been obsessing over, someone had said something about burning everyone in the cottage, including Cameron. The Wallace woman had spoken up at once: *You'll leave Cameron alone! You can trust him; he'll not say anything.*

Jamie sneaked a glance at Ethan, who seemed to have forgotten they'd even discussed it, and decided it was better to let it go. Mr Cameron hadn't been part of what had happened, as far as he knew, and certainly hadn't treated either himself or his mother badly. There was no point raking things up again now, but he would definitely tell his mum, since she was often saying stuff like *it's a small world.* While that might have sounded a bit mad when they were in a city, where no-one really spoke to anyone else, here it started to make more sense, because when Mackenzie arrived to pick him up, Jamie found that Ethan's parents knew him a bit too. Apparently he and Ethan's mum had both been at Abergarry Juniors at the same time.

Mackenzie had brought his brother with him, and there was a slight but noticeable coolness as Ade and Mr Cameron shook hands, but it seemed to come only from Ade's side. Mr Cameron looked a bit puzzled by it, but smiled in a friendly enough way.

'Nice to see you again, after all these years,' he said. 'The last time was probably the leavers' disco in the upper school hall.'

'Aye, more than likely,' Ade said, and turned to Jamie. 'Right, squirt. Ready?'

'Yep.'

They'd spent a cheerful hour or so yesterday, when Ade had turned up looking for Mackenzie, and Jamie liked him a lot – his being around seemed to have made Mackenzie happier, too. Jamie looked at the Camerons' family photo in the hall, and wondered what it would have been like to have had a brother. There was no chance now; his mum had explained that her chemotherapy, and the tablets she'd had to take, meant she couldn't have any more children. It would probably have been nice, though.

He and Ethan exchanged *seeya tomorrow*s, and Jamie crawled into the back of Mackenzie's car. As he looked back for a quick wave he saw that his friend's dad had come outside, zipping up his jacket, and was watching them with a thoughtful look on his face.

'Why don't you like him?' he asked Ade, who twisted in the front seat to look at him in surprise.

'Ben?' I'm sure he's a nice enough bloke.

'Then why were you iffy with him?'

'Was I?' Ade turned back. 'I didn't mean to be.'

'Come off it,' Mackenzie put in, as they turned back onto the main road to Abergarry. He caught Jamie's eye in the mirror. 'Ade had a mad crush when we were at school, on that awful woman who kidnapped you,' he explained, ignoring his brother's snort. 'But back then she and Ben Cameron were joined at the hip.'

'You knew about them then?' Jamie asked. 'Why didn't you say anything?'

'I knew about Ben and Sarah, but didn't know Ben was Ethan's dad, until just now.' Mackenzie shrugged. 'He seems decent, and he couldn't help getting involved in what happened any more than you and your mum could. Anyway,' he went on, directing this at Ade now, 'it was Don Bradley she was romantically involved with, not Ben. He was just her best mate.'

'Aye, fair enough,' Ade conceded, a little grumpily.

'You wouldn't want to go out with a horrible woman like that anyway, would you, Ade?' Jamie asked.

'Of course he wouldn't,' Mackenzie said. 'He only fancied her; he didn't *like* her.'

'I do have a type,' Ade agreed, throwing Jamie a little grin. 'I ended up married to someone who looked a lot like her.'

'Really? Where is she?'

'Turned out she was cut from a similar cloth. Took pretty much everything when we got divorced. I'm telling you, it's a mug's—'

'Ade,' Mackenzie broke in, 'the lad's eleven, aye?'

Ade subsided and gave Jamie another little grin over his shoulder. *Never get married,* he mouthed, and drew a finger across his neck with a little shake of the head. Jamie grinned. No fears on *that* score.

Ade remained in the car while Mackenzie walked Jamie back into the house, and Mum came downstairs with a book in her hand.

'You staying?' she asked Mackenzie.

'I'm just dropping Ade back to the pub. I'll be about an hour, okay?'

'Okay.' She looked shyly pleased, and Jamie looked away when she slipped her arms around Mackenzie's waist and kissed him. 'See you later.'

After his shower, Jamie was going to tell her about Mr Cameron and his old friendship with Sarah Wallace, but she was in too good a mood to spoil, so instead he told her about Kyle's dog, and how Kyle seemed so much happier in the photo than he did now.

'It must have been so nice for him to get a brother and a dog at the same time,' he said, watching her from under half-closed eyelids as he rubbed between his toes with the towel. 'Imagine getting a brother *and* a dog—'

'You can stop there, miladdo,' his mum said, but there was a faint smile on her face. 'Just because I can't give you a brother doesn't mean you're entitled to a dog. Besides, we rent this place and I'm pretty sure there's a no pets policy on the lease.'

'But you'll check?'

She looked at him wordlessly for a moment, and he held her gaze, making his eyes as wide as they would go, until she sighed. 'I'll check,' she said, 'but that doesn't mean—'

'Great!' Jamie tugged his slippers on and settled back against the sofa with a contented sigh. 'I'm gonna call him Sonic.'

Maddy pulled up outside her father's house and sat watching the lighted windows for a moment. She had bundled Tas's sleepy form up in his duvet early that morning and dropped him to his grandad's while it was still dark, before driving out to the Glencoe police station once more, and she wondered what her father had told the boy about Gavin. She had only managed a brief phone call when she'd realised she'd be gone all day, and hadn't been able to explain what was going on; now she knew for sure, and could explain it in hideous detail, it wasn't helping at all.

Behind the closed sitting room curtains she could see a shadow as her father passed the window, and it all looked far too normal for the turmoil that was going on in her head. The silent question on his face when she went in almost made her break down in tears; only the thought of Tas hearing her stopped them.

Tony touched her arm. 'He's upstairs,' he said in a low voice. 'I made up his room, just in case. So is Gavin still...is he—'

'Charged. Remanded at Inverness now, awaiting trial.' The words, spoken in a low voice, still landed hard; she couldn't believe she was saying them about good old reliable Gavin... But then she'd learned a lot about him in the past day or so.

Tony led her into the sitting room. 'I never thought it would come to this,' he muttered. 'Not Gavin. What have they got on him?'

'Pretty much everything except a witness to the murder itself. Including, would you believe, a hand print? Not just fingerprints, oh no. A whole *hand*. He says it's from when he thought he was going to throw up, and he leaned on the sodding car!'

'Oh, Jesus.'

'He said he nearly threw up and was glad he didn't, and I thought he was acting weird, then. He must have remembered he'd done it.' Maddy sighed and sat down, rubbing at her eyes. 'I could do with a cuppa, Dad.'

'Mum!' Tas came thundering down the stairs and ran over for a hug. 'Is Dad here?'

'He's away for a few days. You're going to stay here with Grandad tonight. Is that okay?'

'Aye, I know. We went back for my school things after lunch.' He wasn't the slightest bit put out, or even curious, and she supposed he was used to both his parents doing vanishing acts now and again, though not usually at the same time. 'I like staying here. We can walk to school.'

'Good. Off you go and choose a story, I'll be up in a minute.'

Tony went to make the drinks, and she followed him into the kitchen. 'I've got to start my community payback tomorrow,' she said, turning a couple of mugs right-side up on the counter top. 'I don't know how the hell I'm going to get through that. Not now. There's so much going on.'

'I'll be helping out at the agency,' Tony reminded her, 'and Tas is welcome to stay for a few days, while you settle into your routine. Go and see Gav, love; there's a visitor slot for remand prisoners from half six. If I remember right from visiting someone else,' he added, arching an eyebrow at her, and when she glared at him he gave her a little smile. 'What, too soon?'

She appreciated his attempt to help her relax, but there was a pain building behind her eyes, and her own answering smile was weak. 'I know I should go, but there's nothing helpful I can say to him.'

'He probably just needs reassurance he's not been abandoned.' Tony turned to face her, leaning back on the counter. 'Do you think he did it?'

Maddy opened her mouth, but found her immediate and instinctive denial had dried up, and she could only shake her head. 'I'm going up to see Tas, and when I come down I'll tell you everything I know.'

Later, with Tas in bed and his school uniform neatly laid out on the chair in his room, Maddy sat in her customary fashion in the sitting room, with her legs tucked beneath her in the chair, and told her father everything. Since he already knew about Gavin's arrest it was only when she reached the part about her own questioning that she faltered.

'They looked delighted when I turned up,' she said, remembering. 'Apparently I'd saved them a lot of bother, as they were planning on speaking to me anyway.'

'And what did they want to know?'

'Exactly what Gavin had told me.'

'And you told them all of it?'

Maddy blew on her tea, as a way of avoiding her father's keen eye. 'Almost all of it,' she said at length. 'I didn't correct his reason for meeting Lumsden; it was business, after all, of a kind, and I don't want us to involve Kilbride any more than we have to. But now I'm not so sure telling them the truth was the right thing to do.'

'Of course it was!' Tony stared at her. 'You can't go withholding evidence, not in your position!'

'Oh, but it's okay in yours?' Maddy saw him flinch, and felt bad. 'Look, it doesn't matter, I told them anyway.'

'And why was it the wrong thing to do?'

'He told me he saw the body but left it there. He told *them* he'd been there, but left before Lumsden arrived. So of course, when they put my version to him, he had to change his story, and now he looks guilty as hell for having lied in the first place.'

Her father's face remained impassive, but she knew him well enough to recognise his thinking mode. 'They'd have had to have more than your statement to charge him,' he pointed out. 'That handprint, for starters. If you'd lied on his behalf they'd have known about it the second that print was matched to him, and then you'd have been in it just as deep. It's safer to tell the truth, Mads – you know that, then they can't trip you up. They took his clothes?'

'Aye. And impounded the car. They found what they needed from the car to place him at Three Sisters, but his clothes will be clean; he didn't touch Lumsden. And there was no other connection between them apart from the advisory stuff Gav did for Kilbride in the summer.'

'You said you thought maybe Kilbride himself had paid someone to do the job?'

'It crossed my mind. Still seems feasible; had to be someone who knew he'd be there at that time.'

'Not exactly a tenuous connection between those two though, is it? I mean, if Lumsden was *only* Kilbride's driver and personal assistant you could almost brush it off. But he was married to Kilbride's daughter, and that brings the whole thing under a much darker umbrella, you have to admit.'

'I don't see why. By that token, the fact that I did a job for Kilbride would bring me under it too. He could have approached me to do it just as easily, to pay off Gav's debt. Or Donna could have.'

'Which is why you have to be *very* careful, especially if you've driven Gavin's car at any point.'

'No, never have.'

'Good.'

Tony sipped his tea, and Maddy had the sense that, just as she had, he was using the time to collect his thoughts. 'You never answered my question,' he said at last. 'Do you think he's guilty?'

Again, she couldn't answer right away, but as her mind turned over everything Gavin had said, she remembered the look on his face. 'No,' she said. 'I don't. I think he was unbelievably stupid to have just driven away without telling anyone what he'd seen, but I don't think he's got it in him to—'

'Maddy!'

She almost dropped her cup as the voice yelled from the hallway. She turned to see her brother, his face uncharacteristically flushed and upset, appearing in the sitting room doorway.'

'Quiet!' she said, pointing to the stairs, 'Tas is in bed. What's the matter?'

'Thanks to your feckless shit of a fiancé, I'm back where I started.' Nick came in, barely glancing at his father, and perched on the edge of the sofa, as if too restless to sit properly. 'I can't believe it!'

'I don't know what you're on about,' she said. 'What's Gavin done to you?'

'He got engaged to my sister,' Nick said, 'and then got himself arrested. I'm back in uniform and off the case. So yeah, tell him thanks for that.'

'But if they've made the arrest, surely the investigation's over anyway.'

'Not by a long chalk,' Nick said. 'Not until they've got a conviction. This was my best chance in years to make any kind of headway in that force... The chief was decent enough about it, but it makes no odds. Claire McAndrew said you'd told her you were my sister, so she couldn't wait to drop me in it with him. She's got her eyes on the prize there.'

'This is the new bloke who's in charge, is it?' Tony spoke calmly. 'I'd not worry, lad, he was keen enough to get you on board; I'm sure he'll select you again.'

'I'm supposed to hope someone else dies then, am I?' Nick said, nettled. 'And it might not be a raging bastard next time. This would have been a win-win.'

Tony looked sympathetic, but philosophical. 'If you want a chance at DS, you're better off transferring to a bigger station down south.' He paused for a second, then added, 'like Mulholland did.'

Maddy looked at him, deeply relieved. 'That's where he's gone, is it?'

'Aye, apparently. He's still on extended leave, but he put the request in a few weeks back. Or so Farly tells me.'

'Vince McFarland's still at Abergarry? I thought he'd retired when you did.'

'Nope, still hanging in there. Getting more disillusioned by the day though.' He looked at Nick. 'Cuppa?'

'Aye, go on.'

'So how do things stand with Gavin at the moment?' Nick asked, while their father went to the kitchen. He sounded calmer now, accepting that it was hardly Maddy's fault, but there was still a heavy, morose air hanging over him, and she hoped this wouldn't set him back too much.

She told him what had happened, and was slightly comforted when he too insisted she had done the right thing, and that there was almost certainly more behind Gavin being charged than him being forced to admit he'd lied about seeing Lumsden's body.

'Can you find out what?' Maddy asked him.

'If I hear anything, maybe. But don't ask me to go digging.'

'Of course not. You did your part when you helped with the Don Bradley thing. I won't ask again.'

She exchanged a glance with her father as he handed Nick his drink. She understood, from the warning look on his face, that her brother had no idea she knew about what had happened in 1993; that he had found himself in the terrible position of having to kill the innocent Dougie Cameron in order to protect his father. His already fragile state of mind would be shattered. She gave a barely perceptible nod, indicating she would say nothing, and her father looked away again, satisfied.

Nick had carried the burden of that secret for twenty-five years, periodically relieving the immense pressure only with a short-bladed knife, and a supply of antiseptic cream and plasters. More recently, that pressure had been eased further by finally telling his father what he'd done, and why, but it didn't follow that he'd be glad to know his sister had been brought into it too.

'So, Nick,' Maddy said, 'can I take it you and Max are back on?'

'It's been shaky,' he admitted, then his solemn face broke into a smile. 'But yes, we're okay.'

It was good to see her brother unwind as they talked. Even the news that he'd been bumped from the investigation team didn't seem to matter when he talked about the possibility of getting a new place, closer to Inverness, should his partner get the job he was after.

When she looked at the clock she realised they'd talked the evening into night; she had an early start, and a gruelling day ahead. She shuddered, but in truth the prospect compared so favourably to her time on remand, and to what Gavin would now be going through, that she couldn't help almost relishing the thought of getting started. Though how long before the novelty wore off would be anyone's guess. She'd give it about an hour.

Chapter Seven

'They've charged him with murder,' DS Muir said, when Donna opened the door to her on Monday morning. She accepted Donna's invitation to come in, bringing DC Forbes in her wake. 'He's on remand in Inverness. I thought you'd be glad to know right away.'

'That's...a relief,' Donna said, although she'd thought she'd have felt more elated. It was quick work, at least; no dragging out, and subsequent waning of determination or interest.

'The witness report gave us what we needed to carry out a search of the Galbraith home and impound his car,' Forbes said, his ever-present notebook open while he skimmed the page for the salient points.

'There was heavy rain earlier in the evening, which didn't help,' Muir chipped in, 'but we've now been able to confirm that his tyre marks, and those of the BMW, didn't cross each other's at all once they'd passed the entrance to the car park. It's easy to see there were other vehicles there at various times, but most of them overlap at some point, with the odd exception. The BMW's and Mr Galbraith's tyre marks were both distinct and separate where they parked alongside each other, indicating they were probably there at the same time.'

Forbes waited patiently until she'd said her piece, then went on, 'Faced with this and other evidence, Galbraith changed his story, and admitted to having been at the scene at the same time as Mr Lumsden, rather than before, as he'd originally claimed. So he lied at the outset; never a good look. But it wouldn't have mattered,' he added, with a little pause and a look of minor triumph, 'because forensics found a clear handprint on the driver's side of Mr Lumsden's vehicle. That gave us what we need to place—'

'A *hand* print?' Donna asked, feeling a rush of gratitude that fate was on her side in some things, after all.

'Aye. Seems to correspond with someone bracing themselves against the car. Perhaps to steady themselves while they dealt the blow or blows.'

'That seems pretty careless.'

'The whole attack appears spontaneous rather than premeditated,' Muir said, her tone now holding a cautious note. 'Which is why we're not confident yet that he *won't* be able to get the charge downplayed to manslaughter by reason of diminished responsibility. It was...' She trailed off.

'Brutal,' Donna supplied dully. 'You think Galbraith just lost it then.'

'There's no doubt the initial blow was deliberate, but after that, who knows? Maybe some old PTSD, from something we don't know about, re-surfaced and he went into a sort of fugue state. That might be what his defence throws at it, we don't know. The point is, his prints are on the car and his tyre marks are at the scene.'

'And there's your witness, of course. Will she be called?'

Donna kept her tone even, but to her guilty ear it stood out as if she'd spoken it in a different language.

'That's up to the prosecution, if they can track her down, but it's unlikely they'll put the expense into it if there's nothing more she'd be able to add to what she's already told us.' Muir put away her own pocketbook. 'We'll leave you to it, for now, but you can call us if you need anything. Otherwise you'll be notified of the trial date.'

Donna thanked them mechanically and saw them out, her mind racing; this was it. No more dithering. She picked up her phone and pressed to call her father.

'You made a promise,' she said, as soon as he answered. 'Now it's time to show me you meant it.'

Kilbride arrived less than an hour later. Monday morning had crept on towards lunchtime by now, and Donna's insides were in knots. She told him what Muir and Forbes had said.

'We can't let him try for diminished responsibility,' she finished. 'I won't have him putting the blame on Craig, he's the *victim*! He was just doing his job.'

Kilbride frowned. 'You do realise Craig was more than likely coming the heavy? If he landed even one blow... Well, you said it yourself.'

'Which means any plea like that is going to throw the spotlight onto you as well,' Donna pointed out. 'So you know what we have to do.'

'Aye, well not to worry. I've got it in hand.'

'What are you planning to do?'

'I know someone who's recently been arrested,' her father

said, a satisfied little smile lurking around his lips. 'If he's not charged and remanded yet, he soon will be.'

'Anyone I know? And are they likely to do what you ask?'

'Yes, and yes. It's Ian George.'

'Ian? They found him?'

'With a little help,' he said, and the look of satisfaction broadened. 'He actually found me, in the grounds of my house, and I saw to it that his little act of trespass didn't go unpunished. I made sure he knew I should be his phone call, once he'd been processed, and in return for me fixing him up with legal representation he's put you on his visitor list.'

'Me? Why not you?' She shook her head. 'Silly question. Go on.'

'The sooner you see him, the better. Just tell him you want Galbraith warned.'

'Just warned?'

'In the George brothers sense of the word,' her father clarified, 'which means Gavin Galbraith will be counting his blessings, sitting tight, and keeping it zipped. He'll do the time, don't worry.'

'And Ian's prepared to do the time too, is he? Those places have cameras everywhere.'

'Ian's not likely to get his own hands dirty,' Kilbride assured her. 'He knows people with nothing to lose and a lot to gain from keeping on my good side. Now,' he rubbed his hands together, effectively dismissing Donna's concerns, 'must be nearly lunch time; I'm going to head over to Thistle to treat myself to some of that amazing salmon *en croute* your chef does so well. Do you need anything done while I'm there?'

'I was going in anyway,' Donna said. 'I know,' she added, to forestall her father's protest that it was too soon, 'but I've got to help draft the ad for seasonal staff. It's going up on the website on Wednesday, and in the Courier this weekend. I'm not leaving that to Breda; she'll take anyone. She's too soft, that one.'

'But if it's just waiting staff,' Kilbride began, then subsided as Donna raised an eyebrow. 'Okay, okay. They still have to be a cut above for Thistle – I get it.'

'We'll pick Martha up on the way. She's been so lovely she deserves a bit of pampering for a change.' Donna eased her feet into her work shoes; after only a few days in slippers her toes protested the sudden tightness. 'I've been wondering though,' she added, as she picked up her phone. 'How come Ian was okay with you turning him in?'

'Because he knows first of all that I'm not going to pursue a complaint, and also that there's nothing for him to answer in that business with his brother. Assuming he's right about that, of course. On top of that he'll have earned my gratitude. And his job back.'

'Craig's job,' Donna said, a little tightly. 'He'd better watch himself when he gets out then.'

She locked the front door behind them, and waited in her car while her father settled himself behind the wheel of his own. Her emotions were swinging back and forth more than ever today, making her feel a little ill; one moment she was in the depths of grief, thinking about some stupid little thing she and Craig had done, or said, and the next she was wire-tight with rage and the need for vengeance. She wondered if she could get away with strengthening her dad's *little message* to Ian, but the more serious the assault, the more rigorous the investigation, and if Ian's part in it did come to light her father would be without his protection. Again.

When she pulled into her reserved spot in the Thistle car park, she realised for the first time that the prison was almost directly across the river, and only a couple of streets back. She felt that if she stared hard enough she'd be able to see that cowardly rat Gavin Galbraith; see his misery and his fear. She hoped both were growing more powerful by the minute. With any luck he'd do the decent thing and throw a towel around a shower head—

'Looks like you're fully booked,' Martha observed, straightening her scarf in an eerie echo of that thought, and looking around at the packed car park.

'Morbid curiosity, no doubt,' Donna said. 'They all want a bit of a look at the widow they've read about in the papers. Ah well,' she added with a twist of bitterness, 'it's all been good for business, anyway.'

'You know it'll be next to impossible for you in there,' her father cautioned. 'All eyes will be on you. You go in there looking miserable, and you're bringing the mood down. Smile, and you're heartless.'

'Well I'm damned if I do, and damned if I don't then,' Donna said grimly, and bent to check her hair in her wing mirror. She straightened and fixed her face in as neutral an expression as possible, before leading her father and stepmother into the restaurant.

Her father had been right, of course. As soon as she'd settled them both at the corner table that was always held in reserve for family or special guests, eyes followed her across the restaurant to the kitchen door, through which she passed with a sigh of relief; the noise and chaos in here was infinitely preferable to the lower, but more charged murmurs that had risen in line with the recognition.

She caught her assistant manager's attention, and gestured to the side door and the office beyond. Breda nodded and began wrapping up the conversation she was having with the head waiter, while Donna sat down at her desk and jotted one or two notes on her pad.

'We've had some applications already,' Breda said, closing the door. Her dimpled, smiling face concealed a formidably sharp mind, and her short, rounded form was swathed in colourful knits that made her seem more like a kindergarten teacher than the second-in-command of one of the most highly rated restaurant chains in the nation. She had the kind of gentle Irish accent that gave the impression she was everyone's best friend, and only wanted to please, but Donna knew better than to test that.

Breda took the chair opposite and dropped a buff-coloured file onto the desk. Only then did she seem to remember what had happened. 'Oh, my God, I'm so sorry. I've just been so wrapped up in everything, I—'

'It's fine – don't be silly. The world doesn't stop.' *Didn't it though?*

'Your poor children, too. How are you all?' Breda's soft voice enveloped Donna with such warmth that she felt tears start to her eyes. She wouldn't have believed she had any left to shed. She blinked them back.

'Myles and Chelsea have gone to my mother's, down near Loch Lomond. I'm all the better for knowing the bastard who did it has been arrested and charged.'

'Has he now?' Breda nodded approval. 'Glad to hear it.'

Breda Kelly had worked for Donna for over seven years, and was worth every penny of her generous pay packet; Donna could rely on her for pretty much anything, but, as she'd noted to her father, the woman did have a tendency towards leniency.

'Did you fire Jon?' she asked, and saw a faint flush touch Breda's pale skin.

'I was going to talk to you about that. Why don't we give

him a final written warning instead? Sure, it wasn't his fault the barrel split.'

'No, but it *was* his fault there wasn't another on standby.' Donna sighed. 'And that's not the first time he's left us short on a big night. You've got to toughen up, Bree! It's my reputation that's going to suffer if we get bad reviews.'

'As if! Anyway, these applications.' Breda flipped open the folder. 'I've printed them off, so you can have a look later, but we'd better crack on with this ad so you can get off home again.'

'Why would I want to do that?' Donna pulled the sheets from the folder. 'To be truthful I'd rather be here doing something.'

Breda looked doubtful, but let it pass. 'So, he's arrested, you say? What's his name?'

'Gavin Galbraith.'

'The solicitor?'

'The same.'

'I used that firm for the sale of my house.' Breda sounded scandalised, as if the whole of Willis, Lowry and Kitson had been involved, and it somehow undermined the legitimacy of her conveyancing.

Donna couldn't help smiling. 'The ad?' she prompted, and the two of them worked on the wording for a while. Then, while Breda fleshed out her notes Donna glanced through the applications.

'Some here with good experience,' she observed. 'They did well to get in ahead of the ad going out. Keen.' She plucked three from the pile and pushed them across the desk. 'Get these in for interview Thursday morning, will you please? Along with your top three from any applications we've received as of six o'clock Wednesday evening.'

Breda noted the names on her pad. 'Gardner, Adoti, Russell. Will do.'

Donna tapped the top application. 'We can sound out this Russell bloke for the bar manager position as well, since you're going to be firing Jon. Aren't you?' she added pointedly, and Breda sighed and nodded. 'Mr Russell's been working at the Spey Heights for six years,' Donna went on. 'There's no way he'd be content with a waiter's job.'

'What's he doing applying then?'

'We'll find out on Thursday.' Donna sat back, restlessness sending her gaze on a quick trip around the office, searching for something to focus on.

'Go on home, love,' Breda said quietly. 'There's nothing you can do here. Have they released the...released Craig?'

Donna nodded. 'The post-mortem's done and the inquest's opened. It's been adjourned for now, but at least it means I can bury him.'

'I've got everything covered here,' Breda said. 'Why not go and sit with your ma and pa and enjoy a nice lunch together?'

Donna pursed her lips, then shook her head. 'I've got some arrangements to make,' she said. 'I'll be back in later though. Around eight I expect.' She had the feeling she'd need a stiff drink by then, and definitely wouldn't want to be alone with her thoughts.

At just after six that evening she put her phone and handbag into the locker provided at the visitor centre at the prison in Inverness. She made her way through the search process, surrendering to the pat-down without murmur but hating every moment of it – it wasn't even as if she were visiting someone she liked, and to be put through this physical embarrassment was almost enough to make her turn tail. But she set her teeth hard together and emerged feeling grubby, but relieved. Thank God she didn't need to use the toilet; the thought of being searched before and after that did nothing to put her at her ease.

She spotted Ian, who gave her a rather too-familiar smile as she sat down opposite, trying not to wince at the livid scarring that stood out on his pale face. If he'd crossed her father that badly it was a miracle he'd been forgiven. She couldn't imagine Craig's hands administering such a treatment, not those same hands that had kept his children safe crossing the road, and later touched her with such tenderness. She shook the image away; there was no proof he'd even done it, so why burn her memories down like this?

She looked around the room with nervous distaste. This was a separate visiting time, set aside for remand prisoners, so they were all wearing their own clothes and she was relieved to see Ian was dressed reasonably neatly. One other, though, stood out like an orange in a bowl of lemons.

Ian followed her gaze and nodded. 'Aye, that's him,' he murmured. 'Galbraith.'

There was a woman with him, and she looked nigglingly familiar from the side view – perhaps she was a regular at the restaurant? Her hair was a deep, natural-looking red, tied back in a ponytail and secured at the nape with a wide black band. She also had the kind of profile favoured by perfume manufacturers: all fine bones and clear skin. Her clothes, however, were at the opposite end of the scale to the ones Galbraith wore; faded skinny jeans and a hoodie, and battered-looking Doctor Martens that emphasised the long, slender legs tucked away beneath her chair. She looked to neither side, as if she might find herself contaminated by the sight of so many criminals and their visitors, but focused either on Galbraith or the table top.

Ian was looking at the woman quite intently, unsurprisingly, and Donna shook her head. 'She's way *way* out of your league.'

He shrugged. 'I can dream. So,' he went on, looking back at Donna. 'Your dad did the dirty on me, eh? Why would he do that?'

'You know why,' Donna said mildly, not blinking in the face of that steady stare. Ian had the kind of blunt features that, like Breda Kelly's, veiled a quick and agile mind. She knew her dad underestimated his intelligence, and that was more than likely deliberate on Ian's part, but Craig had warned her more than once to be on her guard around him. Always.

To look at him, with his buzz-cut and carefully maintained stubble, he seemed perfectly made to be someone's muscle. Not huge, but solid. He reminded her a little of Craig in that respect, and she tensed against the twist of pain as she thought about what the family liaison officers had told her of his final moments. She avoided looking at Galbraith again; she might lose it as completely as he had, and she would achieve nothing here by attacking him. His punishment could wait.

'Message from Dad,' she went on, keener than ever now to leave this place and get out into the fresh air. She glanced across at Galbraith's companion, who leaned across the table to clasp his linked hands in hers, before drawing them back with a guilty look at the duty guard, in case that wasn't allowed. The familiarity tugged again.

'Fire away,' Ian said, before she could place it.

Donna kept her voice low, not sure how the acoustics worked in here. 'We're concerned he mightn't plead guilty,' she said. 'He *has* to. Okay? We can't have anything coming back on Craig, or my dad.'

'Agreed,' Ian said. 'I'd quite like a job when I get out.'

'Exactly. So Dad says you'll know what to do.'

'Anything else?'

'It's just as a warning,' Donna stressed. 'Whoever you... whoever passes on the message to him, make sure they know that. Whatever they dish out can be as messy as you like, frightening even, but not life-threatening.'

'Really?' Ian looked sceptical. 'After what he did to your husband?'

'Don't for one minute think I don't *want* it to go further,' Donna hissed. 'But we can't risk a big investigation.'

'Okay.' Ian shrugged. 'You're the boss.' He let his eyes drift downwards from Donna's hair to as far as the table between them allowed. 'Is it too soon to say I wish you actually were?'

Donna narrowed her eyes and considered her words carefully. 'If you ever see Satan strapping on ice skates, call me.'

He grinned, unabashed. 'Fair enough. Tell William I'll be in touch.'

'Good.' Donna stood up and tugged her skirt straight. 'See you soon then, no doubt.'

'Very soon. Your dad's busy dropping charges as we speak, and I'm expecting a visit from my solicitor. I'll probably be out by tomorrow afternoon, but don't worry, I know who to speak to.' Ian stood too, and signalled to the guard. 'I'll be away to my cosy cell then.' He raised his voice slightly. 'Nice of you to come, hen. Give my regards to your father.'

Donna took deep, cleansing breaths despite the gusty rain that blew sideways across the car park on Argyle Street. She was so relieved to be out, she'd have been happy to sit in the middle of the street and just let the wind push the drizzle into every exposed bit of skin. She dug into her bag for her key, and as she pointed it at her car she remembered where she'd seen Galbraith's visitor before: at her own front door, around the time that kid had been snatched from his hotel. She'd been doing some work for Donna's father, she'd said, just like Galbraith had been. But strangely enough she'd been asking about Sarah Wallace, who'd turned up dead just a day or so later... The woman evidently bore some looking into.

Donna slid in behind the wheel and sat watching the car park entrance. The redhead might possibly have been lucky enough to find a parking space in the small prison car park, but if she'd had any sense she wouldn't even have bothered trying. Which meant she'd more than likely be back here at some point. Well, Donna had nowhere to be in a hurry; she'd give it until after the end of the visiting time, and if the woman didn't come into the car park, she'd lost nothing by waiting half an hour or so. If she did, there'd be quite a percentage in finding out where she lived. Just in case.

Less than twenty minutes later she was rewarded. The woman, her coat firmly zipped but her hood still down, as if she shared Donna's need for fresh air on her face, climbed into a Corsa but didn't start the car. Donna flipped her windscreen wipers on to afford a better view and saw, through the rain that splattered the Corsa's driver's side window, that the woman had her head bowed. After a few minutes, however, she sat up straighter, rubbed at her eyes and reached down to twist the ignition key. The Corsa moved out of the car park, and Donna followed.

Chapter Eight

MACKENZIE STARED IRRITABLY at his laptop screen, waiting for the blue circle of doom to stop spinning and the document to load.

'Not what you expected when you joined the agency, is it?' Tony asked with a little grin. 'You never could be arsed with all the paperwork, I remember.'

'Not any better now it's all on this bloody thing.' Mackenzie gestured at the laptop and sighed. 'You sold me the job under false pretences, mate.'

Tony chuckled. 'D'you realise that was ten years ago last month?'

'Christ, was it?' Mackenzie gave up and shut the lid. 'I'll add this to the sheet later.' He scribbled a note on his pad and took a sandwich out of his drawer. 'Want half?'

'Aye, I've just got time before I'm due to meet Mrs Jackson about the daughter's boyfriend.' Tony leaned back in Maddy's chair and stretched. 'Not getting itchy feet after all this time, are you?'

'Itchy in the sense of wanting another job? No.' Mackenzie tore open the packaging and passed half the sandwich to Tony. 'But – you know I told you Ade's back from New Zealand? Well he's full of all these plans. It made me feel a bit, I dunno. Flat?'

'Flat? After what happened in the summer?' Tony snorted, and spoke around a mouthful of tuna and lettuce. 'If you're looking for more excitement after that—'

'Not excitement, so much. Just something different to focus on.'

'So what's Ade got up his sleeve then?'

Mackenzie told Tony about the plans for the estate and the distillery. 'The sales are already going through; both owners are keen to offload their more labour-intensive land, it seems.'

'Oh aye? He's not letting the grass grow, then.'

'The opposite.' Mackenzie picked tomato out of his sandwich and dropped it into his bin with a little grimace. 'He's going to be clearing the ground he's earmarked for the houses, as soon as the planning permission's gone through.'

'Makes sense.' Tony took a swig of his coffee, and Mackenzie noted that his hand was trembling a little as he set his cup down; he wondered if he hadn't expected too much by bringing him out of retirement.

'You okay?'

'I'm fine. Just don't want to spill anything on this high-tech equipment.' Tony indicated his notepad, before returning to the subject of Ade's new venture. 'Presumably he'll have to pull the old house down at Glenlowrie? I'd have thought it would cost more to restore than to re-build after the fire. Surprised it hasn't been done already.'

'It's the bottom end of the two estates he's buying,'

Mackenzie said. 'From what I can gather it's from the old bothy at Drumnacoille, in a more or less straight line across Glen-lowrie, and down to the road.'

Tony didn't answer for a minute. 'I don't know the estates that well,' he confessed at length. 'I'd have to look at Google to get a clear picture. 'Good for Ade though,' he added, raising his cup in a rather shaky salute. 'Here's to new ventures.'

'New ventures.'

'And faster processors,' Tony said, nodding at Mackenzie's laptop. 'Look, I've been dithering a bit. I ought to get off and meet,' he glanced down at his notepad again, 'Mrs Jackson.'

'Chuck the rest of your sarnie over then,' Mackenzie said. 'Can't see it go to waste.'

'You've had that, pal. I'm taking it with me. See you later.'

'Greedy bastard,' Mackenzie called after him, grinning.

He opened the laptop and tried again with his Excel sheet. This time it loaded, and he was soon knee deep in the Clifford-Mackenzie accounts, so when his phone buzzed he snatched it up in relief.

'Ade. Thank God, I was praying for a distraction… Where are you? Sounds like a racetrack there.'

'It's one car, ya drama queen! I've been up at the estate, but I've come down to the main road to find a decent mobile reception.'

Mackenzie remembered all too well how flaky the reception was up at Glenlowrie, and couldn't help a little shiver as he recalled sending young Jamie off to make an emergency call…and delivering him straight into the unhinged grasp of Sarah Wallace, and back to his prison in the hills.

'Why are you calling then?' he asked, pushing the memory away with an effort. 'You lost?'

'Get knotted,' his brother replied, amiably enough, then his tone turned more serious. 'Look, can you spare an hour? I could do with an opinion on something. I might just be over-reacting. Can you meet me up at Glenlowrie?'

Mackenzie's hand tensed on the phone, but he forced himself to relax. 'I suppose.'

'You did say you wanted a distraction,' Ade pressed, and Mackenzie could hear the smile back in his voice. 'There'll be a pint in it for you too. I'll meet you at the turning off the main road. You can leave your car there and I'll drive you up.'

'You don't need to, I'm—'

'No, it's not that.' Ade audibly exhaled, and it sounded a bit shaky. 'I'll explain when you get here.'

Half an hour later Mackenzie locked his own car door and climbed into the passenger side of Ade's second-hand jeep. He soon saw why his brother had advised leaving his own car at the entrance to the estate; the winding main road that led up through the hills was still being maintained, but after a few minutes Ade took a turning onto a side path that only the jeep, or stout walking boots, were equipped to deal with.

'I don't remember this,' Mackenzie said, leaning forward to peer more closely through the trees. 'Where does it lead?'

'Right through to the river, but it's been left to grow out.'

'You'll have your work cut out clearing this lot.'

'At least it's not in sight of the road, so there'll be no complaints about bright yellow diggers.' Ade flinched in sympathetic apology as they drove over a fallen branch, and he threw a quick glance at Mackenzie, who'd clutched at his shoulder. 'Sorry, mate.'

'That's another pint, and counting.'

'Sorry,' Ade said again. 'Look we're here now.'

The jeep crawled through the last of the overgrown bushes and trees, and into a clearing. In the shelter of a group of tall trees, a weather-battered hut stood almost hidden. Nearby, the river flowed through the clearing, fed by the Linn of Glenlowrie; the waterfall at the top end of the estate close to the cottage where Mackenzie, Charis and Jamie had all come so close to death just three months ago.

Ade was already out of the jeep and walking over to the hut, and Mackenzie followed at a distance, looking around him doubtfully. 'This is the land where you're going to build?'

'Not just here, no; it's a bit close to the river.' Ade pointed up the path. 'Further up that way there's a natural flat spot, high enough to avoid risk of flooding. But we're going to have to clear all this ground as well, which is why I've come up here now, to see what kind of job it'll be.'

'So what did you want me to look at?'

'Not look. Smell.' Ade tugged at the door of the hut, which had probably belonged to the fishing gillie when the estate had been in its heyday, and it came free with a grating creak of the hinges. He stepped back though, rather than in, and Mackenzie was disturbed to see him take a few deep breaths.

'It's bound to stink a bit,' he pointed out, coming closer, but he stopped as the smell met him several paces from the hut, despite him being upwind of it. There was the thick stench of mould and decaying canvas, as he'd expected, but underlying it was another, more pungent reek: rotting vegetables and sewerage, with an even heavier edge of putrid eggs... There was no mistaking it.

Mackenzie turned away, his eyes watering and his stomach clenched against the roiling nausea. 'Why the hell did you call me, instead of the police?' he managed at last, when he had himself under control. 'It's bloody obvious what that is!'

'I don't know, do I? I've never smelled a... Look, I just needed you to tell me, and now you have.' Ade peered into the gloom of the shed. 'Besides, it might be a fox, or even a deer.'

'Was the door locked when you got here?'

'Aye, padlocked. But the wood it was bolted to was rotten.'

'Probably not a fox then.' Mackenzie couldn't help the withering tone, but he relented when he saw Ade's dismayed face. 'I suppose something could have been trapped in there before the door was closed the last time,' he conceded. 'Maybe when they put the place up for sale.'

'Exactly, so shouldn't we check before we bother the police? We don't want to drag them all the way out here for a false alarm.'

Mackenzie reluctantly agreed, and Ade let the door stand open for a few minutes before they ventured in. The smell clung to everything, and he mentally said goodbye to his favourite sweatshirt, knowing the first thing he was going to do when he got home was bin it. Or burn it.

'No dead foxes or deer,' he said, looking around.

There was a shabby-looking tea chest that served as a table, and on it were three shallow pools of wax, each with a black fleck in the centre that had once been a wick. A pile of rotting canvases in the corner had probably been used as makeshift shelters for the gamekeeper and his assistants, and the layer of mildew that covered the pile was thick and furry. But the smell was not coming from them.

Ade crossed the wooden floor in just a couple of paces, and stopped as the board beneath his boot creaked. He looked down, then back at Mackenzie. 'I reckon it's down there,' he said in a low voice. 'This board's loose.'

'Still think it's a fox?' Mackenzie asked grimly. He wasn't even close yet to becoming used to the smell, but it had faded a little as he'd looked around. It returned, however, as Ade applied pressure to the plank, and he pressed the back of his hand to his mouth and bit the skin there, hard. The distraction helped for a moment, and then he could speak again.

'Definitely down there.'

'Think we should pull the floorboard back, just to be sure?' Ade asked.

'Knock yourself out, but I'm pretty sure I've seen, and smelled, all I need to. We don't want to screw up a crime scene.'

'I'll be careful. I just need to be certain before I call anyone.'

Mackenzie stepped outside and stood watching from several paces away, while his brother worked at the board with the toe of his boot then bent and got his fingers beneath it. He'd only levered the board up about a foot before he dropped it again and joined Mackenzie outside, his eyes reddened and watering. He didn't have to confirm what he'd seen, and Mackenzie didn't ask.

'This isn't even my land yet,' Ade said as they climbed back into the jeep. 'D'you think I should let the owners know?'

'The police'll do that. They're going to need to talk to them anyway.' Mackenzie rubbed his hands along his jeans, as if he could rid himself of the stench that had seeped into every pore. But it only seemed to release what had crept in among the fibres of his clothing, and, beyond lowering the window, he tried not to move again until they reached the foot of the estate.

Ade made the call to the police, and when they arrived Mackenzie went to sit in his own car while Ade directed them, and the pathologists, to the shed. He found himself looking closely at the attending officers; even knowing his nemesis Don Bradley was dead, and that Bradley's sidekick Mulholland had transferred out, he was still unable to quell the uneasiness the memories of this place had pulled back to the surface. Mistrust of the police was high on the list.

He was glad to see Nick Clifford had been drafted back onto the team though; Maddy said he'd been gutted to have had to give up his secondment on the Lumsden murder, but at least now he had a second bite at the cherry. Nick raised a hand in greeting, then followed the pathologist's van along the trail Ade had indicated.

Ade came over to Mackenzie's car after the officer had finished with him. 'Apparently there's nothing else we can do for a bit,' he said. 'They're going to find us later if they need anything. Thanks for coming out.' He patted the roof and stepped back. 'I'm going back for a shower and change. You?'

'Same, then back to the office.'

'Okay if I come over later?'

Mackenzie nodded. 'We need to talk about that caravan you're picking up tomorrow.' It seemed odd, and disconnected, to be talking about something so mundane, but it helped suppress the queasiness. He started up and eased the car out onto the main road again, trying to ignore the way the disturbed air wafted that sickly smell of death through the car. He added a full valet to the list of consequences of this little lunchtime distraction... Agency accounts suddenly didn't seem like such a chore after all.

Maddy collected her mobile phone at the end of her shift and glanced at the screen: a missed call and a text, both from Paul, and a WhatsApp from her father, with a picture of a happily grinning Tas on his way out of school. Her father knew she'd have been champing at the bit all day to contact him, and she smiled in affectionate gratitude at the message. She replied, saying she'd be over in half an hour, then checked Paul's text.

Not urgent, but interesting – give me a call! Then a shocked-face emoji. She called him back.

'What's so interesting? And why the scream?'

'Get this. They found a body under the floor of the gillie's hut at Glenlowrie.'

'What?' Maddy stopped midway through shoving her tabard into the plastic box in the back of the council van. 'Say that again!'

'Ade found it.' He paused. 'Christ, Mads... I swear I can still smell it. We don't know who it was.'

'So not a skeleton then?'

'Unfortunately not, no. But not fresh either. Judging from the stink I don't envy the pathologist's job. Police aren't telling me much, just asked a few questions about why I was up there.'

'And why were you?'

He told her about Ade's ongoing purchase. 'He called me when he first smelled it, didn't want to get the police in if it was just some wild animal that'd found its way in there.'

'Yuck. Sensible though, I suppose. It's quite a trek for a false alarm.'

'Aye. Anyway, Nick'll be off your case a bit now; he's been pulled back onto the team for this one.'

'Thank God! I felt rotten about before.'

'So, how'd today go?'

'It was okay. I'm litter-picking, which is better than cleaning bogs anyway. I even got chatting to this punky, scary-looking girl, who actually turned out to be—'

'Let me guess. Softer than a kitten's underbelly?'

Maddy grinned as she waved back to Hazel Douglas, who was now striding away from the van. 'Total opposite,' she said. 'Hard as bullets. But super intelligent in a questionable sort of a way. Did you know it only takes fifteen pounds of force to dislocate someone's knee from the side?'

'Thanks for that,' he said dryly. 'Good to know.'

'I hope you're taking notes. Right, I'm just heading over to spend the evening with Tas at Dad's, then I'll be off home.'

'Okay, just wanted to keep you in the loop. Oh, did you see Gavin last night?'

'I went over after my shift. He's... He's not in a good way, Paul.' She remembered the haunted look around his eyes that put lines where none had been before. 'I don't think he even wanted me there, if I'm honest. It was as if he thought I didn't fit anywhere in this new situation he's in.'

'Crap. If anyone understands being on remand, it's you.'

Maddy closed her eyes and sat on that memory once more. 'Well he'll be happy tonight, since I'm not going out there to see him. It's a long drive, and I'm knackered. But I'll go again tomorrow, and maybe by then he'll be ready to talk about what we can do to sort this before it goes to trial.'

'Give him my best,' Paul said. 'I'm sure he'll be out of there soon.'

Are you? I'm not. 'Okay. See you tomorrow, maybe.'

Maddy signed herself out for the day and collected her time sheet, then crossed to her car, her mind still on last night's visit and how helpless she had felt in the face of Gavin's despair. She'd tried to make him talk about his options, and asked what his solicitor had said, but he'd clammed up and just wanted to talk about Tas, his parents, and the fact that he was going to lose business hand over fist now word was out and he'd been named. He was expecting the firm to kick him out any day. She'd come away angry, and too upset even to drop in on Tas, reluctant to foist her temper on him – which increased her anger further.

Tonight she composed herself with an effort and kept up her smiling façade while Tas had his tea. Her father seemed the more distracted one now, and while Tas was tidying his toys away she found him in the kitchen looking blankly at the water running into the sink. She reached across him and turned off the tap.

'Would you rather I took him home? I don't mind.'

'What?' Tony blinked and came back. 'No, not at all. He likes it here. Doesn't he?' He sounded worried now, and she smiled.

'Of course he does. I just thought you seemed a bit distracted.'

'Nope.' Tony squirted washing up liquid into the sink and worked up a lather. 'I'm just a bit tired.'

'Are you still okay to work with Paul? He won't mind if you change your mind; we can manage.'

'I said I'm fine – don't fuss.' Tony gave her a smile to take the sting from his words. 'You go and say your goodnights, then get off home and get some sleep. You look as if you need it.'

Maddy went upstairs and gave Tas a hug. He was disappointingly eager to get back to choosing a bedtime story for later, but his hug was as tight as ever and he gave her a smacker of a kiss goodnight before he let her go back down, so she didn't feel too bereft. She was even starting to look forward to a quiet evening with a glass of wine and some mindless TV.

'Thanks again for having him for a few days,' she said to her father as she lifted her short coat down from the peg in the hall. 'I'll drop in for breakfast tomorrow, and then I'll take him back after my shift on Thursday if that's okay? I'm going to see Gav after CP tomorrow, or I'd do it then.'

He waved it away. 'Whenever suits. He'll be fine all week, if you like.'

'He might be, but I'm not.' Maddy picked up her phone and slid it into her pocket. 'Oh, has Nick been in touch? Apparently he's back on the murder investigation team, for that body Paul and his brother found at Glenlowrie.'

Tony stared. 'Body? Whose?'

'They don't know yet. I assumed you'd seen it on the news.'

'Aye, well, you try watching the news when there's Paw Patrol on telly.' Tony shook his head in the direction of Tas's bedroom as he came with her to the front door. 'Go on now, get home in time for a bit of an evening for yourself.'

A bit of an evening... Maddy found a wry smile crossing her face as she parked outside the house, uninviting now with no Gavin and Tas waiting for her, and all the windows dark. It felt strange to be coming home to an empty house, and it would be cold, too; was it even worth staying up, just for the sake of it?

She sighed as she closed the car door and checked the time on her phone. It was only a bit after seven, but it seemed to make more sense to just grab some toast and a cuppa, and get an early night with a book. Maybe she'd even be able to function like a proper grown-up tomorrow if she managed a decent night's sleep.

She stepped over the threshold and picked up the post that lay fanned on the mat, flicking through it in case something important had managed to get caught up in all the shiny advertising literature. Nothing. Not sure whether she was disappointed or relieved, she had just dropped it into the bin beside the door when a tiny sound behind her made her half turn. She got no further.

Chapter Nine

Before Maddy could see who had pushed into the house behind her, she was enshrouded in rough darkness, and her immediate, shocked inhalation delivered a taste of old, wet dust that made her spit reflexively. But she had no time to regret it; her hands were dragged behind her back, and she felt the narrow, hard plastic of a cable tie cutting into her flesh. A heavy blow in the left side of her back drove her to her knees, where she gagged on the musty sacking that was drawn into her mouth with every heaving breath. Dimly she heard the front door closing and the jingle of her own keys turning in the lock, and then she was on her feet again, dragged up by hard fingers around her upper arms that turned her and shoved her onwards.

She stumbled, her muscles unbearably tense, expecting at any moment to come up hard against some object; her mind's eye pictured the short hallway and she guessed she was being guided, none too gently, towards the open sitting room door. Her thoughts raced, searching for a way to use her knowledge of her own home against her attacker, but before she could think straight she was pulled to a halt, and stood shaking and alone as the grip on her arms vanished.

She waited for him to speak, to tell her what he wanted of her, but whoever it was remained silent as he closed the door. There was the familiar sound of the sitting room curtains closing, and Maddy stood as straight as the throbbing pain in her back allowed. The darkness inside the hood lessened slightly as a light came on in the room, but she was still unable to see more than a shadow moving past her. Still she waited, but not a word was uttered. Finally the tension became too much.

'What's this about?' She hated herself for sounding so pathetic, but at least the silence was broken. 'Who are you?'

No response. Just movement that she tried hard to track, as her assailant moved around the room picking things up and then replacing them. She waited, the ache in her back easing a little, but her shoulders screamed when she tried to move, and her wrists already felt raw where the rough edges of the plastic ties rubbed them.

She thought back over all the cases she'd worked on, but none of them had had any deeply personal element; she hadn't been instrumental in sending anyone to prison, or broken up any marriages, as far as she knew. Yet that was where the winding road of her thoughts continually returned. The coincidence was too much...

Mulholland!

A small sound escaped her lips, and the movement stopped. She sensed her attacker was watching her closely, and forced herself to stand very still while she thought about it. Alistair Mulholland was the only one of that awful collection of mutually destructive criminals to have escaped alive that night in August: Andy Stein had been shot dead and left in the tiny back room; likewise Sarah Wallace, then Don Bradley had washed up at the foot of the Linn of Glenlowrie, the gun that had killed both of them still tucked securely inside his jacket.

Mulholland had been the one to pull the trigger though, and Charis said he'd made it away from the cottage in the confusion as the police helicopter had arrived. The only remaining witnesses to those murders were herself, Charis and Jamie – Maddy went ice-cold and started to tremble, as she wondered if he had already visited the Boulton household tonight. Then there was Ben Cameron: not a witness to what had happened in the cottage, but someone who knew all about Mulholland's involvement in it. *And Sarah's best and oldest friend – let's not forget that...*

No. Cameron had been shaken to the core by what had happened; he was devastated, but not vengeful, and more importantly he knew it hadn't been Maddy's gun that had killed Sarah. This wasn't him, Maddy was reasonably sure of that, but he was certainly in deadly danger now, if he hadn't been killed already. Mulholland had made it quite clear he intended to tie up that particular loose end, but when nothing had happened they'd assumed he'd chosen to simply transfer out of the area, and leave Cameron to thank his lucky stars he was still breathing. He probably enjoyed the thought of the quiet family man living his life in constant fear, and the often-discussed hope was that he had seen sense and recognised how another murder would only throw a spotlight on it all again.

But what if they'd been wrong? What if he'd simply been biding his time? Letting it all gradually fade, until something else huge came up and pushed the newsworthy events of the August bank holiday weekend right under the rug? Something huge like another murder.

The movement resumed as the intruder continued his way around the room, and Maddy tried to follow his progress by sound and shadow. She didn't know whether to address him by name, to show she'd realised who he was, but reflected that it might put her in greater danger. Then again, why hadn't he just killed her immediately? Why this...pacing, and waiting? For the same reason he'd left Cameron alone until now? Or for the terrorising effect he knew it would have on her.

The tension was making her feel ill, and her legs were beginning to shake. She tentatively stretched out a foot, to see if it connected with the chair that should be nearby if she'd imagined her position correctly. Immediately, the shadow changed direction and strode towards her; as she opened her mouth to say she only wanted to sit, a hand shot out and those cold, hard fingers locked around her throat. She dragged a thin breath, but even that was cut off as the grip tightened and a shooting pain flashed up through her jaw. As her vision darkened and the world began to swim away she thought of Tas, and a terrible sense of hopelessness fell over her.

The hand abruptly let go, and Maddy staggered to the side, trying to keep her balance as she pulled in air that only scorched her throat. Relief pulsed in rhythm with her frantic heartbeat; she could feel it in her temples and her chest, and even in her fingers. She didn't try to sit again, nor to speak – she knew she'd cough and have to ask for water if she tried that. Instead she just waited.

And waited.

She didn't know how long it had been, but her head was drooping and her arms screamed for release, and still the shadowy, silent intruder kept moving and lifting things. Examining a life he had no business being near. The shape stopped somewhere close to where Maddy thought the TV should be, and she heard the faint scrape as he picked something up. Her mind showed her a couple of family photos, in matched wooden frames; a selection of tealight holders and an oil burner; a Tiffany-styled lamp... She caught her breath as she remembered how heavy the base of that lamp was, and her imagination presented her with a vivid idea of how it might feel if it were to strike the back of her head... A rattle indicated that whatever it was had been put back down, and she breathed again.

She thought about the floor under her throbbing feet, and how just a couple of days ago she, Gavin and Tas had knelt here, watching the boy constructing his space station. She'd been so angry then, with Gav, for ruining what should have been a euphoric time for them all, and now she was standing in the same room, rigid with fear and wishing for that day back again, with all its petty annoyances as well as its enormous and disturbing revelations.

Eventually the intruder sat down. Maddy heard the soft whisper of the sofa cushion, and her legs weakened in response – what if they failed to support her? The memory of that claw-like grip on her throat brought a prickle of sweat to her hairline, and she could feel it echoed in the dampness in the middle of her back, despite the chill.

She strained to hear anything at all, after the death of her initial wild hope that maybe she was actually alone now, but her efforts were rewarded only with the occasional rustle of what sounded like a heavy fabric as the intruder crossed or uncrossed his legs, and the flick of flimsy paper as he turned a page of the TV guide that sat on the coffee table. The time ticked on.

The earlier chill in the room had happened in another life. Maddy's breath had dampened the sacking and then moulded it to her face, and sweat kept it there as she breathed, steady and slow in an effort to keep panic at bay. It seemed clear now that her attacker was waiting for something, or someone, and the only thing that gave her hope was the fact that she had been hooded; perhaps she would still be spared, if she only managed—

Her right knee buckled. Her weight had been on it, and she dipped violently to that side, bracing herself for the impact as she hit the floor, and even welcoming the thought of a second's respite...but she didn't get that either. Yanked upright again she felt a despairing sob escape at last, and a hand clamped itself over her open mouth. The mildewed sacking rubbed against her teeth, and it took all her self control not to try and bite the fingers through it, but she gave a little nod to indicate that her assailant could trust her.

If it was Mulholland, what could he be waiting for? His intention could only be to silence her, so why would he indulge in all this mental torture? True, he was soulless and ice-hearted, and might have been dispassionately curious enough to study her terror in detail before killing her, but the longer he was here, the bigger the risk that someone would discover him. It just wasn't worth it.

To her horror she felt an all-too familiar flutter in the back of her right calf, and she grunted and tried to flex her foot without toppling over again; she had the feeling he wouldn't be so lenient a second time.

'Cramp,' she whispered, and pushed her heel downwards as hard as she could, praying the flutter wouldn't dissolve into the kind of pulsing sensation that meant screaming pain would soon follow. She'd be unable to massage the pain away, with her hands behind her back. She felt her calf muscle harden, just as her assailant's phone buzzed. It must have been a text; no words were exchanged, and, distracted by the sound of someone rising from the sofa, she lowered her foot and the cramp flared into burning life. She gasped at the severity of it, but knew if she screamed she'd suffer much worse than a blow to the kidney.

Even as she desperately flexed her foot again, fighting to balance on one leg, she felt her right sleeve dragged back to her elbow, and then a sharp pinprick on the inside of her arm. The agony in her leg didn't quite eclipse the thin line of fiery pain that drew downwards from just below her elbow, stopping a little above her wrist, but the flow of blood brought a sweep of heat across her face. She had no way of knowing how deep the wound was; if adrenalin, or nerve damage, were blocking the worst of the pain... Blood seeped down to pool in her curled palm and she swayed, her eyes and mouth tightly closed. The sweat-dampened sacking rasped against her face as she shook her head in frantic denial.

After a moment she realised she wasn't growing weaker, so it was unlikely there was arterial damage; she still had no idea how deep the cut was, but it was clearly not fatal. The cramp began to ease, thanks to continued flexing of her foot, and as her thoughts became less scrambled she understood, with real despair, that the text message was all the intruder had been waiting for. Whatever it had said, and whichever way this went now, it would soon be over.

Her assailant moved to stand behind her, and a hand snaked around and tugged at the sacking, but only raised it a few inches, to the level of her jaw. She felt the tip of the blade again, this time in the skin just below her left ear, and her heart slid into a panicked, erratic beat as gloved fingers cupped her chin almost tenderly and tilted her head back. She heard a faint moan and recognised it as her own, final utterance before the lethal kiss of the blade took her away.

There was a faint tug at her wrists, and through the numbness of pure terror, Maddy gradually realised two things: the hand was gone from her chin, and her own blood-drenched hands were now only held together by her tightly linked fingers. The sound of the closing front door broke her paralysis, and she dragged the sacking off her head and hobbled across to the window, but there was only darkness beyond and the faint cough of an engine starting up.

She snatched her phone from her pocket, and got as far as unlocking the screen before she saw something on the coffee table. A piece of paper had been folded and left there; a message? She opened it up, noticing first that the paper was thicker than normal, and then that it was actually a photo, folded and re-folded multiple times.

She glanced at the TV stand, and the empty wooden frame that had held this picture, and then smoothed out the glossy paper to see Tas smiling up at her, familiar and achingly innocent. The weakened paper along the folds neatly bisected his face, horizontally and vertically, like white slash marks, and a tiny, frayed hole had formed between the boy's eyes. Printed in the corner of the page was a single word: GUILTY, and she put the bloodied phone down again with violently trembling fingers.

It hadn't been Mulholland in her house after all; this had nothing to do with him. This was about Lumsden, and the warning was clear; there could be no question of a self-defence or diminished responsibility plea for Gavin now. Did this mean her visitor had been Lumsden's real killer? The relief that accompanied that thought came as something of a shock – had she really believed Gavin had had something to do with it? She must have, although she hadn't admitted it even to herself.

She wasn't sure how long she sat there, staring at the photo, but as the fearful rush of adrenalin wore off, Maddy became aware once more of the stinging along her arm, and the blood that now dripped onto the carpet. Feeling sick, she pulled her sleeve down and pressed it against the cut, not wanting to look in case it was more severe than it felt. Under different circumstances she might have laughed. *Call yourself a trained nurse?*

She realised then that she was only storing up trouble in the form of bits of fabric in the cut, and limped upstairs to the bathroom, where she peeled off her jumper and sat on the edge of the bath, shivering. She draped a cold flannel across her arm and winced at the icy sensation against her hot, bloodied skin, but eventually began to dab carefully and saw, to her relief, that the cut was shallow and shouldn't need stitches. Or an explanation. Just as well; it would have been difficult explaining that one away, and any hesitation would have raised alarms all over the place. A few steri-strips for the deepest part at the top were enough, and with an adventurous five-year-old in the house she was never without such things.

The cable ties hadn't broken the skin badly, but her wrists were grazed and inflamed in places, and burned along the welts. The cold flannel brought some relief, and she re-soaked it and laid it along her wrists while she allowed her arm to dry.

Forcing herself to remain calm, she applied antiseptic and a bandage to the long cut, securing it with a small, fiddly safety pin that she had trouble doing up with her left hand. Then she went downstairs and cut a hole in the bottom of a freezer bag, drew it over the bandage, and returned to the bathroom. She stepped under the shower, and finally released everything she'd been holding so tightly in check, letting the water run down over her bowed head as she wept.

Later she sat on the sofa, wrapped in a towel and covered by her warmest dressing gown, her feet cosily encased in fleecy slippers. She worked out that she'd only been standing in that one position for a little over two hours – it had felt like half the night. Her arm was stinging despite the anaesthetic properties of the antiseptic cream, and she kept her hand wrapped around the bandage, which eased it somewhat. Her right calf still ached, but that was fading now, too.

She stretched her hand towards her phone for the hundredth time, ready to call the police, but withdrew it yet again as her gaze fell on the folded picture of Tas. She couldn't risk it. All she could do was to tell Gavin tomorrow, when she visited him, and watch his reaction when she floated the possibility that it was Lumsden's murderer who had attacked her in her own home and threatened their son. In the meantime she had to try and get some sleep, though she already knew it would be nearly impossible.

She did pick up the phone now, this time to ensure the alarm was set for the morning, and almost dropped it again as it blared at her, the blood-streaked screen flashing up an unknown number. Her heart hammering, in case it was a further threat, she swiped green.

'Hello?'

'Miss Clifford? I'm calling from HMP Inverness. I'm afraid I have some bad news...'

Around an hour and a half later, and by now frantic, Maddy arrived at Raigmore hospital to be met by a police officer at reception. 'He's undergoing surgery,' the woman explained, 'but I'm afraid they're not very hopeful.'

'What do you mean, *not hopeful?*' Maddy, who'd thrown on the first thing she'd dragged from her wardrobe, pulled the long sleeves of her tatty sweatshirt down over her hands in agitation. 'What have they said?'

'I don't have anything further than that, I'm afraid. They—'

'Mads?'

She looked around in relief. She'd called Paul to tell him where she was, not knowing what to expect; just to hear a friendly voice had been enough, and here he was. The officer nodded and stepped back, and as Paul wrapped her in his familiar embrace, Maddy leaned against him and let out a huge, shuddering sigh. 'Thanks for coming all this way.'

'Of course I'd come.' He held her at arm's length and studied her closely. 'You'd better tell me what's happened.'

'He was found in his cell; someone beat the crap out of him.'

'Shit. What've the doctors said?'

'Not much, apparently.' Maddy found a seat and sank gratefully into it. 'He's in surgery.' She was desperate to tell him what had happened earlier in the evening, but was aware the prison officer was still lingering nearby. 'All I know is that they brought him here rather than deal with it there, so it must be bad. Head injuries, they said on the phone. I've probably broken a dozen speed limits getting here... And I might still be too late.'

She heard the hopelessness in her own voice, but at least with Paul she didn't feel she had to temper it for the sake of appearing resilient. 'The officer there said they're *not hopeful*, whatever that means.'

'God, I'm sorry.'

She leaned forward and covered her face with her hands to blot out the hospital around her, but all she could picture was Gavin's head hitting the painted wall of his cell, leaving smears of blood just as she had done on the shower taps. And on her phone.

She sat upright. 'I've got to call Dad.'

'There's nothing he'll be able to do,' Paul said reasonably.

But that wasn't the point. The sudden, terrifying thought that her attack and Gavin's had happened at roughly the same time had made her wonder if Tas hadn't also been targeted. The desperation to know almost obliterated all other thought, but she just stopped herself from pulling her blood-smeared phone from her pocket before she headed outside. The moment she was through the doors she dragged it out.

'Dad?'

'What's wrong?' He sounded concerned, but otherwise perfectly normal, and she felt her free hand unclench in relief.

'What makes you think anything's wrong?'

'Because it's gone midnight, and you're meant to be getting an early night. Are you okay?'

She told him briefly about the call from the prison, and asked him to explain to Tas that she'd have to miss breakfast with him. 'I'm going to have to call my probation officer and cancel tomorrow's CP too.'

'Let me.' Tony sounded subdued. 'You concentrate on Gavin.'

'And...' Maddy hesitated, knowing this would provoke questions, 'I'd like you to keep Tas off school tomorrow, okay? Keep him home with you.'

There was a pause, but her father had evidently decided now wasn't the time. 'Okay. Are you sure you're all right?'

Maddy closed her eyes, fighting an unexpected and unwelcome surge of emotion. *Not now...* 'I'm fine, Dad. I'll let you know when I hear more about Gav.'

She ended the call, spat on her sleeve and wiped the phone screen, then went back inside and slid into her seat beside Paul. 'He's going to call in about my CP,' she said. She rubbed her eyes hard with the heels of her hands. 'Christ on a bike, I don't know what's happening to my life. What gods or demons have I pissed off now, d'you think?'

'Any that value the sartorial elegance you're usually known for.' He eyed her holey sweatshirt. 'That looks more like something Charis would put on.'

'How very bloody dare you?' But she gave him a weak smile. 'You're one to talk. Speaking of Charis, how was she about me dragging you out at this time of night?'

'You didn't drag me, it was my choice. Anyway I was at my home, she's at hers, so she has no idea I'm here. I've left Ade at mine though; he's more shaken up about finding that body than he's letting on.'

'I know how he feels. I suppose he just wants to talk about anything else, to take his mind off it. How're his plans shaping up?'

Paul didn't answer, and Maddy was about to repeat the question but noticed he was staring at her wrist; looking down she saw that her sleeve had pulled back to reveal the raised welt and a raw graze on the bone. Further up, she noticed that the safety pin was starting to poke through a threadbare part of her sleeve. She casually laid a hand over it, as if embarrassed about the state of her clothes, but met his eyes with hers in a clear message: *don't ask.*

She let her eyes drift back over towards the officer, and saw Paul understood, by the slow blink and the slight shift in direction of his gaze. But she also saw a muscle jumping in his jaw, and knew he'd have the full story out of her the minute it was safe to do so.

Maddy turned to the officer – DS Muir, she remembered now – and indicated that it was fine to speak in front of Paul. 'Can you tell us any more about what happened?'

'He'd been sharing a cell with another remand prisoner,' Muir said, 'but his cellmate had been advised to leave, by a couple of other prisoners. When he was allowed back in, he found Gavin unconscious. He raised the alarm, but wasn't able, or willing, to identify the two men.'

'Who can blame him? Why do they let remand prisoners share the same space as convicted ones?' Maddy felt ill at the thought of it. 'It's lunacy!'

'He's on judge's remand, in there for murder,' Muir said, a little defensively, 'and the evidence is pretty strong.'

'I know! But still, why wasn't he kept apart from the convicted inmates?'

Paul spoke reasonably. 'How do you know he wasn't?'

'Oh, come on! No remand prisoner would risk this!'

'What risk? No-one's pointing the finger at them, are they?' Muir shrugged. 'But yes, you're right; the only thing our witness can say is that the perpetrators were wearing prison clothing instead of their own. It's probably all he felt safe saying, the poor sod.'

'You don't seem bothered about what's happened,' Maddy said. 'Especially since Gavin's not been convicted yet.' She wrapped her hand across her arm, hardly aware she was doing it until she saw Paul's eyes on her again. 'Are you familiar with the case, DS Muir, or are you just—'

'I'm family liaison for the Lumsdens,' Muir said, a little coolly. 'I'm *very* familiar with the case.'

'So you're on their side.'

'I'm not on anyone's side, just answering your question.' Muir gave her a polite smile. 'Okay, I've told you all I know. One of our officers will be along to speak to Mr Galbraith if he...*when* he regains consciousness, but in the meantime, if you hear of anything helpful, please let us know.'

Watching her retreating back, Maddy already knew what Paul was going to say, and she was right.

'Why antagonise them, Mads?' he said on a sigh. 'I'd have thought *I* was a pretty good lesson in what happens when you do that.'

'Well, she was just so cool about it all.'

'Of course she was. It's her job. So, are you going to tell me about that?' He nodded at Maddy's arm. 'I'm guessing you didn't get it picking up litter.' He looked at his phone to check the time. 'Look, Gavin's only just gone in, hasn't he? Come and get a coffee, and we'll talk there.'

'Café's closed.' Maddy looked up at him searchingly; she knew she could trust him, but wasn't sure she was ready for the anger she knew lay beneath that quiet façade. 'Promise me you won't go off the deep end when I tell you.' Predictably, his eyes darkened, and she grabbed his arm. 'Come outside then.'

Under the covered entranceway, where she felt fairly sure anyone watching or listening would stand out, Maddy told Paul everything that had happened since she got home from her father's that evening. She didn't look at him as she spoke, but could hear the occasional explosive hiss of breath somewhere above her head, and heard the shuffle of his feet, as if he were ready to take off and find whoever had attacked her.

When she'd finished he leaned against one of the narrow

pillars and folded his arms. His voice was calm enough, but it was easy to detect the tight undertone. 'Do you think it was whoever killed Craig Lumsden?'

'I can't think who else it could have been. To begin with I was convinced it was Mulholland, but seeing that note on Tas's picture, and with what's happened to Gav... It must have been.'

'So you were all set to convince Gavin to plead guilty, but it looks like he's had his own warning.'

'Some *warning*.'

'The text message,' Paul said thoughtfully. 'I suppose that was your intruder's signal that all had gone to plan at the prison. I imagine if it had said something different, you might be the one in there.' He nodded at the hospital entrance, and Maddy shuddered. She'd been so busy re-living the terrifying experience that she'd forgotten to count herself lucky to be out, and alive, and with only a scratched arm and an aching back and leg to show for it.

'You're going to let me look into this, aren't you?'

'No!' Maddy looked around quickly, and lowered her voice. 'That's not why I told you! I told you because you're a friend.'

'Aye, and friends help when they can.' Paul took her hand. 'If it wasn't for you I'd have lost it completely when Kath and Josh died.' He spoke quietly, but no less intently for all that. 'You not only got me through that, but you also got me a job with your dad. The least I can do now is—'

'Get yourself killed?' Maddy interrupted crossly, and snatched her hand away. 'Look, when I thought I'd lost you in the summer I don't know how I put one foot in front of the other. There's no way I'm going through that again.'

'I'll just make some enquiries,' he soothed. 'Find out who put these arseholes up to what they did.'

'And how are you going to do that? No-one knows who they are.'

'Gavin will.'

'There's zero chance of him telling anyone, even if he...' Maddy's voice hitched, and she cleared her throat. 'He's got to go back in there, don't forget.'

'Surely they'd move him to a different remand centre? Maybe closer to Aberdeen if that's where he'll stand trial.'

'We can't risk it. And he certainly won't.' Maddy pulled her sleeves down again. 'Look, you can go home. I'll be okay.'

'Away and raffle yer doughnut,' Paul grinned, borrowing her favourite phrase. He slipped into a broad Glaswegian accent. 'See, I'm goin' nowhere, pal.'

'That was shocking,' Maddy said, but her smile was real now, and for a moment the awfulness of the evening, and whatever was coming, faded a little. 'Right then, get your arse in there and buy me a coffee from the machine.'

As she followed him in through the glass doors, she glanced behind her into the darkness and tried not to think too hard about how her attacker knew where she lived.

Chapter Ten

KILBRIDE LEFT the front door open for Ian George to invite himself in, and wheeled himself back to the sitting room. Ian followed, looking around a little furtively.

'She out?'

'If, by *she*, you mean your cousin, then no. She's upstairs.'

'She's not our cousin, she's our aunt.' Ian shut the sitting room door and faced Kilbride squarely. 'I take it you're up to speed?'

'How could I be? I've been waiting to hear from you.'

'Okay. Well, Galbraith's in hospital.'

'In...' Kilbride stared. 'What the hell did your blokes *do* to him?'

'Not my fault.' Ian shrugged. 'I told them to warn him, and they did. I can't physically control how far they take it, can I?'

Kilbride had to concede that. And at least the man wasn't dead. 'But he knows he's to plead guilty?' he pressed. 'No falling back on diminished responsibility, or manslaughter?'

'Can I have a cup of tea?'

'Answer me!'

'Aye, he knows.' Ian shoved his hands into his pockets and stared out of the window for a moment. 'So... I get my job back, then?'

Two could play at the sidestepping game. 'How badly *is* he hurt?'

Ian shrugged. 'I've got no more way of knowing than you do. I'd been let out by the time it kicked off, remember?' He gave Kilbride a pained look. 'You could have warned me you were going to shop me; I'd not have put up a fight if I'd understood why you were doing it.'

'I'd have been stupid to take the chance. Besides, I dropped the accusation, didn't I?'

'But they might have held me for the fraud.'

'You told me there was no way they could pin it on you,' Kilbride reminded him. 'Not my fault you're so convincing, is it?' He chewed at the inside of his lip. 'Okay. You can have a month's trial.'

'A *trial*? I was working for you before Craig bloody Lumsden got a sniff in!'

'Take it or leave it,' Kilbride snapped. 'You've got a lot to make up for.'

Ian looked as if he wanted to argue, but then subsided. 'I'll take it. When do I start?'

'Now.' Kilbride peered down the drive. 'Ah, good. Donna's here.'

'Aye, well, I'll not interrupt you two. I've got to arrange a more permanent place to stay.' Ian's face had paled even more than usual, and Kilbride's eyes narrowed.

'You're on my time now,' he reminded him. 'You'll stay put.'

Donna kissed her father's cheek when she came in, as always, but her attention went straight to Ian. 'Well?'

'It's done. I texted you, didn't I?'

'I know it's *done*! And did you see the news this morning?'

Ian looked away, and Kilbride picked up his phone. 'It made the news?'

'Local solicitor on remand, fighting for his life,' Donna said, even as Kilbride found the report on his phone. 'Fuck's sake, Ian, what the hell happened to *warning*?'

'Look, I'll tell you what I told your dad: I gave the orders; it wasn't up to me how they were carried out. The guys must have taken against him, that's all, and that's no surprise, is it?' He shrugged. 'Maybe he helped put one of them away at some point.'

'He's not a criminal lawyer, genius! He works in corporate law. Or he did until now.'

'Well some other reason then.'

'Shall I tell you what *I* think?' Donna stepped up to Ian, her face belligerently close to his. '*I* think you recognised that woman just as clearly as I did.'

'What woman?' Kilbride asked, but he might as well have been talking to himself.

'*I* think you decided she needed to be taught a lesson,' Donna said. 'Payback for this.' She jabbed a finger at Ian's scar. 'I think you gave your mates *carte blanche* to do whatever they wanted to, to her bloke, and that you must have absolutely creamed your Y-fronts when I gave you her address.'

'I didn't do—'

'Is this Maddy Clifford you're talking about?' Kilbride demanded, but was once more ignored.

'What happened at her house, Ian? I mean, I assume she's alive, since there are no white tents there this morning, but I wouldn't mind betting you did a bit more than I told you to.'

Ian spoke in a low, measured voice. 'I waited until I had word of Galbraith, and then I left. Just as you instructed.'

Donna gave a huff of disbelief. 'And there was me thinking you were just eyeing her up on Monday. So what did you think, once you realised she was the one who shopped you to my dad? That she was a legitimate target?'

'That she deserved a bit of a fright, that's all. I didn't hurt her. Badly,' he added, and Kilbride closed his eyes and sighed.

'Did she see you?'

Ian finally acknowledged him. 'Of course not. You think I'm stupid?'

'If I thought that I wouldn't have hired you again,' Kilbride pointed out tightly. 'No, I don't think you're stupid, but I do think you're hot-headed and need to rein it in.' He turned back to Donna. 'This news report doesn't give a lot away. What do you know?'

'That Galbraith was taken to Raigmore around ten o'clock last night, with life-threatening head injuries. He's had emergency surgery, and his fiancée,' she shot Ian a dark look, 'won't comment on the reason for the attack.'

'Well there you go,' Ian said with no small amount of satisfaction. 'If she still thought he was innocent she'd be singing to the rooftops about intimidation.'

'Seems pretty clear she's got the message,' Kilbride agreed. 'Look, Donna, don't fret about the Clifford woman. And if Galbraith dies, well then...job done.'

'If he dies, the finger will be pointed at us!' Donna sat down and crossed her legs. It was clear she had no intention of leaving, and Kilbride closed his eyes briefly and moved on.

'So, Ian. You were talking about finding somewhere to live. Can you afford that?'

'Well I was hoping for an advance on my pay. Better still, a few days in one of your thousands of spare rooms,' he waved a hand to encompass the house, 'while I find somewhere.'

'For God's sake!' Donna looked at them both in turn, incredulous. 'Are you not getting this? If Galbraith—'

'Yes!' Kilbride bristled with irritation. 'We know. If he dies, questions will be asked. Questions that we will deal with *if* it happens. Right now there's nothing we can do, so let's just get on, okay? Ian and I have got more immediate things to discuss. Your new ad goes on the Thistle website today, doesn't it? Why don't you go in to work and field phone calls?'

'I would,' Donna said, looking at him steadily and with suddenly glistening eyes, 'but I've got a funeral to arrange. It's on Monday, in case you were interested.'

'Of course.' Kilbride's remorse kindled. 'Let me help you then,' he said more gently.

'No thanks; you and Ian have got *things to discuss*. I'll talk to Martha.'

'Don't sulk, hen,' Ian put in, sounding too bright by half, 'it doesn't suit you.'

Kilbride glared at him. 'She's upstairs, love,' he said to Donna.

He waited until Donna had left, then spoke mildly. 'Don't ever forget she's my daughter. If you upset her once more, you can kiss goodbye to a lot more than your job.' He could see his calm tone had made his point much more strongly than yelling would have done, and gestured to the seat Donna had vacated. 'So let's talk about your living arrangements.'

Ian sat, visibly relieved. 'If you could give me a few days, that'd save me looking for a squat.'

'What's up with the room where you were staying?'

'Oddly enough they took against being yanked out of bed

by the police,' Ian said dryly. 'I've no more savings for a deposit.'

'Okay. You've got until the weekend.'

'Thanks. I'll fetch my stuff today.' He shuffled his feet on the carpet, and Kilbride knew there was more. He waited. He was right.

'That taxi the other night... It wasn't cheap.'

'They don't tend to be.'

'So I was thinking—'

'I thought you might be.'

Ian gave him an irritated look that quickly faded into a pleading one. 'How about a hire car? Just until I scrape together enough cash for a runabout?'

Kilbride pondered for a moment, then nodded. 'I'll pay for a fortnight's hire, but you'll have to pay any excess insurance. And after that you're on your own.'

'Great, thanks. I'll head out to the airport this afternoon; they've always had a decent selection of automatics.'

'Nothing fancy,' Kilbride cautioned.

'Don't worry, I won't bankrupt you.' Ian was evidently surprised it had been so easy to talk his boss into stumping up for a car, but the last thing Kilbride wanted was to have someone tied to him day and night. He chose not to rib the man about his lack of a manual licence; as long as Ian could drive the adapted Qashqai it made little difference to him.

'So where did you stay last night then,' he asked, 'since the B&B kicked you out?'

'In a garden shed about three miles down the road.' Ian sniffed his armpit. 'I could do with a shower too, as it goes.'

'A shed? Hardly the time of year for that.'

'Aye, it was a bit cold.' Ian chuckled. 'But better than where they found that other poor sod.'

'Which poor sod?'

'Bloke they found in that shed up in the hills. What's the place called?'

'Glenlowrie?' Kilbride was jolted. He'd heard about the body being found, of course, but hadn't paid much attention to the details. He felt his skin prickle. 'I used to know the owners, back in the day. I didn't realise it was up there.'

'Aye. He'd been there a few months, they reckon.'

'And do they know what killed him?'

'If they do, they're not saying. Not yet anyway. Probably not the cold though, not in the summer.' He wrinkled his nose, looking absurdly prim. 'Must've stank, aye?'

'Maybe he walked into an old trap on the estate, and just bled out,' Kilbride mused uncomfortably. 'Duncan always left plenty of them around. Who found him?'

'Some guy who's buying the place, wants to turn it into one of those corporate Highland experience-type places.'

Kilbride couldn't help the sharp laugh. He and Duncan Wallace had clashed swords over the same enterprise, on that Hogmanay when everything had changed, but neither of them had ever seen it through. Though for very different reasons. 'Is he local, this bloke with the big ideas?'

'Used to be, according to what they're saying in the Twisted Tree in Abergarry. Grew up on the estate next door, but recently returned. Name of Mackenzie. From what I've heard he's buying part of both estates, and plans to combine them into one new one.'

Ah. One of Frank Mackenzie's boys. The full story tumbled back into Kilbride's memory, after years of suppressing it: Mackenzie's widely acclaimed estate next door to Duncan's; the robbery, and the consequent collapse of Mackenzie's business and home... Then this August just passed, Dunc's tame police officer turning up dead at the foot of the waterfall at Glenlowrie. Not to mention his own life-changing injuries sustained in that same river. All Duncan's plans, and his own, destroyed by greed.

There was something slyly cursed about the Glenlowrie estate, and now one of Mackenzie's sons was thinking of picking up where he himself and Duncan Wallace had both failed. Kilbride sensed the faintest spark of an idea, and he tuned out Ian's ramblings... Accepting that he had unfinished business had never been one of his strong points.

Jamie ran to catch up with Ethan as they headed for the school gate at the end of Wednesday afternoon. 'Is your brother picking you up?'

'Aye,' Ethan said, pulling his helmet from his backpack. 'I'm pretty sure he's hoping I'll fall off if he takes the bends hard enough. All right for him, he's got a brand-new helmet. I've just got this old thing. *And* he's got a new phone,' he went on in aggrieved tones. 'Wouldn't even give me his old one, and it still works fine.'

'Have you had another scrap? Is that how you got that bruise?'

'What bruise?'

'I saw it in PE, when you were on the monkey bars. I hate them bars,' Jamie added gloomily. 'I can't hold on.'

'We had a fight, that's all. Brothers do, y'know.' Ethan sounded defensive now, so Jamie changed the subject.

'D'you wanna come over Friday, after school?'

'Okay. If Mum says I can.'

'I'm trying to get my Mum to buy me a dog. You can tell her about Pickles and how he was, like, your brother's friend.'

Ethan looked at him with a faint scowl. 'That's why you want me to come over?'

'No, not just that. I've got some invisible ink. We can write messages and hide them for each other to find and decipher.'

Ethan brightened. 'Okay. Kyle's here. I'll see you tomorrow – you can tell me about it then.'

Jamie watched his friend speed off out of the gate, to where Kyle was leaning against the wall looking the other way. The teen's hands were shoved into his coat pockets and his hood was up against the drizzle; when Ethan joined him he simply moved off towards the parked moped without acknowledging him, and unhooked his own new, glossy black helmet without a word. Maybe brothers weren't such a great idea after all.

Jamie found his mum, and together they walked away from the crowd around the railings. 'Is that okay if Ethan comes over Friday?'

'Fine, as long as you'll be happy with a chippy tea. I've got some studying to do.'

'Studying?'

His mum grinned at him, as if she'd been holding it in for ages. 'I'm learning photography, Jay! Properly, I mean. I've signed up for an online course, so that next year I can go to college. Maybe even after that I could get a degree.'

Jamie couldn't understand why she was so excited about the thought of going back to school, but she was fine about Ethan coming over, so it didn't matter.

'Will he need picking up?' she asked as they crossed the road. 'Or will one of his parents be able to drop him off?'

'Dunno, I'll check. His brother might bring him on the

back of his moped.' He considered. 'Actually, no, he probably won't.'

'Why not?'

'They've had a fight. I saw the bruise on Ethan's leg, and they didn't look that pleased to see each other after school.'

'Bruise?'

'Not a very big one,' Jamie hurried on, guessing what she was thinking, but he *was* pretty sure it had been Kyle who'd done it, not his dad; the older boy was so grumpy it'd be dead easy to cross him.

His mother didn't say anything for a moment, then nodded. 'Okay. Better check his mum's okay with him stopping for his tea. Speaking of which, we're going to Mackenzie's for ours, so get changed sharpish. And don't forget your inhaler re-fill.'

He caught her looking after him a bit thoughtfully a few minutes later, as he hared off upstairs to change out of his school stuff, and gave a little inward groan. Ethan's dad wasn't like his own; he was one of the nice ones. She'd even liked him herself when she'd met him, though he remembered now that he hadn't told her it was the same bloke who owned that shop. She'd better not say anything to him anyway; it'd be too embarrassing for words, and Ethan would never speak to him again.

An hour later he wasn't thinking about Ethan, or his family – he was too busy laughing at Mackenzie's own brother's 'guided tour'. He and his mum had gone over to Mackenzie's garden for the 'housewarming', and now the four of them were crammed inside the smallest, tattiest caravan he'd ever seen; it was like that one off *Father Ted*, where about eight people had tried to do the Riverdance at once, and the whole thing had toppled over.

'If you follow that corridor down as far as the eye can see,' Ade was saying in hushed tones, 'you might just make out the feature window at the far end.'

Given that it was about four feet away, and the window was a rubber-surrounded rectangle the size of a chopping board, Jamie gave another shout of laughter. Ade winked at him and continued, in a similar vein, to draw attention to the *master bedroom* – a foldaway bed, currently hanging off the wall at 45 degrees; the *exquisite dining area, complete with professionally restored upholstery* – threadbare seating, criss-crossed with parcel tape; and *mood lighting* – a fluorescent tube on the wall, with a dangling cord.

'It's simply stunning,' Charis said, in a super-posh voice, and twisted to look up at Mackenzie. 'Don't you think so, darling?'

'A revelation,' he agreed. 'One can only aspire.'

But Jamie thought he seemed a bit distracted, despite his grin. Probably worried about Tas Galbraith's dad, who was still in hospital and had apparently not woken up yet.

'And now, we eat.' Ade flung open the caravan door, and Jamie watched in disappointment as his mum and Mackenzie climbed down the wonky metal step onto the wet grass.

'Aren't we having tea in here?'

'Good God, no,' Ade said cheerfully. 'Not fit for purpose, lad. The laird has been good enough to lay on a bit of nosh in the manor.' He pointed at Mackenzie's old-fashioned, but modest, two-bedroomed house. 'I think the cooker in this thing needs a bit of, let's just say, *attention*, before I'll feel happy putting food anywhere near it.'

They traipsed into the house. At least Mackenzie never

insisted on anyone taking shoes off, no matter how wet they were, though Jamie saw his mum guiltily eyeing the footprints on the hall rug. Mackenzie had laid four places at the kitchen table, and Jamie could smell something meaty and rich wafting from the oven; he remembered the greasy glass door of the caravan cooker and the flaking black bits on the hob, and found himself agreeing with the decision after all.

Ade kept them all entertained with tales about his engineering work in New Zealand, but they hadn't long started tucking into their lasagne when a knock at the door stopped him mid-story. Before Mackenzie could get up to answer it, the front door creaked open, and Maddy's voice came drifting in from the hall.

'Only me, but I can see you've got guests, so—'

'Come on in,' Mackenzie called. 'We're in the kitchen.'

Jamie looked at his mum, wide-eyed. 'How did she know we were here?'

'She's a PI,' his mother whispered back mysteriously. 'She's got the gift.' Then she shook her head with a smile. 'Wet footprints all over the hall rug, and three extra coats on the hooks, perhaps?'

Jamie felt a bit silly, considering he was the one who was supposed to be a detective-in-training. He looked up as Maddy came in, looking even paler than she usually did. She was still very pretty though, and he noticed Ade sitting up straighter... He buried his grin in a forkful of dinner.

'He's awake,' Maddy said, addressing Mackenzie but looking around at the others. 'Hi, everyone. Sorry to interrupt your meal.' She turned back to Mackenzie. 'I hope you don't mind me coming over like this. I've just come from seeing Dad and Tas, and I'm not quite ready to go home yet.'

''Course I don't mind, ya numpty.' Mackenzie stood up and gestured for her to take his seat. 'How is he?'

'They're keeping him sedated, but they've sent me home, since there's nothing I can do.'

'I was so shocked to hear about it,' Charis said quietly. 'All of it. Terrible thing.'

Maddy nodded her thanks, though Jamie could see she was close to tears. He wished Ade would say something funny to lighten the mood again, but he seemed to have been silenced for once and just looked a bit shy. Mackenzie seemed on it though.

'Oh yeah, that's right,' he said, handing Maddy a glass of orange juice. 'You two haven't met, have you? Maddy, this is my brother Ade. Ade, Maddy Clifford.'

They nodded at one another, and Maddy took a big gulp of her drink. She stared into the distance for a minute, and Jamie could see her gradually relaxing, then she turned to Mackenzie. 'Nice juice,' she said, 'but you're a pretty shoddy host.'

'Sorry. Want some?' He gestured at the lasagne dish, with the big plastic ladle, but she shook her head.

'Nah, it's okay. I'll just eat yours. Don't want to risk you getting fat, do we?' She took up Mackenzie's fork; Mackenzie muttered a swear word, not quite under his breath enough, and took down another plate from the rack.

Charis and Ade exchanged quick grins, and Jamie saw, with relief, that their humour was echoed faintly on Mackenzie's face despite his outward show of grumpiness; he knew the Scotsman a lot better now, but a few months ago he'd have been certain there was trouble brewing.

For a little while, as they ate, they talked about Ade's plans for the land he was buying. At one point Ade started to mention something about the hut, but Mackenzie, standing at the counter eating his dinner since Maddy had done her Goldilocks trick, shook his head. Ade immediately turned the conversation to their dad and when they planned to visit together.

But Jamie's curiosity was piqued, and he made up his mind to corner Ade later on, and ask about that hut. Then the land-line phone went, and it turned out he didn't have to wait that long to find out after all; at the same time, he realised that the grown-ups hadn't known everything either. Until now.

Chapter Eleven

MACKENZIE PUT his hand over the mouthpiece and waved the handset at Maddy. 'It's your dad; you weren't answering your mobile so he guessed you'd be here.' He passed it over, swapping it for his now-empty plate. His relief at watching the tension gradually seep out of her during the noisy, entertaining meal was matched by the quiet pleasure he felt as he looked across at Charis, who was pinching a crispy bit of pasta off her son's plate while he wasn't looking. She caught Mackenzie watching and assumed a wide-eyed, innocent look, so he rolled his eyes, and she crossed hers.

She and Jamie had slid so easily into his life, and so naturally, that it was only now that he could look around and appreciate how his circle of friends and family had grown. He'd never have suspected, just six months ago, that he'd be cooking dinner for anyone but himself, and that he wouldn't have enough chairs to accommodate the people he loved around his table. Maudlin, he told himself, as he turned away to rinse his plate under the tap, but it felt good.

'Christ!' All eyes went to Maddy, and she looked up guiltily. 'Sorry. Go on, Dad.'

Mackenzie frowned and turned off the tap, and everyone fell silent as Maddy finished her call. She laid the handset carefully back on the table. 'That body you found,' she said, and this time Mackenzie didn't cut the subject off. 'They know who it was.'

'Who?'

'It's not public knowledge yet. Nick thought Dad should know though, and every one of us here deserves to, as well.' She looked up at Mackenzie, and her expression was a baffling mixture of relief and shock. 'It's Mulholland.'

Charis's fork clattered to her plate, but there was no complicated set of emotions on her face, only a fierce elation. 'Yes! Thank God!'

Ade looked shocked at her reaction, but then he didn't know the depth of the terror and danger to which she and Jamie had been subjected at Mulholland's hands. The story he'd been told of that weekend had been quite sanitised, Mackenzie realised, all of them having been happier to leave it in the shadows where it belonged, rather than discuss it. He looked at Jamie, whose eyes were wider than he'd ever seen them, and as Charis's hand reached out to grip his, Jamie ignored it and flung his arms around her neck instead.

'We were told he'd transferred down south,' Mackenzie explained to Ade. 'It was the best we could have hoped for, and the best thing for him to have done.'

'So wait, this is the bloke who helped steal Dad's collection off the original thieves? The same one who killed Sarah?'

'Aye, that's him. He was questioned right enough, because of all the testimonies against him, but the murder weapon turned up on Bradley's body. Without any evidence, Mulholland was never charged with anything.'

'He was evil,' Charis said in a low, tight voice. 'He nearly killed Mackenzie.'

'He nearly killed us all,' Jamie added, his voice muffled in his mother's shoulder; he sounded tearful now, and Mackenzie saw her arms tighten around him. He turned back to Maddy.

'Do they know how he died?'

'If they do, they're not saying. Not yet.'

'No, well I suppose they wouldn't. How about when?'

'Dad didn't say.'

'Bloody hell.'

'Couldn't have put it better myself,' Maddy said, and now she looked more relieved than shocked.

'So now we can stop looking over our shoulders,' Charis said, easing Jamie away from her and smoothing the tumble of hair from his eyes. 'It's finally over, Jay. Properly.'

Mackenzie and Maddy exchanged a quick glance, but evidently not quick enough for Ade's sharp eyes, and for the second time that evening Mackenzie gave him a single, silent, *not now*. Ade subsided.

'Will they question us again, d'you think?' Charis asked. 'I mean, we'd be suspects, wouldn't we? Motive, and all that?'

'Probably,' Maddy said. 'Depends when he died.' She played with the half-empty glass in front of her. 'I don't know if Nick will be able to tell us any more, but he'll have wanted to make sure I knew it was Mulholland, at least, and not over the phone. He went to find me at Dad's, but I'd left by the time he got there, so he told Dad instead.'

'And your dad phoned anyway,' Mackenzie said with a little sigh. 'It was a nice thought of Nick's though.'

'He's a nice bloke,' Maddy said, with a defensiveness that

left Mackenzie puzzled. There was no need for that; he'd always got on well with Maddy's family.

'Look,' Charis said, standing up. 'I think we'll get going now, if that's okay?'

'Don't go on my account,' Maddy said quickly. 'I'll be out of your hair in a minute.'

'No, it's not that.' Charis looked at Mackenzie. 'Jay's a bit... Well, we both are. We could do with some quiet time.' She smiled at Maddy, though it was a little strained, then at Ade. 'Happy new home.'

'Thanks. Next time you come over I'll cook for you in the 'van,' he assured Jamie, who only nodded.

By the door, as a subdued Jamie buttoned his coat, Mackenzie took Charis into his arms. 'Are you going to be okay?' he murmured against her hair. In response her hands crept around his waist to link in the small of his back. Her head rested in the middle of his chest, and he felt her cheek rub his shirt as she nodded.

'It's just a bit of a shock. Relieved, but...it just makes you wonder who else is out there. You know,' she glanced back at the other room, 'who was capable of doing it. Burying him like that.'

'It's probably not even connected with what happened to us,' he said, not sure if he believed that.

'Coincidence is a bit much though, don't you think? With him being left on that particular estate?'

'Maybe, but he'll have pissed a lot of people off, for a lot of reasons. Now at least we can get on with our lives again.'

She looked up, straight into his eyes, and he felt his heart tighten at the trust he saw on her face. He pressed his lips gently to her forehead and released her. 'Give me a call if you want to talk – doesn't matter what time it is.'

'I will.'

Ade and Maddy were sitting in silence when he returned. Ade looked as if, for the first time since he'd come home, he couldn't think of anything to say, and Maddy had gone back to staring into space. She shook off her daze as he sat down and poured some water.

'I'm sorry Charis and Jamie had to rush off.'

'Not your fault. They want to just talk about it together. Their – and your – experiences with him were different from mine. Far more intense.'

He was itching to ask whether Maddy had told Gavin what had happened to her, and what his reaction had been, and Ade seemed to sense his presence was creating a barrier. He pushed his chair back.

'I'll be away to the gatehouse now,' he said, sketching a little bow. 'Send word by the stable boy if I'm needed.'

Maddy turned to Mackenzie for a translation, and he shook his head with a little smile. 'He's got a caravan parked out the back.'

'Oh, that's what he meant about cooking in the 'van.' She pulled a face. 'In your poky little garden?'

'It never seemed that poky before, to be honest.'

'It won't be for long,' Ade pointed out. Then he frowned. 'Although I suppose things'll be put on hold while they investigate this murder. Particularly as it's a copper.' He hesitated, and sat down again. 'Actually, maybe you should fill me in on what really happened in the summer. I'm guessing there was a lot more to it than I read about, or even than Charis told me when I asked.'

It had grown quite late by the time they had told their separate stories. Ade had listened with barely an interruption, his face grave, particularly as he learned how Mulholland had exacerbated Mackenzie's injuries, sending him into hypovolemic shock that had almost killed him. He looked at them both in turn.

'So as far as the police are concerned, you both have motive.'

'I don't think we do though, not really,' Maddy said. 'I mean, he'd got away with it. His transfer had been approved, according to Dad, and—'

'Sorry, what? According to your *dad*?'

'He used to be in the service, and my brother still is. Not that Nick would ever use privileged information, unless he had to,' she added. 'He told Dad who it was that you two found, because he knew it would ease my mind, but he wouldn't pass on any other information. Anyway the point is, Mulholland would have been mad to risk bringing it all up again, so I can't see that we'd benefit from risking the murder of a copper.'

'But if that's the only motive the police can come up with, that's what they'll go for,' Mackenzie said. 'I reckon we can both expect a knock at the door.'

Maddy groaned. 'That's all I need, with this hanging over me.'

'What hanging over you?' Ade asked, finishing his drink.

She told him about the community payback order. 'I just hope to God they don't take me back into custody, even if it's just while they look into this.'

'Ade, would you mind buggering off now?' Mackenzie said. 'Sorry. We just need a bit of a chat.'

Ade looked from one to the other and shrugged. 'Sure, no bother. Let the buggering off commence. I've got some cleaning to do anyway, if young Jamie ever wants to eat *chez* Mackenzie the Superior.' He stood up. 'Good to meet you, Maddy. I owe you a debt of gratitude for securing my wee brother gainful employment, and keeping him on the straight and narrow.'

'Quite the job,' Maddy agreed, and Ade gave her a swift grin as he left.

'So what did you want to talk about?' she asked, when the door was shut.

'Did you get chance to tell Gavin what happened?'

She shook her head. 'Not yet. He was never left alone, and they shooed me off pretty smartish anyway.'

'Do you think Nick would be able to find out a bit more about what happened to him? I mean, even if the blokes who attacked him were lifers, with nothing to lose, it would give us a starting place.'

'There's no way the prison would give him access,' Maddy said. 'He's already been booted off the case for being almost-related, remember? And he's said straight out that he won't go digging, but he'll let me know if he hears anything.' She gave him a wry look. 'He's never been one of Gavin's greatest fans.'

Mackenzie could sympathise. 'What about that friend of your dad's? Sergeant McFarland, wasn't it?'

'We can't let him risk his career either. And even if you found out who they were, what good would it do? We know now it was all about the plea.'

'It might lead us to their acquaintances, and then to the person who actually killed Lumsden. The person who did that,' he added, nodding at her arm. She was wearing one of those jumpers with thumb holes, keeping the sleeves pulled well down over her wrists, but she stretched them further, frowning.

'No. We'll have to try another way. Nick won't put himself on the line like that for Gavin.'

'But he would for you.'

'Don't you dare!' Maddy gave him a fierce look. 'He can't know about what happened, and neither can Dad. Promise me!'

Mackenzie battled with the argument that rose to his lips, but he could see it would be pointless. He nodded. 'They won't hear it from me.'

'Good.'

'Come on, it's late. You're going to need a decent sleep too.'

'Fat chance.'

'But worth a try.'

Maddy nodded, but seemed in no hurry to leave, and Mackenzie understood exactly why, although he knew she wouldn't like him mentioning it directly. He began clearing the rest of the plates. 'Need a lift back?'

'No, I've got the car. I'll...I'll head back in a minute. Can I give you a hand with the dishes?'

'How often have you known me to wash dishes on the same night?' He splashed just enough water into the sink to cover the plates, then returned to the table, drying his hands on his jeans. 'Mads, if you need someone to stay overnight on your sofa—'

'No! God no.' She gave a little laugh, which didn't convince him for a moment. 'I'm fine. They've delivered their warnings, haven't they? I've probably never been safer. Tomorrow I just have to make sure Gav knows what it could cost if he doesn't plead the right way.'

He nodded, still doubtful. 'Speaking of Gavin, he could be in the frame for Mulholland too, if he doesn't have an alibi. He's likely to be questioned about it, at least.'

'D'you think so? He had nothing to do with what happened to us.'

'No, but don't you think he'd want to protect you?'

Maddy's face told a story he didn't enjoy. 'Maybe.'

Mackenzie wanted to ask more, but now wasn't the time. She'd tell him if and when she was ready. 'Are you sure you're okay to go home alone?' he asked, bluntly now.

'Are you *trying* to freak me out?'

'Come off it. I'd be bloody nervous; it wouldn't matter how much sense my brain made. We both know you'll be fine, but that doesn't make it any easier, does it?'

For a second he could see her wavering, then she shook her head. 'I've got to do it sometime. What kind of badass would I be if I wimped out now?'

'Badass?' Mackenzie laughed. 'You're about as badass as that tea towel.'

'I've actually shot someone,' she reminded him, 'which is more than you ever have.' He knew she was still traumatised by it, but a glint of humour had come back into her eyes, and he welcomed the step forward.

'Tea towel,' he said firmly. 'A used one. Okay, well if you're sure.'

'I am.' She stretched up to kiss his cheek, and patted his chest. 'Get some sleep – that brother of yours is going to run you ragged the next few days.'

'What did you think of him?' he asked as they walked to the front door.

'He's like you, only better.'

Mackenzie nodded glumly. 'That's what everyone says.'

'Well, it's true.' Maddy softened then, and squeezed his hand. 'Thanks, Paul.'

He saw her to her car, then went back inside in time to

catch the phone ringing. Not for the first time he cursed the lack of signal up here, as he dashed to the kitchen to grab the landline handset. 'Mackenzie.'

'Boulton.'

Mackenzie smiled and took the phone into the sitting room. 'How are you?'

Her voice was quiet in his ear, croaky with tiredness. 'I'm okay. Is it too late to talk? You said anytime, but—'

'Of course it's not too late.' Mackenzie started unlacing his trainers. 'Is the lad all right? I could see it was a shock for him.'

'He's as relieved as I am, but it brings it all back. And it's nasty to think about, you know?'

'Aye, I do. I didn't want Ade to bring it up, but then Tony called and it was a bit late to worry about it.'

'I don't like the idea of talking to the police about this.'

'They won't think you did it. I mean, *I* know you're tougher than you look, but I doubt you and Jamie between you could've buried the bastard.'

'But they might think I'd got you to do it for me.'

Mackenzie hesitated, but there was no point lying. 'They might.'

'Did you try to talk your brother out of clearing that ground?'

'What's this, a dummy run?'

Charis gave a soft laugh. 'If they talk to Ade again they'll ask him that, and it'd be good if you didn't have to lie.'

'Relax. I didn't say anything about it. He even offered to go somewhere else, in case it was difficult for me, and I told him to go ahead.'

'Good.' Relief was clear in her voice. After a brief hesitation she said, 'Can we talk about other stuff for a minute?'

'Anytime.' He wished she were there with him on the sofa,

and imagined her, sitting cross-legged like a pixie at one end, fixing him with her huge blue eyes. 'Fire away.'

'It's just... I never got around to telling you earlier, and I didn't know what you'd think. I've signed up for an online photography course. It could lead to a foundation degree.'

'That's brilliant. Why would it matter what I think?'

'I dunno. I just thought...you might think it was daft. Being a student at my age.'

'Your age? You're not even forty!'

'So you wouldn't object to going out with a student?'

'Boulton, it would do my ego a power of good.'

'I'd still be working,' she said quickly. 'I mean, I still have to pay rent so I couldn't stop that. But it would be...something different. Something for me. D'you get it?'

The image of her earnest face appeared again, and it was so vivid he almost reached out and touched it. 'You wouldn't have to,' he heard himself saying.

'Wouldn't have to what?' There was a long silence, while Mackenzie examined his thoughts, and she spoke again. 'Mackenzie? You still there?'

'Aye.'

'Wouldn't have to what?'

'Pay rent. You could move in here.'

This time the pause was much longer, and he grimaced; she'd been adamant she didn't want to live with him, when she'd moved up here with Jamie. Not that he'd asked, but he'd hoped that these few months had shown her there was more to their relationship than what had developed over one emotionally intense weekend.

'D'you mean that?' she said at last. 'You're not just saying it because of...of what's happened? Because it's all gone a bit Pete Tong and you think I need protecting?'

'I wouldn't dare.'

'How long have you been thinking about it?'

'About thirty seconds, give or take.' Silence. 'Come on, Charis.'

'I don't want you to think I've been sitting around here waiting for you to ask.'

'I don't think that you were—'

'Let me think about it.' There was a wary tone in her voice now, and he belatedly realised why. He gripped the phone as if he were holding her hand, and spoke very quietly.

'I'm not like him. I'm not Daniel.'

'I know you're not.' Charis sighed and he swore he could feel it stirring his hair. 'I trust you, you know I do. I'm just not sure I'm quite ready to...to give up what I have. Not just yet.'

'Okay. I won't ask again until, maybe, tomorrow?'

She laughed again, the sound rich and warm. 'If I ever want you to ask again, you'll know it. I'll make sure of that.'

'Good enough for me.'

'Okay, well on that note I'm going to hit the hay. G'night, Mackenzie.'

'Night.' He dropped the handset on the sofa and sat back with his hands over his eyes. 'Nice one, numpty.'

He fell into bed twenty minutes later, and it took a while to understand why he was finding sleep evasive tonight; he was pretty bloody exhausted, after all. But despite everything: the aching shoulder and chest, from helping Ade hook up the caravan and get it sorted; the worry over Maddy, and the anger that Lumsden's murderer had breached her home; the sense that he could still smell Mulholland's half-decayed corpse; and the worry that he, Maddy and Charis were likely suspects... Despite all that, he had to admit it was hard to sleep when you were grinning like an idiot.

Chapter Twelve

Breda saw the first candidate out, and returned to the desk as Donna typed up the notes she'd scribbled during the interview.

'Well?' she asked. 'What do we think?'

Donna nodded. 'Abiola gets a trial; let's get him in on Saturday night. Who's next?'

Breda looked at the list. 'Deborah Gardner couldn't make it today, so we've got an hour's gap, then Max Russell's due at eleven. After that we've got an afternoon full, with the best three formal applications, as you suggested. We should be able to fill the posts without shelling out for another ad.'

Donna nodded in satisfaction and stretched. 'Any coffee going, while we wait for Mr Russell?'

Breda went off to oblige, and the moment the door was shut Donna sank her head into her hands and took a deep breath. It was exhausting enough putting on the corporate face for the staff, but even more so trying to convince her more vigilant friends and family that she was holding it together.

Calling her mother that morning with funeral arrangements, and speaking to Myles and Chelsea, had nearly broken her. They were so full of questions, and her mother's quiet reproach that Donna hadn't come to see them was pushing away at her even as she tried to concentrate on keeping her livelihood running.

As always, Craig was constantly hovering at her shoulder, asking why she'd been so squeamish about avenging him, and while she was privately glad Ian George's lifer friends hadn't held back, she did still feel twinges of guilt about the way the Clifford woman had been treated. There was still a chance Galbraith might go down the diminished responsibility route, but he could be brought back into line; it hadn't taken much digging to discover that Clifford was serving a community payback order, and once she was back at her duties she'd be easily found. Ian's particular talents wouldn't be needed again though, and he'd had his chance to work off his personal vendetta. Loose cannon like that were more dangerous than useful.

Breda came back in with the coffee. 'Mr Russell's already here,' she said in a low voice. 'Shall I get him to come in now, so we can knock off for lunch early?'

Donna remembered she'd planned to sound this one out for a different job, though she couldn't remember why. 'Good idea,' she said. 'This interview'll probably be a bit more in depth anyway. Better offer him coffee, too, since we're having one. Oh, Breda?' The assistant manager looked back, eyebrows raised. 'First impressions?'

'Very smooth-looking. Nice dresser. I think he's the one who has lots of experience.'

'Okay.'

Breda poked her head out into the corridor and murmured something, and a moment later she ushered in the next candidate. He declined the offer of coffee, and Donna gestured to the seat opposite then consulted the print-outs Breda had given her.

'Ah, yes, the Spey Heights.' She looked up and gave him an encouraging smile. 'You worked there for several years, I gather?'

He nodded. 'Six years, less a month.' His accent leaned towards Edinburgh, and in all respects Donna agreed with Breda: he presented himself beautifully, in a neatly cut suit and with impeccably groomed hair. Understated, calm. Unlikely to be easily ruffled, which was a definite prerequisite for either role.

'May I call you Max?'

'Of course.'

'Why are you looking to leave the Spey Heights?'

'I'm in the process of buying a house on the outskirts of Inverness, and I don't want to have to travel. Particularly in winter.'

'But...seasonal work?' Donna frowned. 'You'll pardon me for thinking you're a bit over-qualified.'

'Not at all.' He gave her the benefit of his charming smile. 'I have every intention of making it permanent once I've a foot in the door.'

Donna couldn't help laughing. 'Confident. I like it.' She sat back and studied him. 'Having said that, I don't think this work will be enough to keep you interested, if I'm honest.'

He gave the hint of an elegant, almost Gallic, shrug. 'That's okay. If and when the interest wears off, I'll start looking elsewhere.'

'Which is why,' Donna went on, 'I have something else in mind that we would like to interview you for.'

He registered interest. 'Go on.'

Before she could say anything further there was a knock at

the door, and she and Breda exchanged irritated glances. Breda rose and, with an apologetic but curious look, admitted DS Muir and DC Forbes.

Donna hoped her start looked more surprised than guilty. 'If you'll excuse us, Mr Russell,' she said to the candidate. 'I'm sure this won't take long; you can just wait in the passage.'

'We're here to talk about the attack on Mr Gavin Galbraith,' Muir said, as soon as the door had clicked shut. 'Do you know anything about it?'

'Only what I heard on the radio. Why, do you know who did it?'

There was a pause as Forbes opened his infernal pocket-book again. 'We're looking into possible suspects, Mrs Lumsden, but we wanted to ask you why you were visiting a Mr Ian George at HMP Inverness on Monday night.'

'He's an old acquaintance. Friend of my father,' she clarified, seeing them exchange telling looks. 'He used to work with Craig.'

'Yes, we knew that. But why did *you* visit him in prison, when your father was the one who'd reported him for prowling?'

Donna's mind wouldn't work; she just looked at them in turn, feeling the seconds ticking by. Eventually she remembered what Ian had said, and seized on it. 'Dad doesn't find it easy to get about without Craig, and he'd already withdrawn his complaint against Ian. He was a bit embarrassed at being so jumpy.'

Muir's lips tightened slightly, and Donna knew she'd scored a half-point, at least.

'He knew I was here working that evening,' she went on, 'and as it's just across the river he asked Ian to put me on his list instead, so I could pass on his apologies in person. And offer him a job, by way of compensation,' she added, as her eyes grazed the application on her desk. It sounded far more likely.

'A *job*?'

'Our advertisement is on our website,' Donna said, pointing helpfully at her screen, 'and in the paper. We thought it might...ease things for a bit if I offered Ian some temporary work. Seasonal, you know. Until he's on his feet again.'

'Why didn't your dad offer him Craig's job?'

'Because he's on a driving ban.' Too late, Donna realised how easy that was to check. 'At least, that's what he told Dad, and I assume he had no reason to lie.'

That tight-lipped look again, from Muir. 'So...you visited your father's prowler in order to—'

'I told you,' Donna said, trying not to sound exasperated, 'Dad had already dropped the accusation. He was...a bit shaken, that's all. After what happened to Craig. When he thought it over he realised Ian must have just been here to talk. He felt pretty bad about it,' she went on, 'especially since Ian's brother isn't around to help out.'

'No, he's serving time for fraud.' Forbes flipped back a couple of pages. 'Ian was also arrested at that time, but no charges were brought. Again,' he added pointedly.

'No charges were brought because he had nothing to do with it.'

'And how did he come by the scarring on his face?'

Donna was powerless to stop the heat creeping through her skin, so she had to admit something. 'That was due to a fight he had with Craig, just before he left.'

'Nasty,' Muir observed. 'Your husband must have had quite a temper.'

Donna bristled. 'It was a misunderstanding. He thought Ian was involved in his brother's fraud, and that it was something to do with my business. He's...he *was*, very protective. But when you think about that, Ian's not likely to be looking to avenge Craig's death, is he?'

'True, but by the same token, you don't think he might have actually been your husband's killer? Revenge maybe?'

'No,' Donna said. 'As far as I know he was in Stirling until last weekend, and only came back when he heard the news.'

'Hmm.' Forbes made more notes, and Donna found herself chewing the inside of her lip almost frantically, thinking everything over. Had she made a terrible mistake? *Could* it have been Ian?

'We'll check that, of course,' Muir said. 'Did he accept the job?'

'I didn't offer it in the end. We had a...a bit of a disagreement, and I left.'

'What sort of disagreement?'

'Just some stupid, inappropriate comment. Of his, not mine. I left before the end of the session. I'm sure that's a matter of record.'

'We'll check,' Muir said again, as Forbes's pen scrawled. It sounded vaguely threatening.

'Look, I was doing Dad a favour because he felt bad.' She checked the time. 'Now, I have a lot of candidates to interview today, so if you haven't got any more questions?'

'Just one. Do you know if Ian George had any old acquaintances inside HMP Inverness? People who might owe him any favours from way back, that he might have mixed with this time?'

'No, how would I know that?'

'You have to appreciate it's odd. You visit him on Monday night, and two days later, the day after he's safely out of there, in fact, the man who you believe murdered your husband is beaten half to death.'

'Take that up with him!'

'We will,' Muir said quietly, and her eyes on Donna's were steady. 'It's starting to look as if you're not prepared to accept anyone except Galbraith as the murderer. Isn't it more important to get the right man?'

'You've got him,' Donna said tightly. 'Which is why I don't have to arrange to have him intimidated. I believe in the system, oddly enough.'

'Aye well, thanks for your time.' Muir nodded at Forbes, and he opened the door. 'We'll let you know if that alibi checks out for the time of Galbraith's attack, otherwise we'll be back for another word.'

'Of course.'

'Excuse me, sorry.' Muir eased past Breda and Max Russell, who'd been waiting in the short hallway that buffered the office from the restaurant, and a moment later she and Forbes had vanished into the dining room.

'Come in, Max. Sorry about that.' Donna gestured for him to sit again. 'Now, let's assume you're already hacked off with clearing tables for minimum wage. How would you feel about interviewing for the position of bar manager instead?'

<hr>

Maddy shifted in the hard plastic hospital seat, and the prison officer by the door glanced at her and looked away again. She frowned; how was she supposed to talk to Gavin about his plea, when she couldn't so much as rub her eyes without drawing attention? She was lucky to be able to visit at all in the middle of the day, and she was grateful for it, but what was the use if she couldn't speak freely?

Gavin's hand twitched, and she dutifully covered it with her own, feeling a little self-conscious. 'Do you want me to fetch someone?'

He shook his head and winced. His face was severely puffed up on one side, his left eye a single, livid line, and she knew, from her nursing days as well as what she'd been told, that he would be immobile and hooked up to the morphine drip for some time yet. But her sympathy for him was the same she would feel for anyone who'd been badly treated, and who now lay helpless, and that realisation both puzzled and dismayed her.

She had tried to think back to that fun casino night, to resurrect the feelings that had been re-born then, but all it conjured up was the reminder that it had indirectly led to him being here, now. She'd wanted to hiss into his ear as he slept: *It's all your own fault!* but now he was awake she couldn't say the words. He was still Gavin. Still the father of her son. Still the man she'd agreed to marry, and gladly too, at the time.

She gave him a faint smile. 'It's good to see you awake at last.'

His good eye slipped closed, and Maddy couldn't tell whether he'd drifted off again, but she removed her hand from his anyway. It felt stupid to leave it there, as if she thought she were the only thing anchoring him to the world. He would recover soon enough, barring unforeseen complications.

Which meant, of course, that he would be sent back to face more of the same, and the more Maddy thought about that, the more she realised, with increasing hopelessness, that there was no way he'd agree to plead guilty. He'd be mad to.

But he had to know what the consequences would be if he

didn't, and in order to tell him that, she had to be alone with him. She got up stiffly and went over to the door.

'Look,' she said in a reasonable voice, 'he's not going anywhere. I'm not going to be springing him from hospital, or pulling out his tubes. He's not on life-support, so I can't kill him by turning anything off, and I frankly don't have the energy to smother him with one of his own pillows.'

Throughout this tight little speech, the officer had been looking increasingly uncomfortable, and Maddy realised how junior he was. She felt sorry for her sarcasm and spoke plainly. 'Could you just let me close this door for a few minutes? You can watch through the window if you like, but he's my fiancé and we have things to say to one another.'

The officer looked past her, to where Gavin lay motionless. He nodded. 'Five minutes.'

'Thank you.' Maddy pushed the door shut and went back to Gavin's bedside. This had to be fast. 'Gav?' She took his hand again and braced herself. 'You know what this was about, don't you?' He opened his eye again, somehow managing to convey a withering look, and she bit back a retort. 'I mean,' she went on, 'you know why you *have* to plead guilty.'

'No way.' The whisper was barely audible, but it still cracked across the air between them, and she hissed in frustration.

'You don't know everything,' she went on, with a glance at the door to check it was still closed. 'It's not just you. The murderer got to me as well, and threatened Tas—'

'What?' Shock made his voice stronger, and he twisted his head on the pillow to stare at her. 'Are you both okay?'

'Tas knows nothing about it,' she assured him, and gave him a brief outline of what had happened. It was some comfort to see the growing outrage on his swollen face and a glisten of remorse in his eye as he took her hand again.

'Christ,' he murmured. He turned her hand over and traced one of the reddened bumps on her wrist, and she obligingly raised her sleeve slightly so he could see the tip of the bandage beneath.

'I'm okay. I didn't know at the time whether it was deep or not, but it's fine.'

'It might not have been,' Gavin said in a hollow voice. 'Mads, I'm so sorry.'

It was on the tip of her tongue to say *it's not your fault*, a purely automatic response, but she bit that back. 'You'd get a lighter sentence,' she said instead.

'I didn't do it! The jury has to see that.'

'And you a lawyer? Just how naïve are you?' Maddy pulled her hand away and lowered her voice. She looked at the door again. 'Gav, listen to me! If you try, and fail... The murderer's still out there, and he knows where I live.'

'So you're happy for me to get this,' he gestured at his head, 'every other day for the next thirty years? Or worse, killed on day one? No.' He took a deep breath. 'I know it sounds mad, but there's only one thing to do for the best. For you too. I'm going to plead not guilty.'

Maddy wanted to scream. 'And if it goes wrong?'

'It won't.'

The door opened and Maddy swung around, with harsh words on her lips that died when she saw her brother. She guessed the prison officer had no idea of their relationship, as Nick held up his ID and deliberately muddied his introduction.

'Mrs Galbraith? DS Clifford. I'd like a word, if I may.'

'With me, or him?'

'With you.' He nodded to the prison officer, and let the door stand open again while Maddy joined him in the corridor. 'Just down here will be fine, Mrs Galbraith. I won't take a minute of your time.'

She followed him to a quiet corner, where he looked uncertain and reluctant to speak. 'What is it? Is everyone okay?'

'Aye, fine. I just wanted to let you know Max got the job.'

Maddy blinked. 'What?'

'The job at the restaurant by the river. Actually a much better position than the one he went for.'

'Very happy for him.' Maddy shook her head, irritated. 'Why have you come here to tell me that?'

'Because the restaurant is Thistle Inverness, and,' Nick flicked a subtle glance left and right down the corridor, 'his interview was interrupted by a visit from some of my colleagues. They seemed to be questioning Mrs Lumsden about the family's potential role in Gavin's beating. I checked in with Aaron Forbes and got it confirmed. I thought you should know.'

'But that means...' Maddy stopped herself from going further, but a cold finger slid down her spine.

'We'll have good reason to be asking those questions of Donna.' Nick looked down the corridor towards Gavin's room. 'The family won't have risked all this on the basis of an arrest, or even a charge. Believe me, Mads, *they know* who killed Lumsden.'

'I suppose they must.' Maddy's head was buzzing now. 'I only have a minute to speak to him. Let me go back in now. We'll talk later.'

It occurred to her how unlike Nick it was to have confided in her in this way, and how much it must have cost him to pass the information on. It seemed to cross his mind at the same time, because he gave her a tiny smile.

'This isn't privileged information. If the officers who spoke to Mrs Lumsden were careless enough to speak in front of a civilian, they can hardly blame him for passing it on. All I did was confirm it.'

'Thank God for Max,' Maddy said with an answering, though distracted, smile. 'He's a keeper. Thanks, Nick.'

She went back in with a pleading look at the prison officer, who pursed his lips and tapped his watch. Closing the door behind her again, she looked at Gavin. One eye closed, the other useless, his face a mass of bruises and contusions and tape holding together a gash that ran from ear to chin along his left jawline, he should have inspired deep compassion in her. But Nick's words bounced around in her head: *They know…*

Gavin turned his good eye on her as she sat down again. 'What did he want?'

'There's speculation that the people who did this to you are connected to Craig Lumsden's family. Just hearsay, nothing official.'

Gavin's pale face slackened in shock. 'Kilbride?'

She nodded. 'I'd imagine plenty of people are eager to ingratiate themselves with him; it wouldn't have been hard to find a willing pair of hands.' She steeled herself again. 'Why would he go to these lengths if he wasn't certain you killed Lumsden?'

He looked at her, incredulous. 'Are you saying you believe them?'

'I'm saying they're pretty sure it was you, and they've gone to a lot of trouble to make sure you go down for it. They'd want the right man, wouldn't they?'

'And are they judge and jury now?' Gavin hissed, his face turning even paler. 'What the hell do they know?'

'That you *were* out there meeting Lumsden on Thursday night. That, presumably, no-one else was, or they'd have been targeted too.' Maddy gripped his hand tightly. 'Was it you, Gav? Tell *me* the truth, at least.'

'No, it wasn't.' Gavin seemed spent now, too tired to fight. He lay quietly for a moment, then shook his head. 'I'm still not pleading guilty.'

Maddy's heart sank. 'And what if you're found guilty anyway?'

'Then I'll ask to be transferred down south. Somewhere the other prisoners don't know Kilbride or Lumsden, and have no nests to feather by beating the crap out of me on a *daily fucking basis!*' His voice had risen again, and he steadied himself. 'You'll have to get yourself and Tas out, while you're still relatively safe.'

'Safe? You're saying it wasn't you, which means there's another murderer out there, so it *could* have been them who attacked me, to protect themselves.'

'I think, from what your brother said, we can assume it was Lumsden's family who did that,' he said, sounding almost pompous in his certainty. 'And at the moment they don't know if their little warning has worked. They're not going to do anything else until they hear my plea, right? So get the lad, and get away now. Once I'm acquitted, I can join you. If I'm still alive, of course.'

'If you think you can get transferred down south, why not make that a condition of pleading guilty? Surely for the sake of avoiding a trial it'd be worth it to them to arrange it.'

'Because I *didn't fucking do it!*' Gavin sucked in a sharp breath and lifted his hand to his head. After a moment he carried on, 'If I plead guilty, my professional life is over, no chance to prove this has all been a stupid mistake. But I'm going to get off, right?'

'Whether you do or not, we'll all have to leave anyway, won't we?' Maddy's voice turned bitter. 'I'll have to abandon the agency, and my family, and take Tas away from school when he's only just started—'

'This isn't all about you, oddly enough,' Gavin said, with that edge of anger back in his voice now. 'I know it'd break your heart to leave your precious agency, and your bezzie pal Mackenzie, but—'

'You *made* it about us! You've put us in danger. Now, because of you, our lives are going to be turned upside down. And that's the best we can hope for!'

'But I didn't do it,' he said again, in a quieter voice. 'You know I couldn't do something like that.'

'I know you lied about being in debt. I know you lied about where you were last Thursday night, and about finding the body. I know you carried on lying, and I know you're bloody good at it.' Maddy rose to her feet. 'Private time's up, I think. Your guard's staring in at us.'

'Maddy, please!'

She was already on her way over to open the door again, and now turned back. 'I'm not saying I think you're guilty of this,' she said, 'but you're guilty of a lot of unforgiveable things. The gambling, the lying, the refusal to take your family's safety seriously... I've got a lot to think about. I'll let you know what I decide's best for Tas, but,' she took a quick breath and pushed the words out before she had chance to talk herself out of it, 'you and I can't come back from this, Gav.'

He paled further. 'What?'

'When you're better we can talk properly, but we both

know we've been limping along for ages. Even before all this. If you were happy you wouldn't have started gambling away all our money.'

'So that's it? You're choosing this moment, when I'm at my very lowest, to...to *dump* me?'

'I can't trust you any more.' She looked at him sadly. 'I'd only be lying to you if I said we could make it work. There are so many reasons, and this is just... Look, this isn't the time.'

'Damned right it isn't! Yet here we are.'

'I'm sorry. It was probably cruel to say it now, but I had to just—'

'Go on then. Get out. Run off with your rugger-loving mountain man.'

Maddy was so startled she almost laughed, but the laugh stuck in her throat. It wasn't even worth arguing that there was nothing between herself and Paul but friendship; he wouldn't understand the subtlety. She yanked the door open, nodded to the prison officer, and walked away.

Chapter Thirteen

Mackenzie showed the two police officers to the seating area at the back of the office. He tried to gauge, from their manner, whether they'd spoken to Charis or Maddy yet, but they weren't giving anything away. They seemed pleased to find Ade there, however.

'That'll save us traipsing all over town to find you.' The woman who'd introduced herself at the door as DC McAndrew smiled at them in turn. 'Quite alike, you two, aren't you?'

'He's uglier,' they said in unison, and McAndrew looked as if she wanted to laugh but felt it was inappropriate.

'Do you know why we're here?'

'I assume it's about the body we found,' Ade said. 'Do you know who it is yet?'

'He's been identified as a serving police officer,' McAndrew said soberly. 'DS Alistair Mulholland.'

'I see.' Mackenzie composed his features, knowing they'd be watching closely. He allowed a little of his distaste to show at the mention of the name, but tempered it with a show of respect for their feelings. 'That must be hard for you.'

McAndrew inclined her head. 'You, Miss Clifford and Miss Boulton all said in your statements that he was involved in the kidnap of Jamie Thorne, as was, now Jamie Boulton, on Saturday the fourth of August.'

'We said he was involved in what came after,' Mackenzie corrected her. 'Jamie was actually snatched by a bloke called Andy Stein, who was acting for Sarah Wallace.'

McAndrew checked her notes. 'That's right. You said that DS Mulholland had been at the crofter's cottage at Glenlowrie, and had illegally detained Miss Boulton there. And that he'd caused an injury you'd received, as a result of a motorcycle accident, to become life-threatening.'

'He did.' Mackenzie massaged his shoulder, which still throbbed from helping Ade.

'And that he left when the police arrived.'

'I didn't say that,' Mackenzie pointed out. 'I was unconscious at that point.' He had the feeling they were trying to trip him up, and he didn't like it.

'His statement said he'd tried to *help* you and Miss Boulton,' DC Byrne put in, 'and that when the police arrived, and he knew you'd be looked after, he left to find his colleague, who'd gone out looking for the little boy. That was his story.'

'Of course it was.' Mackenzie sighed. 'Look, I know they couldn't make a charge stick, but—'

'There was nothing to substantiate one,' McAndrew said, her manner cooling somewhat. 'DS Mulholland was simply acting on the orders of a superior officer. And now he's turned up dead.'

'How was he killed?'

'We're not releasing that information yet.'

Mackenzie sensed he'd lost any brownie points he might have gained by acknowledging the loss to the Service, and felt himself growing tense again; if he was taken in for questioning it would be a hundred times worse, he knew it. The memory of sitting opposite the then DI Bradley, and learning how his wife and son had died, made his stomach twist painfully.

'You're very close to the other witnesses, aren't you?' McAndrew said, looking at her notes again.

'Yes.' Mackenzie saw exactly where this was going. 'I work with Maddy Clifford, and—'

'Oh yes,' Byrne said, and there was a twitch of a smile on his face now, not quite a smirk, but almost, as he looked around the office. 'You're a private eye.'

Mackenzie winced. 'We provide an investigation service, if that's what you mean.'

'And Miss Boulton?'

'We're...close, as you say.'

'Is it true that she's moved up here to be with you?'

'Not to be with me, no. She fell in love with the town when she and Jamie stayed here. Liverpool has some bad memories for her, and Jamie was between schools, in England, at least. So she gave notice on the rent, upped sticks and moved. She has her own place, a job, and her own life.'

'But you *are* in a romantic relationship?'

'Yes, we are.' Mackenzie thought back to last night's phone call, and felt himself relax a tiny bit. Strange how the thought of a stray firework like Charis could have that effect on him, but it worked every time. It didn't last, however.

'If what Miss Clifford said in her statement is true,' Byrne said, 'she and Miss Boulton would have been at risk from Mulholland, wouldn't they?'

'What they *both* said is true.'

'So they felt that having Mulholland out there, free, was a danger?'

'They were uneasy, yes. But he'd put in for a transfer. We all just assumed he'd decided it wasn't worth the risk, and had drawn a line under it. Moved on.'

'Convenient.'

'I'm sure you can check to make sure his transfer request went through the proper channels.'

Ade met his eyes across the table and gave him a warning look; Mackenzie realised he was coming close to losing his temper and that it showed. He'd thought he'd sounded quite reasonable, but it seemed not.

'Would you say you're a loyal friend and partner?' Byrne asked mildly.

'If you mean did I kill Mulholland out of peevishness, because he got away with murder and attempted murder, no I did not.' He'd had enough of pretending to care about their feelings.

'What about because you believed he posed a real threat?' McAndrew asked.

'Are you formally questioning me? Because this isn't—'

'At the moment you're just helping us with our enquiries. You can come down to the station if you prefer?'

'For a nice friendly little chat?' Mackenzie gave a short, humourless laugh. 'I've done that before, and...and people died as a direct result.' Pain tightened his gut again. *People?*

'Oh, right, yes.' Byrne sat forward, looking interested. 'You and Superintendent Bradley had a history. We looked into that.'

'Did you now?' Mackenzie started to feel ill, but folded his arms to hide the way his hands wanted to curl into fists.

'We found that another officer sat in on your interviews back then,' Byrne said. 'A certain DC Mulholland.'

Mackenzie nodded. 'You'll forgive my memory being a bit

clouded by other matters, at the time,' he said with heavy sarcasm, 'but as far as I can recall the other officer just listened. I'd no axe to grind with him, nor he with me. That was all Bradley.'

'And here Mulholland was, helping your old enemy.' Byrne's expression was one of satisfaction, and Mackenzie could have sworn aloud. Instead he gave the two officers a bland smile.

'I probably owe him a debt of gratitude actually. I'm pretty sure he's the one who pushed Bradley into the waterfall.'

McAndrew and Byrne exchanged quick glances, and Byrne nodded. 'Jamie Thorne, sorry, Boulton, suggested the same. He wasn't there, but he said they were arguing a lot beforehand.'

'Well there you go then.' Mackenzie closed his eyes briefly and took the plunge. 'Look, this really is starting to sound like a formal interview. Isn't it time you got around to the point? Gave me a chance to provide an alibi?'

'We do have an estimated time of death,' Byrne said. 'But given the advanced decomposition it's a bit of a large-ish window. You'd have to be very sure of your whereabouts over the course of several days.'

Mackenzie's spirits sank further. He worked alone so much of the time, as did Maddy, and it was rare that he stayed at Charis's, or she with him, so the nights would be impossible to account for too. The connections were hard to dismiss, and despite his attitude he could hardly fault their conclusions: he was their main suspect, and both Maddy and Charis were either next in line, or right there alongside him.

He took a deep breath and let it out slowly. 'When?'

McAndrew checked her book. 'Taking into account the rate of decay, eye-witness reports, and the presence of trace evidence – flora and suchlike – from the area, the pathologist has concluded that DS Mulholland was, in all probability, killed between the ninth of August and any time until around the week commencing the twentieth.'

'That's, what, two weeks?' Ade put in, scowling. How the hell is anyone supposed to—'

'It's okay,' Mackenzie said. His entire body had relaxed, and it was only now that he realised just how tense he'd been; he turned back to McAndrew. 'I was discharged from hospital on Saturday the first of September. At that time I was still largely immobile, and certainly not in any mood to go burying bodies.'

'Of course we can check that, but thank you.' McAndrew made a note. Mackenzie was surprised to see that she looked disappointed, but not personally thwarted, and reflected that he'd unfairly transferred his mistrust of the police, which was all thanks to Don Bradley, onto undeserving shoulders. He made a mental note to park his paranoia from now on; it was exhausting.

'I know you'll have to check this too,' he went on, 'but I can tell you that Maddy Clifford was still on remand until the twenty-seventh, and Charis was in Liverpool, tying things up at her flat before she moved up here in mid-September.'

'We'll still have to talk to her,' Byrne said. 'It's less than a day's drive, after all.'

'Have you *met* Charis Boulton? She weighs seven stone soaking wet!'

'She has a son.'

'He's eleven, and looks nine.'

'Friends, then. An ex-husband too, I understand.'

'Who screwed up his licence and is currently back serving at Her Majesty's pleasure, in HMP Liverpool.'

'You do appreciate we can't rule anything out at this stage.' McAndrew turned to Ade, eyebrows raised. 'And you, Mr Mackenzie?'

'I didn't arrive back in the UK until last week.'

'We'll—'

'Check, yes. I can bring my stamped passport down to the station.'

'Thank you. Was there any particular reason for you to have been poking around on private land on Tuesday?'

'It's like I told your man on the ground,' Ade said. 'I'm in the process of buying that land, and was trying to get a rough estimate of the cost of clearing it.'

'So the present owner knows of your plans?'

'Yep.'

'And they didn't try and dissuade you from looking over it? Tell you to wait until the sale had gone through?'

Remembering Charis's question, Mackenzie couldn't suppress a smile as Ade shook his head.

So they're probably not your murderers either,' he said. 'Have you not spoken to them yet?'

'Yes, but of course they wouldn't have told us if they *had* warned you off, would they? We need to round out the picture.' She sighed, and made a mark next to one of her notes. From the way she and Byrne looked at one another it seemed their suspect pool was drying up in front of their eyes.

'I honestly can't think of anything further I can say to help,' Mackenzie said, with genuine regret.

That relief was still there, but it was tempered now with uneasiness as he considered who could have killed Mulholland, and why. His thoughts turned to Nick Clifford, who might have been able to engineer a false transfer request. He wasn't sure how that might work, but Nick was a serving officer after all, and his secondment to CID might have put him in the position he needed... The Clifford siblings were close, but were they close enough for him to have done something this desperate? Mackenzie's mind was clicking like a roulette wheel. He had to talk to Maddy, and soon.

Kilbride tapped his iPad to enlarge the screen, cursing his tired eyes as he picked up the landline handset. He punched in the number on the screen, and cleared his throat while he waited for it to be picked up.

'Great Glen Land Agents, Shirley speaking. How can I help?'

'Ah, good,' Kilbride said. 'Is this the Abergarry branch?'

'It is.'

'Good, good. You're handling a purchase for me, and I just wanted to make sure you've got my updated mobile details, as I'm a bit fluid in my living arrangements just now.'

'Of course, sir. Can I take your name?'

'Mackenzie.' Before she could ask for any further detail, which he didn't have, he hurried on, 'It's the Glenlowrie estate.'

'Ah yes, the joint purchase with Drumnacoille.'

'Perfect. Shirley, do you see the number I'm calling from?'

'I do, yes.'

'And is it the same as the one you have on record?'

'No, that one ends in 433.'

Kilbride rolled his eyes; he should have expected this. He pulled a number out of the air. 'Is it 07789 454433?'

'No, it's 07879 896433.'

Grinning, Kilbride scribbled down the number. 'That's fine then. You don't need to update it after all.'

'Would you like us to add your landline too?'

'No, this is...my brother's,' he finished lamely.

'But you asked if that number was the same—'

'Thank you very much!' He ended the call, aware he'd started to sweat; Craig had always been much better at this stuff than he was. He dialled the number Shirley had obligingly provided, and hoped Mackenzie wasn't out of signal. He was in luck.

'Mackenzie speaking.'

'The elder?'

'The middle,' the voice said, sounding amused. 'Adrian. Who's this?'

'My name's William Kilbride. I was a friend of your father's a long time ago.'

'Oh aye, I remember you, I think. It's been a long time, though. What can I do for you?'

'I wondered if you had time for a quick chat, face to face. I have a proposition for you.'

The voice turned wary. 'What kind of proposition? I've only been back in the country a week.'

'But you've been busy, I gather. It's a business proposition, concerned with the land you're buying.'

There was a silence. Then, 'Why not? Okay. When and where?'

'No time like the present. Are you near Inverness at the moment?'

'An hour away, give or take.'

'Okay, an hour then. Thistle, do you know it?'

'Aye, but I'm not over fond of taking out a mortgage just for a drink.'

'On the house,' Kilbride said. 'It's my daughter's place. Ask for me at the door.'

A little over an hour later Kilbride took his drink over to his own private booth and waited. Presently the maître d' brought over a tall man, probably in his mid-forties, which gave Kilbride a jolt; the last time he'd seen the kid he'd been about eleven. It made him feel old, suddenly, but he smiled.

'Mr Mackenzie. Thanks for being obliging enough to meet me here.' He indicated his chair. 'It's easier for me if I know I'm definitely going to get a seat, and there aren't any stairs. Now, order whatever you'd like to drink. As I said, it's on the house.'

'You said it was your daughter's place,' the newcomer reminded him. 'Does she know she's buying strange men drinks?'

Kilbride couldn't help smiling at that. 'The proposition I have for you concerns this place, so best not to get too picky.'

'This place?' Mackenzie looked around, suddenly uneasy. 'Mr Kilbride, I'm not sure I've got what—'

'Call me Will.' He gestured to the maître d' again, who returned to take their drinks order.

'And I'm Ade.'

'Good to meet you, Ade. Choose your poison, then we'll talk.'

'Just orange juice for me. I'm driving.'

'The same.' Kilbride nodded at the maître d' and turned back to Ade. 'Okay, not to beat around the bush, I gather you're buying up the bottom end of your father's old estate, and roughly the same acreage of the one next door?'

'I am. Although the Glenlowrie parcel's currently on hold. We can't get surveyors and so forth in yet, because of the investigation.'

'Right, of course.' Kilbride pursed his lips as he thought

over his proposal once more before putting it to the man opposite. He still found it hard to equate his genially composed companion with the distant thundering of juvenile feet from upstairs whenever he'd been at Frank Mackenzie's place. Maybe it was better to start there.

'We used to call your dad Mick,' he said, in conversational tones, but, not being privy to his thought processes, Ade raised his eyebrows at the sudden change in direction.

'I know,' he said. 'I also know you had nothing to do with the robbery, so if you're thinking of softening your ground by talking about me suddenly being all grown up, and a chip off the old block and so on, you don't have to worry. I've no preconceptions. Let's hear your proposal.'

Kilbride smiled at that. Ade really *was* a chip off the old block though; Mick could be just as acerbic when he chose to be. Which had been often, back in the day. 'Right then,' he said, adopting a more business-like tone. 'You want to create the ultimate Highland experience, correct? For corporate clients?'

Ade nodded. 'That's the plan. Exclusive, high-end. No more than four clients at a time, and no-one who isn't serious about living it for real.'

'Did your dad ever tell you I'd planned something similar at one time? Not myself; I didn't have the land. But my expertise was in the marketing side, and developing the contacts. You've been out of the country a while?'

Ade nodded. 'Came back briefly when my brother's family died, but I only stayed until I knew he was going to be okay. Besides that I've been in New Zealand since 1990.'

'Fantastic place. You've not lost your local accent though. What were you doing out there?'

'Engineering.' Ade gave him a brief grin. 'I know where

you're going with this, and you're right; I've got no contacts here and it'll take a while to build a list. My question is, what would your investment amount to?'

'Why, are you interested?'

'I might be.' Ade took a drink and eyed him carefully. 'You wanted to go into business with my father?'

'Sort of. I have no interest in the day to day running of a place like that, but, as I said, I've always been a dab hand at making connections with potential clients, and they usually stay connected.'

'But you said your proposal was linked to this place.' Ade gestured around them. 'And *this place* isn't yours to play with.'

'I have an interest,' Kilbride said elusively. 'Besides, with Thistle it'd be more of a...a mutual back-scratching exercise than a financial one. Advertising on both ends, discounts, special codes, and so on.'

'So, you'd promote my estate here—'

'And in our other establishments.'

'And in return I'd link my place with the chain, and then subsidise meals and so on?'

'Pretty much sums it up. With restrictions, of course, and we'd have to discuss exclusivity.'

'How many other Thistles are there?'

'Two, at the moment - Edinburgh, and Aberdeen. With a potential new site in Glasgow currently under review.'

Ade nodded. He seemed a level-headed bloke and not likely to turn something down without examining it from all sides. 'Impressive.'

Kilbride inclined his head in acceptance of the compliment. 'You'll have my number in your phone now, so call me when you've had a think, and then I can arrange to have a look at your business plan. Projections, margins and so on.'

Ade finished his juice and rose to his feet. 'Sounds good.' He paused. 'How did you get hold of me, by the way?'

Kilbride sensed that, despite the casual question, this might be a turning point; how much skulduggery would the younger man put up with? Eventually he shrugged. 'I used my initiative.'

Ade raised one eyebrow, and Kilbride couldn't help grinning. He quite liked the lad already – he was sharp. 'But,' he added, 'if your estate agent mentions anything about a phone call you supposedly made today, just...go along with it, aye?'

Chapter Fourteen

'TIME TO CLEAR this away and set the table for tea.' Maddy picked up some of Tas's crayons and put them back in the old domino tin that was open at her son's elbow.

'Just let me finish this bit?'

'After tea,' she said firmly. 'Come on – Grandad's nearly ready to dish up.'

'Muuum!'

'Now!'

'Don't shout at the lad,' Tony said in a maddeningly calm voice, as he came into the dining room. 'He's okay for a few minutes.'

'I wasn't shouting. And you told me you were ready.'

The minor domestic squabble was threatening to get out of hand; it was all very well her father coming over all reasonable now, he'd been just as short-tempered as she had been since she'd arrived... Infuriating. Maddy checked her temper, seeing Tas's eyes go from her to his grandfather and back again. She inhaled slowly.

'Look, Dad, you told me to get the table cleared. I was just doing as I was told. As all good children should,' she added pointedly, looking at Tas. 'Now come on.'

Tas scowled and began throwing the crayons into the tin; some of them bounced off the narrow opening and rolled onto the floor. Maddy bent down to scoop them up before they could be trodden into the carpet, and when she straightened she saw her father's frown of concern and almost burst into tears. Her emotions hadn't been this frayed since she'd been arrested, and it was unsettling that she couldn't seem to get them under control.

'Are you all right' he asked quietly. 'I noticed you're not going in for visiting time tonight.'

Maddy shot Tas a look, glad to see he'd slowed down once he'd realised his display wasn't having the desired effect. 'I'll tell you later,' she murmured. 'Let's just get tea out of the way.'

She picked up the colouring things and was putting them in the blanket box beneath the sitting room window when a tap on the glass made her jump. Her heart nearly failed her as she looked up to see a dark shape looming on the other side, and she even took a couple of paces back before she recognised Paul, cupping his eyes to cut the reflected glare from the street lights. He must have seen the livid look on her face, because he stepped back too, visibly alarmed, as well he might be. How could he have done something so stupid, knowing what had happened just two nights ago?

'Paul's here,' she called to her father in a tight voice. 'I'm letting him in.'

'Tea'll stretch to four,' Tony shouted back from the kitchen. 'Tas, set an extra place, please.'

'I'm so, so sorry,' Paul said, the moment she opened the door to him. 'I didn't think.'

'Dad says you can stay to tea,' she said, walking away and

leaving him to follow her back into the front room. Her nerves were still stretched thin after today's hospital visit, and the conclusion she had come to as a result; she didn't need added aggravation.

'Thanks.'

She pulled the curtains closed with unnecessary vigour and turned to face him. 'Thank him, not me.'

'Look, Mads, I really am sorry. I didn't think.'

'No, you didn't.' She relented slightly; he'd had his own share of shocks lately after all. 'Why are you here, anyway?'

'This isn't going to help much, but I need to speak to you about Nick.'

'Nick? Why?'

'Can we go somewhere else?' He glanced through to the dining room, where Tony was helping Tas with the extra place setting. Tony gave Paul a nod of welcome, and Paul returned it, but both of them seemed suddenly awkward in each other's company. Maddy frowned.

'Have you two fallen out?'

'Would he have asked me to stay and eat, if we had?'

'Hmm. Okay, well we can go outside for a minute, if it's stopped raining.'

'It has.' He followed her out to the porch, where she stood staring intently into the shrubbery that lined the path.

'That's how he got me, you know,' she said, noticing his troubled look. 'He was hiding in Gavin's Blue Arrows, and just...followed me in. Anyway,' she went on before he could respond, 'what did you want to say about Nick?'

'I just needed... I had a visit from a couple of officers earlier. About Mulholland.' He stopped, and she looked up to see his face twisted in uncertainty.

'Go on.'

'Have they talked to you yet?'

She shook her head. 'What did they say? Nick's on the team, isn't he?'

'Aye, but it wasn't him who came over. First off, and you'll be as glad as I was, they reckon the bastard was probably killed sometime from the sixth of August, up to a couple of weeks later.'

Maddy's chest loosened in relief. 'So they know I was on remand then, and you were still being nailed back together.'

'Yeah.'

'Thank God.' When he didn't respond she looked up at him again. 'You don't sound exactly delighted.'

'I'm glad we're ruled out, but they haven't checked yet that Charis was still in Liverpool then.'

'Even if she wasn't, what would she have been doing back at Glenlowrie?'

'They can't rule her out just because it's unlikely. And in any case the body might have been killed somewhere else, and moved there.'

Maddy made a soft, derisive sound. 'I know Mulholland was a skinny sod, but there's no way Charis could have got his body all the way up there.'

'Besides which,' Paul said with a warning edge to his voice, 'she didn't do it.'

'Of course she didn't. I was only saying.'

'Which is why I was trying to think of anyone else who might have wanted... Well, you and your brother are protective of one another.'

Maddy drew a quick breath. 'You can't think *Nick* had anything to do with it?' No wonder Paul hadn't wanted to be anywhere near her father when he'd said this.

'I had to talk to you about it. We can do that at least, can't we?'

Maddy gave a short laugh. 'Oh, this day's just getting better and better.'

'Why, what's happened?'

'Never mind. You just explain to me how and why you think my brother might be capable of...' She stopped, knowing all too well what he was capable of. But Paul didn't know that. As her mind went momentarily blank, her father's words, back in August, blasted into the gap: *Any man who's a threat to my family is fair game...* She felt her heart shrivel, and had to force herself to listen to Paul.

'I'm sorry,' he was saying now. 'But look, *someone* killed Mulholland – right after he'd terrorised a lot of people, and killed at least one. You've not been the same since, and especially since you were banged up. We all wanted to help you, and Mulholland was a danger to you—'

'Not just to me!'

'Well no, Charis too, but she was safe down in Liverpool. Nick must have known you were a potential target back then, before...' It was Paul's turn to stop, and Maddy saw his brows draw together. 'Mads, if he died during that fortnight, then his transfer request was definitely falsified. Your dad said he put in for it a few weeks ago.'

'And because Nick's a police officer in that station you think *he* falsified it?'

'Not necessarily. But you have to admit it would be difficult to do, though working in the same station would certainly give whoever did it an advantage. Get the ball rolling, at least, and the rumour mill doing its thing.'

'Which the police will have worked out for themselves by now, too.' Maddy felt ill. 'And Nick will be just as much in their frame as in yours.' She leaned back against the porch door jamb and rubbed her face. 'He had nothing to do with it, I'm sure of it, but if he gets pulled off this case as well, while they investigate him, it'll be the end for him. He'd just about had enough already, until this secondment brought him back.'

'Back?'

Maddy hesitated. To tell him about Nick's self-harming would mean she'd either have to lie and say she had no idea what had started it, or to trust him and tell him everything. She looked at the front door, behind which Tas and her father would be busily dishing up their evening meal in the warmly lighted dining room, and then at Paul, shadowed by the porch wall, the street lights throwing odd patterns across his face.

She remembered the worst times, when she'd been part of his nursing team after he'd been found suffering from exposure at the foot of Aonach Mor; then, when he'd been discharged but he hadn't eaten for days, grief stripping away every flicker of the life that still waited for him. Their friendship had been cemented in trust, and always would be. She pushed open the front door and called down the hall.

'Five minutes, Dad!' She turned to Paul. 'Where are you parked?'

In his car, staring straight ahead and not watching his reaction, it was easier to say it all. At first the words came hesitantly, but eventually she got it out. The way Nick had been gaslighted, she supposed it would be called now, into believing he was saving his father from prison by killing Dougie Cameron.

'He was just twenty at the time,' she said. 'Don Bradley convinced him that Dad had been part of the robbery at Mackenzie's place, and was corrupt.'

'So where does Cameron come into it?'

'He was the one who'd made those fake statuette things for Wallace, so he'd been under Wallace's protection. But once Wallace was dead, that protection was over. That was when Don Bradley told Nick that the man Cameron was under threat from was our dad, and that Cameron was terrified for his life and about to go to the police about it. If Dad went down, as a serving officer he'd likely have been dead in a week.'

'So Nick removed the perceived threat, by killing Cameron himself.' Paul's voice was low and stunned. 'He did Bradley's work for him. I have to say I'm having real trouble believing this. I do,' he said hurriedly, 'but it's just...' He shook his head and didn't finish.

'Imagine how hard it was for me.' Maddy took a deep breath and pushed on. 'There's a bit more.'

'More?'

She told him about her father's pledge to protect Nick, and how he'd said it meant he was no longer the honourable man he'd been. That he'd crossed a line. And she finished by repeating those words that had slammed into her memory just a few minutes ago. *Any man who's a threat to my family...*

Paul was silent. The sounds of an early evening in the quiet cul-de-sac went on: a car door clunking shut, and the lighter sound of its remote lock; a voice shouting from garden to house; a bin being rolled out ready for tomorrow's collection. Maddy's entire body was tense and aching, and the cut in her arm stung as if awoken by the other nerves coming to life. She waited for him to speak, to let her know if her trust had been misplaced after all.

'Do you think either one of them, or both of them together, could have done this?'

'I don't know. I honestly... I never thought Nick could have done what he did, particularly in cold blood and hand-to-hand.'

'It would make sense,' Paul mused, his voice sober. 'They track him down and kill him, then take him somewhere no-one would be likely to find him. Whoever did it didn't bury him very deep; they probably intended to go back for the remains when they'd be easier to dispose of.'

'Damp ground like that, it probably wouldn't have taken too long,' Maddy said, her nausea increasing at the thought. 'What do we do, Paul?'

'Nothing.'

She looked at him; his profile was set and hard and he stared straight ahead. 'We have to let the police do their job, but we don't have to help them.'

'But if they investigate Nick—'

'We could warn him it's likely, I suppose. Only based on what I thought, not what you've told me tonight. You don't have to tell either of them I know about it.'

'And you'll keep it to yourself?'

He turned to her then, and his face was unreadable. 'From Charis, you mean?'

'Aye. And your brother.'

'I'll not say anything,' he promised. 'Even if...' He stopped, and resumed staring out at the road.

'Even if it comes out that Dad or Nick, or both of them, did kill Mulholland?'

He nodded. 'Warn Nick, okay? It should come from you. And maybe watch his face carefully when you do, and let me know what you think. We're being completely honest now, aren't we? So any updates, we share.'

'Okay.' Maddy opened the passenger side door. 'I will.'

'What else has happened today?' he asked, testing her further. 'Come on, you said today was just getting better and better.'

'I had a visit from the police today too,' Maddy said, and pulled the door closed again. 'When I was in the hospital. Only it was Nick.'

She felt as if she'd been talking for hours by the time she'd finished telling him about Max, and what he'd overheard at the restaurant. 'So it turns out my intruder *wasn't* Craig's murderer keeping the focus on Gavin.'

'It might still have been,' Paul pointed out. 'It could be both. You can't rule out one of Donna's family as having been the killer.'

'That's true. But at least this means I'm not looking over my shoulder in two directions. I mean, there isn't some random loony out there looking to shut Gav up.'

She looked around as the front door opened and her father stood blinking out into the dark street. 'We'll talk about this later. But before we go in, and you put your foot in it, there's one final thing. Gav and I are finished. Tas and Dad don't know.' With that she shoved the door open again and hurried back up the path, barely hearing Paul's muffled, *What?*

He couldn't ask her about it in detail once they were in the house, which had been the point, but she wished he wouldn't keep glaring at her across the table as they ate. She didn't owe him any kind of explanation, particularly as she hadn't yet told her family, and it was still too raw to think about anyway; eight years with Gav, and most of them had been pretty good. Now it was over, and it felt like a failure, rather than a tragedy, but she still didn't know whose.

'Are you back on the old CP tomorrow then?' her father asked as he cleared the plates away.

Maddy nodded. 'I need to claw back some hours. I'll visit Gav after. What are you doing tomorrow? Working at the agency?'

'I've got a few things to clear up,' Tony said, 'but I'll be in around midday if that suits, Mackenzie?'

'Aye. Fine.' Paul was clearly trying to act normally, but he was obviously still reeling from everything she'd told him in the car, and he couldn't look directly at Tony. 'I said I'd give Ade a hand in the morning anyway.'

'How's he getting on?' Tony asked. 'Settling back in well?'

'He's a bit shaken,' Paul said, and Maddy saw where he was taking the conversation even before he added, 'You know, after finding the body.'

Her father shot a look at Tas, but that was his only reaction, and it was an understandable one. 'Not at the table, Mackenzie, aye?'

He was clearly still on a short fuse, having snapped twice at Tas for playing with his food, but she had to remember he was in his seventies now, and Tas could be a real handful at times. It was probably best that she was taking the boy home tonight.

Paul turned to Maddy. 'I was thinking: I might take a trip down to see Donna Lumsden's mother at the weekend. Get some of the lowdown on Donna herself after what you told me.'

'Good idea,' Tony said. 'You might get an insight into the whole family.'

Maddy wasn't sure if she was imagining that he was glad the conversation had shifted. 'Where is she?'

'Down near Loch Lomond, according to her Facebook. I'll check the details. You up for it?'

She shook her head. 'I just want to spend a bit of time with Tas after...you know. Everything.' She gave him a pointed look, and he nodded. 'Take Charis and Jamie,' she suggested. 'It'll be a nice trip out for them both. And you.'

He gave her one of his rare smiles, and she guessed things there had warmed still further. She was relieved to find she could still be glad for them, especially knowing now how terrible things had been for Charis and Jamie, with Jamie's father. The boy couldn't have asked for a better substitute than Paul, and it was clear the affection went both ways. It seemed that the new little family of three was finally taking the sunlit path her own had lost, and she tried to banish the flicker of envy. Considering she genuinely wished them well, it was surprisingly hard to do.

When Paul had left, Maddy sent Tas upstairs to get his things together. 'Make sure you leave the room tidy,' she said firmly. 'Don't come down until you're ready for inspection!'

Tas scampered off upstairs, and Maddy told her father to leave the plates and come into the sitting room. Mystified, he followed without questioning her, and when he was sitting down she told him that Paul now knew about Nick. He didn't speak, but she watched the blood drain from his face and had a momentary panic that she might have triggered a medical emergency. When that brief worry had passed she waited for the surge of anger, mentally preparing her arguments and reasons, and hoped her stupid emotions would be up to the job. But after a few minutes of tense silence, during which his face registered no expression at all, he nodded.

'I trust Mackenzie; he's one of the good ones.' He frowned at his knees, tugging at a minute crease in his trousers and brushing the material. Eventually he looked back at her. 'I can see why you're telling me this, and why you told him.'

'Can you?'

He offered her a brief, strained smile. 'I was a police officer for a long time, hen. I get it.'

It was hard to speak, but she somehow found the words. 'And...was he right to be worried?'

Tony sat forward in his seat and grasped both her hands.

He looked her directly in the eyes, unflinching, and his voice was clear. 'I swear on the soul of your mother, my own Sweet Caroline, that neither Nick nor myself killed DS Mulholland. I *swear* it.' He shook at their linked hands for emphasis, and Maddy slumped with relief.

'I'm sorry,' she began. 'After what you said at the hospital I had to—'

'Look, what Nick did to Dougie Cameron, was... Well. It was unthinkable. Unimaginable. And it's marked him forever.' Tony shook his head. 'Now it's marked you and me, too. But do you really think, after the effect it had on him, that he could have done such a thing *again*?'

'No,' she admitted. 'Not when you say it like that.'

'And all that guff I was spouting at the hospital – that was anger. Bravado, if you like. I couldn't kill someone in cold blood, not even Mulholland. There are other ways to make sure he couldn't harm you.'

She looked at him, startled. 'Like what?'

'Like manufacturing some other charge.' He looked almost belligerently defensive at her surprise. 'Yes, I'd do that. I was in the process of getting it done, when...' He stopped. 'When he put in for his transfer and I realised, or thought I did, that he'd accepted it was all over. That no-one was coming after him.'

'When in fact he was already dead.'

'Was he? When did he die?'

She told him what Paul had said. 'So it's a decent sized window,' she concluded, 'and hard to get an alibi together for the whole time. Unless you're in hospital of course, or banged up,' she added. 'Thank God for bike accidents and remand, eh?' Her humour was bleak, but was met with an appreciative, if faint, smile.

'Nick will need warning,' he said.

'I hope they don't throw him off this case too, Dad, I really do.'

'He'll find it hard to come back from again. We'll have to watch him very closely.'

The sound of Tas's feet jumping down the stairs announced that his bag was packed and the room ready for Grandad's inspection, and Tony patted Maddy's leg. 'Come on, hen. Time to paint on that smile for your wee boy.'

Chapter Fifteen

JAMIE SAT on the playground wall on Friday lunchtime, swinging his feet. His mum would go fruit-loops about the scuffs on the backs of his shoes, but they were getting too small for him anyway. He was just getting fed up enough to go and find someone else to hang out with, when he saw Ethan jogging up the path towards him.

'Sorry,' Ethan said, planting himself on the wall next to Jamie. 'Kyle was at the gate. He wanted me to ask, can you come to mine tonight instead? Mum's going to collect us after school.'

'Dunno. How will I get home?'

'Can't your mum pick you up?'

'Why can't you come to mine?'

'Kyle didn't say.' But Ethan looked a bit uncomfortable, and Jamie frowned.

'Is it something to do with my mum? I told you, she won't ask about that bruise. I've put her straight. She knows it wasn't your dad.'

'So can you call your mum and ask?' Ethan pressed, instead of answering.

Jamie shook his head and looked at his watch. 'We've still got half an hour, and Mum doesn't work on Fridays.' He glanced over to where the lunchtime assistant was breaking up a squabble on the far side of the playground. 'I'll run home and ask her, then I can pick up my after-school stuff at the same time.'

'I wish I lived closer to school,' Ethan said enviously. 'Mum wants us to move into town, but Dad won't do it.'

'I'll be back by bell.' Jamie slid off the wall and shoved his bag towards Ethan with his foot. 'Look after that for me, and if Miss Collier asks just tell her I'm in the toilet.'

'Won't your mum go mad if you're out on the street on your own?'

'Not any more,' Jamie grinned as he re-tied his shoelace. 'We're safe now, the mad copper's dead!'

He gave Miss Collier one more look, then set off through the gate and down the road towards the house his mum had rented, at the bottom of town. As he passed on the opposite side of the street to the little arcade where Ethan's dad worked, he saw Kyle's moped on its stand at the entrance, and he checked his watch again; there was just about time to make sure Kyle knew his mum wasn't going to cause trouble with Mr Cameron. It'd even be worth turning up late after lunch, if it meant he could clear up any misunderstandings; they just didn't know about Jamie's dad and what he'd done, but once they did they'd understand.

Jamie waited for a gap in the traffic, and hurried across to Inverlochy Court. Cameron and Son was about halfway up the row of shops, and he pushed open the door, a friendly smile on his face so they knew he was totally fine and not scared Mr Cameron might turn into the Hulk at any moment.

Kyle and his dad swung around at the sound of the bell on the door, and they both looked straight at him as if he'd come to rob the place. Mr Cameron was tight-lipped and angry, and Kyle was biting his lip as if he'd just received both barrels. Jamie had framed his words already, but they didn't come out.

'Sorry,' he muttered instead. 'I was just on my way home to ask Mum about coming to yours later.' He wasn't at all sure he wanted to go to tea now, but he wasn't about to give up a go on Ethan's Sonic game just because things were a bit awkward. Maybe Mr Cameron was telling Kyle off because he'd been horrible to Ethan? That would help things, provided Kyle listened.

'Right, lad,' Mr Cameron said, and he gave Jamie a nod and smile that looked a bit too big for him. 'I hope you can. Ethan enjoys it when you come over.'

Kyle said nothing, just stared at the counter and started fiddling with the box of gift-cards by the till. Jamie flushed as Mr Cameron kept smiling at him, and cleared his throat, eager to back away from the argument he'd walked into.

'I s'pect it'll be fine,' he mumbled. 'Maybe see you later then.'

'Hope so!' Mr Cameron raised his paint-streaked hand in a wave and looked pointedly at Kyle, who ignored them both and kept fiddling. 'Don't be rude, Kyle,' he murmured. 'Speak to the boy, aye?'

The older boy turned to Jamie again and lifted his own hand. 'See you later.'

Jamie closed the door behind him, never more grateful to be outside looking in. When it came to family rows he was all too familiar with the way they went. What if his mum was right? What if Mr Cameron really *was* hitting his kids? He made up his mind to keep a careful watch on all the Camerons, and set off home.

'Didn't you ask him why?' his mum said, when he explained, as quickly as he could, what Ethan had said. He was throwing his jeans and a sweatshirt into his PE bag at the same time, and hunted about for his trainers.

'Didn't get chance,' he said. 'Can I go then?'

'Okay.' She picked up his trainers from under the bed and handed them to him. 'I'll call Justine in a bit. You go back to school, and if you see me at the gate later you'll know they didn't ask her before arranging it, and she's put her foot down.'

'Great!'

'I'll pick you up around seven if Justine says that's okay. We've got a day out tomorrow.'

'Have we?'

'Mackenzie's taking us on a little road trip.' She smiled. 'I'll tell you about it later. Now get back to school before someone notices, or there'll be ructions.'

After school Jamie looked anxiously for his mother, for once glad not to see her.

Instead, Ethan's mum was waving at them both and pointing up the road to where she'd parked her car.

'We're on,' Ethan grinned. 'Come on!'

Before too long they were out on the road and away from the centre of town, but as the mountainous countryside flashed by, Jamie began to feel uneasy and he couldn't work out why; he hadn't felt like this when his mum brought him out to Ethan's before.

It wasn't until he looked at the back of Ethan's mum's head that he realised: when he'd been in their own car he'd been in the front and they'd been talking non-stop all the way, but sitting alone in the back seat he was reminded of the huge expanse of mountainside the American had driven him through, before leaving him alone in the old crofter's cottage by the waterfall... The dreadful loneliness, and the sick-making fear that he'd never see anyone he knew ever again, seemed to creep over him even though this time it was as different as it could be.

He wanted to speak, to break that spell, but Ethan and his mum were chattering away together, and their voices were turned into meaningless noise by the sound of the engine so he couldn't even join in. He swallowed hard and closed his eyes until they arrived, scrambling out with a gulp of relief to find himself in the larger of the Camerons' two front yards.

Kyle was there, tinkering with his moped by the light of a cordless lamp tied to an overhanging branch, but even the memory of that horrible atmosphere in the shop today was better than re-living the terrifying journey into the mountains in August. Ethan led him up to his room so they could get changed, and he brought the subject up.

'Do your brother and your dad argue a lot?'

'Never used to,' Ethan said, closing his bedroom door. 'But since Pickles died they've just not got on.'

'Oh yeah, I remember you said about that.'

Ethan pulled his jeans out of the drawer. 'Kyle says it was Dad's fault, for not keeping Pickles indoors, and for saying we had to stay longer at Gerry and Sam's so he wasn't here to stop him running off.'

'D'you miss him? Pickles, I mean.'

'Sometimes. He was all right, but I never loved him like Kyle did.'

'Why is there a picture of him in your room then?'

'It's a picture of Kyle too.' There was an oddly defiant expression on Ethan's face, as if daring Jamie to call him soft, but Jamie looked again at Kyle's squinting smile and thought he probably understood: Ethan had lost more than a pet when Pickles died.

'I'm going to get a dog,' he said again, yanking his sweatshirt down over his school shirt. 'I'm going to call it Sonic.'

Ethan grinned, back to himself again. 'Better name than Tommy Pickles.'

'And Pingu. What happened to him?'

'I told you, he was hit by a car.'

'No, I mean, did he have a funeral? You can with pets,' Jamie added, before Ethan could scoff at him. 'My aunty Suze had one for a hamster.'

'No, we didn't have a *funeral*!' He seemed to find the idea absurd. 'Kyle didn't want one anyway, said it was stupid. Dad buried Pickles out in the paddock.'

'Really?' Jamie crossed to the window, which looked down onto the back of the property, but it was dark out and he couldn't see a place that might mark a dog's grave. 'Are you allowed to do that?'

''Course. It's our place. We can do what we like.'

'So he just...dug a hole and put the dog in it?'

'Aye. Well, he wrapped it in my old paddling pool first, stop the foxes getting at him.'

'Did you see it?'

Ethan shook his head. 'It was summer, so Dad had to do it right away or it'd have got too smelly.'

'Mackenzie says that body he and Ade found was smelly.'

Ethan's eyes shot wide. 'That one on the news? Mr Mackenzie found it?'

'Ade found it first, but I heard him and Mackenzie talking, and they were saying they could still smell it days after.'

'Yuck!' But Ethan was looking intrigued. 'Imagine it, all slimy!'

'All the skin coming off, and maggots in its eyes...' Jamie added, waggling his fingers beside his own eyes, and they amused themselves for a few minutes speculating how the body might have looked. Then Ethan went quiet and turned to Jamie with a strange look on his face.

'Why don't we have a look?'

'Don't be stupid. How could we—'

'Not at the dead copper!' Ethan came over to the window. 'At Pickles.'

Jamie felt an uncomfortable thrill running through him. Talking was okay – it was even fun, here, in this lighted room with the smell of tea drifting up the stairs and the sound of Kyle dropping a spanner and swearing. But he wasn't sure about doing it for real. He followed the direction of Ethan's gaze, down to the far end of the paddock.

'It's dark,' he observed, unnecessarily.

'Not now, stupid.' Ethan shook his head. When it's light. Tomorrow?'

'I'm going out tomorrow.' Part of him was relieved, but another part of him really wanted to know what the dog looked like, after so long in the ground.

'Sunday then? It won't look the same as that body, 'cos Pickles has been wrapped up, but there might be maggots.'

Jamie sensed that Ethan was feeling the same mixture of revulsion and excitement as he was, which was a relief. It'd be pretty good to talk about at school, and everyone would want to know about it. 'Maybe we can take a photo,' he suggested. 'Use your phone or something.'

'My phone doesn't take decent pictures.'

'Well ask Kyle if you can borrow his, then. You said he's got a spare.'

'I can try, I suppose.'

Ethan's mum chose that moment to call them down to tea, and as they looked at each other, Ethan made a barfing noise. Jamie laughed, and Ethan joined in, and they went downstairs trying to out-barf each other until Ethan got a look off his mum.

'Sunday,' he mouthed behind her back as she turned away, and Jamie nodded.

Donna ended the call and laid the phone down carefully, trying not to read too much into the way Chelsea had just spoken to her. The girl was devastated – of course she was. It had only been a week since she'd learned her beloved father had been bludgeoned to death; she couldn't be expected to have come to terms with it any more than Donna herself. But to declare that Donna didn't care...

She checked the time, but knew it wouldn't have mattered anyway as she unstopped the bottle – tonight wasn't a night for observing niceties. She poured the Malbec until the glass was full and took the bottle with her to the sofa, her already blurred gaze falling on the family photo on the wall. Herself and the kids, then aged five and seven, and in front of them, cross-legged on the floor like the biggest kid of all, Craig.

It was only amongst his own that he ever dropped the tough-guy behaviour and relaxed; it had been too risky to ever let anyone else see what she and the children had seen: a man who actually, honest to God *giggled* over Monty Python films, got all irate when the wrong contestant got booted out of *Bake Off* and refused to allow anyone to speak to him during *PopMaster*. No matter where he was.

Donna took a slug of her wine, her eyes stinging even more now. Chelsea was hurting, yes, but there had been no excuse for that barb. They couldn't come back yet, it was as simple as that, and she'd tried to explain: things were going to be hectic here until after the funeral, at least, and then they were going to be tense until after Galbraith's plea hearing. After that she'd be able to concentrate on the kids, and on Christmas... Getting through *that* was going to take every ounce of strength she possessed as well.

'Your granny loves having you there,' she'd said to Chelsea, 'and it's good for... Well yes, of course I love having you here too!' She hadn't been able to say the right thing for saying the wrong one, and it was a relief, albeit a frustrating and painful one, when Chelsea had abruptly ended the call.

Now Donna sat back on the sofa and drank half the wine in a couple of gulps. She let go of all thoughts of Thistle, and her dad's idea to bring that new business on board – it would be months before that was even feasible anyway, plenty of time to think about it – and even of Chelsea and Myles. She pushed staff acquisitions to the back of her mind too, and just allowed herself the luxurious agony of remembering Craig.

Their meeting, back in '93, when they'd both been at some party, and she had taken one look at him and decided his girl-friend wasn't worthy of him; the way she'd later claimed an engagement gift by persuading her father to hire him as his personal assistant; their wedding; the births of the kids... The memories paraded in front of her as if they were on a video screen, and she drank and smiled, then drank and cried, and re-filled her glass.

The front doorbell barely penetrated the protective haze she had created, but after it was repeated a few times she sighed and put down her glass. There was only a dribble left anyway, and nothing remained in the bottle; she'd need a fresh one.

She pulled open the door to find Martha standing there. Little, mousy Martha, the divorcée who'd somehow managed to worm her way into the Kilbride family by being constantly at William's side as he'd recovered from the Hogmanay accident. Despite him still being married to Donna's mother back then. How had she done it? She felt mean for thinking like that; Martha had been kindness itself, from day one, and especially since Craig's...

'Come in,' she said, standing aside. She was aware she'd drunk that first bottle quite fast, but it was still a bit of a surprise to feel herself reeling slightly as she followed Martha back into the large sitting room. On her way to the sofa she picked up another bottle, and a glass for her stepmother.

'Not for me, love,' Martha said. 'I'm driving.'

''Course you are.' Donna applied the corkscrew and set to work on her own behalf. She glanced at the label as she did so, and noticed the alcohol content: 14 per cent; no wonder she felt a bit unsteady. 'What brings you out here on a nasty November night?' She gave a brief grin at the unintentional alliteration, and repeated it appreciatively under her breath, but Martha didn't look impressed.

'I just wanted to see how you were doing,' she said quietly. 'It's been a week now, and everything's been so—'

'Fucking in*sane*,' Donna supplied. 'Did you know my kids think I don't care? Just because I've been tied up with police interviews, and work, and funeral arrangements... I mean, I can't afford the luxury of sitting here and sobbing my heart out all day every day, so that means I didn't love Craig, right? It's obvious.' She sloshed more red into her glass. 'Sure you won't have some?'

'Quite sure.' Martha got up to pour herself some lemonade instead. 'The funeral's Monday, so Will tells me.'

'Yep. Kids will be back on Sunday to remind me what a bitch I am.'

'Don't be silly. They love you. They're just confused, and grieving. Probably homesick.'

'*I'm* confused and grieving,' Donna pointed out. 'Who's listening to me?'

'I am, love,' Martha said, and patted her shoulder as she passed her on her way back to her seat. 'You just talk away.'

Donna wanted to, but the words were locked away now. She just shook her head. 'Doesn't matter. Thank you for coming though.'

'Of course.'

'You've been so nice since it happened.'

'I liked Craig.' Martha sipped her lemonade. 'So will this solicitor they've got in custody admit to the murder, do you think?' she went on, before Donna could question that.

'I bloody hope so.'

'Even if he didn't do it?'

'Of course he did it! The evidence is all there.'

Martha raised an eyebrow, and the silent query was almost lost as she took another drink, but Donna saw it. 'You don't think he did?'

'I'm not saying that. But wouldn't you rather make sure the right person gets sent down?'

'They've got the right person.'

'They've got *someone*, granted. Is that enough? I mean,' Martha paused, frowning. 'I mean, is this you hitting out at the wall because you stubbed your toe on the curb?'

Donna stared at her. 'You think it could have been someone else? Who, Ian?'

'No. Not Ian. You know he was still down south.'

'So who then?'

'I don't know. I'm just saying. There might well have been...others, that you haven't considered.'

'There was no-one else due that night. I checked Dad's Excel sheet.'

'I meant people who were dealing directly with Craig and not your father.'

'Oh, I see. So that's why you're here, is it? To distance your-self and Dad from all this?' Donna stood up, grasping the arm of the sofa for balance. 'I knew you were lying when you said you'd liked Craig. You should probably leave now.'

'You're not listening.' Martha stood too, and she seemed less inconsequential now. Her eyes had lost that washed-out, distant look, and bore into Donna's with surprising strength. 'Your husband was working independently of Will.'

'What do you mean, *independently*?'

'Will found out that some of the clients you were sending him never reached him.'

'Never what?'

'Craig was using his contacts at the casino, and Will's money, to set up his own lending system,' Martha said slowly, carefully, as if she were talking to a distracted child. 'He was skimming off the interest the clients paid back. Much higher than Will ever charged, by the way,' she added in a sour voice, 'and replacing the original sum of money before Will knew it had gone missing.'

'So... They were actually dealing with Craig, not Dad?'

'Not that they ever knew that, of course. Where do you suppose he was getting the money to keep you and the bairns in such fine style? He's been doing it for years.'

'I paid for most of this!' Donna gestured at the room.

'But Craig was never short either. Little treats for a family like this don't come cheap.'

'He earned his money, looking after Dad, and working for him.'

'Not that much. Think about it. It's a miracle your father didn't start asking you about it. But of course, he wouldn't, would he? You'd nothing to do with it.'

Donna's thoughts were whirring so fast she couldn't quite fit this into a slot. It sat awkwardly and wouldn't make sense. 'But...if that's the case, why didn't Dad say something about it?'

'He didn't want to believe it, so he chose not to.'

'Then how did you know about it?'

Martha gave her a strange, distant little smile. 'It's surprising what you learn when you're part of the furniture.' She put her still half-full glass on the table. 'Well, as I said, I was just passing by, and thought I'd drop in and see how you're getting on.' She squeezed Donna's arm as she passed her, and Donna followed her to the front door.

'Wait! That can't be right. There's no way Dad would just let it go like that, without doing anything.'

Martha took her time fishing her car keys from her bag, then turned that oddly revitalised look on her again. 'Perhaps he did do something, love,' she said, and patted Donna's hand. 'Haven't you thought about that yet?'

Chapter Sixteen

It was roughly a two-hour drive to Helensburgh, where Donna's mother lived. Now and again on a trip like this, especially along the A82, Mackenzie would find himself wishing he was back on two wheels instead of four; it would have been so good to have brought Charis down here on the back of his old Z900, feeling her arms gripping him as they hammered up the straights, and hearing her laugh as they slowed again to take the bends.

But that bike had come off even worse than he had, after their unscheduled flight and hard landing in the valley at Glenlowrie. Besides, as well as the strain it would have put on his shoulder, he wouldn't have wanted to leave Jamie behind, so they'd piled into his second-hand Mazda after breakfast and set off for the Trossachs. Like a real family.

Helensburgh lay on the far side of Loch Lomond, but the weather didn't lend itself to admiring the huge stretch of water; rain pelted the windows, and Charis gazed past Mackenzie at the world-famous loch through the pattern of small rivers that were blown horizontal along his window.

'We can come back down another day,' she said at length, settling back contentedly against her seat. 'How much further?'

'Isn't it his job to ask that?' Mackenzie jerked his head to indicate where Jamie sat dozing on the back seat, lulled by the warmth of closed windows and a smooth ride.

'If he's going to sleep on the job, I'm happy to step in for him.'

Mackenzie grinned. 'Okay, about quarter of an hour.' He took the turning off the A82, and they trundled along the narrow B road for a while before coming back out into wider countryside.

'So much space,' Charis murmured. 'I still can't get used to it.'

'In a good way?'

'Oh God, yeah,' she assured him. 'A very good way.'

'What was your place in Liverpool like?'

'My flat?' She gave him a sideways look. 'You don't want to know. Not after looking at this.' She waved at the farmland they were passing through. 'To be fair it was okay, for what it was. But this is... Well. I'm here, and that tells a story.'

Jamie stirred, sat up straighter, and wiped the condensation off his window. 'Is that Loch Lomond?' he asked in a sleepy voice.

Mackenzie smiled. 'No, lad. That's just a reservoir. You slept past the loch.'

'Can we stop at Green Welly on the way back? Me and Mum went there when we came here before, and when we were coming back up.'

'Easy, tiger,' Charis said. 'We've not even got there yet.' She turned to Mackenzie and put on an exaggerated pleading voice. 'No, but can we?'

He hesitated. The travellers' stop at Tyndrum had always

been one of Josh's favourite places, and he'd not been back there since the last time with him and Kath. He realised Charis had gone quiet, and he glanced at her to see that, as always, she had guessed at his reticence. Her face was grave and she gave a minute shake of her head, giving him the chance to say no without incurring any complaints.

He thought about the times he and his family had eaten in the restaurant, and about the bright gift shop packed with just the right mixture of decent gifts and cheerful tat. Josh had torn around it like a madman every time; no matter how well he knew the place, each trip out there had felt like a holiday to the boy.

Sharing it with Charis and Jamie today would be bittersweet, but Mackenzie had the slowly growing feeling it would actually be good for him. He nodded and returned his gaze to the road, swallowing past an unexpected lump in his throat.

'Yeah, why not? I think that'd be the perfect end to the trip.'

They pulled up outside a large house near the waterfront, and Charis lowered her window. 'Looks like she did fairly well out of the divorce,' she observed. 'All these places are enormous. And sitting in their own grounds.'

'Aye well, Kilbride couldn't have afforded to try and screw her over,' Mackenzie said, unclipping his seat belt. 'She'll have known what he was doing. I'm surprised she's not been fished out of—'

'Um,' Charis put a hand on his leg and glanced back towards Jamie. 'I get what you're saying. No need to be graphic.'

They hurried up the drive, pushed on by the driving rain and the wind coming off the Clyde at their backs. The door was opened before Mackenzie could knock, by a woman who must have watched them approaching.

'Mrs Kilbride?' Mackenzie said, holding out his hand. 'Paul Mackenzie. We spoke on the phone.'

'Of course. Come in.' The woman, a tall and commanding presence, impeccably dressed, stepped aside to let them in. She didn't mention the wet footprints left in the hall, but Mackenzie guessed there would be someone to come along at some point after they'd left, and that the prints wouldn't survive long.

'This is Charis Boulton,' he said, 'and her son, Jamie.'

'Nice to meet you.' For all her prim appearance, Kilbride's ex-wife didn't seem to have any put-on airs about her. Old money, presumably, and with nothing to prove. 'Can I fetch you a drink, Mr Mackenzie? Miss Boulton?'

Presently they were sitting in a neatly furnished sitting room, clutching fine china teacups, and Mrs Kilbride had called to her grandchildren. 'Myles is probably a year or two older than you,' she said to Jamie. 'Perhaps he can show you his collection.'

Collection of what, it seemed rude to ask, so they just waited, making small talk about the journey down from Abergarry. After a few minutes, two children came in. Myles was actually the same age as Jamie, but Mackenzie and Charis were used to the assumption that Jamie was younger than he was. Chelsea, a couple of years older, was pale and red-eyed, and barely spoke. She followed the two boys as Myles carted Jamie off to his room, and Mrs Kilbride looked after her worriedly.

'Poor girl. Devoted to her dad. She had a row with her mother on the phone last night. Been crying ever since.'

'How long are they here for?' Mackenzie asked, trying not to jump on the information about Donna too quickly.

'Only until tomorrow afternoon. It's the funeral on Monday, so I would think they'll stay at home after that. They've schoolwork to catch up with, after all.' She gave Mackenzie a knowing look. 'You said on the phone that you wanted to talk to me about Donna. Don't beat about the bush; I'm sure you've got places you want to be.'

He smiled. 'Thank you. If I ask anything that makes you uneasy, or you'd rather not answer, please just let me know.'

'Of course I will.' Mrs Kilbride looked at him as if he were simple. 'Don't imagine for one moment I won't ask you to leave if you cross a line.'

'Good,' he said briskly. He was used to all kinds of interviews, and luckily not fazed by her manner, though he sensed Charis stiffen slightly beside him. 'Okay, let's start with the reason I'm asking.'

'Please do.'

'I've had information that the police have spoken to Donna about an attack on a prisoner. The man is charged with killing Craig Lumsden, and was warned against any plea but a guilty one.'

'And your question is?'

'In your opinion, as her mother, do you think it's likely she had anything to do with it?'

Mrs Kilbride pursed her lips. 'I never liked Craig. I never approved of the way William used him for carrying out his dirty work either. But William has a lot of influential people who were loyal to him, and any one of them might have wanted to ingratiate themselves with him.'

'That's not what I asked,' Mackenzie said quietly. 'Is

Donna the type of person who'd threaten someone to plead a certain way in court?'

'She's the type of person who loved her husband, for all his faults. Some women will overlook a man's true nature for love, Mr Mackenzie. How do you think so many men are able to cow their wives into doing whatever they want them to?'

Charis put her cup down, and he saw her hand was trembling. His heart shrank as he looked at her face, the eyes suddenly bright, the mouth drawn into a tight line. 'I'm just going to make sure Jamie's not bothering your grandchildren,' she said quietly. She looked at Mackenzie and nodded, indicating he should just carry on and not worry, and as she levered herself off the deep, two-seater sofa she pressed his hand. 'Back in a bit.'

When the door had closed behind her, cutting off the sound of raised voices from upstairs, Mackenzie faced Mrs Kilbride again. Are you saying you think Craig was somehow controlling your daughter?'

'Not at all. I'm saying he might have thought he was. And William might have thought so too, but Donna loved him. *That* was plain to me, as her mother. So yes,' she added thoughtfully, 'it's possible she might have used her father's contacts to make sure his killer didn't wriggle off the hook.'

Mackenzie nodded and moved away from the subject for a moment.

'Why didn't you like Craig?'

She made a ladylike sound of disgust. 'Nasty, rough piece of work. His family moved down to Devon, and most of us were delighted they'd gone so far away. When she told me he was back, and that they'd got together... Well. I remember the party, too. It was the same night that poor Wallace girl lost her parents in the fire on that estate.'

Mackenzie sat up a bit straighter. 'Glenlowrie?'

'That's the one. Made my complaints about Donna's boyfriend-stealing sound a bit ridiculous when you think about it. Poor Mary and Duncan – I knew them quite well, you know. It was at *their* party where William had his accident in 1988.'

As Charis was fond of saying, it was a small world, and getting smaller.

'What about your ex-husband? Are you all right to talk about him?'

'That depends what you want to know.' She looked around her, at the elegant room. 'I've agreed not to discuss matters that arose when we were married.'

'Well again, just stop me if I go too far.' Mackenzie gave her his widest smile, but it didn't seem to have its usual, disarming effect. 'Are Donna and her dad close? I mean, besides their business partnership.'

'Closer than Donna is to me. He spoiled her from a young age. Only child, you know? I could see the same thing happening with Chelsea and her parents.'

'But Chelsea isn't an only child.'

'No, she was first born, though. Craig had two years of watching her turn into the little princess he wanted, and when Myles came along everyone thought he'd turn all that onto his son. But Myles was an awkward little one. Colicky. It took Craig a while to warm to him.'

'But he did?'

'Oh, yes. So Donna says. But by then Chelsea had already grown enough to realise she had her father wrapped around her little finger.' Mrs Kilbride shifted in her seat. 'Anyway, we were talking about Donna and William.'

'Yes, please go on.'

'They're very alike, which can cause problems. William

would do anything for Donna though, which is why he took Craig on when she asked him to. But Donna's got a…a streak of something a bit hard in her. I don't think she's quite the malleable daughter he'd have liked. She's her own woman.' There was more than a touch of pride in her voice, despite her admission that she felt like the lesser parent.

'What about William's new wife? What's her relationship like with Donna?'

'Hardly new!' Mrs Kilbride sniffed. 'They got married only a month after our divorce came through, in 1990. Almost thirty years ago.'

Mackenzie waited while she caught up with the question.

'They get on well enough,' she said at length. 'Donna was just a teen then of course, but she knew Martha would be doing everything she could to get on her good side. She knows which side her bread's buttered, that one. Always has.'

'And does Martha still do that?'

'Pander to her, you mean?' Mrs Kilbride shook her head. 'According to Donna she mostly just goes to lunch with friends, looks after her blighted cats and generally stays out of the way until William wants to wheel her out as the respectable wife.'

'So she's not really on the radar at all?'

'Not really.' Mrs Kilbride put down her teacup. 'If there's nothing else, I need to get the children ready to go out.'

'I can't think of anything at the moment,' Mackenzie said. 'You've been very candid, thank you. Most helpful. Would it be all right if I called you, if I have any more questions I think you can help with?'

'If you like.' Mrs Kilbride went to the foot of the stairs and called up. 'Myles! Your guest has to leave now.' Myles and Jamie appeared and leaned over the balustrade on the top landing. Mrs Kilbride frowned. 'Where's Jamie's mother?'

'She's talking to Chelsea,' Myles called back.

A moment later Charis, obviously having heard, joined Jamie and brought him downstairs. They said their goodbyes and hurried through the rain to the car; when they'd pulled away from the house Charis turned to Mackenzie.

'So, did you get hold of anything useful?'

'Nothing ground-breaking. She does seem to think Donna's quite capable of doing anything it takes to avenge Craig though. Why?' he asked, sparing her a glance as he pulled onto the main road. 'You've got a weird look about you. What have *you* found out?'

Charis's smile was so self-satisfied that on anyone else he might have called it a smirk. 'Well for starters,' she said, 'I've found out that Lumsden and his father-in-law had a *massive* row, not that long ago. Absolutely explosive evidently, so much so that they didn't seem to notice, or care, that Chelsea might have overheard everything.'

'Wow. That's for starters? What's for main course?'

'The row started because Kilbride had found out that Lumsden had been stealing from him for years. Now,' she leaned over and patted his leg, 'you tell me that's not a motive – I dare you.'

Chapter Seventeen

MADDY PARKED up and went around to open Tas's door and help him from his booster seat. 'We won't be long,' she assured him. 'I know where I put it.'

Tas pulled a face as he looked out at the rain. 'Can't I wait here?'

'Nope. Come on.'

He sighed and climbed out, and a minute later Maddy was unlocking the door at the bottom of the steps that led to the Clifford-Mackenzie office. The office itself gave her a strange pang as she switched on the light against the gloomy day and looked around; she missed it already, knowing she'd not be back to work here for weeks yet. On the other hand it was clear Paul and Tony were of one mind when it came to neatness of work-space: it was an overrated concept.

She sighed and looked around for her raincoat; her father had been sitting at her desk while she was away, so Paul had obviously moved the coat off her chair, but it was too much to hope he'd have hung it on the door or something sensible like that.

'Come on, Mum!' Tas drifted around the room, trailing his hand over the backs of the chairs and eventually throwing himself face down on one of the sofas at the back of the room. She followed his progress and saw what she was looking for draped over the back of the matching sofa opposite him.

'Hah! Come on then.' She picked up the coat and pulled it on, then stopped as she heard footsteps on the stairs. Not Paul's – he was down at Helensburgh today.

'Stay there.' Her heart slipped uncomfortably against her ribs, and she stepped in front of the still-prone Tas and faced the door. She'd let her guard slip lately; what if they'd been followed here?

One hand stole to the phone in her back pocket, and her eyes first lit and then moved on from several potential weapons; none of them were close enough to reach. Her breath shortened as the feet stopped outside, then the door opened cautiously and a dark head peered around.

Maddy relaxed and blew out a harsh breath as she let go of her phone. 'Ade! For God's sake, you nearly gave me... What are you doing here?'

His face creased in a smile. 'If this was *Midsomer Murders*, that'd be the last thing you ever said.'

She couldn't return his humour, not after what had happened at her home – but then he didn't know about that, so she couldn't hold it against him. Unlike Paul, the great plank. 'Seriously,' she said, gesturing for Tas to get up, 'what *are* you doing here?'

'I was just slowing down to show my dad where Paul works, and we saw the light on. I knew Paul and Charis were away down south today, so I thought I should check it out. Did you know your door sign's crooked?'

'Yes, thank you. Frank's out and about, is he?' This was good news; Paul would be happy to hear it.

'Aye, we're on our way up to Glenlowrie. We have a lot to talk about, and he wanted to see Drumnacoille again too. Put some ghosts to rest, you know.' He looked sombre as he said it, and she realised it was probably the first time his father had been back to his old home since his stroke.

Ade held out a hand to Tas. 'Pleased to meet you, sir. My name's Adrian, but everyone calls me Ade.'

'You look like Mr Mackenzie,' the boy said, shaking the hand. 'Only not so tall.'

'I'm a Mr Mackenzie too – he's my little brother. And by the way, I'm over six feet,' he added, 'but you're right, Paul forgot to stop growing at the proper time. I'm always telling him off about it.'

'I can't believe you got Frank out of the Heathers,' Maddy said, with a little smile at Tas's shy giggle. 'What does he think about all your plans?'

'He can't wait to get started.'

'And can you? Get started?'

'Yep, thank goodness. Crime scene's closed; they decided the body had been moved post-mortem, and it's too long ago for there to have been anything else to preserve in the area. Tyre marks and so on. So,' he rubbed his hands, 'the sale's going ahead, and I can start looking into hiring contractors and so on before the ground gets too hard to work.'

'Exciting,' Maddy said. It was hard not to respond to the eagerness she could see, not only on his face but in the way he shifted from foot to foot, keen to get cracking on something.

'Why don't you both come up with us?' he said, out of the blue. 'If you've nothing planned, that is.'

Maddy was a bit taken aback, and looked at Tas, who nodded eagerly.

'Can we, Mum?'

'You don't even know where he's talking about,' Maddy said. 'It's just a mucky old estate, and a *very* smelly shed—'

'We're not going to that part,' Ade broke in quickly. 'Just the plot where I plan to build the main house, and a quick visit to the old family pile next door, for Dad. Come on,' he said, adopting a cajoling tone. 'It'll be a nice little ride out.'

'We were going out to Fort Augustus to watch the boats,' Maddy said, looking at Tas again.

Ade pulled a face. 'Filthy weather for hanging around waiting for a lock to open. Right, Tas?'

'*Can* we go, Mum?' the boy asked again.

'I'll even take you for lunch after,' Ade pressed. 'Somewhere dead posh where I know the owner.'

Maddy grinned. 'I didn't know you were acquainted with the bloke who runs the chip van at Drumnadrochit.'

'I've heard nothing but wonderful things about that van,' Ade said, 'but this time I was referring to Thistle Inverness. There's a potential business partnership in the offing, and I wanted to sample the menu myself, rather than trust Trip Advisor, before I take it any further.'

Maddy's interest leapt. If Donna was at the restaurant there would never be a better opportunity to see how she reacted when Maddy rolled up; any hint of guilt would stand out a mile. If she wasn't, well, there'd be nothing lost, and they'd be a fantastic meal to the good. Plus she would be the proud recipient of a mother of the year trophy, judging from the look Tas was now giving her. Things had been tense and difficult for so long, it was time they both had a treat, wasn't it?

'Well?' Ade said. 'What do you say? I'll tell you about the partnership proposal, and you can tell me what you think.'

Maddy already knew what she thought about any collaboration with Kilbride's family, but now wasn't the time to say anything. 'Sounds like a plan,' she said instead. 'Come on, Tas, let's not keep Mr Mackenzie waiting. I think he might explode if he doesn't get going soon,'

It was strange, driving up through the old estate, and she remembered Paul had said the same thing. Memories were weird things: on one hand they provided a deep sense of unease as various sections of the road, and similar drizzly and foggy conditions, brought that weekend vividly back to life; on the other, there was a fierce triumph to be taken from the fact that she was travelling this same road again, and had beaten everything it had thrown at her. Paul was alive, and in pretty good health, and she herself wouldn't be required to head off into the pitch darkness in pursuit of a small boy. Nor was she likely to be arrested at the end of it all. Probably, she amended with an inward smile, after stealing a quick look at the hugely enthusiastic Ade Mackenzie. It was hard to believe he was the elder brother by five years.

The Glenlowrie manor house had been made safe after the fire, but that was all that had been done with it. It stood glaring down at them with smoke-darkened walls, and a roof peppered with gaping holes where it had caved in upon its burning timbers. Ade helped Frank down from the jeep and they both stared at the house silently for a moment.

'Spent many a great day on this estate,' Frank said at length. 'Duncan's birds were good sport, so we'd all get together here, the five of us...' He trailed off, then looked across in the direction of the neighbouring estate. 'My land – *our* land,' he amended, with a glance at Ade, 'attracted a different sort of client. We were big in the whisky trade you know,' he added to Maddy. 'Duncan was keen to get me involved in his plans for those new team-building things, but I was never interested in that.'

'Not new any more, Dad,' Ade said gently. 'But I want to take it back to your values, not Duncan's. The distillery, the shooting and fishing, yes, but the real experience. No guarantees, nothing made easy to cater to the whims of bored executives.'

'It'll cost a bit to renovate,' Maddy said, eyeing the ruin doubtfully.

'I'm not buying this part, just the bottom end, but we can't drive to it yet. We can walk to it from here though, now it's stopped raining, if you're up for it?'

'Frank?' Maddy looked at him, a bit concerned, but he seemed braced enough by the fresh air and the reminiscences, and put up no argument. The four of them set off down the sloping path.

At the clearing, where Ade pointed out to Frank the dimensions of the house he intended to raise there, a bored Tas wandered off and Maddy went with him. In the distance she could hear the river, fed by the waterfall, and Tas looked back at her. 'Can we skim?'

'If there are stones. But not for too long. It looks like the rain gods aren't quite finished with us yet.'

She followed him through the overgrown ferns, along an old and very rough path, and they'd been tramping happily enough through the mud for a few minutes when she realised several of the fronds were broken and hung limply by their stems.

'There's no need to do that, Tas,' she called out. 'Just push them aside.'

He turned. 'No need to do what?'

'You don't have to break them,' she explained. 'We can get past easily enough.'

'I haven't broken any.'

Maddy was about to point them out when the wind gusted off the river and brought with it a wave of something unpleasantly sweet, with an underlying reek of rotting refuse. She wrinkled her nose, then realisation hit and she turned away, her hand over her mouth, trying not to breathe in too deeply. The shed was just ahead.

'Come away,' she called. 'That's not a nice place down there. Let's go back to the car.'

She started away, gesturing to him to hurry after her. The broken ferns were making sense now, and she tried not to think of who had walked this very path, dragging or carrying the dead body with them. 'Tas!'

The boy straightened up. 'Coming!'

'Don't go picking stones up from here – we can look for them further up by the house.'

'It's not a stone, it's a snail.'

'Okay.'

She knew it would be fruitless, after all this time, but as she waited for Tas to catch up, she crouched and stared closely at the path to see if there were any drag marks. Nothing. Perhaps she was jumping to conclusions, and Ade had actually walked down this way himself, dashing the fronds aside as he explored the land that would soon be his.

She asked him, when she and Tas re-joined him and Frank

at the clearing, but he shook his head. 'Nope, haven't walked down that way yet. Anything interesting?'

'Just the shed.'

He grimaced. 'No wonder you didn't stay down there. The police told me the smell would probably linger for weeks yet.'

'It *stunk!*' Tas declared, and even Frank smiled at that. 'Are we going for lunch now?'

'In a bit. Mr Mackenzie wants to go across to the estate next door, but we'll drive it. We won't stay long.'

At Drumnacoille, they left Frank talking to the current laird and walked a short distance away while Ade told Maddy more about what had happened to the family estate; Paul hadn't really told her much, and she'd certainly never heard about the accusations of fraud that had sent Frank into a spiral of despair and caused the stroke.

'It must be so hard for him, seeing it like this.' Maddy looked around at the overgrown walled garden and the pitted dirt road. 'Especially after he'd tried so hard to save it.'

'Aye, that's why I've been hoping to get him on board with the new venture.'

'And he's keen too?'

'Absolutely. It's given him a new lease of life, I think. He's been talking to his old mate Rob Doohan about coming on board with the distillery. They've been getting on pretty well since they were re-united by you and the Scouse Spitfire.'

Maddy laughed. 'Don't you dare tell her I said so, but she's been bloody good for Paul. And even worse, I'm starting to actually quite like her.'

'I won't say a word,' he said, with a speculative little smile.

'What's that look for?'

'Well, I always thought you and Paul were...you know. Right for each other.'

'We are. We're as right for each other as anyone could be.'

'Well then—'

'But not in the sense you mean.' Maddy saw his eyebrow go up and shook her head. 'It's hard to explain. We were together, for a while, and don't get me wrong – it was wonderful. But it wasn't right for either of us. He wasn't ready to be with anyone, and I realised I couldn't afford to lose his friendship.'

'You sound as if you rely on him now, as much as he did on you when he lost Kath and Josh. I thought you and Gavin were engaged.'

'We are. Were.'

'Ah. No *stand by your man* vibe for you then?'

'That's...' She broke off and sighed. 'It's complicated. I can't trust him, that's all. We're over.'

Ade didn't say anything, but she recognised the suddenly interested look on his face and could have bitten her tongue out; the last thing she needed was a new romantic complication, particularly in the form of someone who reminded her so strongly of Paul. She had to nip this one in the bud.

'I don't think it's a good idea for us to come to lunch with you,' she said regretfully, moving away under the pretence of looking at a stone marker by the side of the path.

'Nor do I.'

'You don't?' She didn't know whether to be relieved or disappointed, but she admitted she was a little bit put out. He certainly gave up quickly.

'Definitely not. I mean look at the state of your boots.'

She looked down and saw the mud caking her Docs, then raised her eyes again to see Ade grinning at her. He shook his head regretfully. 'I just can't be seen with you, Miss Clifford. Not in an establishment like Thistle.'

'Sod,' she muttered, and gave in to a smile of her own. 'Just for that I'm ordering the most expensive meal on the menu.'

Even having washed her own footwear, and Tas's, at the water pump by the old trough in Drumnacoille's yard, Maddy followed Ade and Frank into Thistle Inverness with a sense of slightly defensive awe; it had such a reputation that she automatically felt out of place, yet she knew she had as much right to be there as anyone else. Some places had that effect, and they never failed to make her cross with herself.

She kept her attention on anyone who looked as if they belonged there, hoping to see Donna Lumsden and, more importantly, for Donna to see her bold and unafraid. But there was no sign. The dining room was heaving, as big as it was, and Maddy resigned herself to either a very long wait or a chippy tea after all.

But Ade spoke quietly to the maître d', who made a swift telephone call, and to Maddy's surprise they were guided within a few minutes to a table in the corner. The maître d' removed the 'reserved' sign and produced four menus, before taking their drinks orders and disappearing.

'Well colour me impressed,' Maddy said, smiling as she opened her menu. 'I gather they're pretty sure you're taking them up on their offer then?'

'I certainly gave them reason to think it was a possibility. The place is Donna's, but her dad seems to have a pretty hefty hand in the running of it. Not to mention a good deal of clout as to who gets preferential treatment, apparently. Luckily for us.'

'I gather his money got her started.' Maddy looked at Tas, who was struggling out of his coat. 'Come here. Let me do it.' She helped him get his arm out of the sleeve and shook the coat out. 'What's that in the pocket?'

'Snail, I told you,' he said, returning to his chair to hang his coat on it before she could plunder his pocket. 'I found it on the path.'

'It's a bit bulky for a snail,' she pointed out. 'I said no stones too, remember?'

'It's *not* a stone, it's—'

'Oh, my God!' Maddy stared down at the pristine table-cloth, her heart pounding. 'It's him!'

'Who?' Ade followed the direction she'd been looking in, over the top of Tas's head.

'Don't stare!' Maddy breathed. She closed her eyes and tried to tell herself she was letting her overwrought imagination get the better of her, but another quick glance confirmed it: the man she'd been investigating for William Kilbride was standing in the doorway chatting to the maître d' as if they were old friends. Did he know who *she* was?

She was sure their paths had never crossed, but it would have been easy enough to find out who had shopped him, once he was back in the Kilbride fold... A cold feeling crept over her, and she felt sick as she thought about it; if Donna had ordered the attack on Gavin, and the warning to be delivered to her too, this would more than likely have been the man for the job. No wonder he'd taken such pleasure in frightening her. The cut on her inner arm seemed to flare to life as she remembered the slow drawing of the blade down the softer skin there. It began to feel so much more personal now.

'Maddy, what is it?' Ade asked in a harsh whisper, but she couldn't tell him without frightening Tas, so she gave him an embarrassed smile.

'Nothing. Seeing things. Who's having what, then? Tas, do you want me to help you choose?'

Ade's expression spoke volumes, and she knew she'd have to explain later, but for now she kept half her attention on the man she knew as both Ian George and Dave Carnegie, as they gave their food orders to the waiter. Before too long, George/Carnegie passed through the doorway at the far end of the restaurant, and Maddy relaxed and managed to keep up her end of the various conversations that went back and forth across the table.

Frank and Ade discussed the possibilities of the new estate, and she and Tas talked about Christmas. The time passed pleasantly enough, but towards the end of their dessert Maddy began to fret again. Donna now knew Ade was here, and since he said they'd not met yet, she was sure to come out to speak to him. This was, of course, what Maddy had wanted all along, but now she couldn't shake the squirming feeling that George/Carnegie would accompany her.

At the very least, Ade's association with Maddy might put the kibosh on any deal he was planning to strike, so she made up her mind to whisk Tas off to the toilet the minute she saw Donna approach. Her own agenda would have to be put on hold.

'Mr Mackenzie? Welcome to Thistle Inverness.'

Donna had come in from the other side, not from her office at all. But despite being caught by surprise, Maddy had her moment of certainty after all; as soon as Ade had shaken her hand, Donna turned to greet the others at the table, and her face froze as it lit on Maddy's. Her eyes glittered, and she didn't even pretend politeness for form's sake.

'Miss Clifford? How you have the gall to eat at my table I cannot fathom.'

Startled to suddenly be marked down as villain rather than victim, Maddy could only stare at her. A good thing too, with Tas sitting there watching them both with great interest.

'Mr Mackenzie,' Donna said, 'perhaps you'd be so good as to call me during the week? After Monday,' she added, her eyes swivelling to Maddy again. 'We're burying my husband on Monday.'

'Was it you?' Maddy said, almost conversationally. She didn't want to go into specifics in front of Tas, but she could see she didn't have to; Donna smiled tightly, and answered with a question of her own.

'Did it work?'

Maddy goldfished for a moment; she hadn't expected such an easy admission, and had no answer ready. 'How can you justify it?' she said instead, dropping the *faux* friendly tone. 'There's no evidence Gavin did it. And *I* sure as hell didn't, so why—'

'Maddy!' Ade put his hand over hers, and his gaze flicked towards Tas. 'Not here, eh?'

Maddy looked up at Donna and saw a faint flush touch the fair skin of her neck. It gave her pause; perhaps George/Carnegie had acted alone when he'd come to her home, after all. She turned to Tas, somehow finding her smile. 'Get your coat on. We've got to drop Ade's dad back and pick up our own car.'

'But I've not finished my ice cream.'

'*Now*, please.' She stood up, feeling a little better when her height matched Donna's. Some of her calm returned as she took a few deliberate steps away from the table, and Donna followed. They stood in the bay window overlooking the river; it felt almost civilised.

'I don't know how he's going to plead,' Maddy lied quietly, 'but your message was received and understood. Now leave us alone, okay?'

'Look, it was never meant to be so...loud,' Donna said in an equally low voice. 'And for that I'm sorry. But as for evidence, don't fool yourself. It was all there to be found. Your fiancé is a killer, and *my* husband was his victim.'

Maddy steeled herself and looked into her eyes, prepared to deny it once again; she was stunned to see a flicker there just before Donna looked away. What did that mean? Did the woman still even believe it herself? She wanted to say something more, to draw Donna out on what she really thought, but Donna returned to the table, leaving Maddy staring after her in growing astonishment, and a newly kindling hope.

'Your meal is on the house, Mr Mackenzie,' Donna said, her professional smile back in place. 'I do hope you're free next week to discuss the proposition my father put to you?'

Maddy was relieved to see Ade shake the hand Donna proffered; she'd have hated to have ruined what would probably be a lucrative leg up the ladder to the new business. But she resolved to make sure he at least knew what William Kilbride was like, assuming Paul hadn't already given him the lowdown.

As she took Frank's arm to help him with his coat, she saw Donna looking at her with a faint expression of unease, and it added to that sudden flicker of uncertainty that was impossible to ignore. The more Maddy thought about it, the more she realised that Donna must be having second thoughts. Which meant someone else had crept into the frame. But who?

Maddy turned back at the door, in time to see George/Carnegie moving smoothly across the room and engaging Donna in conversation. Donna immediately stepped to the side, and with a jolt Maddy realised she was doing it to distract her companion's attention; she was actually giving Maddy chance to get away unnoticed. Maddy hurried after the others, her heart hammering. *Was* he the one? Because if so he had got away with it once, and he was still clearly bearing a grudge against her.

It was a frightening thought.

Chapter Eighteen

'Hello again.' Mrs Cameron greeted Jamie brightly enough as Ethan brought him into the kitchen, but she looked strained. Another row with Ethan's dad, probably, or Kyle; Ethan had said they rarely stopped these days.

'Dad says it's like living in a family sitcom, only without the com,' he had said, when Jamie had called to ask if it was still okay to visit. 'You can come over for a couple of hours this afternoon though.'

'I don't have to. We can leave it.' Jamie had seized on the excuse; he'd been thinking about it a lot, and the more his imagination gave him to play with, the less he liked the idea of digging up the family dog after all this time. It had been fun to make gurgling, vomit noises in the comfort of Ethan's bedroom, but it was becoming a bit too real now.

Ethan would have none of it, however, so Jamie had appealed to his mum's soft side for a lift over, and here he was. Hoping they'd be forbidden from playing outside, and envying anyone who was sitting in front of the telly this afternoon with slippers on and a plate of crisps.

'Sorry I couldn't offer you a lift either way today,' Mrs Cameron said. 'My car won't be out of the garage until Wednesday.'

'It's no problem,' Jamie said politely. 'Mum dropped me off, and Mackenzie is picking me up.'

'That's the good thing about a Sunday, I suppose. What are you two going to get up to this afternoon?' She was picking through the laundry basket for Ethan's school uniform, and only half paying attention as Ethan fished in the drawer for a pair of heavy-duty scissors.

'Can we go down to the paddock?'

'What on earth for?'

'To collect stuff for the winter garden project at school.' He showed her the scissors. 'We'll need a spade each too.'

Jamie stared at him in part-awe, part-horror; Ethan really had been thinking about this, and had everything prepared. He himself would have been stumped for an answer if someone had thrown the same question at him.

Mrs Cameron squinted out of the window, and for once in his life Jamie prayed for rain but was ignored. 'Okay,' she said. 'Wear wellies though, not your trainers, and get Kyle to unlock the shed so you can get a couple of spades and whatever else you need.'

Ethan shot Jamie a triumphant look and bore him off to his bedroom to lend him his spare boots. Before long they were following Kyle across the yard to the shed, Kyle jingling keys like an old-fashioned jailer leading a couple of death-row convicts to their new forever-home. Jamie was starting to feel as if that were actually the case.

'What do you need?' Kyle asked, fitting one of the keys into the padlock.

Ethan told him, spinning him the same story about the fictitious school project. Jamie had stopped thinking of it as a lie and turned it into a necessary ruse, like on con-artist programmes; it helped him forget about what they were likely to find. He remembered the faint look of revulsion that had crossed Ade's face at dinner the other night, when he had brought up the subject of the hut before being hushed. If even Ade had felt like that, what chance did Jamie have?

He hoped the old paddling pool Mr Cameron had wrapped around the dog would stop it smelling too badly when they uncovered it, but he'd probably only wrapped it loosely...

'I said how about this one?' Ethan nudged him, and he blinked.

'What?' In the meagre light spilling in from outside, he saw his friend was pointing to a large, three-pronged garden fork leaning against the wall. 'I suppose, yeah. Bit big though.'

'The fork will break the ground better than a spade,' Kyle offered, quite helpful for once. 'Depends how much earth you actually want to move. It'll be really soft anyway, 'cos of the rain.'

'Where's the shorter spade that Mum uses?'

Kyle moved towards a collection of tools that lay in a criss-crossed heap in one corner, then stopped abruptly. 'In there somewhere.' He waved vaguely at the pile and stepped back. 'Go on then!' he snapped, losing that brief spell of friendliness. 'Some of us have got better things to do than fanny about in the dark.'

'Scared of spiders!' Ethan teased, and ducked to avoid Kyle's light back-hand. He and Jamie hurriedly started sorting through the tools; it was like a life-sized jack straws game. Jamie pulled at one handle, hoping he'd found the right one, only to reveal a short, hooked blade on the end instead of a spade. 'What good's this to anyone?'

'That's the patio knife,' Ethan said, and shifted it aside. 'Aha!' He tugged a shorter handle free from the rest. 'This is the one.'

He led the way down to the paddock, leaving Kyle to lock the shed behind them, and Jamie trotted in his wake, feeling queasier by the minute. How was Ethan still looking forward to it?

'Are you sure you still want to do this?' he asked, catching his friend up. 'I mean, it was your dog.'

'Kyle's.'

'Well, the family dog,' Jamie persisted. 'Won't it be horrible for you?'

Ethan slowed and looked at him. 'Are you flaking out of it now?'

'No!'

'Well good.'

'I know you didn't like him that much, but still.'

'He was cute enough. But don't you want to *see*?' Ethan's eyes were bright. 'I think I want to be a police pathologist one day, so I've got to get used to this sort of thing.' He looked back towards the house and nodded. 'Right, no-one's coming down after us. Let's get on with it.'

Now that there was no more putting it off, Jamie found he was instead seized with a desire to get it over with. *Stop thinking, just do it...* He went across to where Ethan was now crouching over the little wooden marker his dad had placed in the ground.

Tommy Pickles. Our Faithful Friend. 2007 – 2018.

'What sort of dog was he again?'

'A beagle.'

'Do they live a long time?'

'Aye. To about fifteen... If they don't get hit by a car,' Ethan added.

Jamie wasn't sure he liked that sort of humour, and had begun to have second thoughts about persuading his mum to get a dog after all; it would be awful to think of someone digging up a pet of his just for fun. He felt his chest tightening a bit and checked for his asthma inhaler; he'd carried it in a pouch, together with the spare re-fill, since August. He hoped he wouldn't need it today, but he was glad to feel the bump of it in his coat pocket.

'Come on then,' he said, to cover the nerves that were threatening to let him down at any minute. He'd never live it down at school if Ethan went around telling everyone the famous kidnap boy had been scared to look at a dead dog. 'Let's get to it before someone comes and ruins the fun. Did you get Kyle to give you a lend of his old phone, since he's got a new one?'

'Nope. Mine'll do though. It just won't be great, that's all.'

It was easier than he'd thought it would be, not only to fake ghoulish interest, but also to actually dig through the ground, softened by rain as Kyle had said it would be. He pushed the fork down with his boot, relieved when it went right up to the tops of the tines and didn't strike anything.

He took his time working the fork loose, reluctant to try again too soon, but he needn't have worried; Ethan gave a little exclamation on this first try with the spade, then looked up and gave a little grimace.

'Feels a bit weird. Not soft, and not hard. The plastic's not very thick, I don't think.'

Jamie was certain he'd gone green, but Ethan didn't seem to notice, or at least, he didn't say anything. He himself was looking a bit sick now.

'Look, stop digging, and let's just...scrape,' Jamie suggested.

'What, with our hands?'

'We didn't bring anything small, did we?'

Ethan shook his head. Then he sighed, and Jamie saw him square his shoulders. 'Come on then.'

The boys pulled at the grass that had grown over the little mound. The peaty earth was packed in quite tightly, but it didn't take long before a corner of clear plastic poked up through the mud – Mr Cameron hadn't dug down very far, and it was a good thing Pickles had been wrapped, or the foxes would definitely have got there first.

Jamie looked at Ethan. 'Ready?'

Ethan nodded. Together they dug and pushed the soil out of the way, until they could see almost the entire wrapping. Ethan produced the pair of scissors he'd brought down and prepared to cut away the plastic, but Jamie frowned.

'I thought you said he was wrapped in a paddling pool. What's that?'

Ethan looked down, and shrugged. 'Dunno. There's a label.' He leaned closer and scraped some more mud away. 'Looks like he used the stuff the lawn mower came in, instead. Right,' he brandished the scissors again. 'Let's do it. You hold that bit tight, okay?'

Jamie held his breath, but he knew he couldn't do it for long and braced himself for the smell. But when it came it was worse than he'd ever imagined. He reeled away as Ethan cut through the plastic, and felt his Sunday lunch boiling up through his throat, as unstoppable as a train. Lurching into the bushes he heard a strange sound behind him, but it wasn't Ethan giving in to his own nausea. It was a low cry of mingled alarm and excitement.

'Jamie! *Look* at this!'

'I can't,' Jamie managed, not caring now about what they'd say at school. All he wanted was to be away from here and back home, where everything was normal. 'Just tell me if there are maggots – take a photo if you want, and then shove it all back.'

'No, I mean this…' There was the sound of scrabbling, and then Ethan was beside him, not even making fun of the way Jamie had to spit and wipe his mouth. Jamie looked down, and suddenly the smell was nowhere. Not on his mind, or up his nose, or even in his memory.

All there was, in the whole world, was the gun balanced between Ethan's earth-smeared hands.

Kilbride watched his daughter getting steadily more drunk and wished there was something he could say. His ex-wife was still hanging around after dropping Chelsea and Myles back, and he wished she'd leave; he'd dropped enough hints about the long way back, especially in the dark, but she just kept saying she wanted to be sure the children were well prepared for the funeral tomorrow. Perhaps she was angling for an invitation to stay? He dismissed that thought immediately it popped into his head; Barbara had made no secret of her feelings for her daughter's husband.

'Are you sure you're going to be all right?' she asked Donna, for the hundredth time.

'Quite sure. Thanks again for having them.' Even Donna was becoming less subtle in her hints now.

Barbara turned to Kilbride. 'Are you and Martha staying over tonight?'

He nodded. 'You needn't worry. The kids will be fine.'

'They'd have been fine anyway,' Donna fired at him. She

slammed her empty glass down. 'For God's sake, I don't need the pair of you hovering over me as if you can't trust me to get dressed in the morning!'

That achieved what Kilbride had so far been unable to, and Barbara rose to pick up her coat. 'That's me told.'

'Mum—'

'No, you're quite right. You have your father here – that's all you've ever wanted.'

'Here we go again,' Kilbride murmured, and Donna made a small derisive sound.

'He's the problem.'

Everyone stared at her, and Kilbride felt his heart slip. 'What are you talking about? What have *I* done?'

Chelsea and Myles exchanged quick, nervous glances, and Martha looked deeply uneasy and made a move towards the door in her usual discreet way. At least Kilbride had assumed it was discretion, but Donna called out to her and killed that notion.

'Tell them what you told me, Martha,' she said, in a voice that cut through the room. 'Go on.'

'Go upstairs, children,' Barbara said, looking from Kilbride to Donna. 'It's time you got ready for bed. It'll be a long and difficult day tomorrow.'

'But we've only just—'

'Quickly now.'

They went, but the mention of what was to come tomorrow seemed to have taken the wind out of Donna's sails. She subsided against the huge cushions of her chair as if she wanted to sink back into them and disappear forever. Kilbride's heartbeat settled a little, but a glance at Martha told him she was only too aware that it was a temporary reprieve. What could she possibly think she knew that would have hurt Donna like that?

'Can I talk to you a minute?' he asked, his voice calm.

'Later,' she said with unusual firmness, and, lacking the ability to seize her arm and pull her from the room, he had to be content with that.

Barbara seemed to realise nothing was going to come of this unexpected little mini-drama after all, and slipped her coat on at last. She kissed Donna's forehead, and murmured something quiet that Kilbride couldn't hear, no doubt something about staying strong for the children, and that she was always there to talk to. About three hours away, of course, while he and Martha could be with Donna in under half an hour on a bad traffic day, but whatever kept her conscience clear.

When she had at last driven away, Kilbride turned to Martha. 'Now what the hell was all that about?'

'Craig,' Martha said bluntly. 'And the way he was ripping you off.'

Kilbride didn't speak for a moment. The manner in which she just came straight out with the accusation, without trying once more to leave the room, was just as startling as the words themselves. He looked at Donna.

'And you believe that?'

'Of course she does,' Martha snapped, 'because it's true. Isn't it?'

Kilbride hesitated, then saw no sense in maintaining the pretence. 'Yes, it's true. Did you know, Donna?'

'Not until recently.' Donna pushed herself to her feet and went to get another bottle. Kilbride frowned; she'd end up hungover at the funeral if she wasn't careful, but there was no point trying to stop her.

'How did *you* find out?' he asked Martha.

'Ian. How else?'

Kilbride's mind raced; he'd had no idea Ian had even been aware of what was going on. Was it tit for tat then? Craig had told Kilbride about Ian and his brother, so Ian had to spill the beans about Craig? 'How long has he known?' he asked.

'Not long.'

'Not long as in, before last Thursday?' Donna said tightly. She faced Kilbride. 'Is that why, Dad?'

Kilbride felt his eyes widen at the shock of the accusation. 'Do you mean you think I'd have had Craig *killed* because of it?'

'You've got form,' she pointed out, and he saw her eyes were glittering now, but not with tears. He'd never seen her so angry. 'You've been known to order some pretty severe punishments.'

'Never a death!'

'And you honestly think no-one did die? Ever?'

'I'd have known about it if they had.'

'Would you though, if it was years later? A suicide due to nerves, or remorse, or...or the inability to see any other way out of crushing debt caused by *you*?'

'For Christ's sake, Donna—'

'*Did you have Craig killed?*' Her voice rose to a shout, and Kilbride saw Martha's eyes go to the door, automatically checking the words wouldn't have reached his grandchildren.

'No I did not!'

They faced each other, breathing hard, Donna towering over Kilbride, who had rarely felt as vulnerable as he did right now. He honestly believed, for the first time, that if she'd had a weapon to hand she'd have used it. He felt the press of his own small handgun, in the pocket of his chair, and swallowed, hoping she didn't know about it. What had happened here?

This was his little girl, looking at him as if she wouldn't think twice about putting a bullet in his head.

'Donna,' he said, more gently, 'I swear to you I didn't do it. I wouldn't do that to you, or to the children.'

'And could Ian have taken it on himself to do it anyway, without your orders?' She didn't say she'd accepted his word, but she moved back to her chair, which was a start. 'If he'd discovered Craig was doing exactly the same thing you'd had *him* punished for, but getting away with it?'

Kilbride shook his head. 'You seriously think Ian came up here sometime last week, found out that Craig was due at Three Sisters that night, lay in wait for him and beat him to death? Then made his official appearance days later?'

Donna looked troubled now. 'I don't know. You can't say for sure he didn't.'

'How would he have known about the Excel sheet? That there were hidden columns?'

'I told you, it doesn't take a genius. And,' she added, shooting a look at her stepmother, 'Martha could easily have let him in and shown him your laptop.'

'I did no such thing.' Martha glared at Donna, then turned to Kilbride. 'You're not going to believe that, are you?'

'Why not?' he said heavily. 'You let Donna into my office without telling me.'

'That was different. I wanted to help her find out who was responsible.'

'And you did. Gavin Galbraith is behind bars. Or at least secure,' he added. 'Ian's pals went overboard there, yes. But he didn't do it himself, did he? And he's not a killer.' Kilbride paused, then turned to his wife. 'What did you hope to achieve by telling Donna about what Craig had been doing?'

She avoided his gaze. 'I thought she ought to know.'

'No. You *wanted* me to accuse him,' Donna said, in wondering tones. 'You came here on Friday, specifically to fire me up!'

'I didn't—'

'It was all you talked about.' Donna rose again, and stood face to face with Martha the way she had with Ian: up close, her hands clenched so tightly that her knuckles looked about to break through the skin. 'You said you were just seeing how I was getting on – you sowed the seed, in your usual mild, fluffy little manner, and then you just *left*!' As she spoke the final word she shoved Martha hard in the shoulder, sending the shorter woman stumbling back against the fireplace.

Martha cried out and grabbed at the mantelpiece, but missed, and Kilbride jerked in horror as she went down, striking her upper back on the marble surround. Her head connected with the hearth, but not hard, and she rolled groggily to her knees and twisted to look up at Donna, who was watching her impassively.

'I'll do you for assault,' she gasped. 'You could have killed me!'

'No such luck.' Donna walked away and opened the bottle she'd picked up earlier. 'Why did you want me to blame Dad?'

'It's the gift she felt she'd earned, isn't it, Martha?' Kilbride watched his wife climbing to her feet, wincing, and felt the coldness of realisation spreading through him. 'You've been waiting for something to come between us.'

'Don't be stupid! I've been taking care of you for years.'

'Exactly. You made sure you were there at the very start, didn't you? Ever since the night *this* happened.' He struck the arms of his wheelchair. 'And you've done pretty well out of it too. So,' he said curiously, 'what's changed?'

Donna gulped at her wine and gave him a wintry smile.

'I'm guessing it's because if you go down for Craig's murder, or conspiracy at least, all your business interests would pass to her. Including your lucrative little side deals.'

Martha made her stiff way over to the sofa. 'I wouldn't know the first thing about how to run such deals.'

'No, but Ian would,' Donna pointed out. 'And as Dad's recognised "assistant" he's already got his foot in the door.'

'Bloody hell!' Kilbride sat up straight, remembering. 'The night he turned up at my place... You'd decided to stay the night with Donna. I thought it was weird, but quite nice of you.'

'I was worried for her!'

'And Ian asked if you were around, knowing damned well you weren't.' Kilbride groaned. 'You set it all up between you, didn't you? Arranged to be out so I was alone, and he pretended I was under threat from someone else...' He shook his head. 'Well you won't get Donna to believe I could have had Craig killed. I needed him – she knows that. And yes, he tried to screw me over, but we'd sorted it out.'

'Like you *sorted Ian out*?' Martha shot back, surprising them both. 'We might not be close relations by blood, but we're still family!'

'I still think he could have been the one,' Donna said in a curiously flat voice. Kilbride looked at her; she was staring at a fixed point on the curtain, and the glass in her hand was tilting slightly, dribbling red wine on her trouser leg, unheeded. 'As soon as Craig is decently buried, I'm going to prove it.' She looked at Kilbride then, with unfocused eyes. 'And if you don't help me, I'll know it was by your orders after all. And then I'll kill you.'

Chapter Nineteen

MACKENZIE ROLLED UP TO THE CAMERONS' place at Wester Dean just before the appointed time, and was surprised to see Jamie already waiting. Ethan was standing with him, and both boys looked as if they'd had one massive humdinger of a row.

'You can wait in the car if you like,' Mackenzie said, eyeing Jamie curiously. 'I just want a quick word with Ethan's dad.'

Jamie glanced at his friend. 'Nothing to do with me.'

Ethan nodded. 'See you tomorrow then.'

Jamie hesitated. 'I'll fix it,' he said in a low voice. 'Don't worry.' With a furtive glance at Mackenzie he hurried across the yard and climbed into the front seat of the waiting car.

Mackenzie followed Ethan down the short passage and into the kitchen, where Justine Cameron was now ironing school shirts for the week ahead. A quick pang came and went as she looked up, her ponytail bobbing, and he was reminded of Kath doing exactly the same thing for Josh. She gave him a bright smile.

'Paul! Nice to see you.'

'You too.'

'Can I get you a cuppa?'

He shook his head. 'No, thanks. I just wondered if Ben was around?'

'Aye, in the sitting room with a catalogue and a marker pen.' She saw his raised eyebrows and grinned. 'He's spotted some nifty new stone cutting tool or other, and Christmas is coming.'

'Ah.' Mackenzie smiled back. 'Okay if I go in?'

'Of course.' She slipped the shirt onto a hanger, and showed him back out into the hall. 'I hear Ade's back in town. For good?'

'We think so.' Mackenzie gave her a sideways look. 'Don't tell me you're one of the ones who fell at his feet at school?'

'Och, he was too old for me.' She laughed over her shoulder at him. 'Tasty though – we all thought so.'

'Well he's about ninety now, and looks like Worzel Gummidge,' Mackenzie assured her. 'Can't string an interesting sentence together, and picks his nose with a pencil.'

Justine grinned and pushed open the sitting room door. 'Ben? A visitor for you.' She stepped back to let Mackenzie through, and dug him in the ribs as she turned to go back to the kitchen. 'You're a bloody horrible brother, and I'll tell him so when I see him.'

Ben looked up in surprise to see Mackenzie; he put the catalogue he'd been reading to one side and gestured to the armchair opposite. 'How can I help? Jamie's okay, isn't he?'

'Aye, fine.' Now he was here, he wasn't sure how to start. The door was closed again, but he lowered his voice anyway, just in case. 'I just wanted to let you in on some information, while I was here.' He could never tell Ben that he knew who'd killed his father, but this was the next best thing.

'Information?' Ben's open, good-natured face clouded a little. 'About what?'

'First off, I should say that I know about your part in what happened in August. You making the fake figurines for Bradley and Mulholland to sell on to Sarah Wallace.'

Ben frowned. 'Are you talking to me as a PI?'

'No, just as someone who knows you were put in an impossible situation. I also know that Sarah was a good friend of yours from way back.'

Ben went very still. His eyes remained steady on Mackenzie's, but Mackenzie was an excellent reader of expressions, and he could see the tightness in Ben's jaw and a tiny muscle flickering there. He kept his own voice even and low.

'You'll have heard that the body we found, up at Glenlowrie, is Mulholland?'

Ben nodded, and looked away. 'Can't pretend to be sad he's gone. Like you said, Sarah was a good friend. I know your friends would have been telling the truth when they said Mulholland killed her, even if they can't prove it.'

'It's tough when you know they're not getting justice.' Mackenzie hesitated again. 'Look, I don't know if the police know about your friendship with Sarah, but I wanted to give you the heads-up that they're probably going to want to talk to you. They've already questioned me, and Maddy too.'

Ben's mouth tightened. 'You're probably right. No stone unturned when it's a copper, aye? Different when it's only some ex-pat who came back to claim her inheritance.'

Mackenzie closed his lips against the retort that this was a woman who had ordered a ten-year-old child to be snatched and held captive in the mountains; to Ben she was just an old friend who'd been swindled, and he probably wouldn't want to believe anything else about her. No doubt he already felt guilty as hell, knowing his craftsmanship had been part of the attempt to sting her out of thousands.

'Anyway,' he said, standing up, 'I just thought it was the right thing to do, to let you know. And to tell you that none of us has said anything about the reason you were involved, so if they have that information, they didn't get it from us. But on the off chance they don't, best keep it zipped.'

Ben nodded. 'Thanks. How did he die?' he asked, rising to show Mackenzie to the door.

'No idea. Maddy's brother's on the investigation though, so as soon as I hear anything I'll let you know.'

'Thanks.' Ben cleared his throat. 'And thanks for keeping quiet about me being involved in Bradley's scheme.'

'You were handed a raw deal, having to help defraud your friend.' Mackenzie stepped out into the hall. 'And thanks for having Jamie over,' he added, at normal volume. 'Give my best to Justine.'

'Aye, will do. She's forever reminiscing about her school days.' A smile broke through the sombre expression. 'Must have hit that age, eh?'

Mackenzie smiled back. 'We all get there. See you later.'

Behind the wheel of his car, he snapped his seat belt into place and looked at Jamie. 'Ready?'

'Are we going to yours or ours?'

'Your mum's still at mine, yakking away to my brother, so she'll take you home from there.' He paused before putting the car into gear. 'Are you sure you're okay?'

'Fine.'

'No more arguments between Ethan and his brother?' He saw Jamie's startled look. 'Your mum told me,' he explained, moving out of the yard. 'Big brothers are the worst.'

Jamie didn't laugh, as expected, and Mackenzie didn't like

the troubled look on his face, but if the lad needed to think about something, best let him work through it. He'd tell them when he was ready.

They drove the rest of the way in silence, and he was glad to see Maddy's car parked outside his house when they arrived. He'd wanted to talk to her when they got back from Helensburgh yesterday, but she'd been out, and Charis's snippet about Kilbride and his son-in-law needed some looking into. Charis might already have told her, which would save time.

She had. The four of them were in the sitting room, where Tas was lying on the floor, poking at what looked suspiciously like a snail, and Charis looked in no rush to get home. So, while a still-quiet Jamie went off to get himself a packet of crisps, Mackenzie sat down and listened as Maddy told him what had happened at Thistle yesterday. Ade had explained last night about the run out to Glenlowrie with their father, and about the proposal from Kilbride, but it was a shock to learn that Maddy had seen the man she believed must have been her attacker, swanning about the restaurant as bold as you like, and hob-nobbing with Kilbride's daughter.

'I'm sure she suspects him, no matter what she said to me,' Maddy said. 'So if we can get the police to investigate him properly, Gavin at least has a chance.'

She'd said no more about the state of her relationship, after her throwaway comment at her dad's on Thursday, and he hadn't asked. Just like Jamie, she would tell him when she was ready.

'So what about what Chelsea said?' Charis wanted to know. 'About the argument, and Lumsden screwing Kilbride over? Do you think Kilbride got this George bloke to do it for him?'

'It's possible,' Mackenzie said. 'If we can move the suspicion onto him, and get them both off the streets while they investigate, it'll be a start.'

Jamie had slipped back in, and now sat next to his mother. Predictably, she pinched one of his crisps, but Mackenzie noticed he didn't roll his eyes or try and take it back, as he usually did, and Charis replaced it without comment, giving him a troubled look.

'I told Ben Cameron about the Mulholland thing,' he said. 'Just that the police might want—'

'Oh!' Maddy sat up straight. 'That was it. I knew there was something else I wanted to tell you – I was all caught up in the Lumsden thing and forgot.'

'Forgot what?'

'Nick was telling me, they know how Mulholland died.'

Jamie dropped his crisps and, white-faced, snatched them back up again. His mother frowned. 'I don't know that this is a conversation for right now,' she said. 'Maybe later.'

'I want to know,' Jamie said. 'Was he shot?'

Maddy waited for Charis's reluctant shrug and went on, 'No, he wasn't. He had a deep cut in his leg.'

'A *cut*?' Charis looked baffled. 'That's it?'

'In the thigh though. The femoral artery was severed.'

Mackenzie watched Jamie's face regain its colour, and saw the shoulders slump a little. 'So it might have been an accident?' he said, feeling unease creeping over him, nevertheless.

'Well the death itself was probably an accident, but the wound was...' Maddy stopped at Charis's tiny shake of the head. 'Never mind. Later.'

'Jamie,' Mackenzie said quietly, 'is there anything you want to tell us?'

The boy raised his head very slowly and looked at him, then at his mother. He shook his head.

'Maddy, Ade,' Mackenzie said, 'can you take Tas and show him the caravan or something?'

'Good idea,' Ade said cheerfully. 'I'm getting good at these guided tours now. I'm thinking of buying a mic.'

They left, though clearly burning with curiosity, and when it was just the three of them Mackenzie sat forward and looked into Jamie's frightened eyes.

'Come on, lad. We've been through enough together for you to know you can trust me.'

Charis put her arm around her son's shoulders and rubbed his arm gently. 'It's all right, Jay. You can tell us anything.'

Jamie carefully put down his crisps and stood up. He went across to where he'd left his coat lying across the back of the only unoccupied chair, and slipped his hand into the pocket. When he withdrew it again Mackenzie felt as if someone had socked him a good solid one in the pit of the stomach. For a moment he couldn't breathe, then he held out his hand.

'Give it to me, lad,' he managed. He looked at Charis to see the same stunned, horrified look on her face, and she only drew breath herself when the gun had safely transferred to Mackenzie's hand. He looked it over carefully; it was pretty old, by the looks of it. Not that he was an expert, but at the same time he recognised that it wasn't a recent model.

He turned away from Charis and Jamie, and ejected the magazine, the clunk sounding ridiculously loud in the hushed room. It was empty. He checked the chamber, then turned back. 'It's safe,' he said, and his voice shook a tiny bit as relief set in. 'Where did you find it?'

'Buried in the ground, with Ethan's pet dog.'

Mackenzie and Charis looked at one another; there were too many questions about that, but some more important than others.

'Who buried the dog?' Charis asked.

'Ethan's dad.' Jamie looked at them in turn. 'But the copper wasn't shot, so it can't have been him, can it?'

'No,' Mackenzie said. 'This isn't what killed him. But...' He looked at Charis. 'Didn't you say Mulholland had Sarah's gun when he ran away from the cottage?'

She nodded. 'She dropped it when she was hit, and he picked it up later. It does look a bit like the same kind too. Not one of the newer type, like Maddy's.'

'So if this *was* Sarah's, it means Mulholland was at the Camerons' place at some point.' Mackenzie thought back over his brief talk with Ben. The man had given nothing away, if that was true.

Charis looked at Jamie. 'You'd better tell us what was going on, and why you're the one who ended up with that thing.'

'Ethan was too scared to keep it. He wanted to bury it again, but I thought someone should know.'

'You did right,' Mackenzie said, 'but God, Jamie! This could have... It might have been...' He couldn't finish, so awful was the idea. 'What did you tell Ethan you were going to do with it?'

'I said I'd give it to you.'

'So why didn't you, straight away?' Charis asked gently.

'I wanted to wait until we were on our own.'

'And what would you have done if Maddy had said the copper *had* been shot?'

Jamie shrugged. 'I don't know. I like Ethan's dad, but he's always cross now. Ethan says it's only since the dog died.'

'And when was that?'

'When they were at their cousins' place.'

Mackenzie saw Charis take a short breath and try again. 'When in the year, Jay?'

'Oh. Um, in the summer. Just before they went back to school.' He looked at Mackenzie, who had slipped the gun into his own jacket pocket. 'What are you going to do with it?'

'Well,' Mackenzie looked at Charis, 'it should be turned in, but probably not by me, and since it didn't kill anyone I can hang onto it until all this has died down. The last thing we want right now is to draw more suspicion.'

'It's quite the coincidence,' Charis mused, 'Sarah and Ben being such good mates, and her gun ending up in his garden.'

'Do you think...' Mackenzie felt a slight chill as the thought occurred to him. 'Do you think he and Mulholland were actually working together by that time? They both hated Bradley after all.'

'It's possible.' Charis held out her hand to Jamie and brought him down to sit beside her again. 'Get the others back in, eh? I could do with something lighter to talk about, and it looks to me as if your brother's got a bit of a thing for the flame-haired beauty.'

'He does have a type,' Jamie said, and when Charis and Mackenzie looked at him in surprise, he shrugged, and a little smile finally touched his pale features. 'He said so, didn't he? Sarah Wallace was his type, and remember how I thought she was Maddy once?'

'The lad's got a point,' Mackenzie said, and he ruffled Jamie's hair on his way to the door. His own smile had returned, and he was glad to see Charis looking less shell-shocked than she had been a few minutes ago.

He still felt ill at the thought of the gun going off by accident, if Ben hadn't thought to empty it first. But burying it with a *dog*? He could only assume it had been used to kill the poor thing, perhaps after it had been hit by the car and was suffering. But was it a coincidence that this had all happened at the same time as Mulholland had been at Wester Dean, and could provide the gun, or was it all connected in another way? Perhaps Mulholland had been the one behind the wheel, and that was why Ben had been so jumpy ever since.

Distracted by Ade's lively conversation as they came back in, he was able to put it from his mind for a while. Tas resumed his place on the floor beneath the window, prodding at the snail, and talk moved on to other things; notably Christmas, then Charis's first Hogmanay, and Ade's plans for the *Drumnacoille 25*. After a rare, pleasant interlude without mention of either recent murder, Charis told Jamie to fetch his coat. 'School tomorrow,' she reminded him, 'and I've not ironed your stuff yet.'

Maddy groaned. 'Nor have I. Good thing mine's still wearing polo shirts – they hide a multitude of sins. Come on, Tas. Pick up Speedy Gonzales there, and let's make a move back.'

'I'll find a snail too, next weekend,' Jamie said, 'and we can have races if you like.'

'Races?' Tas said doubtfully.

'It's a thing,' Maddy assured him, and smiled at Jamie. 'Good idea.'

Tas lifted the snail from the floor, and then fished in his pocket and pulled out a rather muddy object that Mackenzie managed to identify as a gardening glove.

'What've you got that for?'

'It's for Chase.'

'Who?'

'Paw Patrol,' Maddy supplied. 'The snail's *actual* name is Chase, apparently, not Speedy Gonzales.'

'But why the glove?'

'He was on it when I found him.' Tas placed the snail back

on the crusted, half-curled palm of the glove. 'I didn't want him to get squished. And he likes it.'

Maddy stopped, and her face took on a strange expression. 'I thought you'd picked the glove up from the back of Ade's jeep. You're saying it was on the path by the sh...by the river?'

'Aye. You kept saying it was a stone, but I *told* you it wasn't.'

Mackenzie saw what she was getting at. 'How near the river?'

'Close enough for the smell to make us turn back,' Maddy said. 'Tas, give it to me please.'

'It's Chase's!'

'No, love, it belongs to someone else,' Maddy said patiently. 'We'll get another one for Chase, okay?'

Mackenzie went through to the kitchen, and rummaged for a freezer bag which he handed to Maddy. She dropped the glove into it and pressed the seal shut. 'I'll give it to Nick.'

'No, best hand it in properly,' Mackenzie said. 'We don't want any accusations of tampering. Just take it in tonight, and tell them where you found it, and when.'

Maddy nodded. And just like that the heaviness of two deaths came back down onto the little group, and thoughts of Christmas and parties, snail races and romantic possibilities, were once again buried beneath it.

Chapter Twenty

DONNA STEPPED OUTSIDE, leaving the revolting mixture of laughter and condolences behind. Laughing at a funeral wake was probably more affectionate than careless, in most cases; people remembered the good times they'd shared with the deceased, and swapped stories that somehow kept that person alive a little while longer. Perhaps it was even necessary, in order to make it through the ordeal emotionally intact. But it felt utterly disrespectful to her, personally, and she knew it showed. She'd always been painfully aware of how people had seen the Lumsdens' relationship from the outside, and her calm, business-like exterior had done her no favours today.

But the veneer was slipping, and no-one noticed as she took herself out through the French window and stood, coatless, in the shelter of a towering beech tree. The kids were the stars of the show today, the ones to be comforted and jollied along; she was just a bystander. The one who'd no doubt be on the prowl for another Craig to keep her in the style to which she'd become accustomed, as the saying went. Most of them had no idea she'd been the one to buy the house, that the kids went to private school on her wages, and that it was her business that had kept Craig in BMWs and golf club membership. Even his own family, few though they were, had conveniently forgotten that.

She glanced back through the window to see her father, head to head with Ian George, who was sitting in Craig's favourite chair and leaning forward intently to catch every word. Her lips tightened and she remembered last night's discussion; despite his promises, it didn't seem likely that her father was going to do anything to uncover the truth of what had happened to Craig. Right from the start she'd been the one to do that; he'd merely supplied the muscle... And look what a pig's ear that had turned out to be.

She chewed at her lip as another unwelcome thought crept in, to sit alongside the multitude that were making her wine headache even worse: what if Ian had contacted her father after she'd spoken to him, and been given a different instruction? Putting Galbraith out of the way while he was still in the frame for Craig's murder would definitely benefit whoever had actually done it. Or orchestrated it. That Ian had gone rogue on his brief with the Clifford woman was under no doubt, and she knew now why he had done it. It was personal with him. But the treatment of Galbraith had been so extreme, and contrary to her own instructions, that it was unlikely he'd have taken that on himself.

Donna dug into her pocket for her phone and did a quick search: *mckenzie & clifford PI abergarry*. There it was: Clifford-Mackenzie. She saved the number to her phone book, for now, and went back indoors where her father had finally noted her absence and was starting to look around for her.

'I just had to get a bit of air,' she said, taking the seat Ian had vacated. 'Why do people put on so much perfume for funerals?'

'How are you bearing up?' he asked. 'Martha was concerned.'

'Like hell she was. She's got a nerve even coming here today. Has she moved out yet?'

'It's not that simple.'

'I'll bet.' His realisation act last night, if it really had been an act, had been pretty impressive, but Donna was finding it all just a bit too neat. She checked that no-one was heading their way, and lowered her voice. 'So what are you going to do, to figure out if Ian killed Craig?'

'Now isn't the time, love,' he said, equally quietly. 'Let's just get all this out of the way first.'

All this? 'And then what?'

'I'll talk to him,' he promised.

'Not good enough.'

'What are you expecting?'

'Get him to confess,' Donna said bluntly. 'Somewhere I can hear him.'

'He's hardly going to do that, is he?'

'He is if he already knows you know about it.'

'That *I* know about...' Her father closed his eyes for a moment. 'I told you, I had nothing to do with it. And anyway, even if he does confess, and you're a witness to it, what could you do? It's not evidence, and there's no way he'd repeat it to the police.'

'Record it.'

'Inadmissible. All it would get you is the satisfaction of knowing you were right.'

Donna sat back, tapping her fingers on the arms of the chair. 'That might be enough.'

'For what?' His face darkened as she didn't respond. 'Donna, no... Don't even think about it. Your kids need you around, not doing thirty years in Cornton Vale.'

'Oh, that won't happen.' She gave him a thin smile. 'Word is that place'll be closed in a couple of years.'

'Don't be flippant,' he snapped. Then he subsided. 'All right, I'll do what I can.'

'Even if it means throwing yourself into the spotlight?'

'I've got nothing to hide.'

She almost laughed aloud at that; only the thought that she'd be adding to the already obscene level of good cheer in the room stopped her. 'Okay, we'll see. In the meantime I'm sure you'll understand if I crack on with my own investigations.'

'What investigations?'

Donna stood up. 'If you'll excuse me, I ought to mingle before everyone decides they've respected my husband enough for one day.'

It was almost four by the time she and the children had the house to themselves again. The final guests trickled out, and Donna's father and a subdued and defensive-looking Martha left soon afterwards. Donna sent the children up to change out of their stiff, uncomfortable formal clothes, and took out her phone.

'Clifford-Mackenzie. Mackenzie speaking.' The voice was low pitched and pleasant-sounding. Professionally welcoming.

Donna pushed the sitting room door closed, cutting off Myles's voice as he complained loudly to his sister about something. 'Mr Mackenzie, I wonder if it'd be possible to speak to you face to face, today?'

'Of course. The office is open until—'

'I'm sorry, I can't leave the house. I have children. It's quite urgent though.'

'I see. Where are you?'

She told him, and the silence down the phone stretched a little. 'That's well over an hour's drive,' he said at length. 'Can you give me an idea of the type of work you want doing?'

'Well I'm not looking for a lost cat!' She took a quick breath. 'I'm sorry, but my husband was murdered. I think I know who did it, and I want you to help me prove it.'

'Surely the police—'

'The police already think they have the right man. Look, Mr Mackenzie,' she said in a steadier voice, 'I know you'll want to help, because you have an interest in this.'

There was another pause, then, 'Am I talking to Mrs Lumsden?'

'You are.'

'Give me your address.'

Donna gave it, then sat down in Craig's armchair – she felt as if she'd been running on fumes since the murder. Her moment of relief was short lived, however, as the kids came down for their tea, and she was obliged to ransack the buffet leftovers and cobble together something reasonably nutritious. They were finishing up at the table when the doorbell rang.

'Stay in here, you two,' Donna said, her heart speeding up. 'I've got a business meeting.'

'Today?' Chelsea looked at her disapprovingly. She looked too much like her grandfather for Donna's liking, at that moment.

'Yes, today,' she said patiently. 'It's still a work day for most people.'

'It was Daddy's *funeral!*' Chelsea scraped back her chair and left the room, abandoning the remainder of her meal. 'Don't you ever stop?' she cried back over her shoulder, as she ran up the stairs.

'I'll stop when *you* stop demanding I buy you the latest bloody iPhone!' Donna yelled back. She felt a twinge of guilt, but today really wasn't the day for tantrums. Myles went up after his sister, also leaving his meal on the table, and Donna sighed and went to open the door.

She wasn't sure what she was expecting; perhaps she'd seen too many 'rumpled PI, one-week-off-retirement' things on TV; morose, bags under the eyes and a drink problem. But Paul Mackenzie was only late thirties, she guessed – maybe forty at a push, at least six-three and broadly built. Best of all he looked as if he'd be pretty handy in a scuffle, which was encouraging; Ian George wasn't known for his wordy approach any more than Craig had been.

Mackenzie's dark eyebrows were already drawn in against the bright light of the hallway as it fell across his stern, unsmiling face, but he had surprisingly kind eyes. After a day when most people had briefly pressed her hand, murmured a polite condolence and then hurried on to embrace the children, that visible kindness almost sent her into a spiral of renewed grief.

'Come in,' she mumbled, wiping at her own eyes and turning away quickly. She led the way into the sitting room and sat down, gesturing for him to do the same. 'Thank you for coming all this way at this time of day. Can I get you a drink? Tea? Coffee?'

He shook his head. 'Mrs Lumsden, you said you thought you knew who had killed your husband?'

'I do. And, as I said, I know it's in your interest to help me prove it.' She took a deep breath and plunged in, knowing what his first comment would be as soon as she reached the relevant part of her story. She was right; his expression abruptly lost its kindness, and the eyes turned harder than she'd have thought possible.

'You're admitting that you had Gavin Galbraith almost killed, and that you had my...my partner attacked in her own home?'

'No!' Donna shook her head. 'I never meant for any of that... Well.' She tried again. 'Look, Galbraith had to be made clear about his plea, and yes, I told Ian to make sure Miss Clifford was warned too, but he wasn't supposed to harm her, or even frighten her. He was supposed to hang around at her house until he heard that everything had gone to plan with Galbraith, then to knock on her door and deliver a, a *verbal* message.'

'A verbal message.' His voice was flat. Disbelieving.

'Yes! Which was that she should make sure he knew the reason for it. To convince him it was the only sensible thing. And I wanted her to know that we knew where she lived.'

That steel had come back into his face again; she felt the first real tremor of nerves and wondered if she'd made a dreadful mistake. 'I never wanted, or told him, to enter her house,' she said, 'never mind tie her up. I told her as much when I saw her on Saturday.'

'So you do know what he did? The cut on her arm, the sack over her face... Not forgetting the way he threatened her son. You've seen the little lad, Mrs Lumsden – he's five years old. *Five.*'

She flinched. 'I didn't realise he'd done that. I didn't know the details. I'm so sorry, Mr Mackenzie, but all that came from him.'

He sat back, his eyes still locked on hers. 'Why though? Why would he risk going back inside if he'd only just got out?'

Donna spoke heavily. 'Because he'd seen her at the prison, with Galbraith. He recognised her as the person my father had hired to find out where Ian had disappeared to, after he'd been caught with his fingers in the till. Her information led to him being dragged back from his second life, and he and his brother arrested. His brother was convicted. She cost him a lot, Mr Mackenzie; he's badly scarred, and has had to resort to all kinds of subterfuge to get his job back.'

She couldn't believe she was defending the bastard, but it was important for Mackenzie to understand how much of what had happened had been Ian's own doing, not hers or her father's. Mackenzie's face was stony again, but she detected a note of exasperated despair about him as he rubbed his hands over his eyes.

'So how do you propose I go about proving what you think you know?'

This was going to be the hardest bit, and Donna wasn't even sure she wanted to pursue it now. He didn't rush her, but she was aware that the silence was becoming uncomfortably long, and finally blurted it out.

'I think it's possible he and my dad might have been in it together.'

'Your dad?'

But he didn't sound as surprised as she'd expected, and she looked at him with narrowed eyes. He shrugged. 'I did hear he and Mr Lumsden had got into a bit of a row recently. Tempers running high.'

'Where did you hear that?'

The door opened. 'From me.'

Donna swivelled to see her daughter standing there. 'I told the lady who was with him,' she gestured at Mackenzie, 'when they came to talk to Granny Kilbride. She wanted to know how *I* was feeling,' she went on in a rush, tears standing in her eyes. 'Which *you* never did!'

Speechless, Donna looked back at Mackenzie, who hadn't moved, and didn't look about to defend himself. 'You went to my *mother's?*'

'Your daughter is crying, Mrs Lumsden,' he said, quietly but pointedly. 'We can discuss this when she's feeling a little better, aye?'

'Don't you dare go anywhere,' she snapped at him, rising to usher Chelsea from the room. Chelsea took the stairs two at a time, and Donna hurried after her. 'Why were you snooping at the door?'

'Because I wanted to see what business was so important, so I looked out of the window and recognised him. He came to talk to Granny on Saturday. We weren't allowed in the room then, either,' she went on. 'Why did you say you thought Grandad had Daddy killed?'

'I don't, I didn't...' Donna shook her head as she half-closed the bedroom door. 'I'll talk to you later. I promise,' she added, seeing her daughter's set face. 'I have to talk to Mr Mackenzie first.'

Back downstairs she didn't return to her seat; she felt more in control standing up, though Mackenzie remained seated, unfazed by the revelation Chelsea had just made. He was flicking idly through his phone, but slipped it into his pocket when she came back in, and waited for her to speak. The fact she had had to find out from Chelsea, of all people, that he had already been investigating her, kindled her annoyance.

'What were you talking to my mother about?' she demanded, going over to close the curtains.

'You. And Craig.'

Donna hadn't expected such candour, and she couldn't think of anything to say for a moment. 'Why?' she managed at length. 'Who asked you to do that?'

'I'd have thought it was obvious,' Mackenzie said. 'Maddy's fiancé is in hospital, thanks to being attacked in a prison he shouldn't even be in. We were bound to try and clear his name, don't you think? But we needed to know a bit more about the two of you. And your relationship.'

She'd thought her capacity for astonishment all used up, but here she was again, incredulous. 'You think *I* arranged Craig's murder?'

'You have to admit, it's something we had to consider. Craig might have been seeing someone else, or even leading a double life. There was every chance revenge was a motive, given the nature of the killing. But no,' he went on more quietly, perhaps seeing on her face some of the pain she felt. 'Having met you, and after speaking to your mother, we don't think that any more. Barbara was pretty clear on *her* feelings about Craig, but she made it equally clear how much you loved him.' He looked up at her, curious now. 'Why were you so convinced it was Gavin?'

'What difference does that make? I was, and now I'm not. That's all.'

'No, now you're just as firmly convinced it was someone else. And what was that about your father?'

'I'm hoping you'll prove me wrong there.' Donna sighed.

'I've just... I've got a lot of messy thoughts going around in my head, and they keep pointing in the same direction.'

Mackenzie nodded. 'Right. And what happens if I prove you wrong about this Ian George character too? Will you go back to pointing the finger at yet another innocent man? Ruin more lives?'

'I have no idea what'll happen if that's the case,' she confessed. 'But I'm not asking you to trust me, Mr Mackenzie. I'm asking you to do a job, and find out if I'm right. Will you? I won't say money's no object,' she said, shrugging, 'but, as unlikely as people think it, my mother was right: I loved my husband. I'd have done, and will do, anything to bring his killer out into the light.'

Mackenzie pondered a moment, then rose to his feet. 'Okay. I'm not sure I can do what you're asking, but I'm willing to try.'

'To carry on trying, you mean.' Donna gave him a faint smile. 'It seems you were already on the case, so I could have saved myself a bit of money here, couldn't I?'

Mackenzie relaxed then and grinned, and it altered his face completely; he looked altogether friendlier. 'You could,' he said, 'except now you get to boss me around. I'm yours to command, Mrs Lumsden.' He put out his hand, and she shook it.

'You'd better call me Donna then.' She glanced towards the door, and the stairs beyond. 'Look, it's been a difficult day and the kids need me now. But I'll call you first thing tomorrow, and we can arrange for me to pass on anything I think might be helpful.'

'Aye. Suits me. We'll discuss my fees then.' He fished in his pocket for a card and passed it over. 'My mobile, the office number, my home landline. Signal's atrocious where I live,' he explained, 'but you'll catch me on one of those.'

She watched him until he'd got into his car, then closed the front door on the encroaching night and turned her mind to more immediate things. Upstairs she heard the sound of faint sobbing, and her heart hardened once more against Ian George and the way he'd broken her family apart. Him and his scheming aunt, or cousin, or whatever the hell they were to each other... She could only hope her father was as much a victim as she was, but until Mackenzie brought the proof to her on a plate, she wouldn't know. And until then she would be on her guard around them all.

Chapter Twenty-One

Jamie trailed into Mackenzie's kitchen in Ade's wake and dropped his bag on the floor. 'Can we have tea in your caravan?'

Ade gave him an apologetic look. 'I've not had chance to make it fit for receiving guests – I've been too busy with the plans for the new estate. Maybe you can help me?'

'Help you clean up?' Jamie pulled a face.

'No, daft lad. With the new place.' Ade pointed to the paperwork strewn on the table. 'I've got to get some plans professionally drawn up and sent over to the council, so they can approve them, but first I have to come up with a rough layout. Time to get creative.'

Jamie perked up. Since handing the gun over to Mackenzie he'd felt a weight peel off his shoulders, but he couldn't stop his thoughts straying to Ethan's home life, the horrible atmosphere between Kyle and his dad, and what it all meant when you put it together. All day he'd been thinking about why the gun had been buried alongside Pickles, and if the dog had really been hit by a car after all. What if Mr Cameron had lost his temper and shot it, and Kyle knew?

He planned to talk about this to his mum after school, but she had phoned the school to say she had to work late today, and Mackenzie would pick him up. Jamie had been looking forward to it, but had instead found Ade waiting at the gate. He didn't mind; Ade was funny. Although he was drawing some faintly suspicious looks from the other parents – as well as some interested ones from a particular little group of mums, Jamie noticed with a little roll of his eyes.

'Paul's been called out to have a chat with a new client,' Ade had explained, 'but he shouldn't be long. You can still come back to his place for your tea though, and your mum will pick you up later. That okay?'

For a moment Jamie had hesitated. His wariness had gone up a *lot* of notches since August, and although he knew he ought to trust Mackenzie's brother, he didn't really know him that well yet. Ade had stepped back, understanding belatedly dawning on his face, though edged with a faint disappointment.

'Sorry. You're right to be careful. Shall I take you down to your mum's offices instead? I'm sure she won't mind; she was expecting Paul to be here for you after all.'

Jamie looked at him, and after a moment he shook his head. 'No, it's okay. I'll come with you.' They'd be walking, which wasn't nearly as scary as getting into a car alone with someone. He was pretty sure he could duck away and attract enough attention if he needed to.

But he hadn't, and now he was in Mackenzie's familiar house. Ade handed him a carton of juice. 'I'm no Jamie Oliver, but I can throw some beans in a pan, and I expect I can burn some toast to go with it, if that suits?'

'It does, thanks.' Jamie pointed at the paperwork. 'What do you want me to do?'

'Well.' Ade sat opposite and placed both hands flat on the table. 'Imagine you're a rich, posh bloke, who lives to impress people.' He paused. 'Done that?'

'Yep.'

'Are you *really* rich though?'

Jamie nodded. 'Super rich.'

'Good. You're coming up here to stay for a week or so with some of those people you want to impress, to live out the ideal Highland experience. You have a lush cabin, fitted out with everything a laird would have around him. Now, what would you want to see when you looked out of that cabin door in the morning? A big pond you could go fishing on, or rolling hills where you could go shooting?'

Jamie flinched at the word. 'Fishing,' he said at once.

Ade gave him an odd look and made a note. 'Right. What else?'

'A jeep, just for me to use. Not a new one, but one that looks like it's been driving across the land for years. But it's not going to break down,' Jamie added, settling into his task, 'because it's really got a brand-new engine in it.'

Ade made more notes while Jamie chattered, and presently they were interrupted by a knock at Mackenzie's front door.

'That'll probably be your mum,' Ade said. 'Want to get it?'

But Jamie had got no further than sliding one foot down off the rail of his chair before the door opened and Maddy's voice came drifting in. 'Only us.'

She came into the kitchen with Tas, smiled at Jamie, then looked around. 'Paul not here?'

'No,' Ade said. 'He's been called out.'

'Oh? Anywhere interesting?'

Ade hesitated, then sighed. 'You'll find out sooner or later. He's gone to talk to Donna Lumsden.'

'Why?'

'She wants him to look into her husband's murder, so he said. Couldn't turn that down.'

Maddy pursed her lips. 'Which means I was right. She *doesn't* still believe it was Gavin.'

'Seems not. He'll be able to fill you in though; he'll be back in a bit.' Ade started to clear the papers away. 'I've got to get miladdo here some tea. You staying?'

'Aye, why not? I'd like to hear what Paul has to say when he gets back. Jamie, why don't you take Tas through and put the telly on?'

In the sitting room Jamie kept one ear strained towards the kitchen, hoping to catch some conversation that he could later relate to his mum hinting at Maddy definitely being Ade's 'type'. It had seemed to cheer both her and Mackenzie up the other day to think about it, and neither of them had mentioned the fact that Maddy was supposed to get married to Tas's dad someday. Maybe that was kaput, as his mum sometimes said.

Tas had the TV remote and was flicking through the channels. He landed on Nickelodeon, and they settled down to watch until tea was ready. Jamie liked Tas, although he was little. He even felt quite brotherly towards him, he supposed, since Maddy and Mackenzie were so close, and he himself spent quite a lot of time at Mackenzie's. The little squirt wasn't too much of a pain, and sometimes actually made Jamie laugh.

A short while later Ade came in, and when he glanced at the TV he gave a weird little shudder and pulled a face. 'Switch that off, lad, aye? Come on in, both of you – tea's ready. I found some oven chips instead of toast.'

Seated at the table, Jamie remembered that look. 'Don't you like SpongeBob SquarePants?'

'Whoooo lives in a pineapple under the sea,' Tas sang, off-key and helping himself to too much ketchup.

'I've nothing against him as such,' Ade said, but he looked a bit pale. 'I just...can't look at those pictures right now.

Maddy laughed. 'What on earth?'

He gave her a warning look. 'Not now,' he repeated. 'I'll tell you later.'

Maddy subsided, but Tas had got the bit between his teeth now, and was chanting 'SpongeBob SquarePants' under his breath.

'Leave it, Tas,' Maddy said, but she too kept shooting Ade curious looks, until he sighed and lowered his voice.

'When Paul and I found that...what we found,' he said, and Jamie's heart quickened. 'Well,' he glanced at Tas, who was paying no attention whatsoever. 'I had a look under the floorboard, just to make sure before we called the police. I didn't see much, but what I *did* see had pictures of that on it.' He jerked his head towards the sitting room and the TV.

'That what?'

'SpongeBob. The bod...the thing we found was wrapped in something that was covered with those pictures. Pink starfish, yellow sponge.'

'What, like a duvet cover?'

'No, plastic. Thick. More sort of like—'

'A paddling pool,' Jamie said with his mouth full, and in a hollow voice. He put down his fork, very carefully.

'That's the sort of stuff,' Ade said. 'Like PVC. I couldn't place it at the time, but it'd make sense, being nautical in theme. Bizarre thing to see, in a place like that. The bloody TV show just brought it all back.'

Jamie tried to finish the mouthful he'd been chewing, but it had turned to rubber in his mouth. Tears filled his eyes, but he wasn't upset, he was bewildered and frightened, and his inability to swallow was making his throat even tighter. The missing paddling pool, wrapped around Mulholland's body? A gun buried with the dog... Even if that hadn't been the murder weapon, it was definitely sinister. Kyle had sneaked back from his cousins' place to see his dog, only to find it had, coincidentally enough, been run over that very day. And he had been at loggerheads with his father ever since—

'Jamie?' Ade was asking, and it seemed he'd said it a couple of times, because everyone was staring at him now. 'Are you all right?'

He finally managed to swallow, but was saved from answering by the arrival of Mackenzie, who looked disappointed that Charis wasn't back yet. He threw the two boys a smile of welcome, nodded to his brother, then turned to Maddy.

'Great news. I've been hired by Donna Lumsden, to help her prove that her dad's new sidekick killed her husband.'

She nodded, her expression brightening. 'Ade mentioned it. Which means Gavin's in with a chance at getting out before he even has to return to prison. This could literally save his life.' Her attention was off Jamie now, which was a relief, but he could see Ade still watching him with a frown.

'Where will you start?' Maddy wanted to know.

'See who he talks to,' Mackenzie said, 'and what contacts he has outside the Kilbride circle. His brother, for instance. You know better than we do how the prison network operates. We just need to find a tiny connection we can work a bloody great crowbar into.'

'Right.' Maddy stood up. 'I'll talk to Nick, see if he has anything he can add.'

'He'll never—'

'Look, he's already bending,' Maddy said. 'He's given us more information than he would ever have done before, and this is pretty special. He can only say no, but if there was ever a time to push my luck, it's now.' She nodded at Ade and Jamie, and turned back to Mackenzie. 'I'll give you a call later, tell you what he says.'

She and Tas left, and Mackenzie and his brother fell back to discussing the Three Sisters murder. Jamie tuned them out. All he could think about was how Sarah Wallace had tried to protect Ethan's dad from Mulholland, and now Mulholland was dead, and everything pointed to it happening at Ethan's place. He desperately wanted to tell them, but as far as he understood it, Tas's dad's actual life depended on them concentrating on this other bloke; he couldn't risk distracting them with this.

When his mum arrived, he jumped up and grabbed his bag. 'I'm ready.'

'Hang on a bit, our kid,' she protested. 'Give me a chance to say hello, at least.'

He subsided, and saw Ade's eyes on him again. He looked more than ever like Mackenzie when he wore that expression – those eyes were a bit greener, but very sharp and, like Mackenzie's, seemed to read a lot more than Jamie thought he was letting himself show.

Jamie's thoughts turned to Mr Cameron again. Friendly, almost always smiling, at least when he had visitors. Then he saw him as he had that first day he'd gone to Ethan's, staring after Mackenzie's car as it had driven away, and not smiling any more. The dog. The gun. The paddling pool. The dead policeman...

Did Ethan know? Had he known all along? Jamie's breathing suddenly became more difficult, and he took a sip of water. His chest felt heavy, and he automatically patted the table next to him for his inhaler, but it wasn't there. A terrified flash took him back to the crofter's cottage, when he'd sucked the last of the medication into his lungs and felt sure he would die there. But there was a movement beside him and someone turned his hand over and slapped his inhaler into his palm.

He fired off the relief and felt his mum's hand on his back, rubbing gently. It had been a while since he'd been caught unawares, and he could see the troubled look on her face. He also saw her glancing with gratitude at Mackenzie, and gathered he'd been the one to pull the inhaler from Jamie's backpack.

'We should stop talking about this stuff now, in front of Jamie,' she said. 'He's only—'

'No. I need to tell you something,' Jamie broke in. He breathed slowly and steadily for a minute, while they looked on with poorly concealed curiosity, and when his lungs felt back to normal again he faced his mum, and keeping his eyes on hers, he began.

'I think Ethan's dad killed that copper.'

Maddy cut off the call mid-way through Nick's recorded message; this wasn't something she could leave on his voicemail – she had to ask him directly. A swift and cheerful response to a text told her he and Max were out celebrating tonight, so she knew it was pointless to hope she'd be able to talk to him later either. She turned to Tas.

'Fancy a quick trip to see Grandad on the way home?'

'Yes! Will he give me a box for Chase?'

'We can only ask.'

In her father's sitting room she accepted a cup of tea and took her usual seat. 'I was hoping you might be able to get your friend Sergeant McFarland to do us a bit of a favour.'

Tony's eyes narrowed a bit. 'Oh aye? Go on.'

She told him about Mackenzie being summoned by Donna Lumsden, and how he hoped to get the inside track on who Ian George's brother was in touch with in prison.

'I don't know how you think he'd be able to do that,' Tony said. He was distracted and irritable again tonight. 'Farly doesn't have access to that kind of information. You want someone who works in the prison itself.'

'It was just a thought.' Maddy sipped her tea. 'You've both said talk flies fairly freely at the station – he might have heard *something*.' She paused. 'Are you okay?'

'I'm fine.'

Silence fell. It was unusually awkward, and after a few minutes, looking for a diversion, Maddy shifted in her seat. 'Have you got a little box kicking around? Like, a shoe-box size?'

'What for?'

'Chase!' Tas piped up. 'He's my pet snail and Mum says the house I found him on isn't his, so I want to get some grass and mud, and keep him in a box.'

'Good idea.' Tony smiled at last. 'Why don't you go and look in the garage? I've not been in there for a while. Can't remember what I've got, to be honest.' He looked at Maddy. 'If you find one you can use, just take out whatever's in it and leave it on the shelf.'

'Thanks.' She stood up and held out her hand to Tas. 'Have you got any spare antifreeze, while I'm at it? I ought to top up.'

'Aye, probably. Have a rummage.'

Maddy and Tas went out into the chilly evening, and Maddy pulled the string to turn on the garage light. There were a few boxes of bits on the shelf, but most of them held oily car parts or were torn down at the corners, and she shook her head at Tas's hopeful look. There was a fairly big one that looked likely though, an old wellington boots box, and she peered inside to see some spanners and an adjustable wrench.

'How about this one?' she asked, lifting it down. Tas nodded, pleased, and she turned to take out the contents as requested. As she did so her eyes grazed a larger, battered-looking cardboard box that looked like it held the contents of the last time her dad had cleaned out the car. She handed Tas the now-empty welly box, and moved aside a few half-empty cans of de-icer and a sponge that had turned into a dry, misshapen yellow brick.

'Ah. Here we go.' She uncovered a carton of antifreeze near the bottom and pulled it out with a little exclamation of triumph. Then she stopped, motionless. 'Take that box in,' she said after a moment, in a distant voice. 'Tell Grandad I won't be a minute.'

The boy scampered off with his prize, and Maddy turned her attention back to the mess at the bottom of the cardboard box. Slowly she pulled her phone out of her pocket and swiped to unlock it.

'Paul,' she said when he answered, and her heart beat so loudly in her ears that she wasn't even sure she was speaking aloud at first. 'I need you to come down to Dad's place. Right now.'

———

She didn't know how she got through the next ten minutes. Tas was sitting at the kitchen table, happily drawing windows on the cardboard box, and her father was helping him, when she heard the Mazda stop outside and went out to meet Paul.

'I was coming to see you anyway,' he began, but she held up a hand.

'Come with me.'

Bemused, he followed her to the garage, and her fingers were shaking so badly she was barely able to grasp the pull string to turn on the light again. She showed him the box, and then pointed to what she'd seen, right down in the corner, half squashed under a plastic oil bottle. He looked, then turned back to her, his face losing all animation. He reached in and snagged the gardening glove with his fingertips, bringing it out into the light.

'Is it the same?'

She nodded. 'Exactly. And it's the left one. Tas has the right one.'

'Jesus...' Paul turned the glove this way and that in the light for a moment, perhaps looking for blood stains, but if there were any they were buried under layers of dried mud. Then he looked at Maddy, and the shocked sadness on his face pulled the rug from under her. She blinked, felt the first tears squeeze past her eyelashes, and then there was no stopping them.

Paul pulled her tight against him, but it took a moment for her to realise he was trying to muffle her gasping sobs rather than comfort her. 'I know how it looks,' he said in a low voice, 'but it's not him, I'm sure of it. Listen to me.'

Maddy shook her head against his jacket. 'I've been ignoring the obvious! I've been so stupid.'

'No, you haven't.'

'I believed him – he swore on my mother's—'

'Maddy! Listen! We've found out something too.' He held her at arms' length, clearly serious about whatever he thought he knew, but it was ridiculous to try and keep alive the belief that her father wasn't responsible.

Paul's voice was even, despite the strain on his face. 'There's some stuff we haven't told you yet, that we've only just found out about, and it all points to somewhere else. Come inside; we can talk to your dad about it.'

'No!'

'As a copper he'll know whether we have enough for the police to charge the bloke who did it.'

'Who?' Maddy shook her head. 'Paul, it was *my dad*!'

'No. It was Ben Cameron.'

Maddy stopped, shocked into silence at last while he explained everything in a few short sentences. When he'd finished she gestured at the glove he still held. 'How do you explain that then?'

'I have no idea. He could have picked it up anywhere. But the evidence against Cameron is a lot more compelling, don't you think?'

'But Dad said he was willing to do anything to protect his family.'

'That doesn't mean he did. We've all said stuff like that, haven't we?' For a second his face darkened with the resurgence of old pain, then he held out a hand. 'Come on, let's go and talk to him.'

In the house once more, Maddy sent Tas upstairs to play. 'We won't be long,' she said, feeling her throat tighten again and hoping her eyes weren't too puffy, her tears too obvious. She rejoined Paul and her father, and saw that Paul had already posited the theory about Ben Cameron.

'We're on the verge of taking the evidence to the police, but Maddy called me down here for something else. So, while I'm here,' he added casually, 'what do you think? Will it be enough to charge him?'

Tony looked carefully from one to the other, and seemed to deflate in front of them. He shook his head. 'It wasn't Ben, lad.' His eyes were on Maddy's as he reached across the table and grasped her hand. 'It'll be hard to prove it, now you've told me what you know, but he doesn't deserve to go down for something he didn't do.'

She felt numb now, and a creeping sense of inevitable loss. 'Dad, please don't.'

'Let me tell you everything. Then you can decide whether you want to go to the police.'

'Tony,' Paul said, a note of urgency in his voice now. 'Leave it, aye? I've already decided. The police can—'

'I'd been following Mulholland since they decided he'd no case to answer,' Tony broke in, sounding almost conversational. 'Not that either of you would have been in a position to know that, what with you being on remand, Mads, and Mackenzie here still in hospital.' He gave a grim little smile. 'I knew he'd put a foot wrong sooner or later. And if he didn't, I had a few ideas on how to provoke him. You understand why?'

Maddy nodded; while Mulholland was still at large, none of them were safe. *Any man who's a threat...*

'So,' Tony went on, his head bowed and his hands now drawn back in front of him, clasped tightly together, 'I made a point of never being too far away to see what he was up to. And who he was talking to. But I couldn't be there twenty-four seven, so that Thursday I took a break and came in to visit you, Maddy. The half past six slot.' He gave Maddy a faint smile. 'That's how I remembered the time, when I told you to visit Gavin, remember?'

She nodded. 'I thought you were twitchy when you visited, but just assumed it was being an ex-copper in a prison.'

'Aye, well, that accounted for some of it,' he confessed. 'There's always someone looking to make a scene. But just after I'd parked up I'd had a phone call from Farly, and he told me that Mulholland had come in earlier to talk to his boss, and he thought I'd want to know. He didn't know what it was about, and I had to consider the possibility that he was spilling the truth about Nick, and Dougie Cameron...' He spared Paul a glance. 'Maddy told me you know about that. Thank you for keeping it to yourself.'

Paul nodded. 'Of course. You've no need to worry on that account.'

'Anyway,' Tony went on, 'back then I didn't know that Mulholland had no idea who killed Dougie. I mean Bradley could have told him at any time. So as soon as I left Inverness that evening, I planned to find him.'

'What did you intend to do?' But Maddy wasn't sure if she wanted to know, and the next minute she was certain she didn't.

'Ask him,' Tony said simply. 'I was going to get him alone, in his house, and sodding well beat it out of him if I had to.'

Chapter Twenty-Two

Thursday 9th August 2018

TONY HAD DRIVEN BACK to Abergarry like a madman, but slowed ahead of the junction that led to Mulholland's estate, and a glance to check for oncoming traffic had brushed over the little car park by the Twisted Tree pub. Don Bradley's prized Land Rover Discovery sat there like a bad memory. According to Vince McFarland, Bradley's widow had been so distraught by the way the car had been impounded and examined, that the moment it was released back into her possession she'd handed the keys and the logbook straight to Mulholland. A step up from the boneshaker he'd driven before; the perks of being best pals with a greedy bastard like Bradley.

Tony cancelled the indicator, drove a little farther up the road and pulled into the car park instead. He didn't have too long to wait until Mulholland came out, and he followed the Discovery at a discreet distance. But Mulholland hadn't taken the turning off the main road to the estate where he lived – he had carried on, up the hill through town, past the Burnside

Hotel, out past the more countrified area where Mackenzie lived, and on towards Fort William.

Tony followed, still hanging back and more than a little curious, but when the Discovery pulled in for no apparent reason, he had to keep driving until he'd passed it by. Mulholland was sitting very still in the Rover, and was clearly watching the house a short way ahead; a fairly substantial cottage that looked as if it had once been part of a larger place, maybe even a farm. As Tony drove past he saw it had two yards; a gravelled one, open to the road, and a paved one nearer the house, and there was a large family car sitting on the gravel. He was moving too fast to read the name on the gate, Wester something, but there was clearly someone home; he could see shadows moving just beyond the paved yard.

It was still light, at around nine thirty, and it was hard to find a place to stop without being noticed. There were no high hedges here, so the bends in the road provided no cover, but a short way ahead Tony came to a blind summit. He stopped the car on the other side, jogged back, and cursed his stiff bones as he climbed the low stone wall and dropped onto the other side, before making his way back through what appeared to be a paddock that led to the back garden.

The Discovery was nowhere in sight, and Tony wondered if he'd made a mistake in assuming Mulholland was coming here. He bit back a muttered oath of frustration, but couldn't remember seeing or hearing the car on the road as he'd cut back through the paddock, so unless it had turned back to Abergarry it was probably still sitting a short way down the road. Mulholland was probably just biding his time, maybe waiting until it got a bit darker.

Tony heard raised voices as he drew closer, but neither was Mulholland's. An adult male and a younger one were thrashing something out, and he slowed, his heart hammering with the exertion, and listened. It sounded as if the kid should have been somewhere else, and that he was determined not to return there.

'You bloody will,' the older voice said firmly. 'Just as soon as I've finished this.'

'Well can I at least take Pickles?'

'What? No! Sam'd never see his cat again. Go and wait in the car, and stick your moped in the back. I can't trust you to ride it back.'

'You realise you've made me miss the last week of the holidays?' the boy complained. 'Sasha's texted me – they're all going down to Glasgow for a final blow-out, and I'm gonna miss it.'

'There'll be others,' the man said, then his voice quietened, and Tony thought he heard real tension in it. 'Come on, Kyle, don't give me a hard time over this. There's a good reason I sent you all over to Sam's house. I promise I'll tell you someday.'

'If I don't go to Glasgow, Sasha'll ditch me and go off with someone else.'

'Oh, for... Just get in the car! I'll be ten minutes – I just want to finish this.'

There was a scraping noise, and then a rhythmic chopping sound. A car door opening, and the sound of rolling wheels; Tony assumed the boy had finally done as he'd been told. He stood still for a few minutes, unsure what to do about Mulholland, but he didn't have to think about it for long; even as the car door closed on this Kyle kid, he heard the faint sound of the Discovery starting up and few seconds later it pulled into the outer yard. The window buzzed down.

'Mr Cameron. Nice to see you again.'

Tony stiffened. This was *Ben Cameron's* place? Shit...

There was a clatter as the man dropped whatever gardening implement he had been using, probably in shock, and Tony abruptly remembered Maddy asking, that night in the hospital, if Ben was safe. She'd seen Nick's blood on Tony's fingers, and that had been her first thought... Now he knew why. He pressed back against the wall of the house, feeling sweaty and sick, and praying the boy would stay put in the car.

The Discovery's car door clunked softly shut, and there was nothing Tony could do as Mulholland's and Ben's voices faded; one angry but slightly wavering, the other pleasant and polite. The front door closed. Tony breathed slowly to steady his racing heart and reached into his pocket for his phone. Before he could get as far as unlocking it, a joyful barking sound came up from the paddock he'd just crossed, and Tony stared in dismay as a small brown and white dog hurtled towards him... *Go away, go away...*

He got his wish. The dog ran straight past, but Tony's horror deepened as Kyle threw open the car door. 'Pickles! Here, boy!'

The dog kept yapping in delight, and a second later there was the sound of the house's front door slamming open again. Tony still couldn't see anyone without risking being seen himself, but his mind's eye showed him Mulholland, striding across the tiled yard and onto the gravelled one.

'Shut that fucking thing *up!*'

'Who are you? And don't call my dog a—' The retort ended in a hoarse scream, and a second later a flat crack split the summer evening air and the dog fell silent.

Tony's breath stopped; he fought for it, and for a second he thought he'd never take another. His chest tightened, so hard and so fast that he actually gripped it as if his heart were failing him, but when no second shot followed he guessed the boy, at least, was safe. He leaned back against the wall, sweat gathering on his forehead and running into his eyes. He gasped a few times – the whole episode had taken just a couple of seconds – and realised he could hear more footsteps on the gravel. Light, scrabbling ones, accompanied by soft panting sobs.

'No,' he whispered in despair. There was no hope of grabbing Kyle and pulling him to safety before Mulholland loosed off another shot, but he had to do something, so he stepped out from his hiding place, preparing to draw Mulholland's attention away from the boy. But he was only a phantom in the world of terror happening in the yard. Unseen, and helpless to do anything.

Mulholland had left the ghastly tableau in the middle of the yard: the dog's small brown and white head glistening with blood, the distraught teen crouched over him and weeping. He was halfway across the threshold into the house again, the gun held before him and levelled at whoever was inside – presumably Ben Cameron.

Tony once more braced himself to step in, but he didn't get the chance. In one movement Kyle had sprung to his feet and snatched up the patio knife his father had been using; it still had a clump of stubborn weeds and earth clinging to its short, curved blade, which fell off as he drew it back and swung it. This detail seemed to stick strangely in Tony's mind, even as he understood what the inevitable end to this moment must be. The arc, waist high to the boy, dipped slightly as it completed its trajectory, thudding into Mulholland's right thigh with a sickening, meaty sound.

Mulholland's scream was even higher than the boy's had been. He dropped the gun, which spun away into the kitchen along the tiled floor, and as Kyle tried to pull the blade free

Mulholland slipped in his own blood and went down, his momentum snatching the handle from the boy's hand. His weight came down on the blade, driving it deeper, and his second scream was breathless and weak.

Tony lunged forward, trying to draw enough breath to tell Kyle to *leave it, for God's sake!* but it was too late; the first blow had done its work. Blood pumped out of the original wound, past the deeply lodged blade, but only for the time it took Tony to grab Kyle by the collar and pull him out of its increasingly feeble arc.

Mulholland slumped, and Tony could see he was still breathing, but that there was no hope of saving him. Kyle was breathing heavily too, and there was a panicky whistle to each outward breath, as if he were trying to scream but it wouldn't come out.

Tony spun the boy away from the sight of the dying policeman and pushed him, almost roughly, through the gate and back towards the car.

'Jesus...' Ben had stepped out of the house.

Tony could see him trembling, even from his place by the gate, and he pointed at Kyle. 'Get him back to where he should be. Now.'

'I can't take him in this state—'

Tony looked at Kyle, who was sheet-white and had stumbled to his knees, his arms wrapped across his chest. 'Then take him somewhere else first,' he said grimly. 'Just get him the fuck away from here.'

'What do I do?' Cameron asked, his eyes fixed on the still form of Mulholland. The blood was barely oozing now, and a welcome calm fell over Tony as his years in the Service kicked in.

'Nothing. Make sure neither of you stepped in anything,

and when the boy's away to where he belongs, you get back here. Don't you dare do a runner,' he added, fixing the stunned man with his steadiest glare. 'Do that, and see I'll find you. Okay? Count on that. Take your time if you have to, but *get back here tonight.*'

Cameron nodded. Slowly at first, then more positively. He seemed to belatedly realise what it all meant, and his face gradually lost the slack-jawed horror and became almost serene. 'Good riddance, you bastard,' he said softly to Mulholland's motionless form. He raised his eyes to Tony. 'I'll not be long,' he said, more firmly now. 'Thank you. I don't know why you were here, but you've... Thank you.'

'See to your boy.'

Tony called out again, as Cameron eased his son to his feet and began helping him to the car. 'Is your shed locked?'

'Aye. Keys are in the kitchen, in the bowl.'

'Good. Go on then.'

He watched the car, with the moped bouncing around in the space that poor dog would never again occupy, creeping slowly out of the yard, then turned back. He stepped over the puddles of blood that had also run into the cracks in the concrete tiles, and entered the dim coolness of the kitchen. It didn't take a moment to locate the selection of keys, and then to find the one that fitted the padlock on the shed.

Half an hour later he had dug a hole at the bottom of the paddock and returned for the dog. He peered into the corners of the shed and picked up a deflated, dusty and cobwebby paddling pool, which looked as if it hadn't been used for years. It was a good size, but he put it aside. Too substantial to waste on such a small dog, and there was a better use for it that he wasn't yet ready to think about.

After a few minutes poking around in a storage box, he

dragged out the clear plastic that had come wrapped around a newish-looking lawn mower, and picked up the pair of gardening gloves Cameron had been using to de-weed between the flagstones. The dog rolled easily onto the plastic, and he folded it carefully, then carried the grim package down the paddock, thanking every star in the heavens that the Camerons lived somewhere an approaching car could be heard a mile off, and all movement ceased until it had passed by.

The dog buried, he turned his attention to the bigger problem, wishing Cameron would hurry up and get back. It was almost completely dark now, and it would be hard to make any headway cleaning the blood off the concrete, but that would be Cameron's job; Tony might feel he owed the man, but that only went so far. However, the debt included finding somewhere to dispose of the body. It was all very well burying a dog in the garden – that was expected, provided no-one ever wanted to see how it had died, but they would have to box clever with the —he double-checked—yes, the corpse of Alistair Mulholland.

He dragged out the paddling pool and opened it up; the tough PVC plastic would just about cover the body if they angled it right. As he began to drag Mulholland's body onto the pool he heard another car, and stopped moving, melting back into the shadows. The car slowed and turned into the yard, and he breathed again. About time.

Cameron came straight over, flinching as he rounded the corner and saw a reality he'd probably hoped he'd dreamed. 'Kyle's going to be okay, I think,' he said. 'Ethan, his little brother, was the only one who knew he'd sneaked away, and we told him Pickles had been run over and to leave Kyle alone.'

'Good thinking,' Tony said. He gestured to the body. 'Right, is there anywhere we can get rid of this?' He saw Cameron glance down the paddock, and shook his head. 'Not on your property. Nor near it,' he added, as Cameron raised his eyes to take in the woodland. 'It's got to be somewhere off the beaten track. Think about it, while we get him covered up.'

Together they got Mulholland onto the plastic, and Tony began to fold the sides of the pool over. 'I'll get his legs in properly; you go and get some… I dunno, parcel tape or something.'

'I've got loads of it,' Cameron said, and he seemed relieved to be able to contribute something useful. 'From sending out orders and so on, you know.' He disappeared into the house, and when he returned he was holding a roll of tape, and the gun.

'This…' he was staring at it with an odd look on his face. 'This was my dad's.'

Tony shook his head, bemused. 'What?'

'Sarah knew Dad had it, and wanted to borrow it. For protection only, so she said.'

'Well,' Tony said grimly, 'now we know for sure this bastard was armed, up in that cottage, and not the innocent party he claimed to be.'

'You never believed that, did you?'

'Not really. What will you do with it?'

Cameron placed it beside Mulholland, but Tony shook his head. 'If worst comes to worst, and he's found, this will definitely tie him back to you. Bury it on your own property somewhere. It was your dad's, not yours, and as far as we know the only thing it's killed is your dog.'

Cameron nodded and put it aside. 'I'll dig down later, and put it in with Pickles.'

'Empty it first. Meantime, have you thought of where we can get rid of this?' Tony nodded at Mulholland.

'Aye. It was thinking about Sarah that brought it to mind.'

'Not the cottage, I hope. Way too risky.'

'No. Further down the same estate though, there's an old gillie's hut. Sarah and I used to go up there to get...' He hesitated, as he seemed to remember he was talking to a former police officer, then looked at the body and shrugged. 'To get stoned, and drink. You know. Like kids do.'

'And no-one else knows about it, and might go up there to do the same?'

Cameron shook his head. 'It's tucked away by the river, and since her dad sacked all his regular estate workers we were the only ones who used it. It's padlocked, and Sarah gave me the spare key so I wouldn't have to wait in the rain if I got there first.'

'So you're suggesting we just...put him in there?'

'Not quite. It's got a wooden floor, but they had to dig drainage channels under it because of where it is, at the bottom of the hill.'

Tony considered, then nodded. 'We're going to have to re-visit in a few months and move him,' he said. 'When it's down to bones and easier to dispose of. But for now it'll have to do.'

'Why are you doing this?' Cameron asked suddenly, and Tony stopped tearing at the parcel tape.

'What do you mean?'

'You're an ex-copper. You're covering up a crime.' Cameron looked troubled, as if he half-thought Tony was testing him. 'Why would you risk everything, even if it means seeing the back of *him*?'

Tony wrestled, for a moment, with the truth that wanted to come bursting out of him. It had been poisoning him for days. *I'm doing it because my son killed your father...* But he couldn't do it to Nick.

'Kyle doesn't deserve to suffer,' he said at length. 'I saw exactly what happened here. You were being threatened at gunpoint, and this bastard had just shot the lad's dog dead for no reason.' He fixed Cameron with a firm look. 'But make no mistake, Ben, he'd still face a trial. And even if he got off he'd be persecuted for the rest of his life, just because of who Mulholland was.'

'But if it was manslaughter—'

'Provoked by what? We can't prove any wrongdoing by Mulholland here tonight – it'll be the same as it was before. And the fact that you and Sarah were such good friends gives *you* the perfect motive too. Your prints are on the gun, don't forget. *Your dad's* gun. And you could easily have shot the dog yourself.'

Cameron had been looking more defeated with every word, and eventually he just nodded, and held the edges of the pool together while Tony ran the tape around the gruesome package.

'We got him into the Discovery, and parked up by Glenlowrie House,' Tony said now. 'We didn't want to disturb that overgrown path your brother found, and risk sparking up the wrong kind of interest in the land. We carried Mulholland down to the shed and dug out the drainage channel a little deeper, put him in, and that was that. We locked the door, and then I checked Cameron had plenty of white vinegar and bleach and told him how to fix the blood stains.'

He sounded now as if he were simply reciting a list of chores he'd accomplished. 'I drove Mulholland's car back to his place, and Cameron followed so he could give me a lift back out here to pick up my own.'

Maddy's emotions had melted from fear to outright horror

and then to relief during the telling. She had believed, right up until Kyle had swung the patio knife, that her father had been leading up to a confession. She looked across at Paul, who withdrew the glove from his pocket and laid it wordlessly on the table.

Tony's face blanched. 'Where did you get that?'

'It was in the box of car crap,' Maddy said quietly. 'It's why I called Paul down here. I didn't know what to do, Dad.'

Tony nodded, his face a mask of regret and remorse. 'I'm so, so sorry, hen. The PVC was slippery. Hard to grip with the gardening gloves on, so I took them off. I shoved them in my trouser pocket, but one of them must have snagged a fern as we were passing. They were pretty high then, in the summer. When I got back into my own car, I was so all over the place I threw the other glove into the back, and just...forgot about it. I did see, when I cleaned out the car, that one was missing, but I assumed I'd picked it up and junked it at another time.'

'And that was it?' Maddy said in a broken voice. 'You just went back to your everyday life?'

'Hardly everyday life.' Tony lowered his head into his hands. 'First Nick, then Kyle... Once that first line was crossed I really went all out, didn't I?' He sighed. 'The minute Mackenzie told me about Ade clearing that ground, I felt like I'd been hit by a steam roller. I went straight around to see Cameron, on the pretence of going out to deliver a client's report, but it was already too late.'

'I don't get why you left the paddling pool up there,' Paul said. 'That would have slowed down the decay as well, wouldn't it?'

'We hoped it would contain the smell better than it did,' Tony said. 'It would have done, if the body had stayed there a bit longer. It was worth the risk, to avoid the smell getting out.'

'Or so you thought,' Paul said grimly. 'Poor wee Jamie's been a total wreck about this. So stressed he had an asthma attack. He's not had one of those since he was kidnapped.'

'I'm sorry for that too,' Tony said, and rubbed his face. 'Christ, I don't know whether I'm up or down. I haven't slept for days.' He looked directly at Paul. 'What are you going to do?'

Paul didn't hesitate. 'If I could think of a way to do it without implicating you, I'd go straight to the police with what we've found.' He paused. 'Can they trace the pool back to Cameron? And if they did, would he drag you down with him, d'you think?'

'I've no idea. With any luck there won't be any usable prints on it. I gave it as good a going over with the antiseptic wipes as I could, and the soil should have done the rest. As for Cameron naming me, he'd probably only do it if he had no choice. He doesn't know what Nick did, so he just thinks of me as the one who helped his son stay out of jail.'

'He could always say he'd thrown the pool out at the end of the summer,' Maddy said. 'Or sold it at a car boot sale. I can't see how they could connect it all, so my vote is to just say nothing.'

'We do need to talk to Cameron though,' Tony said. 'If he's been feeling anything like me, he's likely to go off the rails pretty soon and give everything up.'

'D'you think he'd confess himself, just to make sure it doesn't come back on Kyle?' Paul asked. 'It seems like something he might consider.'

'We need to speak to him, make sure he doesn't.' Tony looked at them in turn. 'So we're agreed?

Paul and Maddy looked at one another; they didn't need to confer. 'Anyone else, I'd have had second thoughts,' Maddy said, 'but Mulholland?' She shook her head. 'I'd not see anyone ruin their life for his sake.'

'Right then.' Tony looked at Paul, and he seemed bolstered by the decision. 'You and I will go down to Cameron's shop tomorrow morning and talk to him.'

'Good,' Maddy said. 'You'll be back in time to collect Tas from school.'

'Well, okay, but why?'

'I'm going to talk to Gav after my shift.' Maddy felt a tremor of nerves pass through her at the thought of it. 'It's time we sorted some things out. I've put it off long enough.'

'You've not seen him since last week?' Her father looked startled. She didn't feel like explaining now, and Paul clearly sensed it and jumped in.

'I'm expecting a call in the morning from Donna Lumsden, to discuss a plan of action. I'll meet you by Inverlochy Court though, Tony, as soon as that's over.'

'And I've got a hot date with a bucket of paint thinner and a scrubbing brush,' Maddy sighed, stretching. 'The Victoria Road play area's been given an interesting new makeover, apparently, but it's not finding the sort of critical acclaim the artist hoped for.'

'Have fun with that,' Paul said amiably, and smiled at the look she gave him. When she saw him out though, his smile faded.

'Are you going to be all right?' he asked in a low voice. 'You know your dad's going to find things tough for a while.'

'Yeah, I know.' Maddy looked past him to where her father was moving about the kitchen, clearing cups. 'It's taking a toll already. Look after him tomorrow, okay? Don't let Ben Cameron's decisions wreck anything for him. You know what'd happen to him if he got sent down.'

'I'll make sure Cameron knows the score.' He dropped a kiss on her forehead. 'Right, I said I wouldn't be long, and Charis will be sending out a search party any minute. Give my regards to Victoria Road.'

Maddy closed the door behind him and went upstairs to find Tas. She couldn't begin to imagine how she would explain to him if his grandfather ended up in the same place as his father, and it was unnerving and quite frightening to realise that there was nothing she could do to make sure he didn't. All she could do was put her trust in other people, and that didn't feel like nearly enough.

Chapter Twenty-Three

KILBRIDE FACED his wife across the room, grateful for the space between them. Martha's face was tight and impassive, even under the onslaught of his accusations, but at least she was sitting down, which put them on the same level.

'I'm telling you,' she said again, with infuriating calm, 'my early attentions to you came from a good place. Granted I probably looked like a gold digger, but, to be brutally honest, back then you weren't nearly the catch your friend was. If I'd wanted the money, and the family connections, Sandy Broughton would have been the one.'

'You tried, as I recall,' Kilbride reminded her. 'But he was having none of it. He liked a girl with a bit of spark about her.'

She seemed to accept this retaliatory barb, and went on in that same, calm voice, 'My point is, and you can believe this or not, I was happy to be with you. I was happy to care for you, after what happened.'

'And to get me to give your cousin a job.'

'Nephew.'

'Never mind that!' he snapped. 'You asked me, and I

provided. And look how he and that idiot brother of his repaid me.'

'They weren't doing half of what your precious son-in-law was up to!' Martha was clearly growing rattled at last. She slid a cigarette out of the pack on the coffee table and snatched up her lighter. She hadn't smoked in years, but it was little wonder she had recently started again now that her sly games had come to light.

'Craig's been scamming you for years, you nugget,' she said around the cigarette, as she flicked the lighter. 'Ian and Neil pushed their luck a bit far, that was all. Neil was the ringleader, and he's where he deserves to be, but Ian never deserved what that thug did to him.'

'And so you got your petty revenge by telling Donna.' He gave her a look of distaste that he knew would hurt her worse than anger. 'Besides,' he went on, 'it's not your place to tell me what he deserved. Craig was family.'

'By marriage! Which means Ian is too.'

'We could talk about this until the cows come home,' Kilbride said, 'but you need to go now. I've got to talk to Ian. Alone,' he added pointedly. Then, seeing the beginnings of real despair cross her face, he found himself weakening slightly.

'Look, maybe there's a chance you and I can discuss this properly, but not if you're constantly hovering like an over-protective mother hen.' Something about her expression stopped him before he could exhort her, once again, to leave the room.

She blew out smoke, and her stare turned belligerent. 'What?'

'You *are* his mother,' he said wonderingly.

'What?'

'Martha, your face just said it all!' Kilbride moved his chair closer. 'Why the secrecy? Does *he* know?'

She looked poised to deny it further, then subsided and shook her head. 'And you're not to tell him,' she muttered. 'He was taken in by Neil's parents as a baby. As far as both of them know, they're brothers. That's how it stays.'

'And who's his father?'

'He was born in wedlock, if that's what you're getting at.' Martha darted a quick glance at the door to make sure it stayed closed. 'But... He made me give the lad over to my sister – it was one of the reasons we got divorced. I've watched out for Ian ever since though; no-one can deny that.' She sounded proud now, if a little tearful, and Kilbride sighed.

'You could have told me,' he said, more quietly. 'I'd have understood.'

'It was easier to keep it to myself. My ex-husband's gone, and so have Neil's parents, so there was only me left who knew. Until now.'

'You know I can't let him stay. Not if he was responsible for Craig's death.'

'He wasn't!'

'Of course you'd not want to think it, but it all makes sense.' Kilbride raised a hand to forestall any more argument; today was likely to be tense enough. 'Let me talk to him, okay? And stay out of the house for a bit. I don't want to be looking out for helicopter mother of the year if things get a bit shouty.'

'And we'll talk about...us?' she ventured, stubbing out her cigarette.

'We'll talk,' he promised. 'After all these years, I owe you that much, at least.'

He watched until her car turned onto the main road, and picked up his phone to summon Ian downstairs. 'And hurry it up,' he snapped. 'We've got a lot to discuss.'

Ian arrived, rumpled-looking and bleary-eyed after a late night – probably celebrating Craig's funeral somewhere – but still with that cocky grin lurking around his mouth. Kilbride's heart hardened at the sight of him.

'You do realise my daughter thinks you and I are in cahoots over Craig?' he began.

'Cahoots?' Ian chuckled. 'Away and join the twenty-first century, *daddy-o*.'

It was too close for comfort, that word, and Kilbride fixed him with a grim look. 'Call it what you like, but I need to know: was it you who killed him?'

'Was it bollocks.' Ian threw himself into a chair. 'Where's the wee wifey?'

Kilbride allowed himself a little smile. 'Why's that always the first question with you? Are you scared to talk to me alone?'

'Why would I be?'

'You tell me. But it's always the first thing you ask. Close, aren't you?'

'She helped me get a job when I needed one.'

'Aye. With me. And now you've lost it.'

Ian stared, his lazy bravado dropping away so suddenly it was almost comical. 'You're sacking me already?'

'You were under trial,' Kilbride reminded him. 'And now that trial is over.'

'It was for a month!'

'Aye, and it terminates at my discretion. Consider it terminated.'

'And what do I do now?'

Kilbride shrugged. 'Up to you. No doubt Martha will give you some money to get away from here.'

'But you can't just—'

'Don't you remember what I said, that day you and Donna clashed over what you'd done to that Clifford woman?' Kilbride's voice turned hard again. 'I said if you upset my daughter once more you could kiss your job goodbye. So pucker up, laddie.'

'Je*sus!*' Ian thumped the arm of his chair and stood up. For a moment Kilbride felt a tremor of apprehension, then he recalled the Glock in the chair's side pocket. Self-defence, your honour… If he had to claim it, it would only be because it was true.

'Look,' he went on, in a more reasonable voice. 'Donna believes you killed her husband, right? Even if you had nothing to do with it, you'd still be putting yourself in a dangerous situation by staying here.'

'Oh, so you're *protecting* me now?' Ian gave him a nasty grin. 'And who's going to protect you if I go?'

Kilbride looked at him calmly. 'Is that a threat? Because I can tell you right now that there are plenty of people ready to point the finger if anything happens to me. Better to just cut your losses, take whatever we offer you and make a new life elsewhere.' The words reminded him so strongly of Duncan Wallace's speech to him, in hospital, that he could almost smell disinfectant for a second. 'It's mutually assured destruction if either one of us speaks up, after all.'

Ian's lips clamped tight, but his eyes blazed, and Kilbride had difficulty keeping his gaze steady. But he did it. And before either of them could say anything further, a new pair of headlights cut through the murky grey day outside. Ian looked, recognised the car and turned back to Kilbride.

'Is this your way of making sure I get out?'

'I didn't know she was coming,' Kilbride said, truthfully. 'But as I said, she's convinced herself we were in it together.'

'Oh aye? And what's she planning to do?'

'She needs you to confess, and then she's going to kill you. She told me as much. She'd do it, too.'

Ian sounded uncertain now. 'She's fucking lost it, pal.'

Kilbride's love for his daughter brought instant denial to his lips, but Donna's chilling words from last night were still reverberating: *If you don't help me, I'll know it was by your orders after all. And then I'll kill you.*

She had lost something, certainly, and her reason was teetering on the edge of the abyss as a result.

'You'd better go,' he said. 'I'll be in touch when it's safe, and we can talk about severance pay. And other conditions,' he added pointedly. 'Use the back door, and don't come back until I call you.'

'I'll be back tonight,' Ian said, as he pulled open the sitting room door. 'And you'd better have cash for me. Screw your "other conditions".'

***

'Have you got him to confess yet?' There was no greeting as Donna came in, no asking him how he was, just those blunt words and an enquiring glare.

'Not yet, no.' It took an effort for Kilbride to remain calm; his nerves were already stretched thin after his conversations with Martha and Ian. Sit down, love, let's—'

'I've hired an investigator,' she said, her pacing increasing speed instead. The face she turned on him was unsettlingly triumphant. 'He's going to *prove* it was Ian, and then that bastard'll get what's coming to him.'

'But you can't,' he protested. 'Even if it *was* him, you can't risk going to prison; it won't—'

'Won't bring Craig back?' She shook her head vigorously. 'No, it won't. But it might take away this...this...' She startled him then, by bringing her clenched fist around and hitting herself in the chest. 'I don't have *room* for it anymore!' The feverish glitter in her eyes broke and spilled over. 'No-one understands what we were to each other, not even you.'

'We do, love.'

'No.' She shook her head again. 'You think you do, but no-one saw him for what he really was. Only me and the kids know, and that was the way he wanted it.' She held up a hand. 'Yes, he could be cruel sometimes, and he was only too happy to carry out your orders. I know what he was. But he was also... He was our *life*. And he's been taken from us.' She leaned over him, and he couldn't help drawing back, despite wanting to pull her close instead. 'Where's Ian gone, Dad?'

'I don't know, but he'll be back later.'

'Good. In the meantime, I'm going to dig up everything I can on him, and pass it to Paul Mackenzie. What can you give me?'

'Give you? Nothing!'

'Former addresses, phone numbers, family members... Come on! I need everything!'

Kilbride tried to think past the wave of sorrow his daughter's grief was bringing him. 'Craig had most of it,' he said at length. 'He's got the employee details on his computer.'

'Why haven't you?'

'I mean the...the other type of employee. I've got the details of all the accountancy firm's staff, he's got the rest. It made more sense that way. I can't be connected, you know?'

'Right.' Donna pushed herself upright, away from him. 'I'm going to call Mackenzie and give him everything, and he's going to prove once and for all that I'm right. And when he does, I'll be ready.'

Before Kilbride could respond, or even register what she was doing, she leaned down again and dipped her hand into the inside pocket of the chair, bringing out the G42 with a small grunt of satisfaction. She shoved it into her coat pocket, and he finally found his voice.

'You've never fired the thing in your life!'

'How hard can it be? Besides,' she stopped at the door and turned that glittering, brittle smile back on him, 'if worst comes to worst I can always batter him to death with it. Fitting, don't you think?'

Donna had dropped the kids at school on her way out to her father's house, so there was no-one at home to pester her as she went into Craig's office and studied the neat desk. The unfamiliar weight of the gun in her coat was a distraction, and she took it out and examined it properly; better to be ready, when the time came.

It was pretty small, and appeared so bland that on first glance it looked almost as if it were moulded from a single piece of black metal. Or more likely some kind of polymer. She checked to see where the safety was, and frowned; there didn't seem to be one. Perturbed, she turned the handgun this way and that, but there was nothing. The trigger had an extra little tab on it, but it looked as though it would depress easily enough when she was ready. Dad seemed quite happy to have the damned thing riding around next to his leg, so it must be safe. She replaced it in her pocket and turned her attention to Craig's laptop.

It didn't take long to find the extra details that might help Mackenzie with his enquiries about Ian and his brother: parents deceased; home address in Stirling; even Neil's prison number, for some reason; and bank details from when he'd worked for her father before in the odd, hybrid capacity some of them did. She compiled a document for Mackenzie and sent it to print, then reached to hit the power button but paused; there would never be a better time to see if Martha had been telling the truth.

She opened the explorer window and did a search, to include hidden files and folders, for Craig's copies of her father's records. There were duplicates of her father's 'little green books', but it didn't take long to see that, even with her father's extra columns showing, these copies of the Excel sheets had scroll bars that looked unnecessary. She block highlighted several more blank columns and hit the font button, turning it red.

And there it was. Every time a meeting was scheduled for one of her father's pickups, another one showed up in red, with a forty-minute gap on one side or the other. Her heart in her mouth, she found the column for the fifteenth of each month and saw, as she had on her father's copy, an entry for Gavin Galbraith's original loan. A tick appeared every week, up to and including Thursday the eighth of this month. Galbraith was up to date with his payments for her father, so had no real motive to attack his bag man.

Further down in the rows now highlighted red, another name appeared against the fifteenth. But there were no corresponding ticks for the past two months, so someone dealing only with Craig had fallen behind on their payments. Someone was meeting him that night at the Three Sisters lookout point, forty minutes before he'd been due to meet Galbraith. *Someone* had beaten her husband to death, leaving Galbraith to find the body.

Donna looked at the name again, then she closed the document and called Paul Mackenzie, trying his mobile first. 'Hi, Mr Mackenzie. I'm really sorry to have messed you about, but I don't think I'll need your services after all.'

'Have you found the proof you need?'

'I have, yes.'

'And are you going to go to the police with it?'

She paused, thinking it over. 'I'll make sure they know, yes.'

'So Gavin... Mr Galbraith that is, will be cleared?'

Her anger flared again. That was his whole reason for wanting to pin this elsewhere, and it had nothing to do with justice for the innocent victim of a brutal attack. He was just like everyone else; Craig's life didn't matter.

'That's not my problem,' she said tightly, 'I just want justice for my husband.'

'Of course, I'm sorry—'

She cut the connection; she had other things to do now. She'd found the killer – all that remained was to prove it. And then avenge Craig.

It was almost noon by the time Mackenzie called Tony to tell him he was ready, then he locked up the office and headed down the main street to the little open arcade of shops near the end. As he walked, he re-played the story as it had unfolded yesterday in Tony's kitchen, and told himself they'd made the right decision. Ben Cameron was on the verge of letting his nerves destroy his life, and Tony's – and even Kyle's, no matter how much he was trying to protect it; seeing his father go to prison instead of him would be no easier for the boy than being sent to a secure unit himself.

Mackenzie waited under the small archway by the entrance to the arcade, sheltering ineffectually from the drizzle, but he was so used to it he barely noticed it anyway. After a few minutes he wandered up to Cameron and Son to make sure they'd be alone while they talked, but he was fairly confident they would be. They were way past tourist season, and Ben would probably be spending most of his days in his workshop, preparing Christmas orders.

A note on the door stopped his hand, raised to push the door open, and he hissed in frustration.

Closed due to illness.
Please email camerons.abergarry@live.com, or use website
contact form for all enquiries.
Sorry for the inconvenience.

He sent Tony a text then jogged back up the street to the office, where he'd parked his car. His own nerves were jangling now, and he drummed his fingers on the steering wheel as he waited outside Tony's house on Culloden Avenue, wishing once again that he was going to be riding out to Ben's place rather than driving – the twisting roads would have given his adrenalin a decent workout and helped him focus.

Tony appeared, dragging on his jacket and looking as if he'd spent the worst night imaginable. So much for getting the story off his chest. Mackenzie leaned over and pushed open the passenger door.

'You okay? You look dog rough.'

'Thanks a lot.' Tony gave him a sidelong look as he tugged at the seatbelt. 'Let's just get out there. You know where he lives?'

'Aye.' Mackenzie turned back out onto the main road. 'Jamie goes out there to mess about with the younger kid sometimes.'

'Oh yeah – you said.' He shook his head. 'Sorry.'

'Don't be. Just keep it together, or he'll take one look at you and decide it's just not worth the stress of trying to keep quiet. We have to convince him that the pointing finger *will* eventually move on.'

'But should it though?'

Mackenzie slowed a little, and frowned. 'What?'

'Nothing.'

They drove in silence, passing Mackenzie's place as they headed out of Abergarry, and Tony glanced over at it. 'That's your brother's caravan then.'

'It is. Not that he spends a lot of time in it. He'll be moving it out to the new site as soon as the contractors are allowed in, and—'

'I don't know if I can do it again, lad.'

Mackenzie's mouth dried. 'Do what?'

'Ever since Nick told me what he'd done to Dougie Cameron, and I chose to protect him, I've not been able to look myself in the eye, let alone anyone else. I could barely look at Ben either; his dad was completely innocent, he deserved justice. I just... Trying to convince Ben to do the same, to put him through *this*? I don't know if I can do it.'

Mackenzie absorbed this. 'Do you want to go back to town?

I'll see him by myself – I don't mind. But listen, Tony.' He slowed further and pulled into a passing place. 'Kyle was even less to blame than Nick was, but Mulholland was a copper. And the way they'll investigate will bring you into it, and then Nick... It'll all come out anyway. No-one wins.'

Tony didn't answer.

'So what do you want to do?' Mackenzie pressed, trying not to sound impatient.

'I'll come.' Tony straightened and dragged his fingers through his hair to neaten it. 'You're right. Ben's been through enough at the hands of my family; I ought to try and help him preserve his for a little longer, at least.'

They moved off again, but Mackenzie was more worried than ever now, and not just about whether they'd be able to talk Ben out of giving himself up. His old partner seemed to have aged years in the past few months, and today he looked beaten down by the weight of it all. He knew it would be difficult enough for himself to come back from this; for Tony it would be a hundred times worse, knowing what was also at stake for his own son.

At the Camerons' place he had to pull in by the side of the road, since there was no room in the yard. 'Damn, looks like Justine hasn't gone to work yet. Maybe we should have left it 'til a bit later.'

Tony squinted past him at the two cars. 'Maybe she's ministering to the sick.'

'Sick, my arse. Okay, if you go in first he'll guess what it's about, and then hopefully he won't argue when you suggest talking outside.'

Tony nodded. 'Come on then.' He led the way to the front door, and as they passed the two parked cars, one battered looking, the other quite smart, something pecked at Mackenzie's memory but he couldn't place it.

There was no answer to Tony's knock, and he looked back at Mackenzie. 'I can hear someone in there,' he murmured. 'He probably saw it was me and told his wife to keep quiet.'

'Try again,' Mackenzie said grimly. 'Shout, if you have to. We've got to talk to him today, before he loses it.'

He stepped to the other side of the porch and tried to look through the sitting room window, but the curtains were closed. He frowned and looked around.

'I don't like this... Tony?' He followed the path around to the back of the house, where he found Tony peering through the kitchen window instead. 'Are they there?'

Tony adjusted his gaze, and abruptly reeled back from the window. 'Justine!'

He shoved at the door and burst through. A second later Mackenzie followed, and they stumbled to a halt just inside the kitchen where Justine Cameron lay prone in front of the fridge, blood glistening along the side of her head. Kneeling at her side, her husband raised his head, his face pasty white, and stared up at them with wide, shocked eyes.

Chapter Twenty-Four

THE TRANSPORT VAN arrived back at the Abergarry Council Offices at twenty past three, and Maddy collected her signed time sheet. Six more hours down, and the graffiti clean-up had actually been one of the more pleasant jobs she'd been given, despite the fact that some bright spark had found it entertaining to spray most of the tarmac pathway that ran down the sloping length of the park.

There were just three on today's team, one of whom was Hazel, the quick-witted girl Maddy had met on her first day and hit it off with, and the time had passed more quickly than usual. Maddy felt her muscles protest as she waved and set off to collect her car from the council car park, but each day was becoming a bit easier, and she told herself she was at least going to be fit as hell when this was over. Every cloud.

She threw her coat and phone onto the passenger seat and was soon making her way towards Inverness, rehearsing what she would say to Gavin – provided he gave her the chance. Traffic was light, thank goodness, and by the time she passed through Drumnadrochit and started on what she always thought of as the last leg of the almost two-hour drive, she had pretty much arranged her thoughts as well as she was going to.

Her phone vibrated on the seat next to her, and she remembered she hadn't turned the volume back up after receiving it back from her supervisor. She threw a quick glance at the screen and swore lightly under her breath. The school. And she could see now that there were several missed calls before that, too; what were the odds they were from her dad saying he couldn't pick up Tas after all, and then the school wanting to know where she was?

To her annoyance she had just passed a wide layby on the other side of the road, where cars could pull in to look out over the expanse of Loch Ness, but up ahead, just before the road became too twisty, there was a narrow shoulder with a channel that took the runoff from the several small waterfalls that cascaded down to the road.

She pulled in carefully, nosing the front of the car in as close to the channel as she dared, and snatched up the phone before whoever was calling from the school could give up again.

'Maddy Clifford,' she said. 'Is everything okay?'

'Miss Clifford, it's now almost four thirty – we've been calling you and your father since school finished. Tas is getting quite upset. What time will you be in?'

Maddy went cold. 'You can't get hold of my dad? He was supposed to be picking him up today – I'm visiting Tas's father in hospital. Look, could you possibly call Charis Boulton, Jamie's mum, and ask her to take him? I'll try and get hold of Dad. I'm so sorry—'

'And if we can't get hold of Miss Boulton?'

'Then I'll send you the details for my brother. He's a police officer,' she added, as if that made things any better. Her heart was fluttering with fear; her father had never forgotten Tas before, and when she checked the missed calls after the call ended, none of them were from him. All from the school. She shut off the engine with shaking fingers and dialled her father again, and this time she waited until his voicemail kicked in.

'Dad? Please call me back, I'm worried...' She tailed off as, in her rear-view mirror, she saw a car pull in behind her, and the headlights made her blink. She lowered her window as the driver climbed out, and prepared a bright smile, ready to assure them that she knew her car looked as if it were bound for the scrapyard, but that it hadn't broken down.

Something stopped her from ending the call to her father, however, and a second later she thanked that instinct as she looked up, directly into the face of Ian George. Her heart actually stopped beating for a second, and the fleeting thought that this was the worst kind of coincidence was banished by the realisation that it was no coincidence at all. He must have followed her from the moment she got out of the transport van.

She fumbled for the ignition key, but a large hand closed on hers and pulled it away, so she lunged for the passenger side door instead, but was brought up short and hard by the seat belt she hadn't bothered to unclip. A low cry escaped her as she fumbled helplessly with the fastening.

'It's Ian George,' she managed to say into the phone before she was yanked back against her seat by hard fingers that twisted into her hair. She was dimly aware of him checking the road both ways, and a moment later the door was open and she was out in the cold evening air. It was horribly similar to the way Charis had been dragged out of this same car, by her ex-husband, and Maddy could hardly believe she'd fallen for such a trick.

Ian let go of her hair long enough to bring his own arm back out through the open window, and Maddy seized her chance. She shoved the car door as hard as she could into him, and tried to ignore the pain as it bounced back onto her, smacking into her left arm and numbing it from elbow to fingertips. It had the desired effect, however, and Ian stumbled back, his hands going to his face where the corner of the door had caught his cheek.

She levered herself away from the car, making for the middle of the deserted road, and began to run back towards the layby she'd recently passed; her best chance of finding help. As she ran she felt herself tensing up, waiting for a shot. Though, if he was armed, wouldn't he have shot her where she sat behind the wheel? But maybe he just hadn't had chance to take out a concealed weapon before she'd slammed him with the car door. If that were the case she would be on the ground before she knew anything about it.

But it wasn't a bullet that took her down; he must have been right on her tail. He flung a leg out to tackle her feet and she landed hard, knocking the breath out of her lungs as she instinctively folded her injured arm beneath her and landed on it. Seconds later she was up, being dragged to the side of the road, where dense bracken gave way to trees, and barely able to think in a straight line. There was none of the sinister silence about her attacker this time; he kept chanting with chilling monotony as he dragged her: *teach you, teach you, teach you, bitch...* and before long they were in the bracken and he was pulling her by only one arm, up the slope and into the cover of the trees. She urged herself silently to *fight back!* but deep down she knew that, were she to survive this, it would be through guile and not strength; even with him using one arm to pull them both up she was completely outmatched.

The shadows of the trees fell over them like tombstones, plunging Maddy into a dark green nightmare as Ian's fingers sank into the flesh of her arm, sending spears of pain shooting through it. Still stunned from her fall, and from the shock of finding herself here, she struggled to focus her thoughts on what form that guile might take, but all she could really think about was Tas.

'It's all your fault.'

The mantra had changed suddenly, and Maddy was jerked to a halt and shoved against a tree. She looked up at him and saw that blood was streaming from his nose as well as his cheek; she must have cracked him a good one with her car door, and the flash of savage satisfaction helped clear her mind.

They were hidden from the road here, and there was no hope of a rambler passing by; these trees were dense and disordered on their barely manageable slope; natural forest, rather than the regimented larches planted along parts of this road. On the other side, Loch Ness kept its secrets as night fell, heavy and damp, along the shadow of the Great Glen. The occasional hum of a passing car sounded lonely and distant, and Maddy's heartbeat almost eclipsed the sound of the wind in the higher branches.

'You and your spying,' Ian went on, as if she'd spoken. He was breathing hard, and in the sparse green light his eyes glinted like quartz as he stared at her with loathing. 'You cost me everything.'

'Blame Kilbride,' Maddy managed. 'He's the one who didn't trust you. I was just doing a job.'

'Job!' His backhand caught her across the face, but she saw it coming and mitigated the impact by moving her face in the same direction as the blow. But she was unprepared for the fist that sank into her diaphragm a split second later.

If she had been stunned by the fall in the road – that blessed place where help had still been a realistic hope – she was now cursed with the vivid clarity of thought that told her she was going to die. Here and now. Her knees unlocked, and she was vaguely aware of wet leaves on her face, but there was no other feeling. Just the faint sound of her own breath leaving her body in tiny, inexorable grunts, until there was nothing left. Her brain once more screamed at her, this time to *breathe!* but nothing worked.

After an unknowable length of time, though probably less than ten seconds, her muscles uncramped and the air rushed back in, and she realised she was lying curled up on the ground at Ian George's feet. There was pain now, a dull, aching throb centred somewhere between her chest and the pit of her stomach, but beneath that, and the relief of drawing air into her lungs again, real anger had started to find its purpose.

The wet ground soaked through the thin, light shirt she had been wearing on today's sweat-inducing assignment, but she lay still, with her eyes closed. Her head felt oddly heavy, and part of her anticipated the first strike of a boot and was tensed against it, but the rest of her knew that he would wait until he was sure she would be aware of every blow. His own fury had made that quite clear; every wrong path he had taken in life was her fault, and she was going to pay. She would only get one chance, she knew that much, so she would have to be ready the moment any opportunity, however slight, arose.

He was growing impatient, waiting for her to show a sign of awareness; she could tell by the way his boots shuffled impatiently on the ground next to her head. Her arms were wrapped across her waist and she could feel the cut he'd made in her arm over a week ago now, shallow but still stinging with a silver line of pain, while her left arm continued to throb from its brief contact with the car door. She grunted as he nudged her with his boot, immediately cursing herself for the involuntary sound, but it was enough for him.

She opened her eyes in time to see him drop to a crouch beside her, his mouth a hard, narrow line. Too late to turn away, she saw he'd been working that mouth, and now he let loose a thick wad of spittle that struck her lips and made her spit reflexively in return, twisting away and raising her arms to wipe the filth off her mouth with her sleeve.

'Teach you,' he said again, this time in an oddly thoughtful voice. 'How best though, I wonder?'

Maddy's blood ran even chillier. He didn't have the look of someone who was inclined to rape her; there was no desire there at all, either for sexual gratification or physical dominance. There was only hatred, and that wounded, almost betrayed puzzlement: how had he been treated so badly, by such a pathetic creature as this?

She watched the question cross his mind as his eyes travelled over her, and she became even more aware of the shrinking, cowardly sight she presented. Risking another blow, she straightened her legs, feeling with her feet that she was facing down the slope rather than up; it was little wonder there was pressure building in her head.

He didn't respond as she gradually unfolded her body; he just watched. Dispassionate, curious, and still with that betrayed look hovering around his eyes. He made no attempt to stop her as she shuffled to a seated position; he knew there was nothing she could do to overpower him, and was clearly plotting the next phase of his revenge sport.

To her hesitant relief, her feeling of helplessness was receding, to be replaced with the determination that she was going to get out of this alive. Somehow. Tas's image floated across her mind's eye, and the determination grew; she couldn't become just some headline in the Courier: *Local investigator's body recovered in woods...* She had a life to live, and a boy who needed her. She had things she still wanted to do, and being discovered by ramblers or dog-walkers wasn't one of them.

She looked up into Ian's face again; he had tried to wipe the blood with the sleeve of his coat, and now it was smeared like some grotesque mud pack. Her eyes took in the still-livid scarring that Kilbride's enforcer had put there, and she felt the beginnings of a twinge of sympathy; then the bruising pain beneath her breastbone flared again as she moved, and the sympathy died.

Ian leaned in closer and examined her minutely, from her eyebrows to her chin, as if committing every inch of her own face to memory – quite possibly before rending it unrecognisable.

'Stand up, hen,' he said; his use of her father's endearment, although common enough, took her by surprise and she was horrified to feel the sting of tears.

'I said, stand *up!*' Ian grabbed her aching left arm and pulled her awkwardly and painfully to her feet.

'Where's my dad?' she asked him, and her voice was thin and wheezy, the breath still burning in her lungs.

He gave her a genuinely baffled look. 'What?'

It was enough to convince her that her father's failure to answer his phone was unconnected with what was happening, and she was able to once again turn her thoughts to her own survival. She put on a show of hunching over, her free hand pressed against her chest, and although she could still feel the steel of his fingers through her shirt, she sensed a wavering of his attention as he peered down towards the road. She followed his gaze, then, when she knew he had noticed she shifted her own focus a bare inch to the left, and caught her breath in apparent surprise.

It didn't work.

Instead he gave her a slow, knowing grin and gripped her chin in one hand. The other hand reached into his pocket and brought out what was presumably the same blade he'd used on her before; this time he held it up so she could see it with hideous clarity, even down to the crust of dark red on its cheap, grey plastic handle. Maybe the blood was hers, maybe not, but there was no mistaking his intention to add to it. She opened her mouth to speak, but her words halted as he pushed her until her back came up against the tree, and this time he used his body to pin her there. The fact that her arms were free meant nothing; that blade was so close to her skin, she could almost feel the cold air bouncing off the steel. The faintest twitch of a finger, and he would feel it and that would be the end.

She tried once more, dredging up her last reserves of bravado. 'She's coming for you, you know. Donna. She knows you killed her husband, and she's going to—'

'She knows fuck all, I was too late with Kilbride. Now though?' He smiled, and it was horribly disarming. 'I get to take my revenge after all. Stand still, gorgeous, I'm going to *teach you*. No more pissing about with little nicks on your arm – just remember you've brought this on yourself.'

Maddy's stomach knotted in terror as she felt the tip of the blade touch her forehead. Every instinct strained to find a way out, but she knew that if she tried it he would dispense with his little power play and just push the damned thing through her eye. If she were able to keep still, she might at least live. Her instinct still rebelled, but it didn't matter any more; there was nothing she could do as he pressed the blade against her skin, and she felt the first trickle of blood running down to her jaw.

Wester Dean House. 11:20am

Ben Cameron's hand was on Justine's shoulder, and Mackenzie was relieved beyond belief to see the slight rise and fall of her back as she breathed.

'Jesus, Ben, what did you—'

'Look.' Tony gripped his jacket, and he turned to look at the table, where Donna Lumsden sat clutching a handgun of some kind. The weapon was small, compact, almost dwarfed even in her slender hand, but there was no doubting the business-like look of it. It was pointed loosely at Ben, but Donna's gaze was on the stricken woman.

'Is she all right?'

Ben's face twisted. 'Of course she's not all right!' He turned back to Mackenzie. 'She hit her with that fucking *gun!*'

'I meant is she alive?' Donna looked at Mackenzie now. 'You tell me. Cameron, you get away from her.'

Ben looked as if he wanted to argue, but Mackenzie gestured minutely with his head, and he shifted reluctantly away, his hands clenched in a visible attempt to stop himself from reaching out to his wife again. He stood up, very slowly, and took a seat opposite Donna.

Mackenzie noted that he didn't seem at all confused as to why Donna was targeting him, so what was the connection between her and Mulholland? Had she been in love with him? Might this mean that she'd had her husband killed after all, and now she'd discovered that, thanks to Ben, it had all been for nothing?

'She's alive,' Mackenzie said, checking Justine's breathing once more. 'Why are you here, Donna? You hired me to get Ian George for your husband's murder.'

'And I dispensed with your services, if you recall.'

'Aye, you said you had proof of...' His words tailed away; she hadn't said she'd had proof against George though, had she? He'd only assumed it. 'What have the Camerons got to do with your husband's death?'

'Not *the Camerons*, just him.' Donna's face was pale, but her eyes were red-rimmed and watery-bright.

'You can't think Ben had anything to do with it?'

'I don't think, I know. Why are you here, anyway? And who's he?' She nodded at Tony.

'I came here for a chat with Mr Cameron,' Tony said. 'It's not—'

'Was it you?' Ben suddenly fired at him. Then he gave a short bark of laughter. 'What am I saying? Of course it was. It could only have been you; you were the only one who knew.'

'Was what me?' Tony sat down opposite Donna, his eyes still on the gun, but it didn't move away from Ben. 'What are you talking about?'

'I paid you, didn't I?' Ben went on. 'Wasn't that enough?'

Tony frowned. 'Paid me what?'

'You took, and you kept taking. Ben's voice broke. 'I've lost nearly everything—'

'Shut up!' Donna said, her voice hard. 'I can't hear it yet, so shut *up*.'

Mackenzie began to stand, but Donna swivelled the gun onto him. 'Stay there. I need you to tell me when she starts to wake up. You?' She looked back at Ben. 'Not another word. I want your wife to hear it all. I need to watch whatever she feels for you die, right before you do.'

Ben swallowed, clearly with some difficulty, and even from where he sat on the floor Mackenzie could see sweat darkening his blond hair. His own heart was beating uncomfortably hard, and, not for the first time, he wished he was in the habit of carrying his own firearm. Even the unloaded one Jamie had found in Ben's field would have been a visual defence, but it lay safely in the glove box outside in the car. Which brought something else to mind, and he turned to Donna.

'We didn't see a third car outside. Did someone bring you?' *Someone else who knows you're here, and who might return at any moment...*

'It's Justine's car that's not there, not hers,' Ben said, still sending Tony dark, suspicious looks. Betrayed looks. 'It's in being fixed until Wednesday.'

Mackenzie's faint hopes of outside intervention died, and the pecking at his memory, outside, made sense now; that was why he'd had to pick up Jamie from here on Sunday. He kept checking Justine for signs of regaining consciousness, but at the same time he dreaded it; the remainder of Ben's life could be measured in minutes. When his wife awoke he would tell his tale, and when it didn't contain the confession she wanted, Donna would lose it. Either way he was a dead man.

He wondered if there was some way of subduing Justine's natural movement as she awoke, but it seemed unlikely; she was sure to at least groan, and get Donna's unwelcome attention that way. He kept a hand on her back, but because he had to sit slightly twisted to do so, his shoulder soon began to protest and the ache spread into his chest. He reluctantly lifted his hand away and rolled his shoulder. 'She's still out for the count. That's a nasty wound, she's going to need someone to check her over.'

'She'll get it – don't worry.'

'I still don't understand why you're here, Tony said to Donna. 'You've got this wrong, surely?'

But there was absolute certainty on Donna's face, along with hatred, as she fixed her gaze on Ben. 'I'm here because my family owes this one a death. *He* knows why, and now he knows what it's like to see someone he loves get hurt.'

'*That's* why you hit her?' Ben turned agonised eyes on her. 'She's a total innocent in all this! Craig Lumsden was—'

'Don't you dare!' Donna slammed her free hand on the table, making Ben flinch. 'Don't you *dare* speak about him as if you knew him. *No-one knew him!*'

Her own eyes were fierce and glittering, and she was clearly walking a very fine line. Mackenzie could see that Tony was already assessing his chances of wrestling the gun off her, but there was too much space between them. She would get off at least one shot, and it looked like a semi-automatic so she'd probably manage enough to hit them all.

Two things were now perfectly clear; that Donna truly believed Ben Cameron had murdered her husband, and that this had nothing to do with Alistair Mulholland after all. Mackenzie and Tony exchanged a quick, loaded glance; she obviously had no idea that she was on the scene of another murder, but Ben's nerves were going to give way under this pressure at any moment, and even if they made it out in one piece there would be more questions, with Tony certainly implicated.

They needed a change of direction, and Mackenzie glanced down at Justine again. 'Can I at least get this wound cleaned up, while she's still out? There's a lot of blood.'

'Please, let him?' Ben begged. He pointed to the top of the fridge freezer. 'There's a first aid box up there.'

Donna considered, then nodded. 'Aye. Move very slowly, I'm watching.'

Mackenzie rose, and sucked in a breath as a sharp pain shot across the top of his collar bone and into his upper ribs – he was paying the price for helping Ade with his caravan, and just at the time he needed to be at his most mobile. He used his good right arm to lift down the first aid box, and then ran some water into the washing up bowl.

Behind him he was aware of a heavy silence as he knelt back down and began dabbing at Justine's bloodied scalp, then Donna spoke up again.

'What did you mean about payment?' she asked Ben. 'What does this bloke know about you?'

Mackenzie looked around quickly, to see Tony's face set in a carefully neutral expression. 'This wound's pretty bad,' he said, but this time deflection was not working.

'Does he know what you did to Craig?' Donna said to Ben, more sharply. Mackenzie's heart locked up as the gun swivelled to rest on Tony. 'Were you blackmailing him?'

'No! And no.' Tony lowered his voice. 'I swear on the life of all I hold dear, I have no idea what happened to your husband, and I was not blackmailing Mr Cameron. Over anything,' he added pointedly, glaring at Ben.

Ben coloured and looked away, but Mackenzie had abruptly lost interest in what was going on at the table. He stared fixedly at Justine's back, blinked, stared again, and felt a slow sickness working its way up through him. He carefully – unobtrusively, he hoped – worked his finger beneath her jaw, but there was nothing. He pressed harder; still nothing.

He forced himself to continue cleaning the blood that

matted the blonde hair, but now there was a desperate sadness in him, which, in turn, was threatening to disappear beneath a swelling rage at the injustice of it. He loosened Justine's ponytail and allowed her hair to fall forward, concealing the face that would too soon become pallid and dull; all he could do now was keep up the pretence that she was going to wake up, and hope that Donna wouldn't discover the truth. At least, not until they'd found a way to take that gun from her. Ben Cameron's life depended on it.

Chapter Twenty-Five

THE INITIAL, searing pain as the blade sliced into Maddy's skin made her suck in a breath against a scream. The sensation of the blood streaming down her face as Ian brought the knife down, skimming past her eye and onto her cheek, caused her insides to cramp and clench, and suddenly, without warning to either of them, she lurched forward and vomited.

The movement jerked the blade backwards, instead of continuing its planned trajectory down her cheek to her jaw. She was vaguely aware of a tugging sensation as it caught in her hair, and then it was wrenched from Ian's hand as he staggered back in surprise, his boots splattered with the remnants of Maddy's afternoon coffee break.

She straightened, gasping for breath and blinking against the sticky blood that obscured the vision in her left eye. The pain was now a dull, burning, living thing that squirmed along the path of the cut to halfway along her scalp; the blade thudded softly to the soft, wet leaves that were strewn across the ground, and as Maddy swiped at the blood, and smeared it across her face, she realised she and Ian must look like the world's most gruesome twins.

Ian jerked around, peering down between the trees again, just for a heartbeat, then he turned back, and they both stared at the ground where the knife had stained the leaves. Ian darted forward to grab it, and Maddy realised, with a sinking heart, that she'd missed her one chance... Then something flashed into her mind. Hazel Douglas, on their very first day of CP: *Fifteen pounds of force, Maddy. That's all it takes.*

Ian's vomit-splashed left foot was planted alongside hers as he bent down to retrieve the knife, and, with Hazel's solemn words reverberating in her head, Maddy twisted away from him and kicked backwards. Her boot connected with the side of his leg, and she felt it *bend*, inwards, as Ian let loose a blood-curdling shriek and tumbled sideways to the ground.

Maddy whipped her head back and stared for a second, scarcely able to believe she'd done it. There was no chance of getting the knife herself; he already had it in his hand, and any attempt to grab it would bring her within striking range. Instead she turned away again and began to run. She heard him scream after her, and then something landed beside her and skidded alongside her slithering feet as she made her torturously slow way back down the slope. She spared a glance downwards and almost laughed; he'd thrown his precious knife after her, hoping to stop her that way.

She kicked it away, ahead of her and down towards the road. She couldn't hear any sound from him now except for a low, agonised cursing, and even that was falling away behind her. She spared a glance back; he wasn't following. She emerged from the trees onto an open part of the slope, and now the only sounds she heard were her own half-hysterical grunts of effort, and the scuffle of her boots as they slipped and slid over the scree that spilled down to the road.

She dropped to a sitting position and shuffled down, ignoring the myriad scrapes and digs in her palms until finally, in an explosion of fierce triumph, she landed on the tarmac. She'd lost track of how far into the trees Ian had dragged her, and had to look both ways up and down the road before she saw the two cars in the distance. No, not two any more. That was what had distracted him then, when she'd been too busy throwing up to hear, or care about it: another car stopping. Doors opening. Raised voices, perhaps.

The woman standing beside the third car shouted something now to her companion, who had his head shoved in through the open door of Maddy's Corsa; he withdrew it and they both stared at her.

Maddy lifted a hand. 'Please! Help me!' Her voice was barely audible, even to herself, but she saw the man's mouth drop open in shock at the bloodied sight of her, and the couple began moving towards her. For a moment, all Maddy could do was stand still as relief swept over her, then she thought she heard something on the slope behind her, and she made her feet move again, just in case.

Within a few minutes, she was sitting in the back seat of a generously sized SUV of some kind, and the woman was grimacing and pressing a fistful of wet wipes to her blood-streaked face. 'There you go, pet, we've got you now.'

It was a sobering thought that if Ian had been the first one down the slope, these two would probably have been the same sympathetic, ministering angels, and Maddy tried hard to explain that she had to get out, *now*, without sounding ungrateful. She pushed at the door handle, but the woman shook her head.

'Not a chance, love. You're not driving anywhere like that. John'll take you in to the hospital at Inverness.'

'You can come back for your car another time,' John said, and started his engine. 'If you've no money we'll give you enough for a taxi.'

'Thank you, I... Wait! My phone's in my car. I don't know anyone's numbers,' she explained as the woman turned surprised eyes on her. 'I need to call...to call...' She stopped, unable to continue, but wilted with relief as John raised a hand clutching her phone.

'I picked it up off your front seat,' he said. 'It was still recording a message. I hope you don't mind, but I shut it off without thinking. It means the message went through though, so you'd better call whoever it was back.'

Maddy kept the wet wipes pressed to her face with one hand and reached out for the phone with the other. 'Thank you.'

'What on earth happened?' the woman asked as John mercifully, finally, pulled out onto the road. 'We thought it was an accident at first, but did someone *attack* you?'

'Aye.' Maddy didn't want to go into it now. 'Just some nutter who got me to pull over. Turns out I'm exactly the sort of idiot I warn people about.'

She called her father again. Still no answer. She left another message, telling him she was on her way to hospital, but that she was fine and he wasn't to worry, then broke the connection before she could burst into tears. Paul was also unreachable, and she began to feel uneasy about him, too.

A call to Charis, as they were arriving on the outskirts of Inverness, told her that Tas was fine, at least. He was sitting with Jamie having his tea. And no, Paul wasn't there either. Charis's voice trembled a little as she told Maddy this; after what had happened in the summer, it was understandable, but Maddy had no time to soothe the woman's fears now. She thanked her for taking care of Tas, and said she'd be back in Abergarry as soon as she'd been checked over at Raigmore.

Then she sat back and tried not to think too hard about the cut that still bled freely, soaking through a second handful of wipes in a matter of moments. This wasn't like the cut in her arm; she knew that instinctively. It burned, just the same, but in addition to that thin, stinging thread of pain, this time she'd felt the sickening slice of her skin parting, and even the scrape of blade on bone, and she knew this was going to need stitches. Probably quite a few.

Thank God her eyesight had been spared, at least. As if to prove it, her tears spilled over, hampering the mopping up of the blood, and she had to grip her phone tightly to avoid giving in to the delayed reaction entirely.

John and his wife saw her safely into the hospital, then departed with apologetic explanations about coaches and timetables. She took their names so she could find them later and thank them properly, and made her way to A&E where, to her intense relief, she was immediately whisked into a booth.

Waiting with increasing fear, a massive bandage on her torn face, staring at the curtain and half expecting Ian to make a sudden appearance, she managed to call Ade. She could never remember later what she'd said, or asked of him – she had an idea she'd said she was worried about her dad and Paul, and then said something about being careful of Ian George, that he'd put her in hospital but was still out there...

Then she had broken the call and switched off her phone, unable to talk any further without breaking down. Woozy, and finally drained of adrenalin, she lay as still as she could while the nurse cleaned the blood and assessed the wound, but she kept breaking out in a chilly sweat and sour bile rose in her throat whenever she thought about it. The pain was held at bay by local anaesthetic, but it was soon clear that she'd been right; she'd been cut to the bone in places where there was so little flesh. She would need several stitches in her forehead and cheek, and the side of her head was shaved to facilitate still more, where the blade had sheered off its planned path.

'We're going to keep you in overnight,' the nurse told her gently, when it was over. 'The police will want to speak to you in a bit, but you've had a shock, and we need to keep an eye on you. All right?'

Maddy nodded, numb. 'Don't let him in,' she murmured, her eyes drifting shut against her will. 'No matter what he says he is to me.'

'No visitors,' the nurse confirmed. 'Now get some rest. You're safe now, pet.'

Maddy slept.

Kilbride's attention kept stealing to the driveway, expecting to see the headlights from Ian's hire car at any moment, and Martha kept pulling it back with small sounds of annoyance.

'Will you at least *listen* to me?'

'Look, I know you've felt side-lined sometimes, but you have to understand that things—'

'Side-lined? She banged her glass down on the coffee table and sat back, her eyes hard. 'Do you think I never knew you and your so-called friends used to call me *Martha-what's-her-name*? I've never truly been part of your family, no matter what you like to tell people. It's always, *leave us a minute, love*, and *why don't you go out for a bit?*'

'I took Ian on, for Christ's sake, and I didn't even know he was your son!'

'Aye. And now you've thrown him to the wolves.'

'I've done no such thing,' Kilbride pointed out, not for the first time. 'I'm paying him a good sum to bugger off and get himself somewhere safe, before Donna lands on him from a great height.'

'You can't believe he killed Craig!'

'Of course he did.' This time Kilbride's hopes were answered, as Ian's hire car turned into the drive and stopped behind his own car. 'He's here now. Are you going to go with him then?'

Martha hesitated, and there was something on her face he hadn't seen before. It seemed to be a sort of wistful regret. 'Do you want me to?' she asked, in a calmer voice.

'Do you actually expect me to forgive you for what you tried to do to Donna and me? She wanted to kill me! That's down to you. She's right on one thing though; you've played me right from the start.'

'That's not true, Will.' She inhaled slowly. 'Look, we've always worked well together. We can build something on that, can't we? Start again?'

'Why would you want to? After all, I'm the one who's throwing your precious son to the wolves, as you put it.' He looked out of the window; it was almost dark now, but he could see from the outside lights that Ian was taking his time getting out of his car. He turned back to Martha. 'I'm not ready to talk about any kind of future, not until I know Donna's going to be all right.'

'Does that mean you might be ready, sometime?'

He nodded reluctantly, still frowning at the car on the drive. 'Can't deny you've been a good wife,' he muttered. But it was more than that, and it was stupid to ignore it. She was right; they worked, as a couple, and even knowing what she did about his more shadowy side she had always shored him up emotionally. And kept her mouth shut when she had to.

She seemed to read acceptance in his expression, because she persisted. 'It was only when...when you had Craig do what he did, that I decided you didn't deserve to have your daughter hang on your every word any more. You didn't need to do that, Will. He did wrong, but there must have been better punishments. He's *my boy*.' Her voice started to shake, and he dragged his gaze back to her. She swiped furiously at the tears that had started to form on her lashes, and he tried to put himself in her position. If someone had treated Donna like that, would he have done anything else?

'We can't talk now,' he repeated, knowing he'd probably have done a good deal worse. 'But yes, we can talk. Later.'

She nodded and glanced at the window. 'I know you're about to ask me to leave the room,' she said, with a hesitant half-smile on her lips. 'So I'll save you the bother. I'll go and stay in Inverness for a few days. Call me when you're ready to talk things through.'

He listened to her climbing the stairs, presumably to pack a few things, then squinted out through the window again. Ian had the car door open now; his right leg was out, and he seemed to be trying to pull his left leg after him with one hand while he gripped the door with the other. His back was turned but Kilbride could hear a low, rhythmic grunt, and understood the man to be hurt – that gave them a slightly more level playing field, particularly now that Donna had taken his gun.

He wondered who Ian had run up against, and whether they'd ultimately come off better or worse, either way Ian certainly wasn't a happy lad. Kilbride rolled his chair to the front door, and opened it in time to see Ian hopping away from the car and flinging the door shut with a growl of mingled pain and rage.

Kilbride was startled by the blood-streaked features Ian turned on him. 'You'd better come in.'

He went back into the sitting room, hearing the not-too-muffled curses behind him as Ian followed. He had no interest in watching the man hobbling up the path, but that left leg looked to be bulging inwards slightly where the material of his jeans lay against it. It must have been some kind of divine providence that saw him passing his driving test in an automatic back in the day; there was no way he'd have been able to operate a clutch with his leg like that.

The front door slammed with as much vehemence as the car door had, and Kilbride winced, expecting to hear the tinkle of glass as the panel fell out.

'There was no need for that,' he said mildly, when Ian limped in. 'Don't do the same with this door, will you?'

'Where's my money?' Ian sank onto the sofa with visible relief. 'And I'll take a shit-ton of ibuprofen, while you're at it.'

'The money I can do,' Kilbride said. 'I'm allergic to ibuprofen though, so you've had that. Why didn't you get that seen to?' He peered closer. 'And that cut on your face looks pretty nasty too.' He sat up straighter, going cold. 'It wasn't Donna, was it?'

'Was it fuck.'

He seemed reluctant to say who it had been, but Kilbride didn't care – he just wanted the sod gone before Donna landed herself in jail. He needed to talk to her before she risked her future over this nobody, and now he could at least stop worrying that she'd also come off badly in the confrontation.

'I've had twelve thousand transferred into a new account,'

he said, and took a post-it note from the bureau. 'This is the account number, this is the sort code. Let me know where you're living, and I'll send the bank card on when it arrives. Three to five working days, apparently,' he added with an amiable smile. Waiting for the explosion.

Ian looked at the scribbled note, then back at him. 'Are you out of your mind? This is no good to me!'

'I can't get money just like that,' Kilbride reminded him reasonably. 'It's not as if I have a cashpoint in my garden.'

'But this is traceable!' Ian's face was rewarding in its outrage, and the blood was beginning to flow quite freely again. Bonus.

'Aye, it is at the moment. That's *my* protection. Up to you what you do with it when you get it though. Shut the account down, if you like. Spend the lot on prozzies and booze. Or ibuprofen,' he added, with a sadistic little grin as he nodded at Ian's misshapen leg. 'Now get out, and make sure I never see you again.'

Ian folded the post-it into smaller and smaller squares, unfolding them and re-folding. It looked like a nervous habit. 'I didn't do it, you know.'

Kilbride snorted, and let his veneer of friendliness drop. 'I don't believe you. But luckily for you it's in my interest to let things lie as they are, I don't want Donna going down just for the simple pleasure of putting a bullet in your stupid head. So,' he went on, feeling a weight lift off him now that things were evening out a bit, 'Galbraith does the time, and you get off with a warning from me. Take the money and go south, Ian. Way down south. Stay there.'

Ian began pushing himself to his feet, his face twisted in both anger and pain, but Kilbride held up a hand as he heard another vehicle. 'Wait.'

Ian sat back. Kilbride peered past the headlights and saw a familiar figure step out of a ropey-looking jeep. 'Okay, it's only Ade Mackenzie.'

Ian visibly tensed, which was interesting. Perhaps he'd been the one involved in whatever scuffle had resulted in Ian's bashed about face and wonky knee. 'Is he the private eye?' he asked, his hand braced on the arm of the sofa, evidently ready to shove himself upright again.

'No, that's his brother. Ade and I are going into business together – he'll just be wanting to talk about that. But better for us both if no-one sees you looking like that, so I'll get rid of him. You sit tight.'

Kilbride went into the hall once more, aware of Martha hovering at the top of the wide staircase, her wheelie suitcase propped on its base. 'It's only business,' he called up to her as he went to open the door. 'Won't be long.'

Ade Mackenzie smiled as the door opened. 'Hi, Will. Any chance of a word?'

'Not just now,' Kilbride said, affecting regret. 'I've got company. I'll give you a—'

'I won't take up more than a couple of minutes.'

'Really, it's not a good time.' Kilbride tried to convey friendly impatience, but Ade's smile only broadened.

'You'll like this – it's great news. May I?' He squeezed past Kilbride's chair, leaving Kilbride looking after him in exasperation and wondering if he'd misjudged the bloke. If he behaved like this he'd be a real annoyance as a business partner; he was clearly crap at taking a hint, and was striding altogether too quickly towards the sitting room. Will engaged the motor on his chair, something he rarely did in the house.

'Wait!'

Too late, he arrived in the sitting room to see Ade, that

wide smile still fixed in place, standing in front of the sofa. Ian was looking up at him warily, and apparently unnerved by the newcomer's bright cheeriness. Kilbride decided the best way was just to let Ade pass on the news and go.

'So, Ade, you had something to tell me?'

'Would you like to introduce me to your pal there?' Ade looked at Ian with a little wince of sympathy. 'Looks like you've come off worst in an argument with a bus.'

'This is a former personal assistant of mine,' Kilbride said, suppressing a sigh. 'Ian George.' From behind him he heard the front door click open again; presumably Martha leaving, and, relieved, he turned his attention back to his guests. Ade was stretching his hand out to Ian.

'Pleased to meet you, Mr George.'

The moment a bemused Ian took Ade's hand, Ade jerked him forwards and up, and delivered the most perfect Glasgow kiss Kilbride had ever seen. Ian slammed back into his seat, his mouth bubbling with fresh blood and his face slack with shock. Ade wiped his forehead, breathing hard, and now there was no trace of a smile anywhere. His eyes were hard, his jaw tight and his mouth a thin line of suppressed fury as he stood over the large but incapacitated form sprawled against the sofa cushions.

Kilbride felt his chair pulled roughly aside from behind while he was still staring on in astonishment, and two people pushed unceremoniously past him and stood either side of the man on the sofa. The opening front door hadn't been Martha leaving after all – in fact he heard her cry of alarm as she came into the room, but ignored her.

One of the men, the younger of the two, spoke clearly. 'Ian George, I'm arresting you on suspicion of abduction, and wounding or causing grievous bodily harm with intent.'

He and his companion, a uniformed officer of around Kilbride's own age, pulled Ian to his feet again while the plain clothes officer delivered the rest of the caution and slipped the cuffs onto Ian's wrists. Kilbride barely heard a word of it, but despite everything his relief was immense; Donna wouldn't be able to reach Ian now, and do anything to endanger her own future.

Ade looked at the younger newcomer. 'D'you need me to come too?'

The officer shook his head. 'You get off and see Maddy. Give her my love. Sergeant McFarland and I have got this.'

Ade turned to Kilbride. 'I'm sorry, Will. We only came here looking for information, but finding his car outside...' He shrugged. 'You understand why.'

Kilbride nodded, still stunned by the speed of it all. 'You said Maddy. The same girl who did that job for me last summer?'

'Bitch,' Ian muttered, and Kilbride saw Ade's fingers curl at his side.

'Aye. Maddy Clifford.' Ade said the name clearly, directly into Ian's ear. 'Your friend there has put her in hospital and scarred her for life.' The smile flickered back then, but it was laced with that same bitter anger. 'It looks like she was more than a match for this wee coward though, even though he was the one with the knife.'

The contempt was clear on his face, and Kilbride could feel it coming off his taut frame in waves. He looked at Ian, at the blood smearing his lips, at the ugly, misshapen knee, and finally at what he hadn't noticed before, the splashes of puke on his boots. What had he done? Just what the hell had he *done?*

He remembered Galbraith's fiancée, the polite, fresh-faced young woman who'd come here to discuss the job, had sat in that very spot on the sofa, in fact. She'd been so keen to ensure that her investigation was not going to result in violence towards its subject, and he'd reassured her he was only after the money that he'd been swindled out of, and not interested in revenge.

She'd gone away content with that, done her job quickly and efficiently, and now look what had happened to her... Kilbride rubbed hard at his face, trying to banish the knowledge, but it wouldn't go away. If she was indeed scarred for life, as Ade had said, then it was all his fault.

Chapter Twenty-Six

THE DAY HAD MOVED on with agonising slowness. Mackenzie looked at the clock on the cooker, near his head, and saw it was only just after three o'clock; Justine Cameron had been dead for around two and a half hours, and still he tended to her gently, insisting to Donna that it was a good thing she was unconscious; that it would give her a better chance of recovery. He had no idea if he was talking bullshit or not, but he managed it with conviction.

'My business partner was a nurse for five years,' he added, reaching for something to convince her further.

'What about brain damage?' Ben wanted to know. He had aged twenty years in the last few hours. 'Isn't it dangerous for her to be out for this long?'

'She's breathing,' Mackenzie lied, 'so there's oxygen getting around. She'll be fine. She just needs time.' He felt like weeping for the young mother, who'd been so alight with mischief just two days ago, calling him a rotten brother for his tongue-in-cheek comments about Ade. She'd reminded him so strongly of Kath, with her ponytail and her bright, fresh smile, it was unbearable to think they were both gone, so suddenly and pointlessly.

He shifted his position on the floor, wincing at the way he'd stiffened up through lack of movement. He'd deliberately positioned himself so as to shield Justine's face from both Ben and Donna, and he was now doubly glad he'd done so as, with a twist of dismay, he saw through the curtain of hair that her skin was now visibly waxy and pale. He tugged her sleeve down to hide the patches of lividity that had appeared where her arms lay on the floor. 'She's getting a bit cold here on the floor,' he said, a little lamely. *And isn't that the heart-breaking truth…*

'Let me sit with her,' Ben begged of Donna. 'Please!'

'What for? She'll not know you're there.' Donna rolled her neck and massaged the base of her spine with her free hand. 'Stay put,' she clarified, punctuating the words by gesturing with the gun.

'I could do with a wazz,' Tony said. 'It's been ages, and I'm not as young as I was.'

Donna pursed her lips. 'Put your phone on the table, turn it off, and if you're not back in three minutes I'll put one in your friend over there.' She nodded at Mackenzie.

Tony left the room without asking directions, and Mackenzie waited for Donna to ask how he knew his way around the house so well, but she was distracted by Ben, at the way he was suddenly staring hard at Justine. Mackenzie's gut froze, and he tried desperately to signal with his eyes, but it was too late.

Ben let out a tiny huff, as if his lungs had run out of air, and, heedless of the barrel of Donna's gun tracing his movements, he stood up and took a shaky step. Then another.

'Justine?'

Mackenzie held out a hand. 'Sit down, mate, she's fine.'

Ben ignored him and took another step; now Donna was looking at the woman as well. She seemed to shrink in on herself as Mackenzie watched, and then Ben had crossed the kitchen floor and braced his hands on his knees, as if to stop himself from pitching forward onto the prone form of his dead wife. Mackenzie didn't need to look at him to understand the icy hollow that would have opened up inside him; a hollow that would soon be overflowing with the most acute, hopeless, pointless pain. He remembered it all too well.

'Ben,' he began gently, but there was nothing else, and he fell silent.

Ben dropped to his knees and stretched out a hand. He touched Justine's hunched shoulder, let his trembling fingers trail down over her back, barely touching her, as if terrified he would have to accept the truth.

'Oh, Jesus,' Donna moaned softly. 'I've... Jesus.'

'No,' Ben muttered. 'Come on, Jus. Stop pissing about, aye?' A tear splashed onto Justine's shirt, and the sight of it being absorbed into the material seemed to galvanise him. He stood up and whirled towards Donna, heedless of the gun now pointed at his chest. 'Why?'

But the word didn't come out as the roar Mackenzie had expected, and it was easy to hear why: Ben's breath was too short, his throat too tight. Muscles locked in grief and confusion, hurting, constricting. Mackenzie rose to his feet now, too; the pretence was over, and so was the need to stand protective guard over Justine.

'Ben, don't,' he said, taking his arm and drawing him away. 'Sit down, okay? Think about your boys.'

Tony reappeared and took in the scene; for an instant it seemed he might try to snatch the gun from Donna's limp hand, but Mackenzie knew the risk was too great; if there had been a plan when he left the room, it had abruptly come to nothing. He sat down, his eyes not moving from the weapon, but his face registering his own shock at Justine's death.

'Sit, both of you.' Donna came around the table, and holding the gun hard against Ben's ribs, she used it to shove him towards a chair. He didn't wince, though it must have hurt; his gaze was pinned to his wife, his head twisting almost unnaturally as he moved away from her and Donna took his place by her side. One close look evidently satisfied Donna that this was no ruse, and she straightened again, looking every bit as white as the dead woman.

'This is your fault,' she told Ben, who turned his blank eyes away from her, staring at the table. Or perhaps he was seeing Justine, alive and breathing before that single, killing blow had landed.

Tony spoke quietly. 'Why are you so convinced it was him, Donna? A week ago you were just as certain it was Gavin Galbraith.'

'Christ, not you as well.' Donna moved to stand behind Ben and placed the muzzle against the back of his neck. Once again, he didn't flinch. 'Look,' she said, with rising impatience, 'new information comes to light, right? Certainties change; it happens all the time. I've done some of my own investigating,' she threw this comment towards Mackenzie, 'and I know it was him.'

Tony shrugged. 'If you're so certain, why haven't you killed him already, now that Justine won't be able to hear it?'

Mackenzie tensed; this was a dangerous direction to take. But Tony had read Donna accurately.

'Because I'm better than him,' Donna said. '*I'm* going to give him a chance to explain. So you can tell his side of the story for him, when all this comes out and he won't be able to.

So you can explain to his kids. Which is more than *he* did for Craig,' she added, prodding Ben with the gun hard enough to jerk his head forward. 'So confess to your friends now, Cameron, and then *we* can all go home, and you can join your wife.'

Her words were cold, but Mackenzie was sitting opposite Ben, and above the bowed head he saw that her face told a different story. She looked ill, terrified, and most of all distraught as she glanced down at Justine.

'You,' she said to Tony. 'Cover her up, for Christ's sake.' She wiped her mouth with the back of her hand, and her fingers were shaking.

'So why don't you tell us,' Mackenzie pressed, as Tony began searching drawers for a clean tablecloth. 'What makes you so sure Ben killed Craig, and why would he?'

'They were due to meet that night, out at Three Sisters.'

Mackenzie waited, but Donna had fallen silent. 'That's it?' He stared at her, incredulous. 'This,' he waved at the three hostages, 'and...*that*?' He looked past her, to where Tony was laying an incongruously cheerful Christmas tablecloth over Justine's body. 'All because you *think* Ben was meeting your husband, and that means he killed him?'

'I know he was!' Donna jabbed Ben with the gun again, and Mackenzie winced in sympathy, but Ben remained impassive. It was as if he had simply removed himself from it all, leaving only the shell of his body behind. Gone was the friendly, smiling craftsman, the family man, the husband Justine had so clearly loved. In his place sat a wraith.

'You realise you can't do this,' Tony said. 'Ben's not your man. He's not a killer.'

'But you are, Donna,' Mackenzie said, watching her face closely to see what effect his words would have. Hope flared a little as he saw her blench and wipe her mouth again. 'What are you going to do, kill again? Send an innocent man to his death, because you saw someone with that same name in a diary?'

'Spreadsheet,' she corrected absently. 'It was on Craig's spreadsheet. Not my dad's.'

'Which means... What? Do you know how many Camerons there are in this area?'

'I don't know anything about your list,' Ben broke in, coming back to them at last. 'I never had anything to do with your husband.'

'So you're telling me it *was* your partner's fiancé then?' Donna flung at Mackenzie. 'Because he was the only other one out there that night!'

'The only one scheduled,' Tony reminded her. 'Who's to say how many other people knew where he went to collect your dad's dirty money?'

'His new henchman, for one,' Mackenzie added. 'He'd know, if anyone would, wouldn't he? And we know he's got a nasty streak.'

'Anyone who's ever had to meet Craig out there them-selves, too,' Tony said. 'They'll all know it.'

Donna fell silent and switched the gun into her other hand. Mackenzie saw there was no safety on it, and couldn't help flinching as she moved it across.

'I did think it was Ian George, for a while,' she said after a minute. 'Because of what Craig did to him.'

'Which was what?'

They listened without interruption as she told how Ian and his brother had scammed her father, then she fell silent, though it looked as if she had more to tell, but didn't want to. 'What if it *was* him?' she blurted, when she'd finished. She looked as though she herself had ripped away a blindfold that had been blocking her reason as well as her vision. Her eyes were wide, unfocused, her thoughts turned inward, and when she spoke again it was in a small, shaking voice. 'What if I did all this for... for nothing? Taking Dad's gun, keeping you here—'

'Killing my wife,' Ben said dully.

'Oh, God...' Donna stepped away from Ben, and Mackenzie's heart beat faster; he felt all his nerve endings come to life, and his eyes stayed locked on the gun in her hand. He daren't let himself believe that her epiphany was total – she'd come too far. Done too much. *Destroyed* too much. If the chance arose for him to seize that gun, he'd have to be ready.

She crouched beside Justine and laid a hand on the cloth. 'I'm sorry,' she said in a low voice. 'I took you away and I'm so, so sorry.' She looked up at Ben. 'I can't let any of you go though,' she said, her tone bordering on conversational. 'Not yet. I need to think. Just...think.'

The three hostages remained silent as they sat motionless around the table, but Mackenzie felt that Donna wasn't thinking at all, she was remembering. Her face was blank, for the most part, but now and again a flicker of animation told him she was lost in some other time. A time when she'd believed, as everyone did, that their life was going to continue on the same even keel until they chose to change it.

He kept his eye on the gun, and he knew Ben and Tony were both doing the same, but so far no opportunity had arisen that would give them enough time to disengage her fingers from it before she could pull the trigger.

The time marched on again. It was well after four, and they were all becoming stiff and achy when Mackenzie's phone buzzed, and Donna looked up. 'Don't answer it. Turn it off.'

He checked the screen. It was Maddy, and he glanced at Tony, who gestured to his own, now-dark phone in the middle of the table.

'I was supposed to be getting Tas from school today,' Tony said. 'She's probably calling to ask you if you've heard from me.'

'Turn it *off*!'

Mackenzie did so, but the thought of Tas, and school, had reminded him of something else that worried him greatly. His gaze stole to the window, where the daylight was waning fast, and even as his thoughts went over what could happen, he heard the high-pitched whine of a 50cc engine working over-time. It pulled into the front yard and there came the sound of voices; one boyish and light, the other deeper, but still youthful.

Ben rose, horror on his face, and started to go around the table in the direction of the hallway that led to the front door. Tony stood too, and at the same time, Mackenzie saw Donna's look of complete panic. He knew the same thought had crossed her mind: she'd reached the end; she'd crossed a line; she was a killer now and had nothing more to lose.

Tony was closer to the door than Ben, and he lunged towards it; Mackenzie's blood turned to ice as Donna swung the gun away from Ben and a single shot pushed Tony into the door. He uttered no sound, but dropped to his knees before collapsing onto his side, his legs twisted awkwardly, his head striking the stone kitchen floor with a sickening crack.

Mackenzie heard cries of fear from outside, and then somehow he was moving, desperate to get to Tony, to the boys, and at the same time to get the gun away from Donna. He threw himself at her, and felt his fingers close on the weapon a split second before she jerked it, first out of his grasp and then immediately back into his chest. He went spinning into temporary blackness as pain caught fire in the recently pinned bones, and for a second he could think of nothing except fighting the faint that swept hotly over him.

When he could focus again he looked at Tony's huddled shape, praying for a sign of life, but seeing no movement. The spreading blood stain covered Tony from the shoulder to midway down his back, but the woodwork of the door was intact and stain free, and that gave Mackenzie some hope, at least, that there was no gaping exit wound that he couldn't see.

Ben was moving towards the window instead now, and Mackenzie saw that Ethan had come running around to the back of the house at the sound of the shot. Kyle had followed, and now he grabbed Ethan's arm and yanked him away, but Ethan's face was a mask of horror as he caught sight of his father and the woman behind him with the gun. He seemed frozen to the spot.

Ben tried to wave him away, but Donna was on him, and jammed the small but lethal gun into his lower back. 'Come away!'

Ben stiffened, and Mackenzie knew that if Donna pulled that trigger again now, young Ethan would never recover from what he would see hit that window – even if he survived the exiting bullet itself. Kyle once more tugged at his younger brother's arm, and they stumbled away from the window together. A moment later there was the sound of the moped's frantically revving engine as it lurched away, skidding on the gravel.

'They'll call the police,' Mackenzie said, desperation in his voice now, as he looked again at Tony. 'It's time to let it go, Donna. Tony's going to need help. Don't let him die too.'

'Turn around,' Donna said to Ben, and stood back while he did so.

Mackenzie glanced out of the window, now at an angle that allowed him to see the road. 'There's a police car out there already,' he said. 'More than one. It's all over; they've come for you.'

'Already?'

'Someone else will have called them,' Mackenzie said. It had to have been either Maddy or Charis, and he sent them silent thanks, and a fervent hope that he and Tony would both be alive to deliver real ones. 'Let me help Tony. Please!'

She pushed the gun into Ben's midsection, forcing him away from the window and against the wall. There was a sort of defiance about him now; he looked at Justine's shrouded figure, then back at the woman who'd killed her, and a spasm of pain showed only briefly on his face then was gone again. To Mackenzie's dismay it looked as if he had stopped caring about anything now, except bringing this woman down. He looked poised to do something desperate, no matter what the cost, and Mackenzie's heartrate seemed to triple as he watched the different expressions flit across his face.

'Ben,' he said in a low voice, 'think about the boys – they're going to need you.' His glance towards Justine finished the plea wordlessly: *especially now*.

From what he could hear, at least two police vehicles had arrived outside. They were making no secret of their arrival, but given the obvious difficulty in remaining covert out here it made more sense to take the bold approach. He saw black-clad figures moving beyond the window, where the officers had split resources to cover both exits.

'Donna,' he went on, trying to sound steady. Reasonable. 'It's all done now; you know that.'

Donna's eyes were brimming now. 'I didn't mean to kill her.'

'I know that,' he said. It wouldn't achieve anything to remind her that her original intention had been to kill Ben instead. 'But you could still save Tony.'

'Listen to them,' Ben said. 'They've got armed backup.'

'Armed? They don't need that.' Donna's voice was rising, becoming more shrill in her panic.

Mackenzie was about to beg once again to be allowed to check on Tony, but it died in his throat as a knock came at the front door and a voice floated down the corridor.

'Shots were reported. Is anyone hurt?'

'One dead, one down,' Mackenzie yelled, and Donna turned anguished eyes on him.

'Stop it! I didn't mean—'

'Mr Cameron! Surrender your weapon, and come out with your hands raised above your head.'

'What the hell...' Ben started away from the wall, but was stopped by the pressure of the gun as Donna shoved him back again.

'Let him go out,' Mackenzie said quietly. 'He's innocent; he's lost his wife. His kids are terrified. Let him go, aye?'

'No! Let me think!' She turned back to Ben. 'They seem pretty sure he's the bad guy, so...so, maybe he really is.'

'You know he isn't.' Mackenzie shook his head. 'He didn't kill his wife, or your husband. And he didn't shoot my friend.' He looked at Tony. 'The only reason they're focusing on Ben is because this is his place, and they know we were visiting him.'

'So they don't know I'm even here?' There was a flare of hope on her face, but Mackenzie, thinking of Tony, killed it with unrepentant blunt force.

'They didn't, but they will now they'll have seen your car, and checked the plate. Give it up.'

The activity on both sides of the house seemed to kick up a notch without any discernible signals. Just a heightened sense of urgency in the footfalls on the paved yard and the gravelled patch beyond.

A moment later the warnings began. Ben was once more urged to come out, to surrender his weapon, to release his hostages. Questions followed; who was dead? Who injured? What did he want?

Mackenzie appealed again to Donna. 'Let me check Tony.'

'Stay where you are, or I'll end this for all of us right now.' Donna's voice was shaking almost too hard for him to understand her, and of all the expressions he could see on her face when she twisted to speak to him, the most heartrending was her total bafflement that it had come to this. Her eyes were brilliant with tears, and her free hand shook as badly as her voice as she pushed her fringe away from her eyes.

'Step away from Ben,' he urged. 'They can see in now; they'll see you've got him at gunpoint, and—'

'Put down the gun, Mrs Lumsden,' a voice called, electronically magnified and sounding eerily inhuman. 'Step into the middle of the room with your hands raised to your shoulders.'

Donna looked up into Ben's face. 'Do you swear it wasn't you?' she whispered. 'Please... No-one understands. I have to know.'

'I swear,' Cameron choked out, whether in relief or because she was still making it hard for him to breathe freely, Mackenzie didn't know. But his own breath came a little easier as Donna took a step back, bringing the pistol with her.

'Place the weapon on the floor,' the voice commanded. She didn't, and Mackenzie frowned.

'Do it,' he urged. 'These people aren't messing around.'

'I'm not going to shoot anyone,' she said. 'I just need it. To protect myself.'

'But you're not protecting yourself,' Mackenzie said in rising fear, as a red dot appeared on the back of her coat. She turned around and saw it, and now it was bobbing across her chest. 'They can't hear you, they don't know you're not going to use it again. Put it *down!*'

'They'll stop me from finding Ian,' she said in despair, her eyes tracing the minute movements of the insidious red light. 'I have to, to—'

'Donna, for Christ's sake!'

'Mrs Lumsden, put the weapon down! We have the authority to shoot.'

'*Donna!*'

But she only gripped the gun more tightly, holding it to her chest as if afraid someone was going to come in and wrestle it from her grasp.

Ben threw a desperate look at Mackenzie and took a step towards her, probably thinking to capitalise on her uncertainty, but her eyes went to him and curious calm came over her face. She looked over her shoulder at the collection of black-clad officers in the yard, then straightened her arm slowly, deliberately, and placed the gun against Ben's chest.

'Don't!' But Mackenzie could only watch in horror as, to the accompaniment of the sound of smashing glass behind him, Donna's head snapped violently sideways and she crashed to the kitchen floor. Her shoulder struck the corner of the table on the way down, and her body flipped grotesquely to land face-up, sprawled half on Justine and half on the stone flags.

In the second after it happened Mackenzie dropped to his knees beside Tony and checked for signs of life. He encountered a faint pulse and bowed his head briefly in relief, then yelled out for a paramedic, still bent over Tony's crumpled form, and eased him aside to allow the door to open and admit the help they needed. It didn't come.

Even as he reasoned that the police and paramedics didn't know for certain that it was now safe, he saw Ben throw himself down and begin pulling at Donna's limp form, as if seeing her so close to the woman she'd killed had driven the final shreds of rational thought from his head.

Mackenzie left Tony and went over to crouch beside him. 'It's a crime scene,' he began, gently enough, but Ben turned to him, his face awash with furious tears.

'It's my *wife!*' He shoved Mackenzie backwards, and, caught off-balance, Mackenzie landed hard. Pain set his chest alight again and he swore at the intensity of it, but tried again.

'They'll need to investigate. Leave them.'

He looked at Donna's face, the blue eyes wide and now empty, and couldn't help feeling a stab of sympathy no matter what she'd done; he knew all too well how it felt to be driven demented by grief.

There was more shouting from outside, he bent down to bring Ben to his feet, then went to the window, his hands raised as far as he could without wrenching his shoulder.

'It's over!' he shouted. 'We have one in need of urgent medical care!' He glanced back at Donna. 'At least she knew she was wrong to come after you. Come on, we have to—'

'Wrong?' Ben gave him that awful, blank look. 'She wasn't wrong.'

The front door opened, admitting firearms officers who were still on their guard, and as their cautious footsteps sounded in the hall, Mackenzie stared at Ben, unsure he'd heard correctly.

Ben's bloodshot eyes met Mackenzie's, his lips white as he looked around him at the devastation. 'All this *is* my fault. Even Justine.' He swallowed hard and spoke in a whisper under the shouts of warning from the hall. 'Donna was telling the truth. I killed Craig Lumsden.'

Chapter Twenty-Seven

'Mᴜᴍᴍʏ!'

Maddy looked up from her seat as the voice rang down the hospital corridor; a moment later a small shape flung himself into her arms, and all of yesterday's terrors and shocks were, for the moment, held at bay. She could feel a smile curving her mouth, in turn tugging the stitches underneath the padded bandage she wore, and she knew it would be lopsided and strange looking. She was glad he was pressed too closely to see it.

'Have you been a good boy for Charis?' she asked, with an effort, loosening her grip and letting him slither free.

'He's been ace, haven't you, mate?' Charis sat down beside her while Jamie took the next seat along. 'How's your dad?'

Maddy could only nod. The bullet had missed his heart by centimetres rather than inches; it had been too close to think about. The words *he's going to be all right* were stuck somewhere between her brain and her lips, and she knew that if she tried to force them out she'd break into sobs. The thought of what might have happened to him if he'd been left much longer was too terrifying to contemplate.

'What happened to your face?' Tas reached up to touch the huge, fat bandage that covered her left eye, from her forehead to halfway down her cheek. Another bandage covered the shaved side of her head.

'Oh, I just bumped my head on something yesterday,' she said, trying to speak as normally as possible. 'It's only covered up so it doesn't get any dirt in a little cut I managed to give myself.' She looked at Charis, whose evident concern nearly set her off again. 'Where's Paul?'

'On his way. He's been talking to Ben Cameron, said it was important.'

Maddy gave her a searching look. 'I presume Paul told you everything about Ben, and my dad. And...' she left Mulholland's name unspoken, but Charis got it immediately and shuddered.

'Yeah, he did.' She looked nervously around them. 'I know it's wrong to rejoice in any death, but my God, if ever anyone deserved it.'

'Aye, I know what you mean.' Maddy's voice softened. 'Thank you again for calling the police. You saved my dad's life.'

'I told them Ben Cameron was the dangerous one,' Charis said. 'I really thought he was.'

'He must be devastated. His poor wife.'

Charis nodded, her face sober. 'She was so nice too. It's horrible.'

'So sad for those kids, losing their mum like that.' Maddy turned to Jamie, forcing herself to brighten. 'How about you — are you okay?'

He nodded, but he seemed to have lost the spark that

usually managed to peek through. 'Ethan and Kyle have gone to their cousins' place.' He looked as if he wanted to say more, but fell silent again and went back to playing with his fingers.

'You have to feel sorry for Donna Lumsden's two as well,' Maddy said, turning back to Charis. 'They've lost both their mum and their dad, in the space of a fortnight.'

The reflective silence was broken by Paul's arrival. He was looking grim, and his expression darkened further as he caught sight of Maddy. 'How is he?'

This time Maddy was able to reply. 'Still stable.'

Paul squeezed her hand. 'And you?' he said softly. Maddy cast a quick look at Tas and gave a minute shake of her head; he nodded, still holding her hand. She saw Charis looking and almost drew away, but Charis didn't look put out. She just seemed glad that Paul was there.

'What did Ben say?' Maddy asked. 'Was it important, like you thought?'

'I'll say. I can tell you everything after I've seen Tony – it'll take a while. Is he awake?'

'No. He's exhausted.' Maddy stood up and held out her hand to Tas. 'Let's go back to yours for breakfast, Paul. It's the closest out of all of us.' She paused, then asked in an unconvincingly casual tone, 'Is Ade there?'

Paul's mouth twitched, just a little, but Charis actually snorted, the little rat. Maddy glared at her, though with no real animosity. They understood one another better now.

'Yes, I think so,' Paul said. 'Don't tell me he's worn you down after all?'

Maddy flushed. 'He got stuck into my problems without question, got hold of Nick and Farly, and made sure Ian George was arrested. I owe him a lot of thanks for that.'

'I'll make sure he's available for accepting apologies,' Paul promised, and took out his phone. Presumably he thought she hadn't seen the grin that flashed between him and Charis, but rather than making her feel silly it gave her a sense of warmth, and that stayed with her as she followed them out of the hospital and back to Abergarry.

In Paul's kitchen they devoured a mountain of buttered toast between them, and the mood swung between relief that they were all safe, and curiosity about what Ben Cameron had said to Paul that had been so urgent.

'He's going to confess to Mulholland's murder,' Paul said, dropping another two slices on the plate in the middle of the table. 'It's the only way he can protect Kyle. Ethan's agreed not to say anything about Kyle leaving their cousins' that night, and he was the only other person who knew he'd gone. They won't question that. Ben's going to say he acted alone.'

'That's fatherly devotion for you,' Charis said. 'Poor bloke. Bit of a hero when all's said and done.'

'I wouldn't speak too soon,' Paul cautioned. Seeing Maddy's worried look, he shook his head. 'I mean it, Mads, he's not going to implicate your dad. Tony was injured trying to save his kids, and he feels he owes him for that, and for helping him the night Kyle...' he glanced at Jamie, 'did what he did.'

'Thank God for that,' Maddy said. She began to cut up her toast into small pieces; it hurt to open her mouth wide enough to eat properly. She hadn't allowed herself to think about the scars that would be left, but she kept catching Ade looking at her, and the expression on his face was a little frightening at times. She hadn't heard the details of the arrest of Ian George, but there was a bruise on Ade's forehead, with an abrasion in its centre, that told her enough.

'There's something else though,' Paul was saying, pulling her attention back. The group around the table sat silent and stunned as he told them what Ben Cameron had said, those words he'd whispered to the backbeat of the boots approaching down the hall.

'He *admitted* it?' Maddy said at last.

'That's all he said at the time. But he got my number from Justine's phone and called me this morning, said he wanted to see me. He's told me everything.'

'Well you'd better tell us too then,' Charis said. 'Jamie, take Tas upstairs, will you?'

'Mu-um!' His face was a picture of dismay, and Maddy managed a smile without wincing too much.

'Tas can go up on his own, if Jamie doesn't mind him playing in his room?'

'I don't know that I want Jamie to hear this either,' Charis pointed out.

'After last summer I think he can handle it,' Paul said gently. 'I'll not be too graphic, I promise.'

Charis pursed her lips, then nodded. 'Okay. Go on up, Tas. Take a bit of toast with you.'

Tas looked at his mother cautiously. 'I'm not allowed to eat in my room at home.'

'Well you're not at home now,' Charis reminded him with a little smile, ignoring Maddy's frown. 'Neither are we actually, but Mackenzie won't mind. Go on, lad.'

When he'd gone, Paul linked his hands on the table in front of him and, looking only at Jamie, gave him a brief explanation of what had happened to Alistair Mulholland. He left out the gorier details, telling it almost as if he were outlining the plot to a TV programme, where Jamie had missed the first episode. Maddy was curious to see Jamie's reactions; the boy looked interested, concerned, then fascinated, and there was no sign that he was revolted by anything he'd heard. She was glad to see no sign of pleasure either, which he might well have been expected to display after what he'd seen of Mulholland. A glance at Charis showed she was just as relieved about that.

Finally Paul was ready to begin Ben Cameron's story, which picked up where Tony's had left off.

'Ben got everything cleaned up pretty well. Tony told him what he'd need, and explained how to get the stone flags properly cleaned, so by the time his family came back you'd never know anything had happened at all. Kyle was a wreck, of course, and kept himself to himself, but they passed that off as being upset about his dog.'

'Ethan told me he was furious that his dad made him miss the end of the holidays too,' Jamie added. 'And his girlfriend dumped him.'

Paul nodded. 'Well things started settling down, but then Ben started getting texts, demanding payment or the messenger would go to the police.'

'Blackmail?' Maddy shook her head. '*That's* what he was accusing Dad of?' Paul had told her about that astonishing claim, last night at the hospital while they were sitting through that interminable wait for news of her father's operation. It was disturbing to think Cameron could have imagined he'd do something like that, but then he didn't know Tony like she did.

'Anyway, the demands got more and more. Ben mortgaged the shop, but couldn't touch the house as it's in joint names. He ran down his savings account, swapped his car for something rattier – told Justine it was because takings were down, and that the kids needed more expensive stuff. You know the kind of thing.'

'So who could have been doing it?' Ade mused. 'Lumsden?'

Paul shrugged. 'I think so, though it's too soon to know if the demands stopped when Lumsden's clock did.'

'And Ben borrowed the money from Kilbride?'

'Sort of. The loan was arranged by Lumsden himself, though Ben didn't know that. Lumsden stole it from his father-in-law, and was skimming the interest Kilbride should have earned off it. Which was a lot.'

'So there's proof Ben *was* due to meet Lumsden the same night as Gavin was.' Maddy sat up straighter. She winced as her bruises flared, but this confirmation was setting off fireworks in her head. 'And if he confesses, Gav's off the hook? He'll never have to go back inside?'

'Aye, he'll be released,' Paul said, 'and he'll probably be in hospital until then anyway.'

'Imagine the compo,' Charis said in wondering tones, and caught Maddy's disapproval square between the eyes. 'Sorry.'

'But what made him do it?' Maddy shook her head. 'It was such a savage attack. I'd never have thought him capable of something like that.'

'Lumsden had apparently said something about the sins of the father being visited on the children,' Mackenzie said, 'and he just lost it. He had a tyre lever with him, for protection, and he said the cops'll find it in his car and confirm it's the murder weapon. He cleaned his steering wheel, but he was in too much of a mess to do a good job – said the forensics team are bound to find traces in the leather, and in the top of his ignition key. All those little cut-out shapes in the plastic.'

'So no going back then, once he's confessed.'

'Nope. They'll find Lumsden's blood on his coat, from

spatter as well as from his hands. He said he sat with his arms crossed while he was trying to figure out what had happened. It'll all be there, they'll have a field day.'

'All of this means that they'll take him seriously when he confesses to Mulholland's murder too. He's going to hold his hands up to this one, then ask for Mulholland to be taken into consideration.'

'I just don't understand how *anyone* else could have found out about what happened to Mulholland, in order to blackmail Cameron in the first place,' Maddy said. 'From what Dad said it was—'

'It was Kyle,' Jamie said suddenly. Everyone turned to him, and his eyes were growing steadily rounder as they fixed on a point somewhere beyond the table. His thoughts were clearly buzzing at some speed. '*Kyle* was the blackmailer!'

'Where did you pull that one from?' Charis asked, bemused. 'Why would he do that to his own dad?'

'He was pretty angry.'

'But angry enough to cause his family *that* kind of hardship?'

Paul shook his head, and looked with renewed respect at the youngest detective at the table. 'He'd likely have no idea he was doing that,' he pointed out. 'All kids think their parents are bottomless money pits, don't they? At least, those with rambling old houses in their own grounds, two incomes, and a bricks and mortar shop thrown into the mix.'

'Cameron's not likely to be admitting to anyone that he's in desperate straits,' Maddy agreed. 'Least of all his kids.'

'So you reckon Kyle just did it out of, what, spite?' Charis still looked doubtful. 'I don't know that I can believe that.'

'The kid had just *killed* someone,' Paul said. 'His head will still be all over the place, even now. His girlfriend dumped him, which might seem like the least of it to us, but we all know for a sixteen-year-old it can mean the end of the world. Plus, some nutter had broken into his house and threatened his dad with a gun, and on top of that he'd lost his dog and wasn't allowed to tell anyone how it really happened.'

Charis chewed her lip, and shrugged in agreement. 'Yeah, that's a lot to deal with.'

'Ethan said he got a new phone,' Jamie said, 'and a new crash helmet too. But he didn't want to get rid of his old phone, because Ethan only asked if he could have a lend of it and Kyle told him to fu...that he couldn't,' he finished, with a faint flush staining his cheeks.

Charis closed her hand over his and, not quite suppressing a smile, leaned forward to brush his forehead with a kiss. The flush deepened and Jamie backed away; Charis ruffled his hair, the smile fading. Maddy supposed that was in hers and Tas's future too, but luckily not yet.

'That poor lad,' Ade murmured. He'd sat mostly silent throughout this discussion, but now his words gave the conversation a new focus.

'If he thinks he's to blame for his mum's death...' Maddy felt desperately sorry for the boy, shipped off to his cousins' place again to re-live the last time that had happened, and with no-one to talk to.

'Ethan said he'd been snarky with his dad ever since Pickles died,' Jamie said quietly. 'They were always having rows. And Kyle started hitting Ethan, too.' He looked at Charis. 'That's where the bruise came from, not his dad.'

'He couldn't hit his dad,' Charis said, 'so Ethan became the substitute punch bag. Poor kid.'

'So Kyle got a taste for making his dad suffer.' Paul sighed. 'How the hell are we going to let him know he's safe, without anyone finding out? And more importantly that he needs to talk to someone? I dread to think what's going on in the lad's head.'

'By texting his pay-as-you-go phone?' Jamie suggested. 'You can get the number off Mr Cameron, can't you?' He positively glowed under the approving looks from around the table.

'We can,' Paul said, perking up, 'if we're quick.'

'When's he going to make this confession?' Maddy asked.

'As soon as they've let him see Justine one last time. Her post-mortem's this morning, so that'll be later today. I'm pretty sure he won't mind passing that number on; he's going to want to know there's someone looking out for Kyle.'

'Call him now,' Charis said, jumping up to fetch the landline.

Paul took out his own phone and read Justine's number off it, and Maddy tried not to imagine the pain it was going to cause Ben Cameron to see his wife's phone ring and to have to answer it. She couldn't stay in the room.

She pulled open the back door and stood for a while in the doorway, breathing in the dismal afternoon air, and listening to Paul speaking to a man who was about to throw his life away to protect his son. Inevitably her thoughts took her back to August, and to what her father had done for Nick.

Remaining silent about that terrible, twenty-five-year-old crime had taken its toll on him, wearing him down, eroding his sense of who he was and leading him down this increasingly dark path. It had led him first to Mulholland, and then to Ben Cameron's door, and finally to a hospital bed, hooked up to morphine drips and half a dozen monitors that she recognised only too well.

In the peaceful early hours, he had woken and looked bemusedly at her and Paul, almost frightened to see them, as if they were his death bed confessors and he was clinging to life only until his story was told. When the disorientating effects of anaesthetic and confusion had worn off, he'd told them, with tearful relief and see-sawing emotions, that he felt he had finally atoned in some way for Nick's actions.

'I can't bring Ben's dad back,' he'd murmured, 'but I *can* help his boy.'

Maddy twisted in the doorway now as she heard Paul ring off, and from the general wave of relief around that table she understood that Ben Cameron had given him the number of Kyle's pay-as-you-go mobile. There was a further hush as he dialled it, with everyone holding their collective breath in case the boy had already launched the phone into the Ness in a panic.

'Kyle? It's Paul Mackenzie. Don't hang up, just listen...'

Relaxing again, Maddy turned back to stare out over the garden. Ade's caravan still stood there, the eyesore, dripping water from its warped roof, and with its wonky metal step looking like every health and safety nightmare in the book. It should have been so dark and gloomy here, given the weather and the time of year, but as Maddy raised her aching face to the treetops, listening with a new glow of warmth to the low murmur of familiar voices behind her in the kitchen, she saw a glimmer of pure, clean light touching the topmost branches with splashes of gold.

Crossfire

The first book in this series, *Crossfire*, was published by Hobeck Books as ebook and paperback on 6 July 2021.

In this brand new series, under the brooding skies and the sublimely beautiful landscape of the Scottish Highlands, struggling PIs and long-term friends Maddy Clifford and Paul Mackenzie find themselves drawn deeply, and sometimes accidentally, into some very dark situations.

To what depths would you sink to protect your own?

Hogmanay 1987
A prank robbery has fatal consequences.

Five Years' Later
Highlands town Abergarry is shaken by the seemingly gratuitous murder of a local man. The case is unsolved.

Present Day
Ten-year-old Jamie, while on holiday in Abergarry with his mum Charis, overhears a conversation. To him, it is all part of a game. But this is no game and the consequences are far more serious than Jamie ever imagined.

Old wounds are about to be reopened.
Struggling PI team Maddy Clifford and Paul Mackenzie and find themselves involved by a chance meeting. How deeply into those wounds will they have to delve to unravel the mystery?

Available from Amazon.

Praise for *Crossfire*

'Without a doubt, one of the most exciting books I've read!' Shelley Clarke

'Crossfire has stormed into second place in my personal rating system.' Jane Clements

'I loved this book. So many twists and turns which kept me guessng'. H. McLeod

'A gripping mystery.' Yvonne B.

'Nixon can write, no doubt about that!' Johnny Nys

'Beautifully written and an excellent, intricate plot.' Linda

Acknowledgments

My warmest thanks to everyone who's stayed with me on this varied writing career of mine, who've supported me, and kept up the cheerleading when I've found myself running out of voice and puff. Your kind words have meant everything.

On a practical note, I'd like to thank **Transport Scotland** for their information about road traffic cameras, and **Graham Bartlett** (policeadvisor.co.uk) for his patience and for digging around to find out the answers to some odd questions I've had throughout the writing of this one!

Thanks, of course, to **Adrian Hobart** and **Rebecca Collins**; the Ho and the Beck who have continued to offer so much advice and support, and to the entire **Hobeck team** of editors, designers and fellow writers. So grateful to **Jayne Mapp** for her stunning cover designs, too.

As always, my gratitude to my online writing groups and friends, particularly those who've been with me through the same fires, and emerged, picking charred bits out of our hair, but still smiling: **Glynis Peters, Deborah Carr**, and **Christie Barlow.** We are stronger for it. Never forget that.

About the Author

R.D. Nixon is a pen-name of author Terri Nixon, who has been publishing historical drama and mythic fantasy novels since 2013. The initials belong to her two sons, who are graciously pretending not to mind.

Terri was born in Plymouth, UK. She moved to Cornwall at the age of nine, and grew up on the edge of Bodmin Moor, where her early writing found its audience in her school friends, who, to be fair, had very little choice. She has now returned to Plymouth, and works in the university's Faculty of Arts, Humanities and Business. She is occasionally mistaken for a lecturer, but not for long.

Fair Game is Terri's second crime novel in the Clifford-Mackenzie series. The first novel, *Crossfire*, was published in July 2021.

433

Crime Bites includes:

- *Echo Rock* by Robert Daws
- *Old Dogs, Old Tricks* by AB Morgan
- *The Silence of the Rabbit* by Wendy Turbin
- *Never Mind the Baubles: An Anthology of Twisted Winter Tales* by the Hobeck Team (including all the current Hobeck authors and Hobeck's two publishers)
- *The Clarice Cliff Vase* by Linda Huber
- *Here She Lies* by Kerena Swan
- *The Macnab Principle* by R.D. Nixon
- *Fatal Beginnings* by Brian Price
- *A Defining Moment* by Lin Le Versha
- *Saviour* by Jennie Ensor

Also please visit the Hobeck Books website for details of our other superb authors and their books, and if you would like to get in touch, we would love to hear from you.

Hobeck Books also presents a weekly podcast, the Hobcast, where founders Adrian Hobart and Rebecca Collins discuss all things book related, key issues from each week, including the ups and downs of running a creative business. Each episode includes an interview with one of the people who make Hobeck possible: the editors, the authors, the cover designers. These are the people who help Hobeck bring great stories to life. Without them, Hobeck wouldn't exist. The Hobcast can be listened to from all the usual platforms but it can also be found on the Hobeck website: **www.hobeck.net/hobcast**.